Praise for *Like*

"In this braided story about isolated people who are joined by happenstance, the cast's compassion stands out. The novel moves with care toward its rewarding end. Along the way, it subverts assumptions about generational divides...helping to make *Like A Complete Unknown* an engaging novel about second chances."

— *Foreword Reviews*

"Anara Guard writes with heart and power, and hers is a confident, moving novel. You will never think of Chicago in the same way again, or of what it feels like to be a desperate runaway teenager. Her remarkable characters face daunting challenges, realistically and freshly depicted against a backdrop of convulsive social change and pressing moral dilemmas."

— Joseph diPrisco, chair of The New Literary Project

"In this stunning debut novel, Anara Guard weaves together the fragments of a runaway girl's life against the backdrop of 1970s Chicago. Her voice is lyrical and self-aware with a gentle grace that can only come from sympathetic knowing. Intertwining mastery over the bildungsroman and a poetic voice, Guard lulls the reader into her characters' painful, beautiful world."

— *San Francisco Book Review*

"This story of change, transformation, and growth captures not only the social and political milieu of the 1960s, but its pitfall and opportunities. Readers who want a sense of what these times were like and the struggles experienced by those both within and outside of the system will find *Like A Complete Unknown* a vivid, thought-provoking story that captures this world from two different experiences."

— *Midwest Book Review*

"In her impressive debut novel, Anara Guard brings Chicago during the 1960's, when emerging feminism and political upheaval ruled the day, into sharp focus. An unlikely encounter between a widowed doctor who has given up on life and a teenaged girl who has run away from home to find a life sets a propulsive plot in motion. Guard writes with lyrical prose, bringing her characters fully alive in this wonderfully nuanced novel. A remarkable story of persistence, self-discovery and redemption."

— Marcia Butler, author of *Oslo, Maine*

"A compelling and clear-eyed portrait of Chicago during the Vietnam War. She layers the strained idealism of the free love generation atop its ugly underbelly with raw honesty. Although set in the sixties, the novel speaks intimately of our own complex social moment."

— Mary Volmer, author of *Reliance, Illinois*

"Skillfully weaves the music and cultural touchstones of the sixties into a compelling story of a lonely doctor and a naive runaway girl, searching for family and for self. Guard's prose is lyrical and her characters are realistic and fully formed in this close observation of Chicago during the Vietnam War, a time when women had few choices over their bodies or their lives."

— Mary Camarillo, author of *The Lockhart Women*

"Your book is so stunningly observed. I lived through the era you write about, and the detail you have remembered/recovered is so painstakingly accurate. Oh the visceral reality of it—still vivid in my consciousness. Your deeply felt, intimately and power-fully inhabited story felt almost like a personal letter."

— Ronne Hartfield, author of *Another Way Home*

"The moving tale of a runaway girl as she experiences the chaos, danger, and ultimately, the beauty of Chicago's counter-culture in 1970. A gripping story that lingers in memory long after the last satisfying page is turned."

— Lois Ann Abraham, author of *Tina Goes to Heaven*

Praise for *Remedies for Hunger*

"These short stories are snapshots of urban life, intertwined with scenes from the country or the odd suburb . . . stories about children, con men, hippies, sweet fathers, and negligent mothers. Anara Guard picks out the secret jewels of the hardscrabble life where the domestic scene reveals the larger landscape. Her subject is the mystery of childhood, the certainty of death and the shining light somewhere in between with all its startling beauty."

— Lisa Page, Director of Creative Writing
George Washington University

"Anara Guard has an eye for the offbeat detail, the peculiar utterance, lending her stories a realism that is not only magical but also quirky and funny. She conjures a kind of enchanted landscape whose perils are navigated by characters who must contend with the oddness of their reality. These darkly whimsical stories of misfits—a girl who doesn't know left from right, a mother who bleaches her children's eyebrows, a realtor showing a house to a bear—unfold in delightfully unexpected ways."

— Abby Bardi, author of *The Book of Fred*

Praise for *The Sound of One Body*

"These fine stories offer brief, knowing glimpses into lives in transition. Anara Guard is a writer to be read again and again."

— Bret Anthony Johnston, author of *Corpus Christi: Stories*

"These strong, haunting stories are like small wounds, nothing fatal, but nevertheless permanent; not scars but bruises won in battle, each one a glancing blow that leaves a distinct mark, and a memory of the pain we can inflict or endure when we're not even looking."

—Robert Goolrick, author of *A Reliable Wife*

LIKE A COMPLETE UNKNOWN

A NOVEL

Anara Guard

New Wind Publishing
Sacramento, California

New Wind Publishing
Copyright © 2021 by Anara Guard.

Library of Congress Control Number: 2021918379

ISBN 978-1-929777-25-9 (paperback)
ISBN 978-1-929777-27-3 (ebook)

Cover design and collage by Richard Ljoenes Design, LLC
Photographs: Chicago Union Stock Yards by Library of Congress; Vietnam War protest via Wikimedia Commons; girl silhouette, suitcase, and painter's palette by Shutterstock.

Like A Complete Unknown/ Anara Guard. -- 1st ed.

New Wind Publishing
Sacramento, California 95819
www.newwindpublishing.com

"Chicago was the garage sale of all the contradictions America could contain."

— Charles Simic, "Fearful Paradise"

July 1999

Did you roll your eyes at me just now, my daughter? Of course you did. At thirteen, it seems required that you find me embarrassing, old-fashioned, even humiliating. But I was once the center of your life, the hub to your gaily spoked wheel, and you're not so far away from those years that you fail to notice how I flush with emotion as I read the return address on this thick envelope that arrived in the morning mail. My pulse quickens but I make no move to open the flap.

"Who's Jesse?" you ask, leaning over my left shoulder, the ends of your hair tickling my ear. You stand on the rungs of my chair and your weight threatens to tip it over but I don't bat you away. It's rare enough these days to have you come so close to me. I smell your lemony shampoo and feel the heat that emanates in a slow fever from your body, a little more each day until it will overtake you and fill you with desire even before you know what, or whom, to shine that burning light upon.

I hesitate to answer but you've already lost interest as you reach for a glossy magazine among the pile of mail on my desk, claiming it as your own. Even a year ago, you would have declared, "Dibs!" but now such childish slang is behind you. A few heavy steps—not that you weigh much, but you seem incapable of landing softly on anything—the door slams, and I watch through the window as you walk in a crooked line across our small patch of yard and collapse into the hammock with enough force to sway the small trees from which it hangs.

It takes several minutes for you to arrange your legs, for they are strangely long and don't seem to bend in the same ways any more. You think they're too thin and perhaps they are, but all of this is temporary, my dear: your awkward limbs and my gray hairs, the extra weight I carry around my middle that makes you cringe whenever it is the least bit exposed, even the fire that burns within you and ebbs within me. As soon as we become comfortable and familiar with our bodies, they change. I had only just memorized the soft pink of your gums when they were marred by your first tooth cutting through. And then, when I had accustomed myself to your pearly white teeth (do you remember that nursery rhyme? "Thirty white horses upon a red hill, now they tramp, now they champ, now they stand still . . .") they began to loosen and fall out. We buried them beneath your pillow, one at a time, where they vanished in the middle of the night.

I keep them in a small enameled box, the one with a picture of a unicorn on its lid, but teeth don't age well. After a few years, they cracked and broke into tiny shards. Perhaps their calcium was affected by the other fossils I save in that box: two shriveled and mummified umbilical cords, the same color and texture as hashish. When you were four and five, you liked to look at the blackened remains with me, sometimes daring to touch them with a hesitant fingertip while I told you the story you like best of all: the tale of your birth.

One of your bare feet protrudes from the woven hammock and I am seized with the painful knowledge of how brief childhood is, how little time we have left before you must leave me. You push with your toes against the tree trunk to keep some momentum going, rocking, rocking as you turn the magazine pages. Do you feel a need to be comforted as you study those airbrushed limbs and cheekbones? Oh, Hannah, turn a skeptical gaze upon those glistening models and all their unwelcome advice.

I turn the envelope over and make a slit with the butter knife I keep on my desk. Five folded pages: a long letter this time. My fingertips brush over the handwriting like a blind woman reading Braille.

In our yard, the hammock has slowed its pulse. The magazine lies upside down on the damp grass. Your hand dangles listlessly, and I know that you're easing into a sleep where you will not dream of me. You are curious about many things, but not about who I once was. You cannot imagine that your mother has known adventure and loss and peril. That I loved people you've never heard of. But that too will change: someday, you'll want to know.

Chapter One

People everywhere just want to be free

Katya slipped off her loafers and let her bare toes trace patterns upon the linoleum's smooth surface. She reveled in this hidden rebellion: while appearing obedient above the kitchen table, below it, she could do as she liked. In the girls' washroom at school that day, she had studied how American girls applied pink gloss to their lips, how they brushed dark mascara onto their eyelashes. She didn't dare borrow any of their make-up but had rolled the waistband of her plaid skirt up until her knees peeked out below the hem. Then, she waited outside the locker room for Ivan to emerge, his hair in damp curls from the shower. In the shadow of a tree whose leaves had turned October orange, they reached for each other. She kissed his cheek and then his mouth. His lips were supple and wet, and he slipped his hand beneath her blouse before she swatted it away . . . As she trudged home, she tugged her skirt down to look respectable again.

"Katya!" Ma's voice held an edge of impatience. "Tata wants you pass the *golabki*." Her mother was usually the one to ease any friction that rose during dinner, calming everyone as easily as she ironed the wrinkles from their clothes. But tonight, her face was taut with unspoken anxiety.

"Sorry, Tata." She mumbled as she pushed the platter of cabbage rolls toward her father.

"What you do at school today, Katya?"

Ma's question set her stomach quivering. Why this sudden interest? What was going on? Her parents never visited her school: it was too big, too American, outside their neighborhood. Integrated. Full of kids from families who spoke English all the time and sent their kids with lunch money instead of leftover *kielbasa* in a brown paper bag. Kids who were allowed to watch "Laugh-In" and go to the movies by themselves. Nervously, she rubbed the scar on her chin. Ma should swat her hand away like always, reminding her not to draw attention to the jagged white mark. ("How you gonna get good husband, with your face like that?") But her parents seemed oddly intent on adding salt and pepper to their plates, while the kitchen hummed with tension like a radio tuned shy of a station.

At last she offered, "My collage is going to be in the art show." Assembled from photos cut out of the pages of *Life Magazine*, a young soldier's face stared out from the center of the poster. His eyes were dark and haunted. Around him, she'd pasted images of helicopters hovering over a burning jungle, and charred remains of Vietnamese villages where the hut roofs were round like their hats, and a pair of muddy combat boots. She had to labor over those boots, using nail scissors to cut around their intricate shapes. And when Miss McCoo came to examine her progress, she rested her hand on Katya's shoulder for a moment.

"Good work," she said. "I want to hang this one in the school show next week." Warmth blossomed through Katya's chest. Maybe her teacher understood how helpless she felt about the war. Perhaps she had noticed the tiny words inked like black stitches along the edges where the pictures overlapped: "No more. Peace now. End the war."

All over Chicago, students wore black armbands in protest or staged walkouts from their classes. But in Katya's neighborhood of Polish meatpackers and stock-yard workers, U.S. flags waved from the front porches. Every other rusty Skylark sported a "Better Dead Than Red" bumper sticker. Her neighbors would never do anything critical of their adopted country. Only traitors burned flags or gathered in a public square to shout against the government; those were dangerous actions and, besides, you should be grateful for the freedoms of America.

"You made college?" Tata frowned in confusion.

"No, *collage.* You take pictures from magazines and glue them on poster board with other things, like maybe ribbon or buttons or words."

He snorted. "This is not art! Art is painting like Rembrandt, like da Vinci. Only genius can make art! Why these schools waste your time with scissors and paste? Remember when they wanted Piotr take those music classes? I tell them: My boy is not musician! They say, music is for all boys and girls. But now look: your brother at university to learn business. What he need trumpet or drums for?" Tata speared a piece of lamb with his fork. A pearl of blood gleamed against the white fat left on his dish.

After her brother left for college downstate, the lop-sided square that her family made around the kitchen table had formed a new shape: like a knife with a sharp point. She missed his cheerful, gangly presence and how he winked at her when he up-ended the orange juice to drink straight from the carton. Her eyes clouded with tears.

"Katya, not again!" Tata scowled at her, his thick eyebrows like a dark cloud on the horizon. He thought he knew her sorrow. "Already we have decided: why girls need to go to college? Someday you marry, you have babies, you make your mother happy."

Katya dropped her head until her hair created a light brown curtain around her face to hide her unhappiness. She longed to attend art school but she knew her parents would never agree to that. And now, Ma set down her glass of hot tea with a thump. Whatever was brewing within her was ready.

"Tonight, you come with me to work, daughter."

Katya gaped. "To clean offices?"

"Is time you learn the real world, my girl. We need a good helper. Olga is in hospital with the new baby."

"But Ma, you work all night! I have a test tomorrow. How will I stay awake?" Tomorrow's history quiz already promised to be a maze from which she'd have trouble emerging. Her parents exchanged a look, a whole conversation without words.

"Obey your mother," Tata growled.

Katya's arms and legs grew heavy with dread. Ma looked away as she said, "Tonight, we work. Fetch a scarf; the van comes soon. And put your shoes back on."

* * *

Mr. Wojcek's battered blue van was crowded with *żony* who welcomed Katya with toothy smiles: Mrs. Slezak, Mrs. Nowicki, Mrs. Kowalski. These were mothers of neighborhood girls she'd grown up with, all attending

"Make pretty pictures at home," her mother remarked evenly, as if they were discussing what to eat for
breakfast.

"Ma, please! Don't make me do this!" She grasped
her mother's arm, but Ma pulled away.

"You help the family now with money for Piotr's
university. No more talking."

Stunned, Katya followed her mother into the elevator and slumped against the wall, watching the numbers
blink on and off. Mrs. Slezak was right: there was no
thirteen. If only she could find that missing floor, a space
between the numbers where she could escape. But then
what? Where could she go? She gritted her teeth, trying
not to cry.

Outside, the women lit cigarettes and chatted together as they waited for the van. Katya sank to the
chilly curb and picked at a bit of paper towel stuck to
her shoe. Hopelessness stabbed her like a stitch in her
side from running. Knowing that she must return here
tomorrow night and every night to come was unbeara-
ble. She'd never be allowed to go to art school. But there
was no point in protesting or complaining: her misery
would find little sympathy here. Ma and her friends
were glad to have their jobs. And, after all, they had
spared her the toilets. This time.

"Come gather round, people . . ."

Faint sounds of music and voices drifted toward
her. From out of the shadows, almost as though they'd
stepped through some invisible doorway, came a
shaggy-haired boy in blue jeans and another with a huge
round Afro. They sauntered down the middle of the
empty street; beside them strolled a girl whose bare legs
scissored beneath her short skirt. As they passed below

the streetlamp, light glinted on the girl's silver earrings and danced upon the shiny surface of a guitar. They looked like angels in a Renaissance painting, their mouths open in song, and their voices, deep and sweet, rose in harmony.

"Your sons and your daughters are beyond your command . . ."

As the trio drew near, Ma and the other workers huddled together, but Katya scrambled to her feet and teetered at the edge of the curb, holding her breath. If only they would come all the way over to her! If they crossed the street and reached her, something magical would happen, a spell would be broken. She yanked the kerchief from her hair and waved it wildly. The taller fellow beckoned to her in exaggerated motion as if she were far, far away. He cupped his hands around his mouth and called, "Come along!" while his friends grinned and continued to sing, "The times they are a'changin' . . ."

Katya stepped off the curb.

A horn blared, startling her. Mr. Wojcek's van pulled so close that she felt the engine's heat as she scrambled back to safety. The young people retreated back across the street, laughing like they'd never been in any danger.

"*Czas iść!*" Ma commanded: time to go. The cleaning women prodded Katya into the van, clucking and scolding: those young people had no business being out so late, carrying on, making trouble. And Katya: why had she beckoned to such ragged strangers? Numbly, she fell into a window seat and leaned her forehead against the glass. Her new friends were fleeing, already halfway down the block, and then gone, beyond the grownups' command.

As the van rumbled toward home, Katya clasped a single thread of hope: that the merry singers somehow knew her longing. *Wait for me,* she thought. *I'll come back and find you.* Over and over, she made her wish: *Take me with you. Wherever you're going, I want to follow.*

Chapter Two

We've gotta get outta this place

In picture books, you leave home with your belongings stuffed into a striped bandanna, fat and round as a balloon, tied to a long pole. Katya had no pole and no striped bandanna, but she knew where to find the battered suitcase that her parents had brought with them years ago from Krakow. On another occasion, its worn corners and tattered lining might have struck her as sad, but not tonight. This satchel had traveled thousands of miles; it would be an experienced companion for her. She hefted it in one hand and quietly eased the closet door shut, then tiptoed down the hall back to her bedroom.

She hadn't slept after the van brought her home. Her mind kept reeling with the night's images: wet patterns made by the mop's gray tresses as she pushed it across the floor, the dark circles beneath Beata Zajac's eyes, those young singers' bright faces serenading her under the streetlight. And her own unhappy reflection gazing back at her from every window of the office tower. She heard her mother's voice echoing *no more school*, then *no more*, and then just *no*.

At 4:30, the decision pressed upon her, daring her to take its hand and say: *yes*. Her mother would be fast asleep, her father not yet up. But in an hour, he would be drinking strong tea before meeting other workers to walk to the stockyards together. Now was the time. She set the suitcase upon her rumpled bed and spread it open, releasing a pungent odor of mothballs and an invitation to be filled. Without turning on a light, she packed: notebooks, sketch pads, pencils and charcoal, and then clothing. No room for favorite books or for Skarbus, the battered cloth pig who had kept her company since she was a baby. She kissed his threadbare nose and placed him back on the pillow where his single eye stared at her, forlorn.

Turning away, she snapped the suitcase latches shut. The sound was like a crack of lightning in the quiet house. In a panic, she shoved the suitcase beneath her bed and scrambled under the covers. Her heart hammered in her chest with dread. But all remained quiet and, after a time, it seemed safe to get up again. What had she forgotten? She surrendered two notebooks in order to cram in a pair of sneakers and her hairbrush. She'd have to buy some things later, for she didn't dare risk leaving that obvious clue: an empty spot beside the bathroom sink where her toothbrush belonged.

She dressed in extra layers: two pairs of knee socks, two pleated skirts, two blouses covered by a sweater, and sat on the edge of her bed, sweating. There was nothing else to do but wait in the dark and listen to her own rapid and uncertain breath until her father's alarm clock rang in the next room. She heard his groans, her mother's murmured response. The bedsprings creaked, his footsteps scuffed to the bathroom, the faucet squealed as he turned on the water. As water gurgled down the drain, her resolve weakened. It wasn't too late yet: no one need know that she had flirted with the temptation to leave. She could still change her mind, strip off the excess clothes, and go to school like always.

loaves of rye bread, orange Halloween cookies. Wordlessly, Katya pressed her finger to the glass case, pointing to prune *kolaches* and cream-filled *paczek*.

"Which one, honey?" Mrs. Pulaski huffed. A fine dust of sugar dotted one pink cheek as if she had placed it there with a powderpuff.

"Both, please." Did her voice sound shaky?

"Okay, honey. Same bag?" The flesh on the baker's arms wobbled as she pulled the trays from the case. Katya considered for a moment whether to ask for two bags, to pretend that one treat was for a friend, but Mrs. Pulaski wouldn't judge anyone for eating. The warm wax paper bag felt like a blessing in her palms and she gave thanks in Polish to make sure the baker understood.

Down the block, she found a doorway where she could enjoy the first bite of the round *paczek*. Rich custard squirted into her mouth as her teeth sank into the soft sweet dough. When she'd licked the last bit of chocolate from her fingers, she reached into the bag again. Flat and square, corners folded like a pinwheel over the sticky prune filling, *kolache* was one of her favorites. Funny how prunes were nasty by themselves, straight from the box or stewed—but baked and covered with a sprinkle of sugar, nothing was better. Except perhaps a custardy *paczki*.

Bits of sugar still clung to her lips as she left the protection of the doorway and headed to the bus stop. Already she felt stronger, her luggage seemed lighter. If she were spotted by some neighbor peeking past her lace curtains—if later, Mrs. Novak or Mrs. Petroski interrogated Ma, "Where was your daughter going when I saw her with a suitcase out so early on Friday morning?"—well, then, so be it. Katya had money in her pocket, sweet rolls in her stomach, and somewhere, she was certain, her rescuers waited for her.

Chapter Three

One is the loneliest number

Katya thought she would recognize last night's office building when she saw it again, but there were too many to choose among: steel, marble, and granite; old and new; brown, silver, black. The bus crawled up one crowded street and down another while she sat, uncertain and confused, until the driver called out, "Randolph Street. Chi-caw-go Public Liberry!" Surely, the library would have maps of downtown, some aid to help her locate the street she sought. She lugged her heavy suitcase down the aisle.

The massive stone building occupied an entire city block. While other people entered without hesitation, Katya lingered at the bottom of the stone steps, watching the door open and close until a young mother approached the entrance, each outstretched hand clutching the arm of a small, tugging child. Picking up her suitcase, Katya followed the woman inside and then collapsed onto the nearest bench, feeling her heart lift out of her body. Just last Sunday, St. Stanislaus' Church had seemed ornate but, compared to this palace of Aladdin's riches, it was shabby and plain. Huge bronze chandeliers illuminated green and gold mosaics that rose up the walls, along the broad marble stairways, and across a vast domed ceiling. Abalone gleamed in elaborate curlicues twining into endless garlands and wreaths. Embedded in the soaring ceiling were letters formed by mosaic tiles and she tilted her head back to squint at the unfamiliar words. Latin, for sure, or was that Greek? Astonishingly, no one else paused to look up. They stood in line at a long wooden desk, waiting for the disinterested librarians to stamp their books.

Forgetting the maps and eager to find a spot to sketch, Katya ventured up the broad staircase, trailing her fingertips along its cool marble balustrade. At the top of the stairs, she wandered into the Children's Room where shelves of books lined the walls, stretching the length of one chamber and into the next. Little children squatted around a librarian who sat on a low chair in a patch of sunshine, reading aloud from a picture book. A handful of mothers had pulled their chairs together in one corner where they whispered among themselves.

Her feet made no sound as she crossed the green carpet. At the far end of the room old favorites welcomed her from the shelves, their titles on the worn spines as familiar as friends: Black Beauty, Little Women, Heidi. *National Velvet* lay open on a nearby table, waiting for her to arrive, and she sank into an armchair to read. The sun warmed her head; the librarian's sweet voice was rhythmic and soothing, and, far away, a palomino horse whinnied. It nuzzled her shoulder with its soft nose and shook her.

"We don't allow sleeping here," the horse said. An unfamiliar face peered at her: dark eyebrows pinched above tortoiseshell glasses. The librarian pointed to her suitcase, whispering, "You might miss your train."

"Oh. Yeah, my train." Katya retreated down a corridor and found the Ladies Room. Locked in a stall, she counted her money. Between her own small savings and what she'd taken from her mother's housekeeping fund ("borrowed," she reminded herself, "I'm going to pay her back someday,") she had sixty-four dollars. It seemed like a lot, and she slipped most of the bills into her knee sock, keeping only a few dollars in her pockets.

In the mirror, she looked changed somehow, her eyes bigger. As always, the scar gleamed white, a persistent reminder of the painful day when she'd tried to ride Piotr's three-speed bike. He rode no-handed, gracefully shifting his weight as he pedaled. It looked so easy: surely, she would be able to glide as he did, straight as an arrow. But despite his shouts of encouragement, she wavered and wobbled down the block until the bicycle veered wildly into a brick wall and she'd limped home with scraped knees and a gash in her chin. Ma (who believed doctors were unnecessary extravagances) treated the wound with iodine, band-aids, and two Saint Joseph's orange-flavored baby aspirin while she forbade her daughter to ever mount a bicycle again. Only tomboys rode bikes and who'd want to marry a tomboy?

Pushing her limp hair away from her forehead, Katya wished she had thought to pack barrettes. But she could buy them, along with some lunch, for her stomach seemed to have forgotten those morning pastries. And then, she would begin the hunt for her new friends.

Outside, blinding light refracted off the sharp edges of stone buildings. Taxis blared their horns as they pulled up to the curb in a long yellow row and the sidewalk was a river of people rushing past, jostling her with their elbows, bumping against her clumsy suitcase. Squinting from the top of the library steps, she tried to peer over the crowds in search of a lunch counter or drugstore.

"Girl, you in some kinda trouble."

Was that a question or an acknowledgement of the truth? A lanky teen in jeans and a denim jacket perched beside her. Her frizzy hair was white-blond, invisible eyebrows and lashes surrounded pale blue eyes, tiny specks mottled her milky skin. Her colorless lips scowled as she said, "And you better stop staring at me or your troubles gonna get a whole lot worse."

"I'm sorry, I . . ." Katya mumbled.

The girl stretched out her legs, creating a barrier that she dared Katya to step over. "What's your name?" she demanded.

"Cathy." It sounded foreign in her mouth. She'd never used the American version of her name and stuttered over the diphthong so that it came out sounding like "Cat-tee."

"Okay, Catty," her companion smirked. "Now, ask me."

"What's your name?" she echoed, obediently.

"Jo-Jo the Albino. See what I did there? I don't tell you my name, I only tell you what I'm called. How old're you?"

"Seventeen."

"Now I know you a lie!" Was it so obvious? Her cheeks burned as the other girl stood up. She was taller than Katya and wore a crafty smile that didn't reach her eyes. But it was a smile, and that removed some of the ominous tone from her words. "But tell everybody you eighteen, you just look young for your age. Cops pick you up, you gonna be sent to the bad girls' home for sure."

What did she mean, the Bad Girl's Home? Katya couldn't stop herself from glancing over her shoulder in case an officer lurked nearby. Her mouth went dry as she croaked, "Where is that?"

The other girl unwrapped a stick of Juicy Fruit and folded it in half before placing it on her tongue. Her teeth were nicotine-yellow against that pale skin. "Downstate. Near the prison in Dixon. Where'd you say you from?"

"Indiana." The lie emerged smoothly this time.

"Huh. No wonder. You shore aren't a city girl. Look like some kind of refugee." Jo-Jo kicked the suitcase. "And where you think you going?"

Katya stayed silent, thinking of the dark street down which the singing youths had scampered, beckoning for her to follow.

The girl brought her strange speckled face close to Katya's as she hissed, "You a runaway!" Then she reared back and laughed, giving a high hoot that caused people to turn and stare. "I'm gonna teach you a thing or two now." Again, her words sounded menacing but her grin softened them as she hefted the suitcase in one hand. "We gotta get you a knapsack instead of this big ol' clunky thing. Come on!"

She grabbed Katya's arm, tugging her down the steps and around the corner onto Michigan Avenue, where afternoon light glared against the broad sidewalks and shiny windows. Jo-Jo's long legs navigated the sidewalks with ease but, even without the burden of her suitcase, Katya struggled to keep up, her overstuffed satchel bouncing painfully against her hip. As they dodged buses and taxicabs, her new friend tossed information over her shoulder. "Go to the Why-Double-You-See-Ay if you need a cheap room, but be sure to tell 'em you're eighteen. And better get yourself a fake ID.

It'll cost you maybe twenty bucks but you gonna need it." Katya, out of breath, wished she could stop to write down the advice.

At last Jo-Jo halted in front of an Army-Navy store. Its windows were crammed with khaki-colored tents, folding cots, camouflage netting, rows of knives, camping lanterns. "See those knapsacks? Eight bucks and they got all kind of pockets for your little things. Carry one of them around and you're gonna look like a tourist from Europe insteada some runaway gal from the Indiana Dunes. You go in and get it, and I'll watch over your stuff out here." The tall girl straddled the suitcase with her long legs and folded both arms over her flat chest. That vacant blue scrutiny still made Katya uneasy but, clearly, nobody would get the suitcase away from Jo-Jo.

It took a few minutes to find a clerk among the revolving racks of Army jackets and pea coats. Katya pointed to the knapsacks and the clerk used a long pole with a crook to snag one. Colored pencils would fit nicely in those snug side pockets, and her sketch pads could be protected in the main pouch. She fished eight dollars out of her sock and, with a surge of confidence, slung her new pack over one shoulder as she pushed through the front door.

Jo-Jo and the suitcase were gone.

Chapter Four

My kind of town

Quiet, please!" Dr. Epstein pounded the podium with his gavel. "Thank you all for coming. I now bring the October 1969 meeting of the American College of OB-GYNS, Chicago Chapter, to order."

Robert Lewis slipped into a chair near the rear of the Palmer House's elegant ballroom, relieved he hadn't arrived late. Fresh from the barbershop, his skin still prickled and, as he nodded to the men seated around him, Bay Rum aftershave filled his nostrils. While the chairman droned through the rituals of the minutes (approved) and agenda, Robert gazed about in search of familiar colleagues. He recognized only older faces in the crowd and every year, there were fewer and fewer of those, giving him the sense that he too was disappearing somehow. What had happened to all the physicians with whom he'd once practiced at Rush Hospital? Some were dead, others retired. He imagined them golfing, as cartoons often depicted, or sunning themselves on Florida beaches: men with deep tans and healthy physiques. His former peers enjoyed big houses and expensive haircuts; they were grandfathers whose families visited them frequently. Stop with the self-pity, he told himself. Perhaps it was the remnants of his hasty trip to the barber that continued to irritate him. With an effort, he focused again on the chairman's words.

"We have a guest from the Chicago Police Department who wishes to address us. Officer Reilly, the podium is yours." The officer hitched up his pants and approached the microphone warily.

"Thanks, doctor. I'm sure it isn't news to anyone here that unseemly illegal acts are being perpetrated on pregnant ladies here in the city of Chicago by unknown parties." He pronounced it "Chi-CAW-go," as Southsiders tended to do. "And I don't need to tell you that abortion" (he stumbled uncomfortably over the word, his cheeks reddening) "is punishable by fines, prison time, or both." He paused to let the weight of his words sink in while his audience of doctors regarded him impassively. They knew the law: no physician in the State of Illinois was allowed to perform an abortion unless the mother's life was in peril, not even if she had been raped. Violators risked arrest and losing their licenses to practice.

But women had always found ways to end unwanted pregnancies. Those with enough money and connections could reach a sympathetic physician, sometimes traveling to New York, Canada, or even Puerto Rico for the procedure. Poorer women took more drastic actions: gulping quinine, castor oil, bleach. Some swallowed raw eggs—twenty or more. They threw themselves down flights of stairs or douched with solutions of lye. Their boyfriends struck them in the stomach, hoping to "jar something loose." Tea of black cohosh was rumored to work, as were various potions and tinctures that could be bought from hole-in-the-wall shops in Chinatown or Little Village botanicas.

Worse off were women who risked their lives at the hands of unskilled abortionists with their sharp and unsterile instruments. Like many of the men seated beside him, Robert had seen the infections and fevers that resulted, the perforated uteruses. He recalled the shame and panic that flooded a patient's face when she learned that, even after everything she had done, she was still—irrevocably—pregnant. Some women had to be placed on suicide watch. With an aching heart, he remembered two girls who had waited until they were discharged and then jumped into the Chicago River.

Officer Reilly throttled the microphone as if it were a fleeing vandal, collared at last. "We've been hearing rumors lately that some new kind of illegal ring is at work, and we'd appreciate your help in finding them." Robert had heard these rumors too. At the last OB-GYN meeting, there was much discussion in the halls about a secretive network of abortionists who covered their tracks well, their identities shielded so closely that no one could discover the ringleaders. But, whoever they were, they took good precautions and practiced careful medicine: fewer women were showing up in emergency rooms with ruined uteruses or harboring infections after an incomplete D&C. In all of Cook County this year, only a dozen women had died after illegal abortions, less than half the usual number.

"So, if anyone's got information on these criminals, we want you to speak up and help us send them to prison where they belong."

Silence descended over the plush ballroom. The chandeliers twinkled overhead, casting a soft light on the rows of men in dark suits. No one raised a hand. Nor would I, Robert told himself, if I knew who they were. He rubbed the back of his neck, wishing the barber had wielded his brush more carefully and whisked away all the snippets. Reilly wiped his brow with a checkered handkerchief. He leaned in, too close to the mic so that it issued a shriek of feedback. "Look! We know the gals can't be doing this nasty business by themselves." The detective's florid face twisted in frustration. "There's gotta be at least one doctor among the ringleaders! That makes a black mark on all of ya. Do I need to remind ya that abortion is a felony?"

A rumble of muttering rose: was he threatening them? A voice from somewhere to Robert's left called out, "We voted last year! This body does not support the current law!" Dr. Friedman returned to the podium and took the microphone back from the officer's sweaty hands. "That's correct. Our national body passed a resolution affirming the right to therapeutic abortions, provided in hospitals. But this isn't the time or place to re-visit the issue. Thank you for alerting us to this prob-lem, Officer. We must return to our agenda now." The police officer cast a dark look at the audience and stomped off the stage to a smattering of tepid applause.

No doubt Officer Reilly was aggravated, but he had no idea of how utterly frustrated a physician felt when he couldn't meet his patients' needs. Women with un-planned pregnancies often seemed to bring ghosts with them to Robert's private practice; fear and dread clung to their ankles, slowing their reluctant steps. The unborn child they had spent weeks wishing out of exist-ence formed a palpable presence in the room and others lingered there as well, like a shadowy photo album of disappointed faces: their boyfriends, parents, friends. All the selves they had assumed they would inhabit someday—girls who would be more accomplished, more educated, more loved than they were now—

wavered behind them, fading away as his test tubes and blotter paper divined their new undeniable fates.

These thoughts kept Robert unsettled and he paid little notice to the treasurer's report, membership numbers, or plans for attending the national conference in New York. He peered around the room at the younger men and the few—very few—women, wondering who among them might be brave enough (and foolhardy enough, he thought) to offer these safer, cleaner abortions.

During a break, he greeted old colleagues, briefly joined in reminiscences of the days when he had worked beside them. But he declined to volunteer for tasks, even when Dr. Lerner urged him to lend his talents to the By-Laws Committee. Could there be any less interesting topic than bylaws? Surely, Dr. Lerner must regard him as equally dull. When the meeting adjourned, he spurned two offers to gather at the Lockwood Bar for a beer, choosing instead to walk alone down Michigan Avenue. It was nearly six o'clock and people rushed past him, eager to catch their buses and head for home. They waved farewell to their friends, calling out, "Have a nice day," even though the day was almost over. This saying struck Robert as both odd and sad; if your time hadn't been nice yet, it was likely too late now.

He caught a whiff of rich, beefy aroma as he passed the Artist's Snack Shop. One Christmas, he and Phyllis had dined there just as "The Nutcracker" finished a performance. Young ballerinas in their black and primrose leotards jammed the long counter, their faces still heavily made up, their slick hair pulled back in identical tight buns. They wolfed down enormous hot fudge sundaes and banana splits slathered in whipped cream.

Cushioned in the booths beside their families, smaller children gaped at the chattering dancers while the divas gestured at each other with long silver spoons, pretending to ignore their star-struck audience.

On an impulse, he entered the revolving door, pushing against his own reflection: a short, stout man in a gray topcoat who looked even older than he felt. The restaurant was half empty; art students in paint-splattered smocks lounged in the booths, along with a couple of CTA bus drivers on break. He eased onto a stool at the counter and removed his hat.

"What'll you have, hon?" A middle-aged waitress wiped the already clean counter with a damp cloth, handed him the menu, and flipped to a new page on her pad. Her smooth motions were well-practiced.

"Coffee, please. And the beef stew."

As she filled his cup, Robert read the name stitched onto her powder blue uniform above the spot where most people mistakenly thought their hearts were: *Louise.*

"Cream?" She sounded amused. Chagrined to realize he'd been staring at her chest, he shook his head and busied himself with unfolding his paper napkin but when he glanced up, she still stood before him, smiling. Warm brown eyes in a broad, lined face, nut-brown curls threaded with gray. He looked down, unable to hold her gaze, until she moved away and when she returned to place the bowl of stew before him, she didn't linger.

Left alone, he was able to pick at the splinter that had kept snagging his mood. It wasn't true that he could do nothing to aid those patients who became distraught to learn they were pregnant. Of course, he wouldn't perform any procedure himself, but there were certain medications that could be effective: methergine, ergometrine, some other preparations. Perhaps he should consider writing those prescriptions, at least once in a while. But, he argued with himself, his current clientele came and went like the nameless pigeons that visited his windowsill, barely distinguishable from one another, jostling for a bit of space, then flapping away. He didn't know them well. Would they adhere to the instructions that were vital for the abortifacients to succeed? Could he trust them to be discreet?

Robert swallowed the last bite of stew. Once again, he had scarcely tasted his meal. If only he could speak with Phyllis. She had been his wise counsel, his helpmeet, and he had looked forward to sharing even the small troubles and triumphs of his practice with her each evening. But there was no one to whom he could confide his worries now.

Maybe he could let girls who were utterly hopeless know about this new elusive network; then they could choose for themselves whether to find their way to it or not. But how? He had no idea of what to say, or where to find these illegal services. It would be additionally cruel to dangle such a small sliver of hope with no further guidance. Besides, even attempting to refer them for an abortion could place him at great risk. Just last year, two physicians downstate were charged with facilitating criminal abortions; the D.A. seemed intent on bringing them to trial soon.

No, he told himself as he placed a small tip for the friendly waitress beside his empty dish, he could not jeopardize his practice. Not when it was all that he had left. It was unfortunate that Robert could offer his patients so little, but heroics were not for men like him.

Chapter Five

Darkness, be my pillow

Don't panic, Katya told herself. Jo-Jo is gone, and nobody knows where you are. The people rushing past mustn't know how scared you are. Don't cry. Clutch your new empty knapsack as if it can steady you while the maze of unfamiliar city streets stretches around you in all directions. You've never seen such masses of people tearing by, swinging their briefcases, hurrying to subway entrances, yelling for taxis. Everyone else knows where to go. They press around you without noticing you. Maybe you've died and turned into a ghost. You need to end up someplace else. Anywhere is better than this naked bit of sidewalk where Jo-Jo guarded your suitcase before they both vanished. People seem to step around the empty space where it once stood, as if no one will place their foot near the invisible hole.

Think, Katya, think! It's not too late yet: you could find the right buses to take you back home. Come up with a story for where you've been all day. But what about the stolen suitcase and all your belongings? And Ma's missing grocery money. Let the crowds carry you forward. There's too much to explain. If you go back now, they'll never let you out of their sight again. No school, no art. Nothing but vacuum cleaners and the midnight view from deserted office towers.

Keep moving. You can do this. You still have money hidden in the socks sticking to your sweating body. And the few things in your green school satchel: hairbrush, sketchpads, some pencils. Jo-Jo said to go to the Why Double You something and there, straight ahead, neon letters running down the side of a weathered brick building spell out: Y W C A. But what if it's another of her tricks? Find a spot between a parking meter and a stop sign to watch the entrance. Young women pass in and out through the big wooden door, some carrying backpacks, others looking like office workers in their neat white blouses and pencil skirts. At last, you dash across the street and up the steps to where an iron-jawed woman in a black witch's hat sits behind a metal grille. For a startled moment, you feel like Gretel, about to enter the perilous gingerbread house, until you remember that this is Halloween Night.

Say that your luggage was stolen, your ID, too. The witch gnashes her teeth. "Six bucks a night for a shared room, thirty for a full week." Holding your breath, you give her six dollars. With black gloved fingers, she slides a card beneath the grille. "Sign here. Four girls to a room. No visitors, no food in your room. Smoking only in the lounge."

Your hand trembles as it forms the letters. How grade-school your writing looks: that round *C* and the loopy *Y*. No one could believe this signature (you choose Drew as your last name, stolen from Nancy the girl-detective) but the key is pushed toward you. A tiny stifling elevator. Four narrow beds, two skimpy closets, and a scorching hot radiator. The three other girls are older than you, maybe in their twenties. Two are from Belgium, which you think might be somewhere near Spain. They took a Greyhound from New York to Chicago. "Tomorrow we hitchhike to California." The idea seems impossibly dangerous; isn't that asking for trouble? They laugh, unconcerned.

Shove your satchel and useless knapsack beneath the lumpy pillow for safekeeping and tiptoe down the corridor in your socks. No shampoo in the shower, so you scrub your dirty hair with a ridged bar of soap and hope for the best. The water is only tepid but you're so tired, you almost fall asleep leaning against the shower wall. Wrapped in a thin towel, you dart back to room 515. No nightgown: it was in the stolen suitcase along with so many art supplies that you want to weep at the loss. You'll have to sleep in underpants and a shirt, half-naked like the Belgians in their startling white lacy bras and panties. Try not to stare.

You've never slept in the same room as other people before, but it's better to have them here. The fearful thought of how alone in the world you are now squeezes your heart. Today's sights race through your mind: the library's rich mosaic patterns, your hand as it reached into Ma's cupboard to take her savings, Jo-Jo's stained teeth and colorless lips. In the distance, a voice calls, "Lights out," and the room snaps into darkness. Then, a scratch of matches and the scent of smoke. The Belgian girls sit by the open window and trade a cigarette back and forth as they talk in low tones. It is somehow comforting not to understand what they say, not to hear their plans to stand by a highway with their thumbs pointing west. Their voices are soothing, their words unknown, and at last you fall into a sleep that feels like a capture and a release.

Chapter Six

Can this really be the end?

On the first morning at the YW, Katya woke to an empty room, the Belgians already gone to their perilous destination. She found a Greek diner nearby and slipped into a back booth. She'd never eaten in a restaurant by herself and her voice trembled as she asked for fried eggs, toast, and a glass of milk. But no one gave her a second look and, after wiping her plate clean with the last bit of crust, she relaxed enough to order a glazed donut too. As her hunger subsided, she dawdled as long as she could, delaying the moment when she must step out of the warm restaurant, alone. When she ran out of excuses and paid her bill, she chided herself not to spend so much again: her money had to last until she could find her friends.

She walked two blocks in one direction before turning left and then left again, finding her way back to where she started. Widening her range, she made another circuit, three blocks each way this time, and then four. For hours she hunted for that spot where the young minstrels had beckoned to her, searching the crowd's faces for anyone who looked like them, keeping an ear cocked for the sound of a guitar. But the sidewalks were jammed with strangers and nothing looked the same as it had that night. At the end of the day, she counted her money carefully, struggling over the calculations before finally paying the desk clerk (less scary now that she was dressed in a plaid jacket) for a full week.

Months later, when she first saw a yin-yang symbol, Katya would recognize in it the shape of these days downtown: how they were half dark/half bright, freedom wrapping around fear that curved around a heady sense of liberation. Without a map, she memorized the shape and pattern of the city, figuring out that odd numbered addresses were on the east and south sides of the streets, and learning how to slip unnoticed into the clean ladies' rooms in the basements of big department stores: Marshall Field, Carson's, Goldblatt's. To help find her way, she paused to trace outlines of landmarks into her notebook: the Prudential Building with its huge carved rock, the black monolith of the Hancock Tower, and the drawbridges that crossed the murky Chicago River. It seemed impossible that such massive structures could rise up, revealing hidden undersides and then, bells clanging and gigantic gears grinding, lower down again to appear like ordinary streets. Wabash Street was where the elevated trains screeched overhead, sending down a shower of rust as they hurtled around the curve at Van Buren. But further south remained a mystery; that was the direction from which she'd fled and she didn't dare explore too far, afraid that somehow the miles might vanish and she would find herself just around the corner from home. And although she wished she could return to the library's opulent rooms, she avoided the corner of Randolph and Michigan where she might encounter Jo-Jo again.

On her third day, a new roommate (Italian today, Germans yesterday) paraded in from the showers, naked. Katya ducked her head and pretended not to watch Gina scoop those impressive breasts into a black bra. Without needing to stand before a mirror, she threaded earrings through the nearly invisible holes in her earlobes and an idea took shape in Katya's mind. If she could get hold of wire and beads, perhaps she could make simple earrings and sell them. In a phone booth, she riffled through the Yellow Pages and found the Jewelers Building on Dearborn Street. Up the rickety elevator to an office no bigger than a closet, with only a single glass case displaying assorted old wristwatches, plain gold rings, and a few silver chains. The shop-keeper, a droopy-eyed old man with pants belted around his ribcage, greeted her warmly, as if he didn't mind how little money she had. An hour later, she left with spools of copper wire, a small pair of cutters, four vials of colored beads, and a head full of tales about his brilliant grandchildren.

That evening, she experimented with shaping the wire and lost herself in the pleasures of stringing beads. Several tourist girls wanted earrings with the colors of their home countries' flags and no one objected when she asked for fifty cents a pair, and then, seventy-five. Each day, as she walked, she cast her eyes up to the faces of unsmiling strangers and down to the curbs and gutters, picking up anything useful: string, discarded bus schedules and, once, the miracle of a tarnished half-dollar. Feathers were plentiful; she added grackles' purple-black sheen and wrens' soft brown trim to her creations. Other travelers offered to trade if they could no longer cram all their clothes into their knapsacks and Katya was thrilled to barter for her first pair of blue jeans. How Tata would have disapproved: "You trying to be farmer now?" But the denim hugged her legs like a second skin and she felt more confident, less like a schoolgirl.

Still, her cash dwindled too quickly. After buying necessities—toothbrush, underwear, socks—how little she had left to pay for her room. She ate only one meal a day, always at the same diner, staring out the window at passing pedestrians, still clinging to a faint hope of spotting the trio who had launched her on this journey. But those free-wheeling folks had traipsed the streets at three a.m.; too fearful to prowl alone in the dark, how could she ever cross their path?

On her sixteenth birthday, Katya felt worn and alone. Her feet were bruised from hours of plodding upon concrete and granite, and she ached for anything familiar. To cheer herself up, she abandoned her hunt and allowed herself the gift of a day at the Art Institute. For a moment, she stood outside its doors, shivering in the November chill, while she studied the youth who were lingering by two life-sized lion statues that flanked the entrance. The boys' Army jackets matched the lions' weathered green patina. As usual, she didn't recognize their faces and, turning away from that expected disappointment, she pushed through the doors into the temple of art. It was a pay-what-you-wish day but the museum guard glared at her as she dropped a single precious penny into the box.

Katya basked for hours among the Impressionists' vibrant colors and the cool flat tones of Manet and Lautrec. She puzzled over Pollock's abstract explosions and shivered at the weird, melted confusion painted by Salvador Dali. Old Masters called to her to copy their work, and she labored over the thickness of their lines, the curvature of jaw and forehead. Pencils and charcoal were all she had to work with now, and she had to keep her drawings tiny. Had Jo-Jo sold all her paintbrushes and sketchpads—or simply thrown them away? The thought burned through her and she pressed too hard, breaking the stick of charcoal in two.

Frustrated, she gave up sketching and wandered down stairs into the basement. In a hallway at the rear, a huge wooden door gaped ajar revealing a large room cluttered with a dozen paint-spattered easels. The sharp odor of paint and turpentine drifted toward her like an invitation. Katya itched to stand at one of the easels, to study a live model. Behind a desk slouched a young woman dressed entirely in black, ebony hair piled upon her head in a topknot carelessly skewered by a chopstick. And in front of her stood a placard bearing the most marvelous phrase: *School of the Art Institute.* Figure drawing, oil painting, *plein air* . . . the classes this school must offer! Heart racing, Katya approached the desk.

"Hey." There was no response. Determined not to be invisible, she tried again. "It's my birthday today."

"Yeah?" The other girl exhaled the word in a stream of smoke. Katya had never heard anyone sound so bored.

"I just want to know . . . about your school." She tried to sound nonchalant, as if she didn't care too much about the answer. The jaded clerk's gaze raked her with scorn. She gestured lazily, the cigarette in her hand threatening to set that bird's nest hair on fire.

"It's an art school," she sighed.

Stung, Katya flushed. "Yeah, I know that. But how do you get to go here?"

"Well, talent." She flipped a colorful brochure across the desk. "Fill out an application and submit your portfolio. If the work is good enough . . .well, you *might* get in. But we're very selective."

Katya did her best to stare her down. She had nearly filled her sketchbook in a few weeks, carrying it with her everywhere. There must be fifty drawings in it, maybe more. "How many pieces do I need for a portfolio?"

Her opponent rattled off the answers. "Five watercolors, acrylics, or oils. None larger than thirty-six by twenty-four. Canvas should be stretched, not rolled. Or, ten drawings, each one matted. If applying for sculpture, six color photographs, ten by twelve, of your work." Then the final blow. "Two recommendations. And, of course, your high school transcript." She stubbed the cigarette into a black ashtray.

Katya fought an urge to weep as she mounted the stairs. Perhaps someday she could create a portfolio of paintings, but she would never graduate from high school, never have a transcript. Who would recommend her? The dream of art school seemed further away than when she'd lived at home. She couldn't fill out forms that demanded an address, a phone number, her real name. As she left the museum, she dropped the worthless pamphlet into a trashcan.

Chapter Seven

What is and what should never be

The days ran together, each one gray and endless, and yet too short. While it was light outside, Katya wandered the streets, no longer sure what she sought or where to go, her only goal to sell earrings and bracelets to any woman who looked friendly enough to approach. She grew adept at spotting pierced ears and sympathetic smiles. If anyone asked, she claimed to be an art student, raising money for supplies, which wasn't far from the truth. Each afternoon, as the sun sank, Katya's mood sagged along with it. Downtown emptied out then, its workers and shoppers vanishing like water down a drain. Shadows lengthened in every chilly corner and the pigeons huddled together on the elevated tracks' girders as if they dared not descend. Only the Theater District stayed brightly lit, garish neon glows cast from the marquees. Katya would hurry back to the YW, worried about being stopped by a patrolling police car, afraid of thugs who might lurk in dark alleys, and always—always!—fearful of the van filled with Polish cleaning ladies who could recognize her and take her back home. Each day the unwelcome dark arrived a little earlier and still there was no sign of her friends, no guitar music wafting down the street toward her. Her memory of them was fading and she could recall only fragments: the lilt in their voices, the girl's graceful walk, how carefree they had all seemed. But they had vanished into the city's vast corridors and she knew it was unlikely she would meet them again. All she could think to do was fashion and sell enough jewelry to keep her room until something else came along. Something better.

One morning, leaving the labyrinth of office buildings and stores behind, she walked east to watch Lake Michigan's steely waves lap against the shore. Sailboats, shorn of their canvas, rocked idly at anchor. Slack ropes clanked against the masts, sounding like church bells that had cracked and lost their tone. Two yellow school buses pulled up, disgorging their loads of slouching boys and giggling girls. She'd taken a field trip like that in junior high and remembered being delighted by the aquarium's delicate jellyfish as they wafted past the glass, waving *hello, goodbye, hello.* But these kids were heading to the Field Museum. She trailed at the end of their line, through the doors and down a flight of stairs, following closely enough to be mistaken for a straggling student. They dropped brown paper bags onto long tables, then disappeared into a gallery and promptly began to shriek. She peeked around the corner to see what caused the commotion: Egyptian mummies, with the wrappings removed to reveal their shriveled and blackened feet. And while the students screamed and elbowed each other, Katya snagged two lunches and hurried outside.

A block away, she examined her loot. One bag was labelled "Darlene" and the other, "Charlie." Charlie's mother had spread peanut butter on Ritz crackers and wrapped them in wax paper, Darlene's mom mixed black olives into her tuna salad. Not the lunches that Ma used to make for her: white bread instead of black rye, and no leftover sausage. Katya picked the olives out and tossed them aside. Maybe a squirrel or pigeon would want them. What was Ma doing now? Had she called the police? Yesterday, Katya had written a postcard and asked one of her departing roommates to mail it from somewhere out west: Kansas, Utah, anywhere for a postmark. *The weather here is good. Don't worry. Kocham cię. I love you.* Maybe that would keep the cops from her trail.

A boy approached, brandishing a bunch of purple and green peacock feathers. "Want to buy one?" His grimy T-shirt bore a faded peace sign and a flare of acne covered his face. Feeling sorry for him, Katya gave him a quarter and the other half of the tuna-and-olive sandwich. As she walked through Grant Park, the peacock feathers seemed to act like a magic charm: hippies playing frisbee smiled at her like she was one of them now. And she smiled back—especially at the boys.

Her childhood fairy tale books had been decorated with pictures of long-maned princes on horseback, knights whose locks tumbled from beneath their shining helmets as they defended the princess. From the first time she spotted a boy whose hair spilled over his collar like one of the Beatles, longing stirred within her. Now, her knees melted at the sight of these young squires in purple velvet who lounged on the grass and strummed their guitars with fingers hidden beneath their lacy cuffs. No trapping seemed too old-fashioned or feminine for them: plumes of ostrich feathers sprouted from a hat; small brass bells dangled from belt loops. They adorned themselves in costumes of colorful headbands, paisley shirts, fringe and fur.

The city was their theater and at center stage was Buckingham Fountain. Brightly colored water cascaded over the fountain's splendid wedding cake tiers and gushed from the mouths of bronze seahorses ringing the shallow pool. Every so often, jets turned on and a spout of water shot one hundred feet into the air as the tourists cheered and applauded. They tossed coins into the pink marble basin, making wishes for their own continued health and happiness. When a light rain began to fall, the visitors sprinted to their cars but Katya pulled her sweatshirt hood over her head like a cat burglar. Ignoring the rain and the fountain's spray, she plunged both hands into the cold water and scooped up as many coins as she could reach before running away, her stolen treasure jangling like an alarm. The peacock feathers were bent and wet, but with her new plunder she could eat a good meal and buy another night at the YW.

As usual, she picked a booth beside the diner's chilly window and lingered as long as she could. As she slurped the last greasy spoonful of oxtail soup, a young guy in a denim jacket paused at a phone pole, taped a flier on its surface, and moved down the block. The text was large enough to read from where she sat: rally to end the war, noon tomorrow, at Civic Center Plaza. She knew the spot: it held a strange abstract statue that managed to resemble a bird, a horse, and a woman's face all at the same time. Picasso himself had designed it. A good chance to hawk jewelry during the rally; she could make more earrings and bangle bracelets tonight. And at last she would be doing something against the war, more than her childish school collage had ever done. With a rush of new optimism, she left two dimes next to her empty bowl like a down payment on a miracle, a token of hope.

* * *

It might have been a mistake to arrive at Civic Center Plaza so early, but Katya wanted to be sure of finding a good spot: a concrete bench near the Picasso statue where the sun could provide some warmth. She had stuffed all her belongings into her knapsack and satchel, along with a blanket lifted from the twin bed, telling herself that when she made enough money for another night's stay, she'd bring it back. She draped the blanket over the bench and stowed her possessions beneath it, out of sight. Jo-Jo had at least taught her to be cautious.

The plaza remained empty for what seemed like hours and she kept busy arranging the small collection of handmade jewelry along with some sketches. The best pair of earrings she had kept for herself. Fashioned from yesterday's peacock feathers, the soft fronds caressed her neck when she turned her head or shook the hair away from her eyes.

At last, workers arrived to set up a stage and hang a long banner above it: *Bring the Troops Home Now!* She clutched her hands nervously when blue paddy wagons drove up, rolling right past her, but the cops were busy unloading long wooden sawhorses and no one looked her way. People began to appear, a few at a time and then, as if gates had been flung open, they poured into the square from all sides: hippies and old ladies, priests in white collars, men on crutches and some in wheelchairs, girls in rainbow dresses and nuns in black habits, children, and hundreds of young people. Some wore their hair loose or bristling around their heads like wiry halos; others looked like Piotr and his college friends, dressed in chinos and suit coats. Cardboard signs adorned with peace symbols waved above the crowd's heads: *Resist the Draft. Hell No Don't Go! Not My Son.* A dozen men with grim faces and faded Army jackets stood beneath a huge banner identifying them as Vietnam Veterans Against the War, their arms linked together.

Never had she seen such a huge crowd, not even at the Polish Constitution Day parade. Surely, the president would have to listen to these shouts and clamors for peace, to the drumbeats and chants. She forgot to call out, "Buy some earrings? Bracelets?" as people swarmed by but, moments later, it hardly mattered. A thrumming in the air grew louder as police helicopters loomed overhead. Their rotors beat against the air and the sound boomeranged back, echoing whup-whup-whup-whup. People flinched and ducked as if they expected something terrible might rain down upon them from the skies and the cops pressed forward with their sawhorses, hemming the crowd in. It was all too tight, too tense. Katya couldn't catch her breath. She stood on top of her bench, trying to find some air above the throng.

A young man bounded onto the stage and seized a megaphone. His voice was fervent, cutting through the copters' ominous throb. "The military-industrial complex has the weapons, they own the politicians. They can buy the vote, they can buy the judges! But they can't buy our hearts and minds!" As if they could hear his words, the helicopters rose up, disappearing over the courthouse, and a huge cheer followed in their wake, driving them further away. The crowd surged toward the speaker, ignoring the sharp wind that raked across the plaza. Katya watched the wind lift his long blond hair and the fringe on his suede jacket; she saw how he swayed in rhythm to his own words, light on his feet like a dancer. She couldn't follow everything he said but she caught snippets of swords and plowshares, victory and defeat. It seemed like he directed his voice over the square to her, and she felt like she had when she kissed Ivan behind the school, wanting to melt and burst awake at the same moment.

"We're not going to overthrow the system with pennies, people! So, dig deep into your pockets, brothers and sisters. If we all help out, if we all come together, we will be a force greater than the system. Power to the people!" He chanted, "The PEO-ple . . . u-NI-ted . . . will NEV-er be de-FEAT-ed." As hundreds of voices picked up the rhythm, he jumped down from the stage, vanishing from her view. A group of singers replaced him at the microphone. Katya squatted and wrapped her arms around her knees, huddling against a chill that snaked down her collar. Two blue-jeaned legs appeared before her.

"Support the cause?" That rich hoarse voice, now softer, was even more inviting and his fringed sleeve beckoned to her as he held out a coffee can.

"I don't have any money." It was mostly true, but she blushed as if he'd caught her in a lie. Her fingers shielded the scar on her chin. He grinned and brushed his fine hair away from his forehead. A silver ring glinted on his pinky finger. Impulsively, she pointed to her wares. "Want to buy a bracelet for your girlfriend?"

To her surprise, he reached for her hand and placed it upon his chest. His warmth radiated into her palm along with the steady beat of his heart. "I'm Harlow," he said, smiling.

"Ca-Cathy," she stammered.

"Hang tight, Cathy. I'll be back." He turned away to rattle his donation can at a group of college kids who looked warm in their pea coats and fishermen's sweaters. She pressed her tingling hand against her cheek, knowing she would wait for him.

Chapter Eight

Be my baby now

As they drove north in Harlow's rattling brown Volvo, the street-lights turned on before them like beacons: an invitation to keep moving ahead. After each time Harlow slid the gear shift into place, he would reach over and touch her. Shift, touch, shift, touch—upon her cheek, her hand, the back of her neck. With each caress, she seemed to rise up, surfacing from beneath the sea. Some force within her called to his fingers to brush against her, and Harlow recognized the signal even when she had not.

He took her hand again as they climbed the stairs to a third-floor apartment. A knot of people was gathered in the living room, deep in conversation. Harlow didn't stop, only waved to them, so Katya did the same and then felt foolish. Did she think she was the Constitution Day Parade Queen, saluting the crowd with her white gloved hand? But the others scarcely glanced up to acknowledge her presence.

In a long dim corridor lined with posters, Harlow paused to introduce her. Somehow he knew she'd never met them before. "That's Che," he said, with pride. "Then comes Malcolm, Huey, and down at the end, Trotsky and Lenin." Their unfamiliar faces looked dour to her—Malcolm's threatening stare, Lenin's fierce eyebrows. Only Che's faraway gaze beneath his red beret hinted that he saw a horizon somewhere.

"C'mere, Cathy." Harlow's smile was dazzling in the murky hall. He pulled her to him, pressed his moist lips to hers and she kissed him back, gently at first and then more hungrily. This was what she had longed for; it was the true beginning of her new, free life. Her heart pounded as they entered his bedroom: a mattress on the floor surrounded by stacks of books, candles atop a wooden fruit crate, a flowered bedsheet pinned across the window. As she dropped her knapsack to the floor, she knew she wouldn't turn back now.

Harlow brought out a small silver pipe and a lighter. "Hash," he said.

"I know," she replied, although she didn't. Katya didn't know anything about drugs. *Newsweek* said that the Manson family had smoked hash before they went on their killing spree. Would it turn her into some kind of ferocious, vicious creature? But surely, Harlow wouldn't offer it to her if it was dangerous. She tucked her hair behind her ears and lifted the pipe to her mouth.

Hash resembled tar but it tasted like iron and dirt. Dark smoke continued to coat the inside of her throat even after she coughed it out. But she took another puff and another until her head bobbed above her shoulders, huge on her spindly neck, as large as the unsmiling heads on the posters; she pictured it floating down the hall to join those other images. The thud and pull of rock music drifted in from somewhere.

She hadn't been touched in such a long time, not even by herself . . . but now, Harlow kissed her and she was tugged back to her body, his wet tongue sliding into her mouth. When he stroked her hair, she wanted to purr, the strokes felt so lush. He raised himself on one elbow and as he opened his lips, she was sure he would speak words of love.

"I made a lot of dough for the Young Socialists today," he said. "Wanna know how?" Disappointed, she could think of nothing to say. "Holding out an empty can to beg for donations is no good. Nobody feels compelled to give. They gotta feel that urge, you know?" She nodded, feeling other urges, wanting him to kiss her again. Harlow's secret was that he first tossed a handful of pebbles into the can. "Then shake it right in their faces!" he crowed, leaning closer to her. His warm breath was a little cloud against her cheek. "Makes 'em feel uncomfortable. Like everybody else already threw in and why aren't they doing their share?" He unbuttoned her blouse. "My pebbles are seed money for the revolution!"

"Like stone soup." Her thick tongue was unfamiliar in her mouth, her words slurred together. Sounds rhymed and chimed in her mind.

"What's that, babe?" Harlow's lips slid down her neck, moving to her bare collarbone. She drifted above her body even as she vibrated within it.

She meant that his pebbles were like the old children's story. Three soldiers fooled villagers into cooking a delicious soup by placing round rocks in a large iron pot and adding water. "Soup. Stone. Soup." A thought slowly bubbled into her brain: it sounded as if a stone was in her mouth. Harlow unzipped her jeans and she raised her hips to help him remove them. One of the villagers said the soup would be tastier if it had potatoes and he brought an armful of them from his cellar. She slipped her arms beneath Harlow's shirt, explored the soft hairs that curled on his chest. Another villager brought carrots, with their feathery green tops still

attached. Their bellies touched, skin to skin. The villagers poured from their homes, bearing all their hidden
foods: ripe tomatoes and precious salt, sweet cream.
Harlow licked her nipples. The soldiers stirred the soup
with a long-handled spoon until it was ready. He thrust
inside her, hot and stinging and delicious; there was
enough for everyone; and they ate until they were full.

* * *

The next day, although they hadn't talked about it, Harlow gave her two empty fruit crates to stash her things
in and stated the house rules: pay your share of the rent;
no smack allowed; only use the phone when absolutely
necessary. Katya wondered what he meant by "smack"
(hitting? Surely not kissing?) but was more worried
about the rent.

"What if I can't pay it?"

"Don't worry, babe. You can make up for it in other
ways." He winked. Flustered, she asked why not to make
phone calls.

"Phone's tapped. FBI, Red Squad, all those guys
want to know what we're up to. If you do have to use it,
don't say anything!" How to talk without saying anything was another mystery, but she had no one to call
anyway.

Over lunch she met her new roommates: Vicky (in-
timidatingly pretty with sleek black hair) and Michael
(shaggy-headed and a thick mustache). Katya tried again
to tell the story of stone soup. Harlow shook his head.
"Man, that's the way it always goes down! Soldiers
taking advantage of the peasants." Katya wanted to point
out that the soup-makers carried no weapons, they were

just hungry and footsore, trying to get home to their families, but Harlow began to explain socialism so she picked up a pencil to doodle as he spoke. When she re-focused, he was saying, "Think about it. We got thousands of buildings in the city, each one with six or ten or a hundred apartments. Like a giant beehive full of little cells. And every apartment's got a stove and a fridge and a TV, maybe a stereo, a phone. Everybody's got the same stuff: dishes, guitars, speakers." Michael, picking out a blues tune on his guitar, looked up and nodded. Harlow elbowed Katya. "Your mom have a coffee pot?"

"Sure. One of those glass percolators." The memory stabbed her, like a stitch in her side.

"Yeah, whatever. The point is that your house had one, and the house next door had one, and the house next door to that. On and on through the whole neighborhood, the whole fucking city. Everybody owns the same bourgeois stuff. Worker bees, stuck in a grind to buy it all. We fill all the rooms with more stuff. Yours, his, hers." Harlow pointed his fork at each person around the table. Katya noticed that he didn't include himself. "We're brainwashed not to share because it would bring down capitalism if we got smart and started co-operating. It's like the city is one giant hive, but instead of working together like bees do, we each hoard and drink our own honey."

Katya was pretty sure that bees made honey, not drank it, but there was no chance to say so. Harlow went on. "We've got to start sharing the honey because, come the Revolution, there'll be no more private ownership. So we gotta figure out how to co-operate."

Michael interrupted. "I don't know, man. What makes you think people want to share like that?"

"We already do it. Our whole building shares the washers and dryers in the basement, right? Anyway, socialist theory tells us: collective ownership is the future." He kept talking about common production by the labor masses, not noticing when Vicky murmured to her, "But we always do the laundry, not the guys."

A few days later, Harlow and Michael were inspired to go through the apartment and take all the doors off the hinges so they could live more collectively, like bees. Michael laid one door across a pair of sawhorses for a table but the rest were left leaning precariously against the walls. Finally, after some protests by the girls, the guys agreed to allow them to pin up an Indian bedspread as a curtain for the main bathroom.

On many mornings, Katya was still curled in bed beside Harlow when Vicky would walk down the hall. The only one with a straight job, she needed to get to work early. Just as Vicky passed their open doorway, Harlow would throw off the covers, arching his back and laughing while Katya squealed and grabbed for the sheet to cover herself. Of course, Harlow had good reason to be so proud. His body was beautiful: taut, covered in fine golden hair like a lion, and as tan as if he'd spent the summer working as a lifeguard. He was always happy to pose nude for her, so that she could practice life drawing. But why did he have to show off to Vicky?

Chapter Nine

Don't let the stars get in your eyes

A brisk morning wind blasted down Adams Street, scattering newspapers and leaflets. A wad of paper skittered across the street and bounced against Robert's ankles but as he bent to retrieve it, clutching his fedora against the litterbug wind, the ball rolled away from him, picking up speed as it escaped. Defeated, he pushed through the reluctant door of the Shenandoah Building, an invisible hand blowing stray leaflets in with him. Easter hats on sale at Montgomery Ward, six exotic dancers at the Cheetah Lounge, an urgent call for another rally against the war. He grunted as he gathered them up from the tiled floor. Once again, the trash can had gone missing from the lobby and there was no place to deposit the loose papers. The whole building seemed to sag around him. When Robert had first opened his office in 1954, the Shenandoah was a prestigious spot, sitting proudly among the other presidential streets: Washington, Monroe, Madison. A Sullivan-style entrance greeted visitors, with elaborate designs of leaves and vines twining across the lobby's vaulted ceiling. On one wall, a hand-painted wooden sign listed the physicians, dentists, and lawyers, along with their office or suite number, although there'd been no need to consult the directory, for Franklin, the elevator man, knew them all. "Looking for Mr. Feinberg?" he'd say, pulling the clanking scissor gate aside. "Oh, yes. Suite 1401. Going up." Franklin stood, one dark hand resting on the large brass knob to guide his lift to a gentle stop, always precisely level with the floor.

But fifteen years on, jobs and workers had moved to the suburbs and Chicago's downtown streets were gap-toothed with vacant storefronts. The Shenandoah's tenants changed, adding accountants and losing lawyers. The vines faded; one night the lobby chandelier disappeared. No one bothered to mop into the corners of the hallways and the toilets were stained with rust. Locks on the bathroom doors required a key kept tied to a clipboard.

Franklin was gone too. The new elevator was equipped with a steel door and a column of square buttons whose numbers glowed orange when pressed. The occupants glumly watched the numbers light and dim at each stop. With no one to greet you or to advise you to watch your step, there was nothing to say. This morning, Robert had the lonely elevator to himself. On the seventh floor, faint light strained through a grimy window at the far end of the corridor; the "El" train shrieked half a block away, rattling its panes. He tucked the crumpled papers beneath his elbow as he unlocked a door on which was painted in gold letters, *Robert W. Lewis, M.D., OB, GYN* and *The Women's Bureau.*

A "bureau" might be a spacious suite containing a whole team of personnel dedicated to the care and health of female patients. But behind the frosted glass were only Mrs. Watkins and himself, occupying a waiting room, exam room, and his office with the coat closet converted into a small laboratory, complete with autoclave. Mrs. Watkins made the appointments, answered the telephone, typed out bills, and greeted—if that wasn't too strong a word—those patients who found their way to the seventh floor.

"Good morning, dear," he said to the black-and-white photograph that kept vigil on his desk. Phyllis's steady gaze greeted him with her usual composure, the necklace he had given her on their tenth anniversary sparkling against her white throat. The office blinds clattered as he raised them halfway, disturbing a fine layer of soot that had sifted through the window's gaps. He turned on the hotplate and scooped freeze-dried coffee granules into a cup. While the water heated, he stepped into the next room to pull a fresh length of white paper over the exam table and place a clean gown where it would be convenient for his first patient. Little else to do other than to tug on the white coat that he could no longer button across his belly, unplug the hotplate, and drop two lumps of sugar into his Sanka. He had readied his share of the Women's Bureau for the day ahead. Not the waiting room: that was Mrs. Watkins' domain.

His chair creaked as he settled, cup in hand, to review the date book: Miss Natalie Patterson at nine, Miss Sally Johnson at one-thirty, Miss Jill Epstein at four. The slimness of his schedule wasn't unusual; most patients didn't bother making appointments anymore. They found the Women's Bureau in the phone book or heard about it from a friend, and then just showed up as if they knew he wouldn't be too busy to see them. And he never was.

Not like the old days when brides came in for premarital visits and again shortly after their honeymoons. "My husband . . ." they would boast, waving their left hands to be sure he noticed their small diamonds winking in the light. Robert counseled patience:

don't rush, give time to this new partnership. Let your marriage grow, he would say. Get to know one another. But new wives all wanted to get pregnant right away, as if their happiness could be snatched away if they didn't somehow cement it. Perhaps this rush was a legacy from their own mothers, war brides who had romanced and married in weeks, sometimes days.

Robert had enjoyed delivering babies back then. Now, he provided gynecological services and prenatal care through the first two trimesters, before referring mothers-to-be to Chicago Lying-In Hospital. He told himself his fingers were too unsteady to handle forceps or to perform an episiotomy. In truth though, Phyllis' death had hollowed him out, and every birth cracked him open anew. It was the joy did him in: that radiant happiness of new mothers and fathers, how tenderly they held their infants, and the babies' fawn-soft skin, toes like seed pearls, their gauzy unfocused eyes. Unable to abide such happiness in the midst of his grief, he surrendered his hospital privileges.

"Good morning, Doctor," a reedy voice called from the outer room.

"Morning, Mrs. Watkins."

He heard her exclaim faintly as she reached to hang her coat on the hook behind the door. After so many years, he knew all her sounds that emanated from the waiting room: how she muttered as she trimmed the anemic spider plant by the window, and the way that she thumped her index cards three times upon the desk to align their edges. Those cards were part of a system she had created herself, with a code to indicate the date a patient first appeared in the office along with the source of their referral: Yellow Pages, another physician (infrequently used), or elsewhere. So many Lake View College girls, she assigned them their own code: LV.

The front door opened: high voices and rustles as if a flock of chickadees had arrived. "Doctor," Mrs. Watkins poked her gray head around his doorframe, "Miss Patterson is here."

"Thank you. Please send her in." He stood and offered his hand to both of the identically dressed girls who flounced into his office. How often a young woman in tattered dungarees and sandals brought along a companion dressed in the same outfit, and one who favored high heels and a teased bouffant would inevitably have a friend styled like her shadow. Some kind of protection must be assumed by appearing to have a twin, some strength in knowing that you were doubled, and so wouldn't be singled out for the cruel attentions that sometimes come to those who stand out from the crowd. The pair before him now sported tight blond ringlets, aqua mini-skirts as bright as a neon sign, and thick black lashes that were surely artificial.

"I'm Nat. This is my friend Sharon," one girl tittered, jerking her head at her double.

"Your *best* friend," Sharon said. She snapped her chewing gum and stared at the colorful posters of the reproductive system decorating his walls.

"I need some birth control!" Natalie announced. Sharon giggled. Robert wasn't surprised by her declaration. Today's young women usually blurted out their burning question: Can I have the Pill? Did my lousy boyfriend give me the clap? Are you going to tell anyone I was here?

He motioned for them to sit down. "Let's have a chat first. Are you sexually active?" His standard question. "By which I mean, do you have intercourse?"

"Yeah. But only one time!" Robert waited. Natalie gnawed at a cuticle. "Well, maybe twice."

"I'll need to examine you before providing you with contraception. We can talk about the birth control pill versus a diaphragm or even an IUD." Of course, she would want the Pill; they all did these days, nothing that would require any planning ahead. "But we must run a test to determine that you're not pregnant first."

In this single regard, the Women's Bureau was up-to-date, even ahead of other clinics, for Robert proudly offered the Wampole's two-hour test which could accurately detect pregnancy only four days after a missed period. He directed Natalie to the restroom to provide a urine sample: down the hall, past the elevators. No, her friend must stay behind; he needed to be certain which girl actually produced the sample. After Natalie returned and handed over the warm cup, he checked her blood pressure. It took him several tries because the girls kept prattling to each other, making it difficult to detect the quiet throb of his patient's pulse. When he released the bulb valve and the air sighed out of the pressure cuff, he felt himself deflate as well, unwilling to spend one more minute in the company of these chatterboxes. The internal exam and Pap smear could wait. He suggested the girls go shopping and come back later for their results. *Their* results: now he was regarding the pair of them as one entity.

In the silence after they departed, Robert berated himself for his sense of relief. He wondered, not for the first time, whether it was time for him to retire. But then, as always, he pictured his empty house and his evenings spent in front of the black-and-white TV that brought the endless war, scorched and incandescent, into his unsettled dreams. And the same unanswered questions nagged at him: where would he go each day? What else could he possibly do?

Chapter Ten

A hazy shade of winter

Had there ever been such a frigid winter? Katya could only remember ten or twelve winter seasons but, still, this one must be setting records. The city was caught in a hard freeze like prey in the mouth of a beast with lockjaw. Wind whistled around the ill-fitting windows and sent icy drafts across the floor, straight to Katya's mattress. All through the long months, the radiator valves hissed and shrieked, and the pipes clanged like an unseen janitor hammering against them from his basement furnace room. Sometimes the apartment became so overheated that she had to open the windows a few inches, letting in a blast of cold air. Other times, she pulled on two pairs of socks to keep warm as she huddled beneath the blankets with Harlow.

He never asked where she came from or how old she was. No one in this new life asked nosy questions or gave a last name; they simply accepted you with a nod and a smile. The apartment's living room was a gathering place for friends and strangers to smoke pot, listen to music, discuss politics. Sometimes they were just passing through, intent on reaching California, Ann Arbor, Austin. All through the night they would share their utopian dreams for a peaceful world, planning a new society for Spaceship Earth. When it was too cold to hitchhike, they stayed for days until they could find a ride, sleeping on the couch and floor, or bedding with Vicky or Michael if they were willing.

Katya was grateful for their company, even though she sometimes wished for just a bit of private space for herself, a single door that she could close. What a luxury her childish pink bedroom had been; now she learned such frivolities were only for bourgeois people. But her family hadn't been rich, and wasn't her father a member of the working class? She didn't ask Harlow to explain it even though she figured he would be proud to know his girlfriend came from the proletariat. He spent most evenings downtown at the Young Socialist Alliance. Katya refused to join him there. She wouldn't confess how boring she found his political meetings, couldn't explain her fears about Mr. Wojcek's van prowling the streets, with that empty seat intended for her. When she stayed silent, Harlow would get pissed off and leave the apartment without her.

She didn't mind much. There were plenty of other people to talk to and all those visitors meant chances to sell things she made: headbands, roach clips, earrings and bracelets, even a sketch or two. Still, she never made quite enough to pay her share of the rent and Harlow always needed to chip in for her. In exchange, she crocheted a Christmas present for him, even though he said they shouldn't be suckered into those middle-class traditions. On Christmas morning, she presented him with a long, lumpy blue scarf and tried not to mind that he had no gift for her.

The holiday was cheerful anyway, the apartment exuberantly crowded with friends and strangers. Big Jim cooked a goose, somebody else baked yams for the vegetarians, and everyone crowded around the door that served as their table. After dinner, they brought out guitars and harmonicas and kazoos to play by candlelight. For a few moments, she wondered what had become of the three music-makers who had first beckoned her into this life . . . Wherever they were, they had helped her to escape from drudgery and she silently thanked them for it. A lighter flared for a cigarette and laughing faces appeared out of the gloom, illuminated for a moment before being cast back into the shadows. Like gathering around a campfire, she imagined, or how it must have been back in caveman times, before television.

A few weeks later, there was no more television in the apartment. Late one January night, Bonyman, a scrawny hippie on the road from Texas, was tripping on acid when a Chop-O-Matic commercial came on. He thought the Chop-O-Matic could slice up brainwaves as well as vegetables and, in a frenzy, he tossed the TV set out the window, yelling, "I gotta protect us, man!" Even when the set lay smashed on the sidewalk, he still feared that its powers might penetrate through the brick walls of the building. He dumped a bucket of water onto the broken pieces and only calmed down after ice froze around the shards of glass and plastic, encasing them in a protective layer.

January inched forward, each day unpredictable and yet much the same. Freed from the demands of school and her parents, now the weather held Katya captive much of the time. How had she walked to school in such biting winds, especially since girls weren't allowed to wear pants? Without a good winter coat—that's what Ma would have called it: "a good winter coat"—she dared not brave the long treks to the Free Store or Sunlight Health Foods. With shame, she remembered how

Ma had made sure her children were outfitted with good coats, warm mittens, rubber galoshes to pull over their shoes. She sewed their mittens to either end of a long piece of elastic, threaded through the sleeves of Katya's coat. And when Katya still managed to lose one, Ma hadn't scolded.

She missed that warmth now—not only the wool and corduroy, but how Ma forced her to wear a hat with flaps. "Put lower," she would say, "you want to freeze your ears?" Too late, Katya saw how Ma had cared for her, loved her without saying so. She huddled by the hissing radiator, drawing pictures of mittens lost in snowbanks, waiting for spring.

Sometimes people teased her as she practiced techniques she'd learned in her high school art class: cross-hatching, shading, experiments with perspective. How delighted she was to discover that smudging graphite with her thumb created shadow while the white spaces on the paper gave the illusion of light. Nicknames of "Scribbler" or "Little Miss Picasso" were like a quick hug, a recognition of who she was. She gave many drawings away, eager to trade for nothing more than a compliment or a moment of admiration, while keeping her art supplies beneath the mattress or stashed in the cloth satchel that she kept with her at all times. Not that anyone meant to rip her off, but they tended to pick up her good colored pencils to write a note or draft a speech, heedless of how precious—and expensive—those objects were.

Rip-off was one of the many new words she'd learned, along with bread, dough, and moola for money. Stealing was what the Establishment did: it waged war, polluted the earth, and exploited workers. Harlow said, come the revolution, the Establishment would be over and everyone would own everything communally. No more lawnmowers locked in garages all up and down the street. Leave your doors open all the time; if somebody needs a crockpot or a hammer, they'll walk in and borrow it.

"But what if they don't bring it back?" she wondered aloud.

"Who cares?" Harlow shrugged. "Go to somebody else's crib and borrow another one." Katya thought that might be a little chaotic but he said, "We can't be defined by our possessions, babe. You think you own them, but before you know it, they own you." And nodded in agreement with himself.

Near the end of February, as rent loomed due again, Katya felt sick. Her throat burned as if she had swallowed a cinder, and she grew nauseous at the thought of eating. She lay in bed, silently longing for the warm lemon-and-honey drink that her father used to make when Harlow slouched through the doorway with a paper bag holding a dozen lemons. He knew exactly what she wanted without her needing to say so. In moments like that, she knew they must have been destined to be together. While she drank the hot lemonade, he read her palm.

"This is your life line. It goes all the way across your hand, so you're going to live a long life. These three rings around your wrist? Each one means twenty-five years. And this is your heart line." He ran his tongue along the width of her palm, curving up between the base of her fingers.

"What's that?" she rasped.

"It shows," he inserted his finger between hers, stroking back and forth so that she shivered with pleasure as if his lanky body were already between her legs, "that what you need is a good screw." He grinned, bent to nibble her earlobe, and that was the end of the palm reading. In the next room, someone was playing Beatles records. As she wrapped her legs around him, pulling him closer, the record began to skip and the song stuttered, "It's only love—it's only love—it's only love—" until at last somebody silenced it.

* * *

As the snow finally melted and the sun began to give off warmth again, the apartment grew emptier. The visitors packed up and took off, gypsies returning to the road, leaving behind overflowing ashtrays and a strange silence. At last, Katya could approach Vicky alone while Harlow and Michael were in another room, going on about Spiro Agnew.

"I'm late." She whispered as if she were back in the confessional with Father Ignatius, but Vicky heard and knew what she meant.

"How late?" They sat cross-legged on Vicky's bed, folding laundry together. Vicky's room was the smallest, just off the kitchen, nearly filled by her four-poster bed and matching dresser with a large mirror.

Katya hesitated. "I'm not sure."

"Don't you keep track of your period?" Vicky's dark eyebrows drew down in a scowl.

Katya rubbed the scar on her chin. She didn't want to admit that she paid little attention to when her period arrived or how long it lasted. Every time that shocking red bloom appeared, she rinsed her underwear in the bathroom sink with a sense of shame, like she'd been caught at something. The first time it happened, she'd run crying to her mother, thinking she must have hurt herself somehow. Ma provided scant explanation. She showed Katya how to wear the elastic strap and bulky pad, and told her to always wrap the evidence in toilet paper and hide it at the bottom of the wastebasket. "Now you a woman, Katya. You got to be careful, talking to boys." (As if talking was the problem!)

"I know I had one near Christmas. Oh yeah, and around when Bonyman broke the TV?" she guessed. Katya hoped that Vicky would tell her it was no big whoop, everybody missed their period sometimes, maybe because of stress or sickness. Or for any reason except the one that neither of them was saying out loud. She picked at a loose thread in the bedspread.

"But that was *January*, Cathy." Vicky sounded exasperated. "We're halfway through April!" She sighed. "Do you feel sick, like you need to puke?"

"Sometimes." Another secret: how often she bent over the toilet, retching.

"Okay, don't freak out. You can get tested at a clinic downtown."

"You mean, like a doctor's office?"

"Yeah, a doctor's office." Vicky was becoming impatient. "Called the Women's Bureau. And, you know, if it does turn out to be bad news, there are things you can do."

Katya stared at her. How could she possibly go to a doctor, all by herself? But Vicky wasn't finished. "I mean, you have some *choices*. There are places that can take care of it for you. If you know the right people."

"Abortion?" Katya whispered the sinful word.

Vicky gave a quick nod. "It won't be cheap. Maybe three hundred bucks. Still, it's better than . . ." She didn't need to explain more.

Michael's voice boomed down the hallway. "Phone for you, Vicky." As she stood and straightened her miniskirt she gave Katya a hard look. "Ask for Jane," she commanded as she left the room.

Who? Katya couldn't think of anyone with that name. And ask Jane what? She wrote in tiny letters inside the back cover of her sketchbook: Jane, Women's Bureau. And next to the words, she penciled the impossible sum of three hundred dollars.

Chapter Eleven

Can't find my way home

Fudge, fudge, fudge, boom-boom-boom . . ."
As Katya lay on the cool linoleum floor, she listened
to girls' voices chanting outside in the soft spring air.
Her neighbors who lived in a basement apartment were
paying her ten bucks to unlock their door when Ma Bell
came to fix their telephone, and the cash would come in
handy. She didn't like to ask Harlow for rent money
again, especially when he was so busy organizing another boycott, this time against grapes.

Don't think about grapes right now. She'd thrown
up for the second time a little while ago and now she
hoped that the repairman wouldn't arrive too soon. So
many foods were disgusting: strings that hung from a
ripe banana, snotty egg whites . . . even the memory of
foods she had loved when her mother cooked them, like
golabki kapusciane, stuffed cabbage leaves, or the cold
beet summer soup, *chlodnik.* Ma would pour extra cream
on top of the soup from a pitcher shaped like a little cow.
Its brown tail formed the handle and the cream poured
through its open mouth. It was a silly thing but still, re-
membering it now made Katya want to cry.

She rolled over. On a patch of bare sidewalk visible
through the tall barred window above her, skinny dark
legs in white sneakers hopped in place. Jump ropes
slapped against the ground like a rapidly ticking clock.
Double Dutch, she thought. When I feel better, I'll stand

up and watch those girls jump. At her parish school, girls skipped rope out on the blacktop during recess, chanting their rhymes; the nuns kept a careful watch to make sure that everyone got a turn. But when she transferred to a public high school, she found a small huddle of black girls showing off a syncopated style, clutching a rope in each hand. They spun the ropes toward each other—left, right, left, right—while they shouted to the jumpers. Tight black pigtails sprang from the sides of their heads, their hair slicked into place with Dippity-Do. Their friends swayed rhythmically on eager feet, waiting for just the right moment to spring into the swishing ropes and show off their moves. The Double Dutch corner was a lively unsupervised spot. Off to one side, a few white girls still jumped alone with their single strand. No one bothered to watch *their* tricks.

At lunchtime, Katya would take her sketchbook outside and lean against the chain link fence to watch the Double Dutch competition. Boys stood in the shadows where they could sneak a cigarette and admire how the girls' skirts lifted and fell, lifted and fell, as they leapt into the air. Now, outside the basement window, the unseen jumpers continued with their rhyme, words marking time with the rhythm of the rope.

Fudge, fudge, fudge! Boom-boom-boom.
Call the judge. Boom-boom-boom.
Momma's got a brand-new baby!

The last word was sung with great emphasis, drawing out the first syllable for an extra beat and then shouting the final sound as the rope struck the ground: Baaay-BEE!

She'd heard this song before, but hadn't listened to the words. Why would you call a judge when a baby came? What did fudge have to do with it? Did the booming mean a drum or was it a nonsense word to make the rhythm?

Not a BOY. Boom! Not a GIRL. Boom!

Just an ordinary baaayBEE!

Katya slipped one hand beneath her blouse. Her belly was the same yielding surface as always, still concave as long as she lay flat on the green linoleum. Could an ordinary baby be growing somewhere beneath her belly button? Was she one of those girls who got "in trouble"? The possibility filled her with anxiety.

Wrap it up in tissue paper!

Send it down the elevator.

First floor: Stop!

Second floor: Stop!

The girls' voices were merry and carefree. Two sneakers hit the sidewalk flatfooted at each *stop*, toes facing the window. She could see a small dark hole in the canvas of one shoe. As the song continued, imaginary elevator rising, Katya found herself holding her breath and silently counting along.

Eighth floor: Stop!

Kick it out the door!

The ropes dropped to the ground. Voices rose in raucous laughter. Six shoes hopped and skipped carelessly over the snaky tangle. In a moment, the girls had switched places and another pair of sneakers began jumping to another familiar chant. "Teddy bear, teddy bear, turn all around. Teddy bear, teddy bear, touch the ground . . ." A brown hand brushed the pavement, following the directions, but Katya stopped listening. She closed her eyes to focus on her body, wishing she could see inside the dark spaces where something might—

please not!—be growing.

One Christmas Eve, the gift that Piotr unwrapped was a "Visible Man Body Kit." The package promised All Vital Organs and a Handbook Written by Medical Authorities. Inside the box, little beige pieces of plastic waited to be painted. The liver was meant to be turned purply red, intestines a lurid shade of coral, and the tiny gallbladder, oddly, should be tinted green. All the parts had to be glued into place: heart inside lungs, stomach under heart, and then nestled into the clear plastic halves to form an entire man, head to toe. Each night, after supper was cleared, her brother had assembled the man together, applying airplane cement with toothpicks while she sat beside him, dizzy from the fumes and the secrets that were being unveiled.

If only it had been a "Visible Woman Kit," she might know what was happening inside her body now. Although the plastic model might not have revealed all the right parts. Just like Barbie's boyfriend, Ken, the Visible Man had disappointed her. Between his legs, she found only a vague, unfinished bulge. Katya had brought her curiosity to a lonely corner of the school library, to consult World Book Encyclopedia's *H* volume where transparent pages layered upon each other illustrated the Human Body. She studied how the blood vessels branched, red and blue, through that mysterious area between pink thigh muscles. And although she'd heard Piotr's friends ("Pete," they called him when no parents were around) snickering about boners, she knew there was no bone down there.

Still, she hadn't known what boys hid beneath their clothes until she met Harlow. Living with him, she had witnessed his cock's surprising ability to change shape and size, how it could become animated and beckoning, then deflate into a tired, slack version of itself. Sometimes, in her dreams, she sensed what that kind of transformation might feel like and she became larger, more vivacious—a girl who was unequivocally brave, who could lose her temper in fury, who might assert her will. But when she awoke, she was still small, the same pale color as the sheets tangled around her and she couldn't imagine what it would be like to have a body that altered so radically. Until now. Everything would change if her body had betrayed her, if she were to grow fat and round, to swell like a parade balloon.

The doorbell rang, interrupting her thoughts: the phone repairman at last. She pressed the button to buzz him in through the front entryway and stood on her toes to squint through the peephole. Hat, clipboard, Illinois Bell stitched upon his crisp gray shirt. She unlocked the door and pointed at the silent apparatus on the wall.

"How long's it been out?" He lifted the receiver and unscrewed the mouthpiece, revealing a surprising mass of colorful wires crammed behind those little holes. She wanted to ask why so many different colors, but kept quiet so that she could watch. After a few minutes of fiddling, he held the handset out to her.

"Let's try it out. Here, call somebody." The phone was the nauseating fleshy shade of Silly Putty, and her stomach lurched at the idea of touching it. With one fingertip, she dialed the seven digits she had memorized in kindergarten. As the phone rang at the other end, she pictured the squat black instrument that sat on a table between the sofa and her father's green armchair. Four rings, five . . . the repairman moved the handset to his ear.

"Hello, ma'am. Just testing the line. Thank you." He hung up before she could decide whether she wanted to listen to Ma's voice or to say anything at all.

As Katya locked the door behind the repairman, she remembered the last time she'd seen that little china cow pitcher: on the morning when she'd wobbled on a kitchen stool as she stole her mother's money. She couldn't go back. Not even if she was a girl "in trouble."

Chapter Twelve

Within you and without you

In the closet that served as his laboratory, Robert divided the urine sample in half so that he could run the test twice, ensuring there would be no errors. Today's Miss Carter must not drink enough water: her urine was the color of goldfish. With funnel, filter paper, test tubes and a bottle of hCG antiserum, he devoted himself to the quiet tasks of measuring and titrating until lunch time. Then, as was his usual habit on Mondays, he walked to Stouffer's, a restaurant favored by ladies and known for excellent service. Phyllis used to meet him for lunch there each week. They would be welcomed by name and given a table halfway down the room, not too near to the drafty kitchen door nor the large windows looking onto Randolph Street. Phyllis would show him what she had bought that day: a pair of gloves wrapped in pink tissue paper, flowered hairbands to send to her niece. And then, from the depths of a green Marshall Field's shopping bag, a box of Frango Chocolate Mints would emerge.

"Now, how did those get in here?" she would always ask, widening her eyes in mock surprise. "Someone must have mixed up the packages."

Robert played along. "How lucky! Frangos happen to be my favorite candy."

"Well then, this must belong to you!" And she would hand him the slim box and he would slip it into his jacket pocket, never taking his gaze from her bright face. It seemed to him that their ritual was a perfect expression of love: how she thought of him as she hovered over the glass counter in the candy department, choosing what he favored; the delight she took in "discovering" the box at the bottom of her bag, and the surprise they both feigned; the happiness in her eyes as she gave it to him. He patted the box once or twice during the meal as if to assure himself that it was still there. Back at the office, he would offer mints to Mrs. Watkins (proud of her slim figure, she never took more than one) and doled the rest out to himself throughout the week so that on Monday morning, shortly before meeting his wife for lunch again, the last one dissolved on his tongue.

If he had cared to date after Phyllis was gone, his weekly visit to Stouffer's would have provided him with plenty of opportunities. The dining room was filled with coiffed and gloved ladies; as he followed the hostess through the crowded tables and took his customary seat, they watched him like sparrow hawks. But he ignored their hungry smiles, the fingers fluttered hopefully in his direction. Instead, he raised a glass of ice water to silently toast the empty seat opposite him. He remembered the last time she sat there, how her thin hand was as white as the rice pudding that she slowly spooned to her lips. She'd had no appetite but wanted to please him and their waitress who hovered anxiously nearby. That server had long since retired. The brunette who waited on him today was new, she hadn't known Phyllis, had never seen him dine with anyone. Robert tucked the cloth napkin into his collar and ordered the day's special without bothering to ask what it was.

* * *

His next patient, a pseudonymous Miss Johnson, seemed unsurprised to learn that she wasn't pregnant. Had it never occurred to her that she was taking risks by having sex without precautions? Sometimes he wished he could rebuke his careless patients. He imagined himself snapping, "Cross your legs instead of your fingers!" But instead, he offered his usual counsel as he wrote out a prescription.

"One pill each morning, you understand? Make an appointment to return in a month's time so that I can check your blood pressure. Remember, you must take the Pill every single day, not only when you plan to have sexual relations."

Miss Johnson rummaged in her purse, uninterested in his advice. What could he possibly know about sex? After all, he was old, over sixty. Even if he bumped into her on the street tomorrow, she wouldn't recognize him. Robert slumped in his desk chair, feeling heavy and listless while he listened to Mrs. Watkins settle the bill. He hadn't bothered to ask Miss Johnson whether she received any pleasure from the acts in which she engaged. Some of his younger patients laughed at the kinds of questions that he used to pose to the brides. Back then, he had earned a reputation as a progressive gynecologist who took pride in his gentle, careful ability to describe the intimacies of marriage. Perhaps it wasn't as important for this generation to learn to satisfy each other if all they sought was a fling. If it was only some boy having sex with a girl who'd caught his eye or the other way round. Not enough thrills? So long, see you later, move on to somebody else.

But when a couple had committed themselves, when they vowed to create a life together and share a bed for thousands of nights until they ran out of time and breath—then, mutuality mattered. Neither partner should respond to the other's touch with resignation or dread or indifference! Each one ought to welcome sex, and to dedicate themselves to the other's joyful, wet fulfillment as he and Phyllis had done. These young kids didn't know what they were missing.

Robert stood to spread a new sheet of paper over the exam table. He could almost recall the cool Frango mint on his tongue, mingled with rich chocolate. But he pushed the memory aside: he knew he would never taste that sweetness again.

* * *

His final patient of the day. He hoped Miss Carroll would welcome the results, but her drooping shoulders signaled her expectation of defeat.

"The test shows that you are pregnant." He paused to let the news sink in. Once in a great while this news was greeted with a smile. A look of triumph might flash across that girl's face as if she now knew exactly what to do and he could almost see the young man in her mind, standing on the horizon, as she galloped toward him like an eager pony. But usually, Robert was the herald who crushed dreams, ended education, ruined lives. "Based on the date of your last menstrual period, about twelve weeks along."

Miss Carroll stared at him, the color draining from her spotty face. "I can't be."

"I'm sorry. The test is very accurate." He pushed a box of tissues toward her before tears began to drip down her cheeks.

"But . . . how am I going to tell my parents? They don't even know I have a boyfriend."

"I'm sorry," he repeated. "Will he support you?"

She shook her head, looking toward the window as if it might offer an escape. "I'll have to leave college."

"Many families come around and find ways to welcome a new addition together. I hope you'll return for prenatal care. Or I'll be glad to provide you with a referral to another obstetrician for the remainder of your pregnancy."

Miss Carroll plucked nervously at her skirt. "I've heard there are places I could go . . . where they can help . . . if you just *can't* have a baby."

He knew what she hinted at. From memory, he recited his response, aware that he sounded stiff and bureaucratic. "I'm sorry. No physician in the State of Illinois is allowed to provide an abortion unless the mother's life is in imminent danger."

"Just tell me what to do!" Her voice rose in panic. "I'll do anything!"

Robert spread his hands on the desk in a signal of finality. "The procedure is legal now in New York State and in Florida." But from the distraught look on his patient's face, he may as well have said Mars or Venus.

Chapter Thirteen

Don't know why you say goodbye

May presented a balmy gift to the city: one of those rare azure mornings when the sun shone down, blessing each street corner, every water tower and drawbridge and news stand. Lake Michigan shimmered like a mirror and the lakefront overflowed with students ditching class and workers claiming sick days, basking atop the blocks of concrete that formed the breakwater. As Robert strolled to the Shenandoah, he wished that he could join them. Alas, his obligations were not to be tossed aside so lightly. Mrs. Watkins would be at her usual post and expecting him to do the same. But as noon approached, he was struck again with that rash desire to do something uncharacteristic and spontaneous. On such a glorious day, eating a liverwurst sandwich at his desk was too pitiable to consider. He strode into the waiting room to make his announcement.

"I'm going out."

"Out?" Mrs. Watkins uttered the word in the tones of a prisoner who cannot fathom what lies beyond the walls. "Where?"

"To lunch."

"But . . . it's Tuesday!" Indeed it was, and there was nothing more to say about that. When he didn't reply, she added, "What about our patients? What if we have a walk-in?"

The doctor settled his fedora upon his head. "Have them make an appointment. Or they can wait; I'll be back by one-thirty." The door swung shut behind him and as his footsteps echoed down the corridor to the elevator, Mrs. Watkins might have heard him whistle.

Freed from routine, he veered ·left instead of right, happily bumping elbows with other people equally overjoyed to be released. Across Michigan Avenue, tour buses lined up to discharge their gawking passengers outside the Art Institute. Art students lugging their black portfolios pushed through the revolving glass doors and disappeared, while dozens of young people sprawled upon the broad steps as if they were in their own living rooms and not out in public. The museum's grand entrance was guarded by a pair of majestic lions whose long tails had been rubbed by visiting schoolchildren over so many years that they gleamed brightly in the sun. As he waited to cross the street, Robert's eye was drawn to a lanky fellow casually leaning against one of the lions, his crown of shaggy brown curls vivid against the muscular green body. A harem of girls crowded around him, competing for his attention. What was it like to be that cocky and attractive, that confident? Robert had never been so self-assured, not even as a young man. Watching the tableau, he recalled the statues' nicknames: one was called "Defiance," while the other—like the lad who posed against it—was "On the Prowl."

"Spare change?" A tall, dark-haired girl accosted him. A yellow daisy was painted on her cheek. The panhandler stood in front of him, blocking his way. As he hesitated, she demanded again, "Got any change, mister?" The traffic signal turned green but his feet would not move; he found himself unable to decide whether to reach into his pants pocket in search of a quarter or to tell her to get lost. Why was she begging on the streets? This was Chicago, not Calcutta! Giving up on him, she darted across the intersection even as the light changed to red and drivers honked and shouted their disapproval.

Robert's sense of adventure evaporated amidst his indignation. Turning away from the museum, he retreated to the Artists' Snack Shop down the block. To his surprise, that friendly waitress, Louise, smiled as if she recognized him. But perhaps this was how she welcomed everyone. Still, he waited until a seat opened at her section of the counter.

"How's the world treating you today, hon?" she asked. Before he could figure out his answer, she hollered over his shoulder, "Hey!" Robert swiveled around on his stool to spot a group of long-haired kids in shabby clothes heaping sugar and lemon slices into paper cups. The kids glanced at Louise and rushed to top off their loot before scurrying for the door. "Leave some for the paying customers!" she yelled after the young bandits. One of them doffed his cap to her as they spun through the revolving door.

"Hippies!" she said, sounding more amused than angry. "They come in every day and help themselves to what they call self-serve lemonade. Sometimes they steal used tea bags out of the cups before we clear the tables. They believe in free love, free lemonade, and no tipping." With a wink, Louise padded away to serve other customers but as he finished his sandwich, she returned, bearing a generous slice of pecan pie. She set the plate on the scuffed countertop and pushed it toward him with the tips of her fingers as if she were having a last-minute doubt whether he would accept her offering. "I thought you might like this." She rubbed her thumb against an invisible speck on the stainless-steel rack that held the menus.

"Thank you." Robert sat up straight and tasted the pie. Brown-sugar filling melted down his throat, sending a sweet warmth into his body. "It's wonderful," he said, holding her gaze. Her face brightened with pleasure as she smoothed her curls. How astonishing! She was flirting with him. He'd forgotten what this felt like: his pulse quickening, the hint of promise. He drew a deep breath just as a bell chimed, summoning her to pick up a new order from the kitchen window. While he savored the rest of his dessert, he watched Louise move behind the counter, appreciating how her capable hands lifted the plates and how her hips rolled beneath her uniform. How glad he was that he had ventured out of his office today.

But when he returned to the Women's Bureau, he found Mrs. Watkins in a state of agitation. She came out from behind her desk to clutch him by the arm just as he crossed the threshold. Yes, he was running a few minutes behind, but that shouldn't account for the frown with which she greeted him.

"Just like I thought: we had a walk-in. I've put her in your office."

"But why?" There were three unoccupied chairs in the waiting room.

"She's . . . not suitable. Doesn't even know what day it is. I didn't trust her alone in the exam room and I didn't want her hanging around out here." Mrs.

Watkins pressed her lips together as she handed him a patient index card. Clearly, she wasn't about to say more. Curious, he entered his office to take a look.

A girl sat cross-legged on the floor, giving him a clear view of her bare feet, blackened with grime. Light brown hair shielded her face as she bent over something in her lap while Phyllis' portrait lay before her, staring up at the ceiling.

"Good afternoon," he grumbled as he reached to return the photo to its rightful spot. The girl raised her head, showing him a young, serious face. Bedraggled peacock feathers dangled from her earlobes. Clear complexion, hazel eyes. With high cheekbones and deep-set eyes, she resembled a pixie—except for the crooked scar on her chin: a wound that hadn't been properly sutured. A quick glance at her card: Miss Cathy Jones claimed to be eighteen years old but surely, she couldn't be more than sixteen. Mrs. Watkins had added a black *X* in one corner: some kind of demerit for those dirty bare feet.

"I'm Dr. Lewis. Won't you sit down?" He pointedly nudged the chair closer to her. She rose and perched rigidly at the edge of her seat, clutching a sketchpad close to her body.

Robert leaned against his desk and composed his face to be neutral, non-judgmental. It seemed important that he not sit where the furniture would create a barrier between him and this waif. "What brings you here today?"

Miss Jones slowly surveyed his office, taking in the wall posters and anatomical models depicting the female reproductive system. "This is the Woman's

Bureau? The whole thing?" Her voice was low but he caught the error.

"Yes, the Women's Bureau," he corrected, unable to help himself.

"I thought it might be all women here. Maybe somebody named *Jane*?" She seemed to place emphasis on that name.

He shook his head. "Didn't you see my name on the door when you arrived?" He took care to keep his voice gentle. Even after years of explaining that he *was* the Women's Bureau, he was pained by how let down this girl looked. A scene leapt to mind from an old movie shown on television every spring when Toto pulled aside a curtain to reveal that the wizard was a short bald and altogether fallible man. Robert ran one hand over his own thinning hair and nudged a box of tissues toward her, in case she began to cry.

"No Jane here. Just me," he said, spreading his empty hands. He tried to smile. "And Mrs. Watkins, of course." The girl frowned, rubbing the scar on her chin. Even her feather earrings fluttered like they wanted to leave the room. The pad of paper slipped from her lap and landed on the floor. Robert reached to retrieve it and caught his breath in surprise: it was a crayon portrait of Phyllis, copied from the black and white photo. But now, that beloved face glowed with life: her cheeks were a healthy pink, her hair restored to a rich brown, and her eyes the exact shade of sea green that he remembered so well. How had the girl known to get that right? The nose wasn't perfect, and Phyllis herself might not have appreciated how wide her mouth had become, but Cathy Jones had somehow managed to revive the essence of his late wife.

"It's lovely. You're very talented."

She ducked her head and blushed at the compliment. "Well, I like to make things more colorful, happier, you know?" For the first time, he caught a hint of an accent. Not German. Eastern European?

"Are you an art student?"

"No!" she blurted, then clamped her lips together; she'd said too much. Robert waited, sensing that she had more to tell. She gazed at the floor and out the window before saying, softly, "My parents made me quit school." She shook her head as if to chase away a bad memory or perhaps to show that she disagreed with their decision.

"That's too bad. I see real promise here." He handed the sketchpad back, saying, "Will you tell me why you came in today? I'd like to help you if I can." She regarded him for a long moment. At last her thin shoulders eased, decision evidently made.

"I need a test 'cause I missed my period a couple times."

"Have you had intercourse?"

His usual question brought a faint smile. "Well, yeah! I have a boyfriend."

"And what forms of birth control have you been using?" Cathy looked away and gave no answer. He knew that meant no contraception and as he reached for her left wrist to time her pulse, tried another tack. "Will he be coming by to pick you up?"

"Harlow?" The name was out before she could catch it and she stammered at her mistake. "No, he doesn't know I'm here. I mean, he's over at the Young Socialists."

"Tell me about him." Her pulse was steady but she was quite pale and her fingernails showed ridges that could signal anemia. Too soon to suggest a blood test though; he must tread lightly so as not to scare away this delicate girl.

"Oh, he's cool. He's really fine, and smart. And he knows a lot about politics and other stuff ..." She seemed to run out of attributes before adding, "He wants to change the world, you know?" She shot a quick look at him, gauging whether he took her seriously.

"That's good. A lot of change is needed, don't you think?" She nodded vigorously, the feathers on her earlobes swaying in agreement. "Does he love you?"

"Yeah!"

Her answer was too quick, too sure. Girls always thought that love was what motivated their young men. If only that were true! Suppressing a sigh, he explained what would come next—she was to void into a cup for the pregnancy test and he would conduct a physical exam in the next room. He'd have her results in a few hours, after which they would talk some more.

"What kind of exam?" Her pink cheeks and strained voice told him that this must be her first visit to a gynecologist.

"We'll take it step by step, and I'll explain as we go." He retrieved a plastic cup from the cabinet and escorted her to the waiting room. "The lavatory is down the hall." He watched her drift from one side of the corridor to the other, the lavatory key dangling from its clipboard, and the wide hems of her jeans whispering against each other. The shoeless sprite was in no hurry: she craned her neck to look up at the ceiling, bent over to study the faded designs in the tile floor. At the end of the hallway, her slight frame was briefly silhouetted against the window while she struggled with the key. The clipboard clattered against the door and she disappeared inside.

He returned to his office to wait and wonder. That scar. Parents who forced her to drop out of school. And the fact that her boyfriend didn't know she was here pricked at him like a warning. Maybe she was dawdling in the lavatory, humming as she examined the frosted glass in the window. Or staring wistfully at the Modess sanitary napkin dispenser on the wall. If he was the kind of man who prayed, he might send up a wish that he would not have to deliver bad news to her. Please don't let her be pregnant. Not this one.

At last she shuffled in with the plastic cup trembling in her fingers. "I want to ask a question."

"Be my guest."

She pointed to the photograph of Phyllis. "She's dead, right? Wait! That's not my question. What I want to know is, when did she die?"

His answer was very soft. "Almost eight years ago."

To his surprise, her face brightened. "Okay then! That's good. After seven years, all the cells in your body die and get replaced by new ones. So, in a way, you're not even the same person and you don't have to be sad anymore."

He hid a smile behind his hand. What an odd girl! Telling him, a man of medicine, how the human body worked! Her theory wasn't correct, of course, but it was a generous thought and a genuine attempt to release him from his grief.

She wrestled her sketchpad out of her satchel and placed it on his desk. Carefully, she removed the portrait and handed it to him.

"Here. You can keep it."

Speechless, he held the paper by the edges, Phyllis smiling up at him as he tried to compose himself. "Thank you. This is wonderful. I think it deserves to hang in a special place." They both pointed to a spot opposite his desk where he could admire it from his chair and, at the same moment said, "There."

"Jinx!" Again, that elfin grin lit up her face, even as it tugged against her crooked scar.

"But now the artist must sign her work before going into the exam room."

She beamed. "Nobody ever asked me before." Robert unscrewed the cap from his best fountain pen. She bent over the portrait, taking her task seriously. The first stroke formed a straight line and she paused as if she'd made a mistake. He opened his appointment book to pretend he hadn't noticed, listening to the pen scratching furiously for a minute.

"Okay, catch you later." She slipped from the room. Her signature had been partly crossed out and amended, a crooked "C" to match the white line on her chin. Robert waited to hear her call that she had changed into a gown and was ready for him to enter the exam room. But instead, the elevator signal rang and he knew that Cathy Jones had fled.

Chapter Fourteen

Four dead in Ohio

Katya emerged from the doctor's building into a warm afternoon, the air tender against her skin, the usual stench of bus exhaust and trash cans swept away by a lake breeze. She crossed Wabash Street, keeping an eye out for shards of glass on the pavement. Maybe she should go back to Lincoln Park to try and find her shoes. Earlier, she'd smoked pot there with Birdie and Theresa and some guy whose name she didn't remember; the stuff had been surprisingly strong and she wasn't sure where she had left her sneakers. But the high had done its job: it helped her brave going to the clinic alone. To her relief, she'd found nothing worse than that dragon lady at the front desk who'd glared at her and made her wait in the office. The doctor himself was nice in the ways she imagined grandfathers must be: kind, gentle, old-fashioned. A little sad, though. But he wanted to give her a physical exam and she didn't like the sound of that. Somehow, he would reach inside her; just thinking of it awakened the nausea that accompanied her so often these days.

A crowd of shoppers emerged from Florsheim Shoes, battering her with their bags of shoe boxes. Katya pressed her back against the plate glass window to let them pass, unwilling to let them interrupt her thoughts. Anyway, what would the doctor be looking for? He said her pee would tell him if she was pregnant. *I can't be, I can't be.* The phrase clattered through her mind, day and night, like an endless freight train hurtling down the track. Doctor Lewis didn't seem to know who Jane was, but even if he had, how could she raise three hundred bucks? *I can't be, I can't be.* But if she was, maybe Harlow would be happy about a baby. There was plenty of room in the apartment and Vicky could help too.

Think about good things. The old doctor's praise for her drawing thrilled her although she'd nearly goofed up her signature, starting to write her real name by mistake. She didn't feel badly for lying about her name and age; those were necessary parts of her life. Even Harlow didn't know she was sixteen. But the doctor's question stung: did Harlow love her. He must; why else would he have invited her to move in? Okay, he hadn't exactly invited, but he did want her to stay after their first night together. He never said she should go; he made room for her; they shared a bed; they made love and, every time, she said that she loved him. To make sure that it wasn't just sex. Harlow would smile and kiss her. But he never repeated those words to her. And sometimes, when he came back late at night, his skin and hair held scents that she didn't recognize—not his patchouli oil nor the shampoo that she liked best. She worried then about where he'd been, and with whom.

"Hurry!" Someone jostled against her, yelling, "The rally's starting." Katya tried to shake off her grip but the other girl (she recognized her now: Shorty, who lived near them on Belmont) tugged her along the sidewalk. "They're shooting us! Come on!"

"What're you talking about?" Suddenly, the sidewalks had become choked with masses of shoppers, workers, students. She and Shorty had to shoulder their way through the crowds. "Who's shooting? Where?"

"The fucking pigs!" Shorty sobbed. "In Ohio. The National Guard fired at the students. They *killed* them! Four people are dead. We've gotta get out in the streets, now!" She pulled Katya around the corner into a Civic Center Plaza that was jammed with people, as if everyone had heard the news at once, like an electric current running from one distraught person to the next. Someone tied a strip of black cloth around her upper arm. A bedsheet strung between two poles declared "They Can't Kill Us All" in weeping red paint. In front of her, four crosses were scrawled in white shoe polish on the back of a gray sweatshirt. Other protests had been loud, even festive, but this crowd seethed with anger, trembled in mourning.

Harlow's familiar voice blared over a bullhorn. "The government is coming after us! Students at Kent State were armed only with their signs and their righteous belief that this war is wrong! Are we going to take it??"

"No!" howled the crowd in response. Their grief and rage thrummed across the plaza like thunder on a sultry summer day. As always, Katya was struck dumb with admiration at Harlow's ability to rouse people, how he could soothe or stir, agitate or appease with his voice. She kept pressing through the tightly packed bodies, trying to move toward the stage, but the crowd surged forward with her, their fists beating the air, everyone drawn to Harlow's urgent call, so that she seemed to make no progress at all.

"They're running scared now, people! We're such a threat to the Establishment now, they'll do anything to stop us. But We. Will. Not. Stop." A thousand voices roared in appreciation. "No more business as usual! We're taking it to the streets. They might kill me but hundreds will rise up to take my place." His echoing words struck the walls of the Federal Building like a hammer against stone. Cold fear gripped her. Could someone shoot Harlow? He often said all the good ones got killed: Dr. King, Malcolm, Bobby. A line of helmeted cops stood in menacing formation before the doors of City Hall, billy clubs twitching in their black-gloved hands.

"No going to work tomorrow! No going to school. We're going to shut this city down. Strike! Strike! Strike!"

On all sides, people were sobbing and taking up the call to strike. Katya shoved the broad back ahead of her, pushing against the four white crosses drawn on his gray sweatshirt, but he did not yield and her palms came away sticky with white polish. She yelled for Harlow, her voice unheard in the tumult, and then shrieked in pain as someone trod on her bare toes.

"Come here." In her ear, a quiet voice. "Come to us." A gentle arm wrapped around her shoulders and she was pulled into a circle of silver-haired women clad in long indigo skirts. They wore small peace symbols on buttons pinned to their collars and pendants lying upon their bosoms. While others shouted and shook their fists in the air, the blue and silver women remained still, shielding her and, within the protection of their circle, Katya could breathe again. Her vulnerable feet were safe, surrounded by their sturdy shoes that held fast to the ground, resisting the tide of the crowd's movement.

Harlow's voice continued to trumpet above their heads. "We will never surrender! We will not stop; we will not move." And the circle of women began to sing, "We shall not be moved." Their voices were sweet and harmonious, others nearby picked up the tune, and the song spread through the crowd, expanding over the plaza until the words tumbled against the granite walls and echoed back, in tumultuous agreement: "Just like a tree that's standing by the water, we shall not be moved . . ." All afternoon, the heartbeat of mourning and anger pounded beneath the sun's glorious, oblivious gaze. Whenever the bullhorn voices preached vengeance and the mood began to turn dark or menacing, her ring of protectors lifted their voices in song again, pouring oil on troubled waters. We shall overcome. Down by the river side. Where have all the flowers gone?

At last, as color drained from the sky and long shadows chilled the plaza, the protesters began to disperse. One of the women brought out a sandwich wrapped in wax paper. At the sight of it, Katya realized how weary and famished she was. It was an effort to take the sandwich. "Will you be all right now?" the woman asked.

"Yeah, thanks." As she bit into the bread, she spotted Harlow moving through the dwindling ranks. "There's my boyfriend!" The circle seemed to hesitate and then moved apart slightly, like opening a door to allow her to step through. As Katya hurried away from her safekeepers, it occurred to her to turn and ask, "Who are you?"

The sandwich woman smiled. "We're Quakers, my dear. The Society of Friends."

A society of friends: how lovely that sounded. She had once searched for a small group of singing friends with the hope that they would bring her into a new life.

The Quaker women called out to her, but their gentle voices were lost, and Katya ran to catch up with Harlow.

Chapter Fifteen

I want to hold your hand

Robert wanted to return to the warm afternoon air in order to recollect the pleasant exchange he'd had with Louise over lunch and to puzzle over the young, scarred artist. He made an excuse of needing a trip to First National Bank As he left his building, shouts and the sound of drum beats echoed through the canyons of skyscrapers. Another anti-war protest must be taking over the plaza at City Hall; to avoid those unruly crowds, he walked six blocks out of his way. Only a single teller window was open at the bank; by the time he got back to the Bureau, it was nearly four and he still needed to complete the Wampole's test. He removed his hat as he entered, ready to apologize for his tardiness. The waiting room chairs were empty. Mrs. Watkins was working on a jumble puzzle as she often did when there were no tasks to be done.

"Is Miss Jones in my office?" he asked, hopefully.

Mrs. Watkins did not look up. "No but I suppose she'll be running in with those filthy feet any time now."

He closed his office door with particular care, determined not to reveal how annoyed he felt. Had Mrs. Watkins always been so querulous, so detached from the patients? Or had the years worn upon her, rubbing away all the soft and rounded parts of her nature, leaving only sharp edges? When Phyllis passed away, Mrs. Watkins had been helpful. It was she who had brought the obituary he composed to the Tribune Building, walking it over herself to make sure it reached the correct department. She hung a discreet black-edged sign on the door while they closed for a week, purchased appropriate notecards from the stationers for him to acknowledge the sympathy cards and flowers, and she attended the funeral. But she hadn't wept, and she pretended not to notice when he did.

The young wives used to talk to her. They showed off their wedding rings and new hats, sometimes asked her for advice. Those were the patients who called in advance to make appointments and who paid their bills on time. The changes in his practice must grate upon her: unmarried girls, Negroes with big Afros, hippies, his sliding scale fees. Dirty feet. Perhaps he should speak to her about her attitude. But they'd never had conversations like that. Still, he wished she would be less judgmental. How intimidating she must seem to someone like the delicate young artist.

He examined the signature on her drawing, that first vertical pen stroke now a tall T in the middle of her name: *CaThy* followed by a faltering *jones*. Cathy Jones, whose Wechsler results in the test tube showed that unmistakable tint: a sign of new life, but likely not of hope.

Robert had learned long ago not to offer congratulations or even to say, "The test is positive." Once, when he had done so, the young woman—whose name was Rita, he remembered now—was momentarily elated. "Thank Gawd!" she exclaimed. "I was so afraid I was knocked up!" When he clarified that he meant she was pregnant, Rita burst into tears. "But positive means *good*," she'd wailed. "And being knocked up isn't good!"

He shifted uncomfortably in his seat at the memory. How he'd wished on that awful day that his wife was still alive. They could have discussed together how best to talk to patients. Not that Phyllis' own physician had told her anything; instead, he called Robert's office with the grim results. "Bob," he said. "It's malignant. Prepare for the worst."

But there is no way to prepare for the worst. She was only forty-seven when she died; the hole her death created felt as large as the one where her remains had been buried. Standing at the graveside, the sight of that damp chasm had made him ill, it was so black and vacant and looming—so unlike Phyllis. Robert had lurched away even while the pastor was still speaking. His shoes squelched against the wet grass until, at the edge of the cemetery, he vomited behind the headstone of a Lieutenant John Marshall, killed in Korea, June 8, 1951.

He picked up Cathy's colorful drawing, admiring again how she had managed to capture something of Phyllis' personality. Glancing up from the paper, the rest of his office appeared dull in comparison. The walls needed a fresh coat of paint, the veneer on his desk bore a veil of scratches, his gray raincoat sagged on its hook.

Mrs. Watkins rapped and opened his door. "It's five o'clock, Doctor."

"She's still not back?" He craned to look past her as if the girl might somehow materialize in the waiting room.

"No. And if you want my opinion," (he didn't, but there was no point in saying so) "that girl was high on drugs."

Robert grimaced. He would have to find a way to address Mrs. Watkins' shortcomings. But not today. "It's all right. You may leave."

"Aren't you coming, too?" Her penciled eyebrows pushed higher on her forehead in surprise.

"No, I'm going to . . ." What? There was nothing to do, no excuse he could give. "I'm just going to sit here a little while." He could almost hear how forcefully Mrs. Watkins refrained from speaking her mind as she retrieved her handbag from the desk drawer and as the outer door banged shut. Her footsteps snapped down the corridor, the elevator chimed, and the office fell quiet again.

In the early evening light, the proof of Miss Jones' condition dimly glowed pale green, like the phosphorescent numbers on the alarm clock that sat on his bedside table. What had become of poor Rita, who'd misunderstood what positive meant? Or all of his other patients whose lives were tainted by that gleam of chartreuse— and by his inability, his unwillingness, to help them? Robert rested his empty useless hands upon his appointment book and waited for Cathy Jones to come back. He wanted her to tell him again that he was no longer the same man who'd lost his wife; that he didn't need to mourn; that now—at last—he could change.

* * *

Robert juggled the hot foil tray of his TV dinner. No matter how many times he heated the darn things up, he never seemed to anticipate how flimsy they were; if he didn't hold the tray with both hands, a corner would collapse and empty its segment of green peas or apple cobbler onto the floor. What relief when he managed to set it down on the little folding table without burning his fingers or splattering the carpet. He turned on the television set and settled into his armchair with everything in place for another ordinary evening: napkin on lap, dinner on tray, and all the troubles of the day on display while he ate. But he had already missed most of the evening news, having remained at the Bureau for another hour in the vain hope that Miss Jones would appear. Walter Cronkite's image shimmered onto the screen only in time to sign off with his usual phrase, "And that's the way it is."

No doubt it was unwise to dine like this each evening, scarcely tasting the rubbery Salisbury steak with its overly salted sauce while subjecting himself to images of combat helicopters and napalmed villages. But the television kept him from thinking about his barren house, the empty closet where Phyllis' dresses had drooped until he summoned the strength to donate them to charity. If he weren't alone, he might not have continued to sit in front of "The Adventures of Daniel Boone," followed by "Ironside," the detective who managed to solve crimes even though he was confined to a wheelchair. Phyllis might have enjoyed that program: she liked Raymond Burr. But she was gone before it first aired. How time could move so slowly and yet vanish so quickly was an unending puzzle. Each day inched along, his routine unvarying and familiar—but entire weeks and months disappeared without his even noticing. Seven years since he'd heard the sound of her voice. He feared he was forgetting her soft intonations, how she'd always mispronounce a few words. What were they? "Vicie versa." Yes, and something else. He'd never pointed out the errors to her, instead tucking them into his memory as a private pleasure, but they were slipping away from him. At least now, when he closed his eyes, he could see her face in vivid color again, thanks to that barefoot girl.

* * *

Before the alarm rang, Robert sat up, already awake, and rubbed his face with both hands, feeling the fresh bristle of whiskers scrape against his palms. While his coffee percolated, he retrieved the morning *Sun-Times* from the stoop and stood in shock at the headline: "4 Kent State Students Killed by Troops." On the front page, a young woman knelt beside a prone body, her hands lifted in horror. Her open mouth appeared to be shouting, "Why?" He read the article before pouring his coffee. Peaceful marchers shot dead by the National Guard; ten students injured, some so seriously they might be paralyzed. Just the other day, President Nixon had called protesting students "bums." Now, Guardsmen—scarcely older than the protesting students themselves—were firing upon them, not with rubber bullets or tear gas but with live ammunition. Live, meaning deadly.

Distressed, he paged through the rest of the newspaper until a small item on an inside page stopped him. "Dead Baby Found in High School Bathroom." His eyes raced over the few lines. A newborn infant in a trashcan, umbilical cord still attached, wrapped in bloody paper towels. Police were questioning students and teachers at the high school, and area hospitals had been alerted to notify authorities if any patients matched the profile of the presumed mother. It was a sharp reminder of what could happen to young, scared pregnant girls. All morning, Robert hoped that Miss Jones would show up at the Women's Bureau. She seemed more vulnerable now than the day before; he wanted her to know about her condition as soon as possible, for her own health as well as for the baby's. The portrait of Phyllis, healthy color on her cheeks and lips, seemed to urge him to find its creator. But where did an anonymous barefoot girl spend her days?

While Mrs. Watkins was in the ladies', he retrieved Cathy's index card from her file box and dialed the telephone number Miss Jones had provided. While the phone rang, he rubbed the offensive black X on the card's corner with his thumb.

A man's rough voice. "Belmont Auto."

"Pardon me?"

"Belmont Auto Repair. What can I do fer ya?"

Robert cleared his throat. "There isn't by chance a Cathy there? Or a Miss Jones?"

"Nope, sure isn't. Ya want your car detailed, pal?"

"No, thank you."

Was there any hope that she'd given a real address? He called the public library and asked them to check a reverse directory. Sure enough, there was no such house number on Racine Avenue. So. No way to trace her. What now? He could not close the lid on his growing unease. What was her boyfriend's name? Arlo? He was fairly certain she'd mentioned young socialists. The White Pages listed a Young Socialists Movement in the Loop, only half a dozen blocks from his own.

After work, Robert found the address on Lake Street. The elevated train shrieked above him as it hurtled around the sharp curve. Up two flights of steps he panted to where voices spilled from an open doorway in what sounded like a lively debate. Half a dozen people were crowded into a room already crammed full of desks and bookshelves. The walls were papered with political posters; the air reeked of cigarettes and the inky odor of a mimeo machine spitting out fliers. A serious-looking man blocked Robert from entering the room. No wild-haired hippie: with a bit of ironing, he and his button-down shirt could have blended in at any office. His gaze landed on Robert's shoes as if they gave a clue to the wearer's character or purpose.

"Yes?" He did not sound friendly.

"I'm looking for Harley. Or maybe Arlo." The rest of the room paused; all eyes were on Robert now. The young man exchanged a meaningful look with his colleagues. Only the clank of the mimeo drum continued to keep time.

"Never heard of him. Either one of 'em."

"What about a girl named Cathy?"

"Nope. That's all, we have work to do." Before Robert could think of another question, the door was closed and locked. Behind the frosted glass panel, murky figures moved about as they returned to their tasks, leaving him no choice but to descend the rickety stairs.

Chapter Sixteen

I don't want to fade away

Katya rolled away from the funk of Harlow's armpit; the smell made her queasy. She settled onto her back beside him and began to braid the ends of their hair together into a loose plait. His locks were almost as long as hers but paler, a shade for which she had no word. Maybe like a field of ripe wheat but she wasn't sure, having never left the city to see such fields. Anyway, their shared braid was a glad sign that she and Harlow were meant to be together. And if they were going to have a baby, it would be beautiful, with his blue eyes and golden hair.

"What're you thinking about?" She liked to ask this question, never knowing what his response would be. Harlow's long lashes fluttered as he gazed at the ceiling.

"All kinds of stuff." His voice was husky, still strained from the Kent State protest. "I'm wondering how those little pygmy blowgun darts work. If the Weathermen started using them, could they take out Henry Kissinger? Think so, baby?"

"Harlow, maybe you shouldn't call me that." She pinched the end of the plait between two fingers to keep it from unraveling.

"Call you what?"

"Baby."

"Yeah? Why's that?" He sounded bemused. Katya murmured her secret. "Because I think someone is getting ready to enter the world. Somebody we can both call 'baby'."

"What the *fuck*, Cathy?" Harlow bolted upright, yanking their joined hair so hard that Katya's head jerked off the pillow. Their love-plait burst apart as he wrenched his body away from hers. "What the hell you talking about?"

"It's just that . . . I think . . . I might be pregnant. Her voice trembled. How could he look at her with such anger and suspicion?

"Aren't you on the Pill?" His face flared deep red, his mouth was twisted in a scowl.

Katya gaped wordlessly. Harlow was the one who knew so much more than she did; they'd never talked about pills or birth control.

"You don't know for sure?"

"No, but . . . I missed my period a few times and I've been feeling kind of sick for a while . . ."

"Well, shee-yit, girl." He let out a deep sigh. "Why'd you come at me with all this crap if you don't know what you're talking about? Messing with my head like this!"

She wanted to say, "I thought you'd be happy." She had stupidly hoped that when she told him, Harlow would embrace her and make promises to her, that this heavy ache would evaporate from her body. Then she could feel happy, too. He rummaged in an ashtray beside the bed, plucking out a roach to light it.

"Look," he began. But he inhaled and held the smoke for a long, silent minute so she had to wait, holding her breath along with him. The bit of paper smoldered between his stained fingertips. He seemed oblivious to its heat, staring at her with a terrible expression, as if he had a bad taste in his mouth. Finally, the smoke drifted from his lips like a sneer as he spoke. "Let's not freak out. So, go get yourself tested, *baby*."

Her cheeks burned. She hated to be treated like she was just a kid. But then she went and did stupid things like never thinking about birth control. Like dreaming that Harlow might want to have a baby with her. Maybe stupidest of all, getting pregnant. She wouldn't admit now that she'd already been downtown, peed in a cup, gave it to that kind, sad doctor and then didn't bother to go back.

"But . . . what if I am?" she ventured.

Silence. Harlow turned away as he pulled his jeans up over his naked butt. As if his cock was newly private, off limits to her. "I'm gonna get something to eat. You probably just got a bug or something and that's why you're late. Don't borrow trouble," he said and left the room. Her mother used to say that too. But wasn't borrowed trouble the best kind? If it didn't belong to you, sooner or later, you could give it back.

For an hour she kept to herself, making earrings without paying attention to the pattern or design. Resentment rubbed at her like a stone caught in her shoe. Harlow's mocking words still stung, and she silently argued with him, imagining all the responses she might have made: *I* wasn't the one freaking out. Don't you care that I've been sick? Why didn't you tell me how to get the pill? She gripped the needle-nose pliers so tightly that the delicate wire snapped and she had to start over. Why should she go all the way downtown again just because Harlow said to? Anyway, she didn't have enough money for bus fare and she wasn't about to ask Harlow for the cash. And then there was the doctor's fee. She hadn't paid him; was her drawing enough?

A festival on Clark Street today would offer a chance for her to sell jewelry and make some bread. But she lingered at the apartment until everyone else had left, so that she could use the phone in private. Harlow always warned that their line was tapped. Still, why would the FBI care about a call to a doctor's office?

A woman's voice answered. "Good afternoon, Women's Bureau." It was the dragon lady.

Katya swallowed, her throat suddenly dry. "Um, I was there and had a test . . ."

"Yes?" She sounded impatient.

"So, I wondered if you could tell me what the answer was. For my test, I mean."

"Oh, no. We don't give that kind of information over the telephone. You need to come in and see Doctor."

She licked her lips and tried again. "Well, okay, can I talk to him then? Maybe he could tell me . . ."

"Doctor isn't in at the moment. And he definitely would want to see you in person to give you any results. You should make an appointment. When can you come in? We have openings on—"

But Katya didn't wait to hear the choices. She hung up. If the phone *was* tapped, the FBI hadn't learned the answer either.

* * *

The fair was a welcome antidote to her troubles. Mimes and stilt walkers circulated among the crowd. Children drew pictures on the sidewalk using fat stubs of colored chalk. Katya found a spot beside a spindly gingko tree. She loved how its leaves were shaped like little green fans. Brushing away some grit before she sat, she was reminded of Harlow's coffee can of pebbles. It was stupid of him not to use pennies. Stones in an empty can don't sound like coins, they just make a lot of noise.

While she sat beside her sparkling displays, she turned to one of the last remaining blank pages in her sketchbook. She would need a new book soon and if she sold enough bracelets, perhaps she could afford vellum paper. Next week she'd go back to the women's clinic— but maybe she wouldn't need to by then. Impossible amazing things happened all the time: John and Yoko had held a peace protest in bed for a whole week. The Woodstock festival last summer had been a marvel with millions of people celebrating together and feeding each other, all for free. And last July, men had walked on the moon. Her whole family had huddled around the television set to watch them, even her father awed by those bold swaddled explorers who had braved that desolate surface so far away.

Miracles could happen and her period could return anytime now. It had to.

Chapter Seventeen

When you're strange, no one remembers your name

On Friday morning, road construction diverted Robert's commute and he found himself stuck in traffic beside Grant Park. He and Phyllis had often come here for picnic dinners and to listen to classical music concerts. Two summers ago, these same lawns and gardens were occupied by thousands of students, priests, hippies, and Yippies protesting the Democratic National Convention until the police charged in, spraying mace and smashing heads with their billy clubs. Robert had never forgotten the gruesome televised images: Gene McCarthy's college kid supporters weeping as they aided their battered and bloodied friends. But today, even at this early hour, young people lounged peacefully upon the grass and the thought struck him: Why wait for Miss Jones to revisit him? Why not go find her himself?

"Robert, you're becoming slow," he chided himself. "It took you three days to come up with such a logical solution." Once at his office, he could hardly wait for Mrs. Watkins to come through the door before announcing with relish that he was going back out. "Since I have no appointments this morning, I'm taking a walk in Grant Park. I'll be back by one at the latest."

The park was only a few blocks away but as he reached Michigan Avenue his momentum slowed. His topcoat was too heavy for such a warm morning, and he grew short of breath as his nerve began to fail. What was he going to do, walk up to every long-haired teen and ask: "Do you know Cathy Jones?" How foolish he would sound, and how unlikely that his questions would be answered. That wasn't even her real name! He needed to think, to work out more of a plan and, just down the street, the Artists' Snack Shop beckoned to him once more.

Louise stood at the end of the counter, deep in conversation with a young woman who appeared to be crying. The waitress pressed something into her hand as she gave her a quick hug. He waited until the young woman left, wiping her eyes, before taking the seat, still warm from her presence. "That's a mighty friendly way to greet a customer," he remarked but Louise poured the coffee without acknowledging his comment. "Maybe you can help me," he began again. "I'm looking for a girl."

"Somebody in particular?" She shifted her weight from one foot to the other, as if they were tender. He nodded. "Your granddaughter, maybe?"

"No. But it's important that I find her."

The service bell rang and she was called away. During the next lull, she refilled his cup and listened to his description.

"She calls herself Cathy. Slight, about yea high, light brown hair down to here. And sometimes she goes barefoot." His description sounded flat, uninteresting even to himself. By making her sound like every other girl wearing Levi's, he was diminishing her. But how could he convey her delicate touch or the way those feather earrings had quivered as she spoke? Or the happiness that blossomed within both of them when she presented him with her drawing? "She has a scar on her chin, right here, and likes to draw. So I thought this place might appeal to her. Its name and all . . ."

Louise thought for a moment. "Can't say for sure if I've seen her, hon. A lot of girls come in and plenty of them go without shoes once the weather turns warm. They don't pay any attention to the rules." She gestured to a sign that warned: No shirt, no shoes, no service. "You try the Art Institute?"

"Not yet." Another reminder of how slow he was to come upon new ideas. "But I will."

"What's so special about her?"

Robert hesitated to say. Still, he needed to let her know there was some urgency to his request. "I'm a doctor; she's a patient of mine."

"Ah." Louise's face grew serious. "Well, like I said, lots of kids stop in for a cold pop or soup-of-the-day. Most of them aren't exactly early birds—there's a whole bunch that shows up after the lunch crowd and again before the dinner rush. After that, I don't know; I'm usually off at four-thirty." As she moved down the counter to a businessman snapping his fingers at her, she called over her shoulder, "You wanna stick around till then?"

"I better not." Robert left his business card beneath the saucer along with a generous tip. If he had turned around as he pushed against the revolving door, he would have seen how she picked up the card and studied it before slipping it into her pocket. And he might have wondered at the curious expressions that played across her face. But he pushed ahead without looking back, determined to start his hunt for the young artist.

All morning, he roamed Grant Park's paths, searching for her elfin face. Teens sprawled everywhere, lazing on the spring grass, already trampled flat. The young people wore ragged colorful clothing as if they were at some outdoor costume party, covered with fringes and lace, accented by political buttons and peace symbols. In their company, Robert felt drab and old-fashioned: his gray trousers and jacket were too formal, his shoes in need of a good polishing. Although no one else was likely to notice or care, those scuffed shoes troubled him.

Strains of guitar music drifted in the air along with the resonant beat of drums. Some people dozed on the ground with an arm flung over their faces to block the sun. Others sat cross-legged in small groups, talking and laughing, clapping to the music. A few frolicked in an odd loose-limbed kind of dance or played with yo-yos. A handful of kids perched on the backs of the green wooden benches with their shoes planted on the seats. As Robert passed, he caught snippets of song and conversations sprinkled with swear words that were delivered cheerfully and without a trace of animosity. The atmosphere of a festival was undeniable, but he worried: had they no jobs, none of them? No classes to attend or families to take care of? Even as a young man, he'd never spent an entire day lolling in the park. His youth had been bent toward education, medical school, and then his practice. Only while courting Phyllis had he dallied. The two of them had strolled arm in arm through flower gardens and by Buckingham Fountain to watch its magnificent sprays of water burst upwards and cascade down again, colored beacons playing upon their luminous surfaces.

Although he paused to peer closely at every light-haired girl, no one spoke to him. Their eyes flicked over him and away. He was old, not of their world, an interloper despite his fond memories of sitting by the bandshell on summer evenings. He should be asking questions, trying to find out if anyone had seen her. But something held him back from breaking the bubble that seemed to have sealed around him, leaving him with the odd idea that if he were to speak, his words would sound like Middle English to them, as if he had stepped directly from Chaucer's time.

His foot caught on an uneven square of concrete and he stumbled sideways, nearly treading upon a bearded man who lay entwined with a girl on a patch of worn grass beside the sidewalk.

"Hey!"

"Excuse me," Robert glanced at the young woman's face: round and freckled. Not who he sought.

"It's cool, man." She spoke in a slow drawl, like emerging from deep sleep.

"Better sober up, pops," smirked her companion. He snaked a hand beneath her blouse and she squealed, fully awake now.

Robert walked on more slowly, checking the ground for tripping hazards. *Life Magazine* said this was the "Now Generation." Did these kids think they could live now without planning for any future? Still, they did appear to be content. Or maybe just hung over. He stopped in a shady spot to remove his hat and wipe his brow. A burly young man in a faded denim jacket tossed his cigarette butt into a bed of purple and white petunias. Some new world this lot will bring us, Robert thought. No manners, no consequences.

But there would be consequences ahead for Cathy Jones, whether he found her or not. The morning paper had carried a disturbing update: "Mother of Abandoned

Infant Found." In a grainy photo snapped outside the Twelfth Precinct, the 17-year-old high school student held a coat before her so that only her broad forehead was revealed. Her hair was dark, her form boxy, nothing like Cathy, who had appeared nonchalant, ethereal. And naïve. It was difficult to imagine how such a wisp could manage the decisions that would inevitably confront her.

It was possible that she might seek out an abortion, whether through the safer network he'd heard of or ones with dirty instruments. But could she raise the funds? And unless she realized soon enough that she was pregnant, it would be too late for the procedure, and what then? Adoption, early marriage, poverty? The morgue? Where was her family? Who cared for Miss Jones? His mind filled with troubling images: bloodied bathroom tiles, a gray umbilical cord throttling a tiny throat, the waxy pallor of a woman who had hemorrhaged. A distant clock struck one; he must return to his office, care for his other patients. Cottonwood seeds drifted past him on a warm puff of air. Robert reached up, grasping at the delicate bits of white fluff, but did not catch even one.

Chapter Eighteen

I heard it through the grapevine

Only Memorial Day, but the afternoon was summer sultry with not a hint of fresh air coming from the lake. Limp bits of grass stuck to the back of Katya's legs and her embroidered blouse clung to her sweaty flesh. She plucked at the orange fabric, pulling it away from her body in an effort to flap a bit of air onto her skin. She couldn't button the top of her shorts now and the zipper threatened to split. Yesterday, she had caught Harlow staring at her belly with an uncertain expression on his face. Neither of them had mentioned tests or babies again, nor had they made love since she shared her secret with him. Harlow kept to his own side of the mattress.

A few trees at the edge of the park cast small patches of shadow and Katya chose one of those to spread her bandanna and two dozen pairs of earrings for sale. She used safety pins to fasten the earrings onto the cloth so no one could pocket them when she wasn't looking. As the day wore on, her bit of shade was invaded by others seeking respite as they waited for Sly and his band to appear on stage. First, two Jesus freaks showed up; they kept trying to tell everyone about the "Good News." Then three giddy teenagers, hoping to score. They unsuccessfully solicited every passing longhair: "Hey man, got any pot?" A bearded hippie and his girlfriend in a patchwork skirt brought a wicker basket with them.

Finally, a black guy dressed like Sly in leather vest and mirrored shades lay down and they all inched over to make room for him.

A pack of shirtless young men, emboldened by beer and the crowd's cheers, climbed onto the speaker towers where they clung like pale apes, refusing to come down. Cops in their shiny blue riot helmets formed a tight line below them; their hands hovered ominously above their canisters of Mace. Rumors flew through the crowd. Some said the concert was at a standstill: the cops wouldn't let the music start until the kids got off the towers. Others claimed that Sly hadn't even arrived in town yet; he was notorious for late performances. But recorded music continued to play over the loudspeakers and a few knots of people danced, oblivious to the heat. Joints passed from hand to hand in sections of the park far from where the cops were positioned.

While she waited, Katya idly drew spiral shapes in the dirt. One night, at a fundraiser for the Chicago 7 Defense, a professor explained that history always moves forward in a rising coil, like a mattress spring or a Slinky. She hadn't understood his talk of synthesis and antithesis, but the image appealed to her. Even when you think you're stuck in a groove, you're not. Your life turns, moving you to a higher level where you gain a wider view. You can look behind and see where you've been, but there's no such thing as going backwards. It comforted her to know that life progressed, sometimes slowly, sometimes at a dizzying pace, but always spiraling upwards. She and Harlow would figure out a way to make this work. Maybe Vicky and Michael could be godparents or like an aunt and uncle.

The Sly fan rolled onto his back, taking up more than his share of the tree's dappled shade, but no one protested and he soon began to snore. The Jesus freaks murmured together, maybe praying, maybe complaining about how hard it was to carry the truth to people who refused to hear it. And then someone began to wail, like a cat.

Katya looked up. The girl in the patchwork skirt twisted around and reached into the basket beside her. With a broad smile, she lifted up what looked like a bundle of damp clothes. "Have you woken up at last, little one?" she cooed. She raised her shirt and pressed the wiggling bundle to her bare breast. The sounds it made! Snucking, gulping, choking. His mother laughed at his sputters; she held him up in the air, jiggling him gently. "Easy, easy . . ."

Katya stared at the naked flesh that seemed to loom before her. Never had she seen such an enormous, round breast; it seemed to fill her entire field of vision. The nipple, rosy and wet, seemed to pulsate in the air. A drop of milk dangled at its tip. As she watched, the drop fell and was replaced by another and another, thin white milk oozing onto the woman's skirt where it spread in a dark wet circle.

"Amazing, isn't it?" the young woman beamed as she juggled her baby to the other breast, hoisting her shirt up to her collarbone. Katya tried to move her gaze to the woman's face but couldn't stop staring at the copious stream of milk leaking from that breast.

"I'm Meadow," said the woman. "And that's River." She nodded toward the grinning man beside her.

Katya forced herself to focus on the wire-rimmed glasses that sat halfway down River's nose. "What's your baby's name?"

"We don't know yet," Meadow responded. "We're waiting for him to tell us who he is."

River chimed in. "He'll give us a sign. Like the first thing he reaches for, or what makes him smile, or maybe tell us in a dream, you know?"

"Oh," said Katya. "Right."

"And when is *your* blessed little one arriving?" Meadow asked. Katya flushed and pulled her own blouse down, trying to cover her straining zipper.

"Nothing to freak out about," River said.

"That's right," Meadow agreed. "You have an adorable little Buddha belly."

Katya glanced at the Jesus freaks; they were arguing over who had dibs to lean against the locust tree's trunk. Meadow placed a damp hand on her knee. "Aren't we lucky? You and me are *made* to do this, to create new life and to feed it. It's the most natural thing in the world."

The nameless infant pulled his mother's breast into his mouth so greedily that her pink nipple and areola disappeared completely and Katya's nipples stood up in immediate response, as if the sight of that nursing baby meant something to them, bypassing her brain completely. A thread tugged at her alert breasts, drawing them toward the child's wet, pink mouth. Again, she plucked her shirt away from her body, gripped by a fear that milk would begin to spill out of her, too.

River said, approvingly, "Looks like your tits are getting ready too." Did these two have x-ray vision or something?

"You know what you need?" asked Meadow. "A pair of overalls. They're the *best*! You can keep loosening the straps and undoing the side buttons as you get bigger. I wore mine for almost the whole pregnancy, didn't I, sweetheart?"

"Right on," River nodded.

Meadow lifted the squawking baby onto her shoulder and patted his back. "They only cost about six bucks. I got mine at the Army-Navy store on Fullerton. You know it?" Katya nodded dumbly: right down the street from Harlow's apartment. Meadow's hand, tapping and rubbing, patting again, mesmerized her. "That bubble just isn't coming up, is it?" Meadow began to bob up and down, jouncing the baby and, as she jiggled, her exposed breasts bounced too, droplets of milk flying into the air. The Jesus freaks stared, openmouthed; the Sly lookalike sat up, wearing the same grin that River sported. Absorbed in clumsy efforts to roll a joint, only the teenage boys remained oblivious to the spectacle.

Katya wanted to flee. She fumbled with her bandanna of earrings. A safety pin sprang open and stabbed her thumb. "Ow!" She stuck her hurt thumb in her mouth and then instantly pulled it out again, embarrassed that she had acted like a baby. Suddenly, she wanted her own mother more than anything. She longed to be held and comforted by someone who had gazed at her with the same adoration that Meadow shone on her baby. When she was little, Ma had tucked her in at night, listened to her prayers, braided flowers into her hair for confirmation. But now, even strangers could see she was pregnant and shame flashed through Katya like a fever, leaving her limbs weak. That professor was right: you couldn't go backwards. There would be no adoring looks from Ma, not ever.

A rumble began to rise from near the stage: "Pigs, pigs, *pigs*." The chanting grew louder, more fervent, with each repetition. Someone hurled a bottle toward the blue helmets and, at the same moment, a scream rang out. The scream and the green bottle seemed to arc and hang in the air as if they were connected—and when the bottle smashed against the ground, the scream, too, would shatter. Katya stuffed her things into her satchel and scrambled to her feet but, in the next instant, Sly's band bounded onstage, and the crowd rose to its feet in a hot cheering surge of relief.

Meadow gripped her arm. "Hold up. Where're you going? I don't need my overalls anymore; I'll give 'em to you. Here's our address. Come by, okay?" Katya shoved the scrap of paper into her pocket and ran from the park until a stitch in her side forced her to stop, stabbing beneath her swelling, pregnant breast.

Chapter Nineteen

A man you must believe

Each time he opened a newspaper, Robert was gripped by dread. He pored through the *Tribune* and *Sun-Times*, fearing that he would be confronted by reports of a young girl's body pulled from the river or the victim of a hit and run. But all he found were more police shootings—two students killed and a dozen injured at Jackson State in Mississippi—and page after page of breathless coverage of Frances Flannery. She was the girl who'd hidden her pregnancy for months, even while she gave muffled birth alone in her high school bathroom. The coroner ruled that the baby had been born alive; Frances was charged with manslaughter, her trial set for later that summer. How he wished that she had come to see him at the Women's Bureau! Her stunned miserable face reproached him from the front page. She too seemed unhappy that he'd failed to find Cathy.

He had told Louise that he would search the Art Institute but the building was so massive, he knew there was little hope of lucking upon her in its huge galleries. Instead, he stopped at the broad stone steps that were clearly a popular spot to "hang out." No sign of Cathy but that scruffy youth with the shaggy mass of hair was once again posed against the lion, with another slender girl pressed tightly against his side. As Robert approached, she peeled herself away from her prize. Tiny bells on her skirt tinkled like fairy warnings.

"What're you looking at?" Her voice was nasal, accusatory: such an ugly tone from a pretty girl.

"Cool it, babe." The youth addressed her but kept his gaze on Robert

"Huck—" she whined.

"Beat it."

Robert feared this was directed at him until Huck swatted the girl on her behind to emphasize his point. "Ow!" She ducked under the lion's tail and slunk away to join another knot of teens while Huck resumed his posture of ease, carelessly scuffing one boot against the granite step. Despite his casual manner, Robert knew the younger man was sizing him up, judging his flaccid belly, his stodgy hat. He cleared his throat but Huck spoke first.

"Whatcha want?" He seemed to expect a confrontation.

Robert blurted out his first thought. "I'm looking for a girl."

"Naw, man, I don't do that." Huck shook his head for emphasis. "No way."

"No, I don't mean . . ." Robert's cheeks flushed.

"Then what? 'Cause whatever it is, I didn't do it."

"I'm not a cop." Huck raised both eyebrows as if he wasn't convinced. "I'm a doctor. I'm looking for one of my patients."

The young man folded his arms across his chest. "What're you asking me for? And I know you didn't just show up; I've seen you checking me out before."

"Well, for one thing, you seem to know quite a few young ladies."

Huck gave a short laugh. Perhaps that pleased him. He pulled a box of cigarettes from his shirt pocket. "You're pretty straight. You a shrink?"

"No, I'm not a psychiatrist. Why do you ask?"

Now it was Huck's turn to hesitate, as he weighed how much to explain to this clueless straight man. "Because a lot of people—when their kid doesn't do what they want, maybe smokes a little weed or skips school—they send the kid to a shrink. Next thing you know, kid's in the psych ward at Michael Reese, slitting her wrists."

"I would think it would be the other way 'round: if she harms herself, then her parents place her in the hospital for treatment."

"You got any kids?"

Robert shook his head.

"Yeah. Well, shows how little you know, man." The youth's tone was mocking, but he smiled as he pushed himself away from the lion's side and stuck out his right hand, saying, "You can call me Huck." Robert moved to shake it, but Huck flipped his open palm up and Robert ended up grasping air above the empty hand.

"I'm Doctor Robert Lewis."

"Like the Beatles song? No shit!" To Robert's confusion, the lad began to loudly sing, "Doctor Robert, helping everyone in need." The sullen girl snickered from her new post. "No one can succeed . . . like Doctor Robert!"

"Doctor Robert" was eager to end this public spectacle. "Can we talk? Somewhere else?"

Huck shrugged. "It's a free country. Or so they say. Then again, you don't get much for free." He waited for Robert to catch on.

Robert eyed how loosely Huck's jeans hung on his thin frame. "How 'bout I buy you a burger for starters? Maybe at the Artists' Snack Shop up the street?"

"Far out."

Was that an agreement? Huck made no movement and at last Robert understood: the youth might be unwilling to walk beside someone so unlike him and his friends. Someone so old, so *straight*. "Why don't I go ahead and get us a booth?" he said quietly and the young man nodded his approval.

Twenty minutes later, Robert had downed two cups of coffee and impatiently puzzled over the art-themed menu. "Rubens" was a play on words for a sandwich of hot corned beef and sauerkraut on pumpernickel. But why name half a tomato stuffed with egg salad "Van Gogh"? The waitress (not Louise, alas, but an Estelle) hovered by his table as Huck arrived at last.

"Keep a hand on your wallet," Estelle advised when she saw Huck shambling toward them. "That's a light-fingered one there, scoops up the tips before we can get to them." She glared at Huck as he eased past her into the booth.

"Thank you for coming." Robert tried to mask his annoyance at how long it had taken the young man to walk a block and a half.

Huck offered no apology. "Gimme a burger."

Estelle shot Robert a disapproving look and flipped her order pad to a fresh page. "Burger comes with grilled onions, fries or potato salad, and pickles. Twenty-five cents extra if you want cheese."

"Cool. I'll take cheese and fries." With a sidelong glance at Robert, daring him to say no, Huck added,

"And a chocolate milkshake. Oh yeah, a piece of apple pie too."

Robert nodded his consent and requested a glass of milk and a burger, no cheese. Please. Although he wasn't hungry, slowly chewing over a meal might be the ideal way to have conversation.

The young man propped both elbows on the table-top. "You look better without the hat. Less like a narc."

"I told you, I'm no cop."

"Yeah, yeah." Huck scanned the restaurant, perhaps looking for someone. Idly, he drummed his fingers on the table in rhythm to a tune only he could hear. Robert studied his companion's lean tanned face. He looked intelligent and wary. Despite how lighthearted he'd appeared when surrounded by his covey of young ladies on the museum steps, his eyes contained something sadder as if he too might have once lost something precious. When the food came, he ate like he was taking part in a hot dog competition, swallowing his burger in four bites, stuffing the fries into his mouth five and six at a time. By the time Robert had seasoned his own burger with salt, pepper, and mustard and replaced the bun, Huck had cleaned his plate.

"The girl," Robert said, pushing his dish forward so that Huck could help himself. "She's maybe sixteen or seventeen years old and might use the name Cathy Jones."

"Never heard of her," Huck mumbled, mouth full of Robert's burger.

"She's small, slight, brown hair past her shoulders, but lighter than yours. A quiet kid, artistic. Has a scar on her chin." Why did he save the most relevant detail for last?

Huck slurped his milkshake through a straw, gazing into space. Was he listening or just filling his belly? Robert went on. "Greenish-brown eyes. Hazel, I guess you'd call them." He did not describe her as he had seen her, like a pixie.

Huck's eyes shifted. "I might be able to find somebody who knows her. What's the deal with her?"

Robert had wondered about this since his first conversation with Louise. *What's so special about her?* He couldn't recall how he had responded, but the girl *was* special to him. Miss Jones was entitled to her privacy and he'd already said too much by revealing that she was his patient. He couldn't reveal that she was pregnant—if she still was. Or that it had seemed as if her bare feet scarcely touched the ground. Or that he might have missed his only chance to help her. *You can't help everyone.* That inner voice sounded like Mrs. Watkins, encouraging him to give up. If he did find her, what then? What did he think he could do for her? It must be obvious to her by now that she was pregnant, so why would she bother to come back to his clinic? He should have said so much more while he had the chance. He should have emphasized the need for good health care, whether she was pregnant or not. She deserved counseling, a family—a pair of shoes! He fiddled with his napkin.

"I have some information that she needs," he said at last. "It's important and I promise I won't lock her up in the psych ward. Or anywhere else."

Huck focused on spooning up his cherry pie. "I can probably find her, man. Sooner or later, all the chicks come to Huck the Rooster." He grinned, lifted his plate and licked the last sticky dribble of pie filling from where it had spilled onto the edge. His tongue was disturbingly long. "But it'll cost you."

Robert's thoughts raced. He knows I'm a doctor; maybe he wants drugs. If I pay him cash, he might just keep demanding more, offering crumbs of information, promising to deliver next time. But if I refuse, he'll get up and saunter out, satisfied with his free meal. And I'm getting nowhere on my own. Taking care to keep his voice low and steady, he said, "I won't pay you. But . . ." the word was meant to keep Huck from leaving " . . . but I can buy you meals. And if there's something else—something legal, I mean—that you need, let's talk about it. Maybe I can help you out."

Huck's face relaxed. "And what about after? Do I get a reward when I find her?"

Robert shrugged, oddly mirroring the gesture that Huck had given him earlier. His shoulders seemed to feel more carefree than the rest of him, as if they knew tomorrow was a long way off. "We'll see," he said. He wrote his office phone number on a napkin. "You can reach me here during weekdays." Then he added his home number, just in case.

Huck chewed on his drinking straw. "You sure you don't have the hots for that girl?" He hooted. "Man, you should see your face! Okay, *Doc*." He rose to his feet. "I'll call if I get some news. But first, you gotta lose those shoes."

"What?" Robert strained to glance beneath the table at his nicely polished black Oxfords. "What's wrong with them?"

"Those are narc shoes, man. I can't be seen with you looking like that. Get some tennies or something, would ya? Gotta boogie." Huck strode away, giving Robert a clear view of the American flag decal, sewn upside down on the seat of his jeans. Right before sidling through the revolving door, he turned and held up two fingers, signaling peace. "And bring your wallet," he added. "I'll be hungry."

Chapter Twenty

It's your thing, do what you wanna do

Katya climbed the stairs quickly, wondering which apartment the sour smell was emanating from. Even her mother's cabbage dishes never stank like that; on such a warm June day, the odor would linger in the stairwell for hours. She cupped a hand over her nose to breathe in the scent she found there: her own sweaty palm mixed with faint varnish from the stairway banister.

She'd gone out early for a walk, dawdling away from the apartment until Harlow and Vicky would be at work, and Michael gone to class. She needed some quiet time to think and hoped that, for once, she would have the place to herself. She wanted a long cool bath with no one barging in while she tried to figure out what to do. Even Meadow, that woman at the concert, could see she was showing but Harlow hadn't asked her again about getting tested and she hadn't told him about seeing the doctor. But first, she had to pee. Squeezing her legs together while she shouldered open the door, she hobbled through the vacant living room to the bathroom and ducked behind a yellow Indian bedspread. With a sigh of relief, she sank onto the toilet seat.

Faint noises floated up from a downstairs neighbors' apartment, like the chanting sounds that sometimes throbbed from the Buddhist Center's open door. "Guh-guh-guh." When she flushed, the chants paused and then deepened again into rhythmic moans that seemed somehow to pulse from down the hall, not through the floor. She slipped past the curtain into the dim hallway where Che stared past her with his tragic eyes. Malcolm X held his hand up, one finger pointed over her head. Those moans definitely came from the rear of the apartment but, except for flies buzzing around dirty dishes piled in the sink, the kitchen was empty.

"Guh-guh-guh-guhh!"

She peered around the empty doorframe of Vicky's bedroom. Harlow stood with his back to her, jeans around his ankles, his bare ass convulsing as he thrust himself against someone who braced herself against the dresser with both hands, both of them facing the large mirror. In the reflection, Harlow's hands cupped Vicky's bare breasts, folded over them like he was protecting her. Vicky's head was tilted backwards, her dark hair splayed wildly over his shoulders, and that guttural sound thrummed from both their throats as if they were counting together: *nine, ten, more, MORE.* "GUUHH!" Harlow bellowed just as Vicky caught sight of Katya, frozen in the kitchen, and screamed. Did Katya cry out too? Vicky thrust out an arm to slam the door closed. But there was no door and no way to shut out what had just been seen.

Katya fled down the hall, back to the room she shared with Harlow, and flung herself onto their mattress. A few moments later, he strolled in, buttoning his fly. He held his chin high as if proud of himself, or maybe ready for a fight.

"What's the problem, babe?" The mattress complained as he sat down beside her. She glared at him.

How could he be so casual, so unconcerned? She tried to stop crying so that she could speak, although she didn't yet know what to say. "Didn't I always tell you I'm not into possessions?" Harlow dabbed her wet face with a corner of the sheet. His voice became gentler as he said, "You don't belong to me, Cathy." Then he added, pausing between the words to emphasize how much he meant them, "And I. Don't belong. To you."

"But, but what about this?" She cupped her hands over her belly with its undeniable evidence that Harlow had once been hers. Even strangers in the park had known it. "We're going to have a baby, Harlow!"

His gaze shifted, unwilling to look at her body. "Might not be mine." He tried to sound casual but she recognized how his voice took on a slight drawl whenever he lied.

"Of course, it is! Who else's could it be?" There had never been anyone else, he knew that. The room was too hot; it tilted around her and her pulse roared in her ears.

"I don't know what you're into when I'm not here. There's all kind of guys been through this place. But hey, it's your body. You can do what you want."

What she wanted was to throw something at him, to slap his dishonest face. And to have her own room again, with a door that she could lock and forever keep him—and Vicky—out. She wanted to go back in time and to have never loved him. She wanted to have taken the pill, to not be pregnant, not be stuck with this reminder of all her stupid mistakes. But she couldn't do any of that and everything was too late now. She covered her eyes with both hands and, in the dark, his words seemed to bray at her: *You don't belong to me.*

No, she thought. And I don't belong here anymore. For some reason, she suddenly remembered the collage she'd made and left behind, abandoned in the school art show with no one to claim it. And then a word rang in her mind, a single syllable that resonated inside her skull, a mantra that lifted her from the bed and propelled her around the room, guiding her hands as she stuffed her things into a knapsack and pillowcase, wrapped a belt around the neck of the pillowcase and pulled it into a tight knot.

"Where you going?" Harlow's voice seemed to come from a great distance.

She meant to answer but the word filled her dry throat, too big to fit. Silently, she jammed her art supplies and notebooks into the green satchel and hoisted the rest of her belongings into both arms. Harlow stepped back, making no move to stop her; if he called out a farewell, she didn't catch it as she ran down the stairs through the lingering haze of cooked cabbage. All she heard was a song without melody, a blues bass line that matched the thud of her steps, telling her: *home, home, home.*

* * *

The doctor's gig had sounded easy enough at first: help the old man find the girl and get fed along the way, maybe even a big payoff when they reunited. Huck had spent a couple days hanging at Oak Street Beach and in Lincoln Park, eyeing girls, chatting them up. Plenty of chicks admired the way his jeans hung low on his hips and how he strode down the sidewalk in his Frye boots. But trouble was, Doc's description sounded like a hundred other chicks on the street: long straight hair, fake name, greenish-brown eyes, barefoot. Yeah, that narrowed it down, all right. Only the scar on her chin stood out, and what if Doc was wrong about that? Huck couldn't get a handle on the man: he hadn't seemed frantic to find the girl, more like worried. There was a sadness to him, and Huck didn't trust sorrow; it was too unpredictable.

And his promised meals were too infrequent. Nearly noon and Huck didn't have enough cash for a meal. A long bank of payphones stretched along the curb and he poked his finger into each coin return slot in search of overlooked dimes. He squatted down to check beneath the phones and in the gutter, but nothing. Shit. Reluctantly, he began walking in the direction of the blood bank. They paid fifteen bucks for your plasma and didn't demand ID.

A group of middle-aged women leaving a restaurant blocked the sidewalk, forcing him to stop as they hailed a Yellow Cab, fussing over who would pay the driver and whether everyone had her handbag. One lady in a bright orange coat and fancy hat motioned for them to get in, clucking at them like a chicken. As aromas of meat wafted from the restaurant doorway, Huck's stomach growled. Fuck it, I'm too hungry to sell my blood. I need some grub now! He sidled up to the woman at the tail end of the group.

"Excuse me, ma'am? I haven't eaten in two days." He gave a wan smile, trying to look hungry and docile, but she recoiled and whipped her arm away from him to hide her handbag behind her back. Her hat slipped sideways on her head; a bunch of fake cherries dangled in front of her face.

"Evelyn, are you all right?" One of her friends moved closer to protect her.

"I didn't do anything to her. I'm just looking for some spare change so I can eat . . ."

Another woman began to climb back out of the cab, crowding into the ones still trying to get in so that the orange lady was almost knocked over. "Ladies," she called, trying to restore order. "Ladies! Move along, young man." She glowered at Huck and flipped her gloved hands at him like she was shooing away a fly. "Just leave us alone." Her purse dangled temptingly from the crook of her elbow. Huck swallowed hard. If he grabbed it, how far could he get? No, the cab driver was staring at him; too much risk.

"Even fifty cents would help out." He closed his eyes to spit out the word, "*Please.*" Something hard smacked into his face. That bitch had slugged him with her purse! The women clambered into their taxi, buzzing with indignation and excitement. As it roared away from the curb, he sagged against the cool windowpane, holding his throbbing eye. On the other side of the glass, tables draped in white cloth and topped with brass lamps filled the room. Waitresses in little caps and lacy aprons moved about while old black men in uniforms carried away trays of dirty dishes upon their shoulders. Two ancient biddies sat with their forks frozen halfway to their open mouths, glowering at him. Steam rose from a gap in the pot pie on the table between them. He could almost smell the gravy.

He turned his gaze to the next table: macaroni and cheese, golden brown and luscious, and at the next, a beautiful piece of roast beef lifted on the tines of a silver fork up to a familiar face. Huck smacked the glass with the flat of his hand. The old biddies scowled at him but he slapped the window again until his quarry raised his head to look.

* * *

About to take a bite, Robert hesitated. Everyone around him had ceased dining, captivated by something thudding at the window. Where a rumpled hippie pressed his unshaved face against the glass. And to Robert's chagrin, he recognized that face.

"This seat taken?" Huck plopped into the opposite chair as hostess and waitresses scurried over. "Nah, I don't need a menu," he said, nodding at Robert's plate. "Gimme the same as him." The hostess looked to Robert for approval. Objections and considerations flew through his mind. This was outrageous, embarrassing, and worse—his Monday ritual was ruined. Huck had invaded the weekly lunch in Phyllis's memory, sitting in *her* chair, scruffy and unkempt. But would Huck create a bigger commotion if he weren't fed? And what if he had some news about Cathy?

It was that hope, in the end, that led Robert to sigh, "It's fine. Please bring my friend what he requests." He endeavored to keep his voice mild, to demonstrate the kind of decorum that was expected in Stouffer's dining room. He knew that curious looks and whispers were being cast his way. *After all these years of dining alone, this is who he eats with?* The server placed another set of silverware on the table at arm's length, as if Robert's companion might have a contagious disease. Huck gazed about at the maroon and gold carpet underfoot, the cherry wood paneling, the gilt-edged dishes on each table.

"So this is where you hide out. Pretty nice. Fancier than the Artists' Snack Shop anyway."

Feeling as if he were accused of some kind of disloyalty to Louise, Robert answered cautiously. "I do eat here sometimes, yes. What happened to you?"

Huck touched the rising welt. "Lady bashed me with her purse. Figured I was going to rip her off."

"Were you?"

"Hell no!" Huck sounded offended at the idea, but it didn't seem so farfetched to Robert.

"Better hold a piece of ice on that eye for a bit. It'll help keep the swelling down. And since this meal is going on my tab, perhaps you can tell me what you've done lately to locate Miss Jones."

Huck looked up from slurping his cream of tomato soup. "Hey, man, why're you so pissed off? You volunteered to feed me in the first place!"

"And you are supposed to be searching!" Robert shot back. He lowered his voice to add, "It's been over a week and you haven't called."

Huck had his own accusation. "You didn't give me much to go on!"

When the waitress brought a fresh plate of roast beef, they fell silent, each unwilling to air their differences in front of her. Robert watched Huck dive into his meal and thought hard. Perhaps this arrangement had been an error in judgement. Yes, the young man seemed intelligent, but he might intend to take advantage of every free meal he could get and nothing more. On the other hand, Huck had somehow tracked him down to Stouffer's. Maybe he did have some useful skills . . .

Huck spoke first. "Look, man, I really have been asking around and watching out for her. I went to the beach, the parks...But—think about it: what are the chances she and I are going to end up in the same place at the same time?"

"You told me 'all the chicks' come to you."

"Well..." Huck looked sheepish. "I might have pumped that up a little." He busied himself with sopping up gravy from his plate. "Sorry about that," he mumbled.

Robert signaled for hot coffee. Everyone deserved a second chance and Huck did appear abashed. "All right, let me tell you what *I've* done." Robert had gone to the local precinct to file a missing person's report. But without a real name, no photograph and no family connection, the desk sergeant refused to file the paperwork. "You know how many runaways are in this town? Believe you me, they don't want to be found." The officer had tossed the form into his trash can like he was shooting baskets.

"Not surprised. Cops don't give a shit—" Huck began. "Sorry." He lowered his voice. "They don't give a crap about us."

"I read the papers and watch the news every day. And I've asked colleagues at different hospitals around the city to notify me if she comes into the ER."

"That's it?" Huck wiped his mouth on his sleeve, earning a fresh glare from his patron. "You can't just read the paper. Doc, you're talking about finding somebody in the counterculture! We fly beneath the radar. Like bats, man."

"But that's what I've engaged *you* for, young man. To be my eyes and ears." Not a bat, he thought.

"It's a damn big city, Doc. Neither of us can cover it all. We need a new strategy."

Robert chuckled. "We? So, does this mean you're fully on board?"

"Yeah, and here's an idea: we print up fliers and post them all over, at coffeehouses and clubs. We need a lot of bulletin boards and store windows, and it's going to take both of us to do it."

Robert reached across the table and gave Huck a hearty handshake. If the other diners gawked, so be it; this would be his last lunch here. Phyllis' ghost had been replaced by a living, breathing person in her chair. There was no need to come back to Stouffer's.

"And you've gotta give me some cash. Don't give me that hairy eyeball. I just need a roll of dimes for phone calls."

"What's the idea?"

"I got contacts, you know. It'll be a lot quicker to make calls than to run all over town. And you should offer a reward on the fliers. That always gets attention."

"How much do you think we should offer?" Robert asked, warily.

Huck smiled as he helped himself to chocolate pudding. "I dunno, Doc. How badly you wanna find her?"

Chapter Twenty-one

I am everyday people

As she neared the bus stop, Katya's steps slowed to match the thoughts that dragged through the thick bog of her mind. Why was it so difficult to think? She sat heavily on the scarred green bench. Its planks were gouged with initials, some of them etched inside of idiotic hearts. As if carving the words could make love permanent. The sun beat down on her head like a punishment. When she closed her eyes, she saw Harlow's pale naked butt pumping against Vicky's body and then those two white globes became Meadow's bouncing breasts, dripping with milk. Sex with him was her past; a swollen body and a squalling baby were her future. Action; reaction. Truth; consequence.

In the distance, church bells rang out, urging people to Mass but she knew they did not call to her. Katya would not be welcomed through those wooden doors. How could she go home now? The school year was over, and she had missed it all. Her parents would never trust her again, never let her out of their sight. She'd stolen from them, run away, and now—undeniably pregnant— she couldn't bring this new humiliation back to Ma and Tata for the whole neighborhood to see. Everyone would know Katya Warshawsky's failure and her lies. Wishing she could leave her worries behind on the bench, she picked up her bundles and walked away, meandering without direction, randomly choosing streets, hoping that a new idea would come to her soon. The words of Dylan's song kept playing in her head, asking her how it felt to be on her own, like a rolling stone. Katya wasn't sure of the answer; didn't a stone always roll downhill? It could end up at the bottom as rubble.

Down a side street near Logan Square, she spotted a brass plaque that lifted her hopes: Friends Meeting House. This old brick building must be where the women who gave her shelter during the Kent State protest came from. Eagerly, she mounted the steps and pulled on the doorknob but it refused to turn. The door was locked, no one answered her knocks, and after a time, she gave up and returned to wandering.

She stopped to rest at a vacant lot where a colorfully painted placard declared: People's Park. *Always open, never closed. All are Welcome.* Nearby, a metal sign had been altered to read *Pleaze Stay ON the Grass!* A thin red string stretched loosely around the perimeter of the lot. Something about that tiny cord sagging between each post stung Katya's heart: such a fragile thread meant to be a fence. Narrow paths were roughly marked by stones and bits of red brick. A broken-down sofa and two La-Z-Boy recliners huddled at the top of a small rise, as if abandoned in mid-conversation. Jumbled wooden crates had been nailed together like a jungle gym, and swinging ropes hung from the low branch of an elm tree. Straggling rows were etched in the dirt of a paltry garden. A wooden popsicle stick optimistically identified some wilted green seedlings as "tomatos."

"They'll be all right once they get a good drink."

A man spoke from one of the La-Z-Boys, his clothing as worn and brown as its Naugahyde. He was old, with long gray hair sprouting from beneath his hat and a full, rough beard. The soles of his shoes were caked in mud, a worn knapsack lay on the ground beside his chair. He moved the lever so that the footrest collapsed with a rusty squeak, and rousted himself from the depths of his seat. Scarcely taller than she was, he appeared plump but that might have been the many layers he wore: a bulky sweater, checked vest, brown overcoat. The heat didn't seem to bother him.

"Good afternoon, missy. I'm Ernest Mann," he said in a soft voice with a hint of southern accent. Katya approached cautiously. He offered her one hand while he tipped his shapeless hat with the other. Perhaps she should curtsy in response to his gentlemanly manner, for he was no wino: his eyes were clear and his lined face was serene.

"I go by Cathy," she replied, returning his handshake.

"Would you care to sit, Miss Cathy?" He motioned toward the empty recliners. "What brings you to the People's Park on such a day?"

"Just out walking." She was unsure why she lied. Sometimes truth felt out of reach. Then a new thought seized her. "Would you like to buy some jewelry? Or maybe a drawing?" She began to rummage through her belongings, searching for her sketchpad to show him. "You can pick whichever one you want. Only a dollar."

He smiled, showing a large gap in his bottom teeth. "But I have no money. Not one silver dime. I live without it."

She sighed. There were precious few coins in her pocket, not much more than bus fare. "Yeah, I'm broke, too."

"Oh, you misunderstand me, missy. I am not broken; I am the wave of the future. We are creating a new cash-less economy. Everywhere, young people like you are offering free food, fixing up old bicycles and giving them away. Soon, everyone will recognize the futility of money."

"I dunno, I wish I had more money."

"Why?" He leaned forward, interested in her answer.

She picked at the stuffing that sprouted from a hole in the seat while she decided to tell a truth. "I could eat more, for one thing." Maybe he didn't notice her little belly or maybe he thought she was plump.

Her companion pulled an apple from his pocket. "Here. Take it. I give it to you freely and of my own free will. You must use your free will in order to be free." The fruit was cool in her hand. She took a bite: juicy and sweet.

"This is how we'll function without money in the future: simple barter and trade." He held out a little pamphlet covered in dense purple writing. *The Money-Less Economy by an Earnest Man.* She wasn't sure whether to start reading right away but set the paper aside and continued to eat as he spoke. "The Bible tells us that money is the root of all evil, and that is true enough. Wars have been fought over it, people are robbed and murdered, lives are lost in the pursuit of more. I used to put on a suit and tie every day and I went into an office and did mindless work just to earn money. But why? I only handed it over to other people to pay for things that I didn't need. Like suits and ties.

"Think about it: you have to get money to buy a car and then you need more to fill it with gas and oil, patch it up when it gets rusty . . . all so you can drive to your job at the factory or office to earn the money to pay for it! So, who owns who?" His eyes sparkled with excitement. "If we didn't have money, there would be no poverty. No slavery. No inequality, no misery."

Katya swallowed the last bite of apple. She didn't want to be rude after he had given her the fruit but what he said sounded too easy—and reminded her of Harlow. But money didn't make him screw Vicky or accuse Katya of sleeping around.

"Toss the core over there. A squirrel will enjoy it, perhaps some birds, and then the earthworms. See, in the natural world there is no waste." She flung the core into a muddy spot among the green shoots. "I see that you are dubious, Miss Cathy. What is the value of a one-dollar bill?"

"A dollar."

"And the value of a twenty-dollar bill?"

"Twenty bucks . . ."

"But the twenty-dollar bill is a piece of paper, same as one dollar. It only has more value because we've agreed that it is worth more. Our monetary system is built upon a simple agreement. It's only a concept, an idea in our minds. And we can change our minds whenever we want!"

"But didn't we start using paper money because it's too heavy to carry around silver and gold?"

Earnest gave a warm smile like there was nothing he would rather do, no place he would choose to be, other than in this broken-down recliner in the People's Park, talking with her.

"Exactly! And that's the agreement: we pretend that these pieces of paper represent gold. But gold only has value because it is desired; if no one wanted gold, it would be worthless. If we were sensible, we would know that apples have more value than gold because you can eat them."

Katya wanted to be sensible. "Are you sure you can't buy any of my stuff?"

He smiled again. "I'm positive. But you may keep my pamphlet. It's priceless!"

She folded the pamphlet into her satchel. "Thanks. I better get going. It'll be dark soon and I need to find a place to sleep tonight."

He spread his arms wide. "Why not here? There are two recliners, and no one to bother us."

It wasn't a bad idea. The evening was warm, she had plenty of extra clothes to use for a pillow or blanket, and nowhere else to go. They sat quietly together as the sky turned purple and a flock of birds settled in a nearby tree, calling to each other: goodnight, goodnight. Earnest closed his eyes and began to breathe heavily. She pulled sketchbook and pencil from her bag and made a quick drawing of him in the fading light. Maybe he wouldn't want to keep another burdensome possession, but it was a trade for his apple and pamphlet. She tucked the paper beneath his elbow and then settled into the other recliner with her knapsack and pillowcase beside her. So little belonged to her now and yet, she didn't feel free.

Chapter Twenty-two

Give me just a little more time

"I have an announcement, Mrs. Watkins."

Robert had composed his brief speech overnight but still felt uneasy about delivering it. Huck was right: the search needed more effort than Robert could give, even during his extended lunch hours. Although he'd printed up several dozen fliers and provided Huck with bus fare to post them on bulletin boards around college campuses and in the windows of record shops and bookstores, the only result had been one call from a self-proclaimed psychic who swore she could find anyone, dead or alive, for $100. Robert had hung up on her. He wasn't likely to find Cathy by occupying a park bench like a spectator at the circus or by returning to the same spots over and over. If there were any chance of helping her, he would have to be braver himself. Still, his decision unnerved him, giving him the sense of stepping onto a rope bridge: although it might look solid, the planks swayed beneath your feet. And now, as his secretary regarded him with disapproval, his resolve tilted. He took a deep breath.

"There's no need for us to sit here all day, waiting for patients to appear. So, I've decided to limit the hours of the Women's Bureau." Mrs. Watkins opened her mouth but snapped it shut again without speaking. Robert plunged ahead. "From now on, all appointments must be made before two o'clock. No more walk-ins after two, either. On beautiful summer days like this, there won't be many walk-ins anyway." He delivered what he hoped would be a benefit. "You can have more free time to enjoy yourself."

She crossed her arms beneath her scant bosom. Perhaps she didn't want any additional freedom in her day, more time to work on puzzles or whatever else she did when not at the Bureau. Robert forged on. "We can post a sign on the door, instructing them to call ahead for an appointment." Her silence indicated how unlikely she thought it was that anyone who made their way up to the seventh floor only to find the office closed would bother to call or come back.

He dealt his final argument. "Your salary will not be diminished, Mrs. Watkins. This isn't a demotion." Mercifully, the telephone rang at that moment and when she moved to answer it, he escaped into his office and shut the door. They each remained at their desks, the door closed between them, until two o'clock arrived. Then he removed his white coat and placed his hat on his head, she draped her typewriter with its plastic dust cover, and they left the office together as if they were of one mind. As he turned the key in the lock, she reached past him to tape an index card on the frosted glass: *Women's Bureau Hours 9:00 A.M. to 2:00 P.M. Appointments are encouraged.* Then, ever helpful, she added a small pad of paper and a pencil to the wall.

"So that they can leave us a note if they wish to make an appointment."

"Excellent idea. Thank you, Mrs. Watkins." She shook off his appreciation as if it might muss up her hair. They rode the elevator down in silence. In the lobby, she said, "I'll see you tomorrow, Doctor." And Robert tipped his hat, acknowledging her surrender.

* * *

He waited for Huck at their usual meeting spot in the park. Although the younger man wore no watch, he usually managed to arrive close to their agreed-upon time. (No doubt his stomach sent him reminders.) Dappled shade created a slowly moving pattern upon Robert's trouser leg. A puff of air toyed with the medical journal he had brought along. He turned a page, aware that he hadn't absorbed any of the findings described by the study. Still, he held the journal as a decoy while his gaze flickered over anyone who might resemble her, assessing and rejecting each possible candidate like a casting director riffling through stacks of audition photos and discarding them one by one: too tall, too old, too heavy, hair too curly. He tried not to stare. Many of these girls went without bras and their breasts swung freely beneath their shirts. All the more reason not to appear as if he might be ogling them. So, he glanced for only a moment or two in hope of catching the shape of a thin shoulder, that white mark across her chin.

A month ago, he hadn't believed that his memory of her would ever waver. But now it was becoming a will-o-the-wisp. The shape of that scar remained vivid, but not the angle of her forehead. Her eyes were greenish, or had they been more of a brown? Trying to picture her was like attempting to remember a word when all you could get hold of was its rhythm: three syllables, starts with a T or maybe a hard G, accent on the second syllable. Or like a song whose lyrics escaped you, keeping only a faint memory of how the melody rose and fell. Sometimes, as he emerged from the depths of a dream, he knew he had fully recalled her there, that she had stood before him while he slept and had taken his hand in her own. He held that hand out before him now as if he might see an imprint, but his palm was as blank and unyielding as his memory. In the distance, small white planes lifted into the air from Meigs Field, heading south to Springfield or across the lake to Michigan. It was just that easy to leave the city, to be weightless and free.

"Hey, man!" Huck called, striding toward him. He slapped a bundle of paper onto the bench next to Robert's leg and declared, "*This* is how we're going to find that chick!" He crossed his arms in front of his chest and stood grinning, hips thrust forward, as he waited for Robert's praise.

Emblazoned across the cover was a lurid cartoon of a pig in a blue police uniform with swastikas below the masthead: *The Chicago Seed*, written in hand drawn, blocky letters. The pig brandished an ugly, phallic-looking club in one hand. Robert started to turn the page, eager to move past the image, but Huck snatched the newspaper back.

"This is our paper, where the counterculture gets the lowdown on what's really going on. Look, look," he flipped through the pages until he found the right one. Headlined "Intercourse" in red ink, it appeared to be a classified ad section. *Wanted: an electric organ, any condition, any type. Must be free or cheap. Call Armando.* And, *Blues band needs singer, bassist, pianist, trumpet and tenor sax. Must have your own equipment and transportation. Call Rudy.* Sections were labeled Rides, Help!, Messages. *Beware – a batch of bad acid with purple dots. Be good to yourself and stay away.*

Huck sat on the bench so near to Robert that his elbow jostled the paper. "Right here." *Cathy Jones who saw a Dr. downtown in May, please get in touch! We urgently need to rap. Box 290.*

The idea that their elusive girl would respond to the one that Huck had posted seemed unlikely. Would she even want to "rap" with him? But his young friend was ebullient. "She sees the message, calls in," he stabbed his finger at a telephone number on the top of the page, "and tells us how to reach her. All we got to do is stop by the Seed's office or call 'em to see if there's a message for Box 290. That's why I needed those dimes. I coulda said there's a reward, like on the fliers, but that might bring out weirdos. You know, there's a lot of freaky people.

He glanced at Huck's eager face, picturing how he must have chewed on the end of a pencil as he tried to figure out what to write, what words would speak to her. "Good idea," he said, and Huck beamed as he settled into his customary slouch. "So, every day you'll call in see if she's answered?"

"Yeah, man, something like that. And I'm gonna need more dimes."

Robert gave a non-committal grunt while he skimmed the rest of the ads: The Revolution needed more people. Two guys with two dogs wanted roommates "who don't mind a little housework." A "groovy two room furnished pad" was available; Blind Al could set up lights and sound systems; turntables for sale; a lithographer sought work. Karate lessons, coffeehouse and art gallery events. And then, near the bottom of the page, a plea: *Bucky (or anyone knowing him). I'm in trouble and need you so much. I don't know what to do, I don't have anybody and if you have left me too, God knows what will happen to me. Bucky, please get in touch. I love you. Margo (from Cleveland).* And a phone number. Poor Margo, another abandoned girl.

Huck pulled the *Seed* from Robert's hands and shoved it beneath his thigh. For a time, they sat together without speaking. Huck reached into his shirt pocket for cigarettes and began to perform his elaborate ritual of slapping the box of Marlboros against one palm. A pair of young women trotted past. One grabbed the other by the waist, pulling her down to the grass where they sprawled in a laughing tangle of bare arms and legs. Did his wayward girl have a friend like that or did she always travel alone?

Robert sighed and stretched his legs before him. Canvas shoes had turned out to be quite comfortable and he wore them every day now, even in the office. The shoes also seemed to make Huck less uptight about being seen with him. What an unlikely pair they must make, the freewheeling young hippie and a man well on the way to old age, bound by his responsibilities: patients, practice, bills and taxes. At Huck's age, Robert had carried a full load of college courses *and* worked part time. If he'd had a bit more freedom then, what different choices might he have made? Yet there was no point in wondering. Perhaps Huck envied him a little too, for his stable routine days, his three squares, and the roof over his head.

"You've done good work, Huck. Shall we get some lunch?"

"You're on your own this time, Doc." Huck flashed a grin. "That fox who passed us—the one with the really short skirt?"

Robert shook his head. Whoever the fox was, she hadn't made an impression on him.

"Over by the water fountain." He tilted his head, too cool to point, and took a final drag on his cigarette. "I gotta go check her out."

"Okay, young man. I'll manage without you."

"Hey, I'll get a taste of something, don't you worry 'bout that!"

* * *

"Well, look who's here!" Louise smiled as she deftly placed a menu, spoon, and coffee cup before him. As usual, she seemed happy to see him, but filled his cup and moved down the counter to another customer before he could answer her question. He stirred the black coffee needlessly, wondering why it was so easy for young people to meet one another. Huck just walked right up to any girl who caught his interest, without wondering what to say, and seemed to have success. When Louise returned to take his order, Robert looked directly at her.

"I'd like a fried egg sandwich. And . . . I'd like to have dinner with you sometime." She shifted her weight from foot to foot while she considered his question. Robert flushed; where were his manners? He should have engaged in small talk first. He added, "Not here, of course."

She laughed.

"I would hope not! I spend enough hours in this place, I don't need to eat here after my shift's over.".

"We could go . . . well, anywhere you like." *Sometime. Anywhere.* How vague he sounded. He decided to press the point. "How about tomorrow night?" From uncertain to eager, his dating skills lurched like a car with no second gear, revving and faltering. Sweat broke out on his brow.

"Anywhere, huh? All right then." She planted her palms on the counter and leaned toward him. "But not tomorrow, I'm busy on Thursdays. How about Friday? I've always wanted to go to Berghoff's."

Robert hesitated. He hadn't been to the storied German restaurant in years but he could picture Louise in its dark walnut-paneled cavern, her bulky white waitress shoes sinking into the thick soundless carpet. His pause only lasted a moment, the blink of an eye, but it was long enough for her to notice. He opened his mouth to reply, but she spoke first as she drew back.

"Unless it's too expensive."

"Not at all." He needed to erase the frown on her forehead, that hurt expression in her eyes. Of course, she wouldn't wear her waitress outfit on a date! "I'd be very pleased to take you to the Berghoff." He mentally smacked himself for saying the name correctly and emphasizing her slight error. "What time shall I pick you up?" The kitchen bell chimed: her signal to move.

"Let me get that egg sandwich ordered up for you. Why don't you meet me here at seven and we can walk over together." She turned to the kitchen window to hoist a tray of platters onto her broad shoulder.

As Robert ate his sandwich and drank the hot coffee that Louise continued to top off, he cherished that word, one that hadn't been directed his way in years, a word full of promise. *Together.* What a beautiful word.

Chapter Twenty-three

Can't get next to you

Even from Diversey Avenue, Katya could hear electric bass thumping out of the third-floor windows and drums pounding like the heartbeat of a huge, wild beast. She stood in the dark for a moment, gazing up at the apartment building. Molly had told her about this party, saying "I'd go myself, Cathy, but I scored tickets for the Traffic concert." Katya had been crashing with her for a few days but Molly's roommate was due back on Monday. Already, Katya's few belongings were piled in Molly's front hallway, her welcome worn out. So, she'd borrowed a loose-fitting dress to help camouflage her belly and hoped tonight she would meet somebody with a spare couch or a mattress to share, a new friend. And hoped not to run into Harlow.

As she rounded the corner at the top of the stairs, a blast of smoke and noise poured from the open doorway to greet her. Rays of colored light rotated upon the ceiling, sweeping over the masses of people dancing inside, tinting them emerald, ruby, sapphire.

Someone shouted at her. "Two dollars to get in!"

Molly hadn't said anything about money but the guy held out a shoebox with a hole cut in its top. Ruddy freckles covered the backs of his slender hands and ran up the length of his arms. He was tall and lanky, with a mane of red hair that bobbed as he hollered, "It's for a good cause!"

"Cool!" Katya yelled back. "This is all I've got." She smiled as she flashed a crumpled dollar bill, hoping he would believe her. He adjusted the embroidered guitar strap across his chest and leaned closer until his breath tickled her ear and she tucked her head to hide her scarred chin.

"Okay, cutie, you get a pass. This time." He grinned and plucked the money from her hand, his freckled fingers brushing against hers. Would his skin smell spicy, like ginger? Or sweet, like orange marmalade?

"Hey," she began, tossing her head so that her earrings would sparkle in the colored lights. But someone else beckoned to him, yelling, "Kenny!" and Kenny moved away. The guitar slung over his back winked at her as its lacquered surface caught the light. All around her, the room heaved like a boisterous, reeling carnival ride. Between gyrating bodies, the drummer's rapid sticks blurred in the air and a solemn bass player nodded his head while a hand held a tambourine high, impossible to hear above the roar. Too shy to dance, Katya pushed further into the fray. Snatches of conversation spun past her: *Rock and roll is the heart of the revolution . . . The biggest rip-off you ever saw . . . Heavy shit, man . . . New Dylan album?* She was buoyed by the sense of being in a boundless community, surrounded by strangers who by the end of the night could become friends. This is what I hoped for when I left home, she thought. I didn't run *from*, I ran *to*. For a moment, the image of the three singers who had first tempted her flashed in her mind, like a single frame caught in the strobe light.

In the next room, people milled about a large table, helping themselves to food from crockpots, foil pans, and platters. Everyone's mouth seemed to be in motion at once, chewing, arguing, smoking. Bottles of beer, pop, and Jack Daniels covered a card table. She heaped lasagna onto a plate and when someone waggled a bottle of Boone's Farm at her like a question, she nodded for him to pour its cherry-red liquid into a chipped coffee cup.

The only empty place to sit was on the arm of an upholstered chair where a couple was busy making out, and to reach it, she had to squeeze behind a pair of men who stood together in conversation, so close that their foreheads almost touched. She sat hunched with her back to the lovers. The plate of food wobbled on her knees while she ate and listened to the men in front of her. The bearded white guy had on one of those embroidered sheepskin vests that she coveted, while the black man wore an exotically printed dashiki. Sheepskin seemed worried. His dark eyebrows drew down toward his nose as he muttered something to his companion.

"Pigs!" Dashiki responded. "Motherfuckin' pigs! They trashed our headquarters again? How many times we gonna put up with this shit?"

Sheepskin shook his head. "Damn straight.

Dashiki grumbled, "Somebody got to teach those fuckers a lesson, and I mean *now*." His voice was throaty, like he smoked too many cigarettes.

As she took another bite, Katya's plate slid off her knees and clattered to the floor and the two men turned to glare at her. The lovers behind her ceased their groping and stared at the mess she'd made.

"Sorry." She squatted to scoop up the noodles.

"You spying on us, chickie?" Sheepskin growled.

"No. Not really. I mean, I don't know what you're talking about." Reluctant to wipe her hands upon Molly's borrowed dress, she began to suck the tomato sauce from her fingers.

"Let the baby be, man," Dashiki said, dismissively. Too late, she pulled her thumb from her mouth, growing hot with embarrassment.

Sheepskin glowered at her. "Never presume innocence," he said. "It's got to be proven. She show up here to keep the revolution alive? Or just pig out on free food like it's a goddamn party?"

"It's not free," she argued. "I paid to get in."

He sneered. "You ever read 'Soul on Ice'? Heard of Stokely Carmichael?" His questions were a test that she knew she couldn't pass.

Dashiki put a hand on his buddy's shoulder. "Be cool, Marco. I told you, she just a baby."

Katya wanted to wash her hands, to get a drink of water and, most of all, to get out of this corner. She edged away, feeling like a child shooed from the grown-ups' affair, and escaped down the hall to the bathroom. It was small and dirty and dimly lit; no one had flushed the stained toilet. In the mirror, her earrings (a pair she had crafted from faceted glass beads) twinkled at her, but her skin looked yellow except for the white scar which seemed to rebuke her for all the mistakes she'd made, every clumsy move, each stumble and fall permanently etched on her young face.

She was still hungry—always hungry these days— but she wasn't about to go back for more food. That room was one more place to keep away from. She'd been boycotting anti-war protests and rallies so that she wouldn't bump into Harlow and see his arm around another girl. But it was so unfair: *he* didn't have to do anything different. He got to keep living in his apartment and screwing Vicky—or anyone else he wanted. There was nowhere Harlow had to avoid, no scars on his unchanged body.

"Hey!" Someone pounded on the door. "You fall in?" She sprang the lock, pushed through the crowd, and scurried to the kitchen, crammed with people sitting on the counter tops and leaning against the fridge. An open back door let in cooler air, and a couple of folks nodded at her as she entered as if they might welcome her presence. Someone passed her a bottle of beer: warm and stale, but Katya drank it down.

At the center of the room, a woman in a cornflower blue dress held court. Her deep neckline revealed the pink curve of her breasts. She pulled a small rectangle of paper from a packet, folded it along one edge, and sprinkled pot into the crease. Efficiently, the woman rolled the cigarette, licked the glue edge of the paper, and twisted the tips. A lighter snapped and flared; she held the joint to her mouth and the room hushed. As she sucked in the first hit, it seemed that everyone else inhaled along with her, holding their breath as she did and gazing at her rosy, quivering breasts.

Katya watched the joint pass around the dim kitchen, its little ember glowing from one mouth to the next. When it was her turn, she gulped the smoke too quickly and had to fight an urge to cough, clamping one hand over her mouth and nostrils. Her torso convulsed but she resisted, determined not to humiliate herself again. As she wiped her streaming eyes on her sleeve, someone nudged her to take another hit. Again she puffed, this time more cautiously, and took another swig of sour beer to ease the burn.

It was good to be with quieter people. Her head was full of bubbles. Bubbly-bobbly. She smiled at the girl beside her, admiring how her arm was covered in silver bracelets that clinked like a tune. Funny how, at every party, there were always more girls in the kitchen than any other room. "Baubles," Katya said. "You're so bauble-y." The girl with the bracelets smiled and nodded like she understood.

Across the room, the open doorway led to a darker, cooler place. There must be a back porch out there. A black night back porch. After the next toke, she aimed for the door, stumbling around the people squatting on the floor. "Zig Zag," she whispered to herself in amusement.

Stepping outside, she entered a quieter dimension. In the center of the porch floor, a brown paper bag cast a yellow glow. Katya crouched next to the makeshift lantern, marveling at how the candle flame didn't burn the flimsy paper.

"Luminaria." Kenny sat on the top step. His halo of red hair radiated in the dim light. She didn't know what he meant but it didn't matter; the word had already wafted away, dissolving in the night air. She smiled at him. His pale fingers seemed to shimmer as he plucked the strings of his guitar. "Hey, little mama. How's it going?"

"It's cool." Her words sounded slow and lazy. She plopped down beside him, so close that she could feel warmth rising from his body. The spots on his hands looked dark but she knew they were really flecks of gold. Earnest Mann said gold only had worth if you

desired it and Katya did: she wanted to touch Kenny's
fine hair and his dappled skin. With a fingertip, she began to trace patterns on his forearm from one golden
freckle to the next. Draw a line from dot to dot and
when you reach the end, you'll have created a picture of
a rabbit or a tree or a treasure chest. As Kenny picked
out a tune, his elbow bumped against her distended
belly. Abruptly, the music stopped. Katya stared at the
invisible star she had been tracing on his skin.

"Girl, better get real!" He stood and his guitar
slammed into her shoulder, twanging its disapproval.
"Nobody wants to make it with a pregnant chick." As he
stalked past the luminaria, its flame guttered and flared,
sending shadows veering across the porch floor before
they melted into the night.

Stung by his rejection, she sat with her pulse pounding in her ears. Deep within her abdomen, something
fluttered like a trapped bird beating its wings against the
glass. Tentatively, she slipped one hand beneath her
dress. There it was again: a warning from the unseen
stranger she carried with her now, this invader who
thwarted all her desires, and who would keep growing
until soon there would be nothing left of Katya at all.

Chapter Twenty-four

Put a little love in your heart

The heavy oak door of the Berghoff Restaurant resisted Robert's efforts to open it. The door couldn't have gained weight or heft since he had last been here a decade ago, and yet he found that he needed to wrap both hands around the twisted metal handle and tug hard. Had he really become that much weaker? At last, the door swung open and he held it for Louise to pass through while he tried to steady his breath.

She had changed from her uniform into a showy dress for their date: swirling patterns of orange and green, with a matching orange belt and a row of green plastic bangles on one wrist. A bit loud, perhaps, for the Berghoff, but he wouldn't dream of saying so. She'd pinned her hair in a way that let her curls drape loosely and her earlobes sparkled with rhinestones.

"You look nice," Robert said. At the coat check window, he handed his fedora to a young woman who appeared suitably Germanic in her green dirndl. She gave him a limp smile along with a small cardboard tag.

"Shall we have a drink first?" He escorted Louise down a short passageway lined with framed photographs of luminaries who had visited the restaurant throughout its history. She paused, stooping to peer closely at the pictures.

"Oh, look!" A dazzling film star of yesteryear posed with her arms looped around the shoulders of two men wearing chef's toques. "It's whatshername!" As she continued to examine each photo, she exclaimed brightly in recognition, but Robert couldn't identify many of the celebrities.

"I haven't gone out much in the past few years," he admitted. "Quite a few, to tell the truth."

Louise straightened up and looked him in the eye. "Do—" she said, "tell the truth. Whenever possible." Surprised and impressed, Robert nodded agreement.

At last, they entered the bar. The entire room—walls, ceiling, and the massive bar itself—was covered in carvings of oak leaves, trees, animals, birds. Half a dozen men sat at the polished counter, puffing cigars. Taxidermied elk and deer heads hung high on the walls. A thick haze of smoke dimmed their glass eyes, giving them dull, hopeless expressions below the huge antlers.

A portly man in green lederhosen stepped in front of them. "Ek-scuse me. This is the Men's Grill." His accent snipped at his words, adding a veneer of menace.

"I beg your pardon?" Robert faltered while Louise stiffened at his side.

"The Men's Grill. Reserved for men only." The obstructionist pointed to a sign above the doorway that confirmed his words. "It is tradition."

"It's traditional to be unwelcoming to your female customers?" Louise's voice was level but there was a granite resolve in her tone. The maître d' ignored her and continued to address Robert.

"In seventy-six years, we have kept the grill for men. Your date is welcome to enjoy our dining room, of course."

"I don't think so," Robert responded. "We'll be taking our business elsewhere."

Louise slipped her hand into the crook of his arm. "To an establishment that welcomes men *and* women," she added.

Half an hour later, they were settled in a large round booth at the Little Corporal. As suited a Napoleon-themed restaurant, the room was extravagantly decorated with over-sized fluted columns and burgundy velvet curtains that spilled down onto the floor. Massive chandeliers twinkled overhead. The waiter delivered menus in the shape of Bonaparte's famous coat, complete with paper epaulets, gold medals, and a red diagonal sash. Louise sat close beside him and they ordered champagne, feeling festive and daring as they raised their glasses in a toast: in 1970, women should be able to go wherever they pleased.

"All that fuss to keep us out of their bar!" she said. "Did you see how the moths had munched on some of those elk heads? Who'd want to drink beer with a bunch of old stuffed animals?"

"Or with stuffed shirts?"

Louise laughed at his joke, and Robert felt that all was well. She seemed comfortable in his company and the time passed pleasantly as they exchanged bits of their life stories. Neither of them was inclined to start at the beginning and try to unreel an entire autobiography. Instead, the conversation dipped and swooped as they sipped their glasses of bubbly and described places they'd lived and movies they enjoyed. He was careful not to ask her whether she'd gone to college; she pretended not to notice how he absently rubbed his left ring finger with his thumb, drawing attention to the empty space.

Then she brought up the war. Not what Robert had expected on a first date, but these were serious times and the war could not be ignored; it was on everyone's mind. "I see the faces of these boys we send over to Viet Nam and they look hardly old enough to shave!" She stopped, swallowing hard. "I guess I don't know your politics. I was a McCarthy supporter myself."

"My first choice was RFK. After he was assassinated, Humphrey seemed the most pragmatic option, but McCarthy would have been all right, too."

"McCarthy never would have expanded the war into Cambodia!" she declared.

He liked how strongly she held her opinions. "At least Nixon can't possibly be re-elected. We'll elect a president with some sense next time . . ."

Their waiter arrived, balancing a heavily laden tray on his shoulder, and their conversation came to a standstill while they ate. Louise was a hearty eater, sampling everything, sometimes closing her eyes to taste. "Well," she said, setting down her fork and delicately wiping the corners of her mouth, "now that we've broken bread together, I'll ask: Did you find that girl you were looking for?"

"No, not yet. But I'm still hoping." He wiped his lips with his napkin, wondering what to say next. How to explain why it was so important to rescue Cathy? Yes, she needed good nutrition, folic acid, blood pressure checks, prenatal care. She should be attending school, not burdened with a baby or estranged from her family. But there was more to it than that. After the Great Fire, Chicago had been rebuilt out of brick and stone, concrete and steel; it was a city of sharp-edges and granite, with little room for tenderness, for such a delicate *naïf*.

She had seen his unending sorrow in a way that no one else had. And then, with her gift of the portrait and her simplistic ideas, she had tried to release him from the burden of his grief. But all that was more than he could say to Louise tonight.

He took a sip of water. "She didn't even have a pair of shoes on when she came into my office. She said she'd never been to a doctor before—can you imagine? And she was shy, hoping that someone named Jane would be there instead of me."

"She asked for Jane?" An expression flashed across Louise's face, too quickly for him to decipher.

"Yes, I don't know why."

"Tell me again what she looks like." Louise listened intently as he listed the few qualities that he could: slight build, maybe sixteen or seventeen years old, light brown hair, hazel eyes.

"And, of course, the scar on her chin. The fact that it wasn't sutured properly bothers me. It seems emblematic, as if signaling that she had a hard, deprived life. Why else would such a young girl run away from home?"

Louise spoke quietly. "She might've had cruel parents or ones who hardly paid attention to her. Maybe she broke too many rules and they kicked her out. Or she was chasing something, a dream, a boy . . ."

"Well, she found a boy somewhere! The urgency is that she's pregnant." It was a relief to say it out loud, to confess the burden that had pressed upon him all these weeks. He shouldn't discuss his patients but he felt the need to tell someone and Louise didn't look surprised. He shared more of his worries. "But she didn't return for her test results. I've never had a patient who didn't want to know the outcome. What if she can't face the reality of her situation? She could end up like Frances Flannery."

"That poor girl, giving birth all alone in a school bathroom! Can you believe how the D.A. is going after her because she won't name the father." Louise slapped her napkin against the table in indignation, rattling her plastic bracelets. "She's not only on trial for murder—but for having a sex life!" The approaching waiter scurried away as he overheard Louise's last words. She pushed her plate aside and crossed her forearms on the table. "You know what I'm going to do? Go to her trial, that's what! See for myself how it plays out on Monday. Want to come with?"

How spirited Louise was, how full of spunk! A bit of hair had slipped out of its barrette and lay draped along the side of her neck. Robert wished he could wrap the soft tress around his finger. He shook his head in dual regret. "I've got patients to see. But if you attend the trial, I hope you'll tell me about the experience."

"Oh, I'm going all right." In the pause that followed, the waiter cautiously re-appeared to pour their coffee and Louise changed the subject. "And if you find Cathy, then what?"

Robert rubbed his chin. "I'm not entirely sure. I hope she'll allow me to assist her, make sure she and the baby are healthy. So much can go wrong without good prenatal care. I could connect her to some services or adoption programs. Get her back in school later. She's talented at art. She drew a portrait for me: of Phyllis, my late wife." The mention of her name hung in the air between them for a moment and then faded as Louise watched him, waiting for him to continue. "Cathy had a little accent. No, not exactly; more like an unusual rhythm, or a different inflection. As if she were used to another language."

"That doesn't help much, does it? Chicago's full of immigrants."

"Right," he sighed. "She could have come from anywhere, gone anywhere." He looked at his companion and brightened. "But looking for her has been an adventure. I get out of my office more, try new things. I've become friends of a sort with Huck, that young man you've seen me with at your café. Claims he's catnip to every girl in the city and always dines out on my dime, but he is smart and seems sincere about helping me find Cathy. And I've made another discovery that's quite wonderful."

"And that is?" She smiled as if she knew the answer but wanted to hear him say it.

"I've met you," he said, longing to reach for her hand. But Robert held himself back. It wouldn't do to be so forward on a first date. Would it?

Chapter Twenty-five

Try some of my purple berries

Your baby's crying." Katya nudged Meadow, but the other woman's response was muffled as she bent into the washing machine. "Hey, he's crying. Don't you hear him?" Meadow turned around and wiped her forehead with the back of her hand. Her dark eyes narrowed.

"Yeah, I do. And what would really be groovy? If you'd go take care of him." She snapped a cotton diaper to shake out the wrinkles, whipping it close to Katya's arm. *Snap.* "You might as well start getting some practice. Your own baby will be here before you know it." She gave a tight smile and then turned her back, wielding another diaper. *Snap.*

Katya grumbled as she trudged up the stairs from the basement. Meadow and River had been a lot friendlier back when she'd first met them at the concert in the park. After Molly kicked her out, she'd found the crumpled piece of paper with their address on it and rode two buses north, hoping they'd take her in. When she reached their large, dilapidated house, Meadow had welcomed her with a cup of herbal tea and the promised pair of overalls. Then she was ushered into the living room, where ten men and women sat in a circle on the worn carpet as if they were about to play a round of Duck, Duck, Goose. With their long hair parted down the middle, they looked like siblings from a big family.

Meadow's fingers gently stroked her arm, River kept one hand on the small of her back. "Who's this?" asked a man with a wooly brown beard as he stared at her body. Resentment bit at her. Didn't she have a face anymore?

"Laura," she declared, thinking of the gutsy, smart girl in the Little House on the Prairie books. She ran around barefoot all day; her parents did everything they could to send her to school.

"Laura is staying with us now," Meadow said. She sounded triumphant, as if she had won a prize.

"But she'll upset our gender balance," complained a woman with a spotty face and terrible posture.

River chimed in. "We need a companion for our baby, someone for him to grow up with so they can walk the same paths of life together. Unless you want to help create the next generation, Penny?" Penny glowered in response.

"We can take that up on another agenda," someone else snickered.

"Welcome, Laura." The bearded man bent over his crossed legs in a kind of seated bow. "I'm Al." The rest of the circle introduced themselves then, too many names for her to remember other than pouting Penny.

Living with twelve other people (thirteen, when she remembered to count the nameless baby) was surprisingly lonely: they were all older than her, with their house rules and roles already set. The past two weeks had been nothing but *do this, do that*. Living in a co-operative household meant long, boring meetings and plenty of work, with extra chores assigned to her in lieu of rent. "Did you remember to rinse the sprouts today, Laura?" "Can't you get that frying pan a little cleaner?"

"Check the job board; we all have to do our share." And yesterday she had caught River gazing at her with a creepy, hungry look.

Now, Katya stomped through the kitchen, not bothering to hide her dissatisfaction. Like all the girls in her old neighborhood, she'd had babies handed to her at church, expected to comfort them while their mothers lined up for communion. She knew the cloying sensation of damp plastic pants and the acrid smell of diapers. Meadow's still unnamed baby squalled in a wicker basket on the floor. She squatted next to the basket with her knees spread apart to make room for her belly and watched him flap his chubby arms. His toothless gums were as pink as bubble gum and strands of drool dangled from his lips. Tears leaked down his scarlet cheeks. If she touched him, she'd be coated with his sticky residue: spit-up, tears, pee, and the flaky stuff on his scalp that Meadow said was "cradle cap." Katya pushed her fingers into her ears and pressed a forearm against her nose to block the stench that rose from his wet gown.

"Hey," she said, softly. With her fingers stuck in her ears, her voice sounded as if she were underwater. "Hey, little no-name. Hush up." His wail rose into a shriek until Meadow dashed into the room and scooped him, too livid to notice the white curds that he hiccupped down her back.

"What's wrong with you, Laura? Why don't you help him stop crying?"

"Maybe he's crying 'cause he's got no name. Ever think about that?" Katya struggled to her feet and angrily stalked through the kitchen. The screen door stuck, and she shoved it hard so that the door ricocheted against the porch railing with a satisfying bang. The backyard was half shaded by two large sycamores whose yellow leaves littered the dirt. A few wet diapers sagged on the clothesline above Meadow's abandoned basket of laundry. Flies buzzed around a heap in the back corner where the household was attempting to make compost. Broken eggshells bulged from the moldy mass like eyeballs. If anybody looked out here for inspiration, they'd end up calling that baby Trashpile or Dirt Patch. The idea of Baby Dirt Patch made her smile. Dollops of dark pulp covered the ground beneath a straggly mulberry tree. Or Mulberry, that would be a cute name. Katya moved beneath the tree's branches, trying to avoid stepping on the mucky lumps, and reached for a berry. Soft and moist against her fingers, the fruit looked like a bunch of fairy grapes, gleaming red and black. Its sweet juice burst on her tongue, but the white core tasted bitter and she spat it out.

Maybe she could make berry juice or jam, like Laura Ingalls did. Something to sell at a street fair. She unbuckled the bib of her overalls and held it away from her with one hand while, with the other, she shook a branch, raining berries onto her head and into her improvised bowl. She sang an old nursery rhyme as she thrashed the branches: *Here we go round the mulberry bush, the mulberry bush . . .* until berries covered her breasts (larger now than they'd ever been) and she hastened back to the empty kitchen to dump her harvest into a stock pot. But there was no sugar in the pantry. White sugar, meat, and alcohol were against the house rules. Now there'd be no jam, and her clothes were mottled with damp purple splotches that might not wash out. But the stains looked like big abstract flowers, which gave her a new idea: boil the berries, press them somehow, and make dye.

Strains of Beatles music wafted from the front of the house but no one came to disturb her. As Katya stirred her concoction, the wooden spoon turned purple-black and the room filled with a fruity aroma. After the fruit cooked down, she poured the mixture through a sieve into a bowl. Although she tried to be careful, hot splatters of juice hit the stove and the tops of her bare feet. She jumped back, nearly upsetting the bowl. How little liquid had pooled in the bottom. Back to the tree for more berries.

By the time the pot brimmed with a dark simmering liquid, the kitchen table was spattered with berry juice and the floor was tattooed in black. Time to try out her dye on a clean dishcloth. There was something unsettling in how the purple seeped into the cotton, rising toward her hand as if it wanted to reach her stained fingers. Like ink from a giant squid on *Sea Hunt* spreading ominously through water. Or watching darkness come too soon. But the dye seemed to work, so she stripped off her ruined overalls and T-shirt and dropped them into the pot.

Looking down, she saw with dismay that she had become a roly-poly person, like Mrs. Pulaski back at the bakery. Her bare belly hovered pale and moonlike beneath her swollen breasts. She cringed at the thought of anyone seeing her like this: half-naked, fat, sweaty. A faded denim work shirt hung behind the pantry door and she slipped her arms into its soft sleeves. The fabric smelled of dough, as if Mrs. Pulaski now held her in an embrace, but the buttons were on the wrong side: it was a man's shirt.

All through junior high, girls had challenged each other. "What are you?" they would demand. "Boy or girl?" Were the buttonholes on the correct side of your shirt? Did the fly over your zipper open the right way? You had to perform certain tasks to prove what you were. *Sit down*: girls keep their knees together while boys spread theirs wide apart. *Cross your legs*: boys place an ankle over their knee, only girls cross one thigh on top of the other. *Look at your fingernails*: splaying them in front of you was a girls' method. Katya always felt ashamed to participate in these games, as if some hidden flaw of hers might accidentally be exposed.

Thankfully, these games stopped in high school, but the gym teacher delivered her own challenge and girls spent many classes walking in circles around the gymnasium precariously balancing textbooks on top of their heads. This activity was called "deportment." When Katya tried to practice at home, Tata had growled, "What for? They think you gonna be Saint Lucia and wear candles on your head?" Was he teasing her or truly angry? It was so hard to know.

Now, she fumbled with the man-buttons, pulling the shirt over the hill of her tummy. The gas flame gave a little hiss as she shut it off. With the blackened spoon, she fished her clothes out of the hot inky water and let them drip into the pot until cool enough to wring out. She carried the shirt and overalls outside and hung them over the line to dry. The shirt—and her hands—had turned a satisfying dark purple, as beautiful as an eggplant or some exotic flower. Flowers: that's what she would create, blossoms that she could make into jewelry. A stack of round paper coffee filters near the percolator would work perfectly. She dropped a filter into her pot. Like a feather, it fluttered into the mixture, blushed pale violet, and sank. She dredged it out with the spoon, dissatisfied with the shapeless result.

She found a canister of salt in the pantry and sprinkled a few grains on the wet paper to see how the salt repelled the color, creating little stars of lavender where the crystals dissolved. But how to fix the colors so that they wouldn't bleed or fade? In freshman art class, they'd used hairspray to protect their chalk drawings but she would have to work with what she had now. She split the dye into two pots and added a bottle of white vinegar into one, half a bottle of cider vinegar into the other. One by one, she formed new shapes. Some, she wet with water first and then twisted them into strange orchids. Others, she folded like accordions into small fans whose edges she touched with ink. She tried soaking the filters in vinegar, then the dye. Or dye first, then salt water, leaving marbled, cryptic markings behind. Soak in salt water, pucker and twist, a quick dip in the dye bath, and then a vinegar rinse.

The table pressed against Katya's belly as she bent over her splattered pots and bowls. Vinegar stung her nostrils, her eyes teared, and both hands bore the color of deep bruises, hues of betrayal, the shade of what's left when you've lost so much. Her dreams of becoming an artist had seemed so remote, as if they had vanished with the three singers from that long-ago October night. She hummed as she worked, and a collection of tiny pansies, violets, and amethyst roses spread across the table.

"Whoa!" Al stood on the threshold, gaping at the ravaged kitchen: the table and counters, littered with dishes, empty vinegar bottles, and cookie sheets full of her drying creations; the floor, stippled with purple splotches, and crusted with salt. "What's happenin' here?" He sounded stunned.

"I'm making art." She tossed more coffee filters into the pot.

"Huh." He waited, but she didn't look up. "Yeah, looks like you're really into it." She plucked a flower from the dye. This one looked like an iris; it pleased her immensely. "Um, you gonna be done pretty soon? 'Cause I gotta make dinner tonight."

Katya swished the iris in vinegar, watching the faint swirl of purple eddy around the crumpled paper. She answered flatly. "Nope."

Al shuffled his feet. "You mean, no, you're not done soon?" Katya ignored him. "This is not cool!" He disappeared and a few minutes later, Meadow leaned into the room, clinging to the doorjamb as if she didn't dare step inside. Her voice was icy.

"We're going to have to order pizza. The money's coming out of the budget to fix the roof. We're holding an emergency House Meeting right now, and you're supposed to be there. And whatever that black stuff is, it *better* not be toxic!"

Katya bent over the table and blew on a blossom to help it dry faster. Even though Meadow had given herself a nature name, she didn't seem to recognize the scent of mulberries.

"You might not give a rat's ass, Laura, but *you* are the first item on the agenda because of this . . . this *disaster*. We're going to caucus on whether we'll allow you to stay in this house. And since you've appropriated our co-operative kitchen for your own personal project and trashed it, and since you don't seem to care about anyone's goals but your own, I think we all know what the consensus will be." Meadow pushed herself away from the doorway and disappeared. Voices drifted from the front of the house: deep murmurs, shriller tones, the baby wailing. Flies buzzed around Katya as she carried the leftover berry pulp outside to the compost heap. The evening sky was the rich color of her flower creations. She knew that tomorrow morning, she'd need to find a new place to live. But tonight, she would string her flowers into necklaces and bracelets, thread them onto wire and turn them into earrings. These creations were better than any other jewelry she had made, worth a higher price.

There was still a little dye left in the bottom of the pot. Rather than dump it down the sink, she poured the liquid into a small glass jar. With a steady hand, she drew a skull-and-crossbones on the lid and pushed the jar into the back of the fridge where it wouldn't be found for weeks, not until it had thickened into an evil looking slime, not until long after "Laura" was gone.

Chapter Twenty-six

Eight miles high

Huck, if you were sick or hurt, where would you go for help?" It was an idea that should have occurred to Robert weeks ago but had only struck him only now, as they stuck fliers on telephone poles around Circle campus.

"I'd come to your office," Huck grinned. "No man, I'm putting you on, I know you only see the chicks. I'd go to one of the Free Clinics like I did when I got cut. They stitched me up real nice." He pushed up a sleeve to reveal a neat white line arcing across his bicep.

"Ouch. How did that happen?" But Huck gave him that hooded look that meant he wouldn't talk. (Or, as he would put it, "I'm not sayin' shit.") "It's free because you didn't pay anything?"

"Yeah, man, it's free if you can't afford it. But they're also *free* like run by our people. They're not in a hospital, not run by The Man. Black Panthers have their own on the west side, but I went to Haymarket. It's in a church near Logan Square."

"Sounds like a good place to check for Cathy. Come along?" He turned to go, but Huck took a final drag before crushing the cigarette butt beneath his heel.

"Nah, I'll finish these fliers and hang out around here. Looks like there's a concert tonight." He gestured at a garish poster beside the flier he had just taped up.

"Suit yourself." Robert unlocked his car door.

189

Half an hour later, he stood before a rundown Methodist church. Its rugged sandstone façade had blackened over the decades; gaps in the roof showed where shingles were missing. It looked like a hulking old man in a dirty coat with bald patches on his head. Shaggy clumps of grass sprouted intermittently in the dirt yard. According to a leaflet tacked on the front door, Reverend Taylor would offer the Sunday sermon "Peace in Our Time" and on Tuesday evening, all were welcome at a potluck community dinner. Robert couldn't imagine many people came to this sagging house of worship. A sign directed him down a short flight of steps to the Haymarket People's Free Clinic but the door was locked and no one answered his knocks.

As he remounted the steps, a red and white VW bus lurched to the curb, its side door slid open, and four young people spilled out. They pulled cartons and bundles from the back and trotted down to the clinic door as Robert called, "Excuse me?" to their backs.

The tallest man paused, cradling a cardboard box in his arms. "Help you?"

"I'm looking for the clinic director. Do you know where I might find him?"

The young man pushed his glasses up his nose to peer closely at Robert. He sported what passed for a short haircut these days, the ends barely brushing his shirt collar. "Tell me what you want and maybe I can point you in the right direction. What agency are you with?"

"I'm not sure what you mean. My name is Robert Lewis, I'm an M.D. with a practice downtown."

"Doctor!" The younger man juggled his carton to offer a hand in greeting. "I was afraid you were from the

board of health or the zoning commission, come to hassle us again. Ethan Fein. I'm an intern at Michael Reese
Hospital. Those guys," he nodded where the others had
vanished inside, "are a fourth-year student, a nurse, and
a med school dropout. Welcome! Come on in."

"I—" Robert began but Ethan marched off. Well,
there would be time to straighten things out with the
director. He picked his way back down the stairs, holding onto the shaky handrail. A metal folding chair
propped the door open. Inside, fluorescent lights and
green linoleum gave a sickly hue to the room, but cheery
efforts had been made: a colorful knit afghan draped
over an old sofa, posters promoting breastfeeding, paper
peace symbols taped to the barred windows. A coffee
urn, hotplate, and record player competed for space on
a table near a hand-lettered sign that warned, "Watch
out for the blue tab acid."

"I tried calling," Robert said as the workers bustled
about, unloading medical supplies into cupboards and
drawers.

Ethan gave a short laugh. "Phone's been turned off.
We couldn't pay the bill. Let's rap back here." He pulled
aside a vinyl shower curtain and waved Robert through.
Several small rooms opened off a short hallway. Ethan
reached inside one and flicked on the lamp to reveal
another tired sofa and several squat armchairs. "Take
your pick. They're all uncomfortable." Robert opted for
the sofa and immediately regretted his choice when the
springs collapsed beneath his weight, his rear end nearly
hitting the floor. Ethan flopped into an opposite chair,
sending small clouds of dust exhaling from its cushions.
"Sorry, what was your name again?" With difficulty,

Robert wrestled his wallet out of his back pocket and removed a business card.

"Thanks, Dr. Lewis. Like I said, we're glad to have a physician here again. As you can see, we operate on the proverbial shoestring and we'll take any help we can get."

"You have no other doctors?"

"The last guy moved away and we had to shut down for a while. But you've arrived just in time—yesterday, the crew and I decided to re-open anyway and trust that we won't get busted. Too many people count on us for health care."

"Where *are* your patients?"

"They mostly show up after work, around five or six. And Saturday mornings." He checked his watch. "Folks'll come in once they figure out we're open again. You probably thought we'd all be hippies, right?"

Robert smiled. "Well . . . I did hear about you from someone who fits that description."

"We treat everybody, whether they have flowers in their hair or head lice—or both."

"And Ethan, you're the director here?"

"Nope. We're run by a collective." Seeing Robert's blank look, he explained. "There's a small, loose group of us and we make the decisions together, mostly by consensus. We're not trying to create the hierarchy of a hospital; nobody's getting paid, so why bother with all that status and bureaucracy? We simply try to give care to people who need it, as best we can and they pay us what they can—or sometimes nothing. If the Board of Health and the Mayor would just leave us alone, we could make a real difference."

This place was so unorthodox, so young. Robert cleared his throat. "What about pregnancies? You see many of those?"

"Sure, sometimes. We can run a basic pregnancy test, check blood pressure, offer prenatal vitamins. But beyond that, they need to go to a hospital for care. Maybe we should send them to your . . ." He checked Robert's business card. " . . . Women's Bureau."

"I'm actually looking for one of my patients. Perhaps your records would show . . ."

Ethan shuffled his foot on the carpet. "Sorry. Don't keep much in the way of records. If we're ever subpoenaed, or hauled into court, we don't want any documents that could incriminate us. Or the patients."

Somewhere, a door slammed. Voices rose from the front room. A serious-looking fellow poked his head around the doorway. "Ethan? We need you for a moment?" His mustache quivered as he spoke.

"Sure, Joel. 'Scuse me." Ethan hoisted himself out of his dusty chair and disappeared around the corner while Robert stayed put, caught by disappointment. No doctors, no director, no documents. What a waste of time to have come here. He couldn't just sit in the waiting room and wait for pregnant girls to walk in. At least he had brought along his fliers and maybe Ethan would post one somewhere. The voices down the hall became more audible, followed by a sharp cry of pain.

"Doctor Lewis! Can you help us here?" He tried to stand, but the broken springs of the couch kept him trapped and he found himself rocking in place without gaining any momentum. Hurling himself to one side, Robert managed to struggle to his feet. In a nearby room, Ethan, Joel, and two others stood crowded together, while a youth was doubled over in the corner, thrashing and moaning. Blood dribbled from Joel's mustache. Ethan looked scared but kept his voice calm. "Kid took something. We don't know what, but he's pretty high. Soon as Joel touched him, kid belted him."

Robert steadied his breath. "All right, let's get this under control. You," he tapped the young woman on her shoulder, "get something cold to press on Joel's nose. Pick up his glasses, they're on the floor over there. Now, did anyone else come in with this young man?"

"Not that I saw. If they did, they dumped him and took off."

How long had it been since he'd examined a male? Decades . . . "Well, well," he addressed the agitated patient, careful to keep an arm's length away. "Looks like you're in a lot of pain. I'm a doctor and I'd like to help. I'm going to take a look at you now." He placed a cautious hand on the boy's thin upper arm which jerked at his touch. "I'm Doctor Lewis; what's your name?"

"Mike," he groaned. "God, it hurts." He couldn't be more than nineteen or twenty years old.

"Okay, Mike." Robert steered him over to an exam table and directed his makeshift assistants to hold Mike there. As if he were in a teaching hospital, he shared his observations with the young staff. "The patient is pale, pupils dilated, legs thrashing. No rebound pain in the right lower quadrant."

"What're you on, man?" Ethan leaned in, keeping a firm grip on Mike's arm. The kid mumbled a long string of words that were unintelligible to Robert. "Right. Mikey got ready to face the draft board tomorrow by taking uppers, downers, and whatever he found in the medicine cabinet."

Mike's eyes rolled like a panicked horse. Robert placed a hand against his clammy forehead and the touch appeared to soothe him somewhat. "Michael? Did you swallow anything else, besides pills?"

"Magnets," Mike groaned. "Buncha tiny magnets."

Robert straightened up. "All right, we need to pump his stomach. It's either that or send him to a hospital. Have you seen this procedure done before?" Ethan said yes, Sandy and Joel shook their heads no. "Well, I guess it's a teaching day. We need tubing and activated charcoal. Bring a brighter lamp, if you have one. And rubber gloves, please." He hoped he still had the necessary skills; it had been many years since he'd mixed the slurry of charcoal and pumped it through a nasogastric tube. Mike gagged and protested throughout, but the young, strong helpers held him down. "Hopefully, some of what he ingested will be absorbed by the charcoal, rather than making its way into his bloodstream."

"What about the magnets?" Sandy said through clenched teeth as she leaned her full weight on Mike's bucking legs.

"If they're small enough, nature will take its course. Let's get him sobered up and maybe he can tell us more about them. Now, use the rubber bulb to create suction and begin emptying the stomach." He handed the bulb around so they could each practice emptying Mike's gastric juices into a bucket. A sour odor filled the room; more than one of the young staff looked queasy, but they persevered. Mike moaned quietly and gradually stopped fighting. At last, Robert pulled the slimy tube from his nose and dropped it into the pail. "Is there a place I can wash up?" As he lathered his hands, he studied himself in the small looking glass over the sink and allowed himself to feel a warm prickle of pride. Not bad for an old guy out of practice.

* * *

The magnets, as it turned out, were very small and Mike had swallowed only a few. "With enough fluids and Milk of Magnesia, they should pass through your system without causing harm," Robert said.

But Mike was not particularly grateful. "You sonsabitches messed up my high. I gotta go for my physical in the morning and I wanted to be flying."

"So they'd reject you," Ethan guessed.

"Damn straight," Mike snapped. "The magnets were my back-up plan. If they gave me an x-ray, they'd think something was wrong with my insides and they'd cut me loose. Now what am I going to do?" His sneer faded and his eyes grew wet. "I'm gonna have to break my fingers." He spread his left hand out like a starfish. "Gimme a hammer!"

"Good God, no!" Robert took hold of Mike's hands. The nails were chewed and ragged. "There must be an alternative."

"He wouldn't be the first to do it," Ethan said, flatly. "Guys do a lot of desperate things to themselves to avoid being sent to Nam. Sandy and Joel can stay with him; let's you and I go outside to talk."

The sunset had left the western sky streaked with crimson. "Let me show you something." He pulled a piece of paper from his pocket. Robert slowly read the list, printed in shaky capital letters: *Asthmatic. Color blind. Homosexual. Bed-wetter. Hearing loss. Myopic. Ulcers. Communist. Addicted to heroin. Agoraphobic.*

Acrophobic. Kleptomaniac. Sex maniac.

"What in the world is this?"

"It was written by a kid last week, trying to get classified 1-Y. Claimed he had all these conditions. He went a little overboard, don't you think?"

Robert handed back the paper. "Did it work?"

"Only for six months. He got a medical deferment, not an exemption. Then he'll have to go through it all again. You wouldn't believe the shit we see. Guys smoke an entire carton of cigarettes to bring on an asthma attack or lock themselves in a roomful of cats when they're allergic. They starve themselves to lose 30 pounds. They swallow drugs, cleaning products, diuretics, No-Doz. Get infections from crappy obscene tattoos. Blow out their knees on purpose."

"Dear Lord." Robert shook his head.

"The kid who wrote this would've had better odds if he'd brought a simpler letter from his doctor. That kind of paperwork can make a big difference. Maybe documenting high blood pressure or asthma or a bad back. There are numerous conditions that lead to an exemption. Even color blindness can qualify . . ." Ethan studied Robert's face, as if looking for a door out of a locked room.

"But . . . doesn't the draft board do a physical exam to confirm those findings?"

"Sometimes yes, sometimes no. Even when they do, those exams can be pretty perfunctory. A lot of doctors in the Army don't want to be there either and they're not always keen on sending more guys into the damn jungle. So, if a draftee has a note saying he's blind-as-a-bat nearsighted, they shine a flashlight in his pupils and tell him to try to read the eye chart. And that's easy enough to flunk. Think you might know any doctors who, uh, could be interested in writing those kinds of letters?"

Ethan waited, hands clasped behind his back, while Robert gazed up at the slashes of red fading into pink. How tragic that anyone would deliberately harm themselves in a reckless effort to control their own fate. But Ethan was asking him to falsify records, to put his medical license at risk, to lie to the government. Robert was an honest man, most of the time. He hadn't forgiven himself for not sharing the truth of Phyllis' diagnosis with her sooner. Although he had told himself it was a kindness to keep the grim news from her, he knew whose pain he'd wanted to avoid.

A siren wailed in the distance: somewhere, there was trouble. Somewhere, help was on the way. Half an hour ago, he'd congratulated himself on his medical skills; now he saw the depth of his cowardice. Lads like Mike might harm themselves in nasty and disfiguring ways. Didn't they deserve to have their health spared? Their lives saved? They weren't so different from his pregnant patients who begged him for an alternative. Robert had seen their despair but had done nothing. Even after he'd heard that someone was providing clean abortions, what had he done with that information? Nothing.

"I don't know whether I can . . ." Robert began.

"Well, if you can't, you can't." Ethan's voice was bitter. "I just hoped—"

"You misunderstand me." Robert placed a hand on the younger man's arm. "The only letterhead I have is from my private practice. Right at the top, it says, 'The

Women's Bureau.' I don't suppose the draft board would accept that."

Ethan chuckled. "Probably not. We've got stationary, and you're more than welcome to use it. Want to start with a letter for Mike?"

"I better examine him more thoroughly first. For all I know, he might have a condition that would disqualify him honestly, and it'd be good to document that in the letter."

"Of course." Ethan's grin didn't waver. "I'll get the typewriter out of the closet for you." He galloped down the steps to the clinic while Robert lingered to watch a flock of pigeons gliding to the church's roof where they formed a long line, silhouetted against the evening sky. Something inside his chest unclenched. Oh, Cathy, he thought, what a pixie you've turned out to be. Look where you've led me now.

Chapter Twenty-seven

Runaway child running wild

Outside the entrance of Piper's Alley in Old Town, Katya kicked off her shoes and sat cross-legged on the hot sidewalk. She spread her bandanna beside her, proud of the dyed earrings she had made. Scents of cinnamon and musk wafted down the passageway from the candle shop, awakening her ever-present hunger. This small neighborhood, teeming with tourists and hippies, was her favorite place to hang out and summer Sunday crowds were the best. The Aardvark Cinema's art films drew moviegoers while the Bijou attracted guys who liked gay porn. Tourists surged through the doors of Ripley's Believe It or Not, the Wax Museum, and the Old Town School of Folk Music. They lingered outside to gawk at the cavalcade of street people prancing up and down Wells Street in their jaunty hats and fringed vests. She wished she could render it all in pastels: the clowns and jesters, kings and queens, the sparkle and flash. But these days she had little freedom to draw. She needed to keep her head up and watch for customers, friendly faces, anyone she could ask, "Got a place where I can crash?"

For a few days, she'd found refuge in the musty basement of a house over on Addison. The girl who lived there, Tricia, had admired—but didn't buy—Katya's jewelry, saying that she'd already spent her allowance on patchouli oil and a T-shirt silk-screened with peace symbols. She wouldn't have any more

money until her parents came back to town. Katya
(astonished that they would leave their teenage daughter alone for a week) had wasted no time in inviting herself over. The narrow house was three stories high, in a
row of similar brick townhomes, and the basement had
its own entrance. Tricia had left it unlocked until her
parents returned and Katya found the door bolted again,
with most of her clothes behind it. No matter: hardly
anything fit her now and soon she would outgrow even
the cut-off overalls.

After that, she tried to sleep on the broken-down
recliners at the People's Park, lying on top of her few
remaining possessions so that no one could rip her off
while she dozed. Earnest Mann and his apples were long
gone. The nights were hot and humid, distant sirens
wailed of disasters—fire, arrest, heart attack—and as she
protected her precious sketchpads and colored pencils
with her body, the difference between "belongings" and
"longings" was smaller than she could hold on to.

Early this morning, a guy with stringy hair and bad
teeth had approached her there. "Hey, girlie. I seen you
out here, all by yourself." Katya had a bad feeling about
him. He was old, at least thirty, and he looked her up and
down with yellow eyes like a possum's. "Need a place to
spend the night? I gotta spot right over there," he said,
jerking his thumb at a brick building behind him overlooking the park.

"Yeah?" she said, stalling for time while she tried to
figure out how to get rid of him.

"I got a stereo and a tv set. Only one bed but, hey!
It's not like you gotta worry about getting knocked up."
He ran his tongue over his scuzzy teeth.

"That's okay. I've got to go somewhere and, um, meet my friends," she lied, smiling so he wouldn't take offense.

"Dyke!" He spat on the ground near her feet. After he left, she held her satchel with shaking hands, knowing she wouldn't return to the Park.

A middle-aged woman stopped in front of her display: hair in a perm, pink skirt and matching short-sleeved blouse. She picked up a copper wire trinket, and opened and closed the alligator spring with her manicured fingers, apparently not recognizing that it was a roach clip.

"How much for this?"

"Two dollars." Might as well ask for a lot; she looked like she could afford it.

"Hmm." The lady replaced the clip but remained where she was.

"I've got other designs too. And these earrings." Katya pointed to her mulberry-dyed creations.

The woman stared at Katya's belly with her forehead furrowed and eyebrows pinched together, her lips pressed in a thin, disapproving line. Without speaking, she turned away and crossed the street. With a sinking heart, Katya knew where she was heading: to the only phone booth on the block. Every inch of its interior was covered in messages, phone numbers, names, initials, swear words. Drug deals and rendezvous were arranged within those plexiglass walls. The Yellow Pages chained to the wall was in tatters, torn into scrap paper to record some vital bit of information. When the accordion door was elbowed shut, a feeble bulb turned on: barely bright enough to guide a drunken hand to insert coins. Katya had checked the floor for lost dimes dozens of times.

Now the woman was in the booth, rummaging in her handbag for change. She lifted the receiver and, as she did so, cast a look across Wells Street at Katya, who knew with terrible certainty that she was the subject of that call. Whether it would be to the cops (vending without a license) or social services (pregnant teenager, squatting on the street) or truant officers (did they pick kids up during the summer?) or some other authority she hadn't yet imagined, Katya wasn't about to stick around to find out. She grabbed her satchel and the rest of her things, not bothering to be careful, tumbling everything together: shoes and sketchbook crushing sticks of charcoal into powder. With a last glance at the informant—who pointed accusingly at Katya as if the person on the other end of the line could see where that sharp finger aimed—she dashed around the corner and ran as fast as her bulky body would allow.

Two blocks later, out of breath and her belly aching, she ducked into an alley, confident that Mrs. Nosy Whoever-she-was wouldn't follow her there. Nice people—straight people—didn't venture into alleys, not even in the daytime. This one held a long line of woven wire fences, broad anonymous garage doors, trash cans and smelly dumpsters. Weeds had sprouted and grown huge in the narrow passageways between shed and fence. She crouched in a niche beside a ramshackle lean-to to unwrap her bundle. Damnit. Some of the earrings were smashed. Not that she could sell them in Old Town now. It was all so messed up. That busybody might return to Katya's corner, and whoever she'd phoned could be searching for her, too. Another spot on the map marked off now, like the People's Park, and Harlow's apartment, and all of Saint Stanislaus Parish. Those library steps where Jo-Jo had stolen her suitcase, and downtown streets where Mr. Wojcek's van roamed at night... Somehow this vast city was shrinking and tightening around her, becoming a maze with more and more dead ends. She leaned her forehead against her knees, breathless with misery.

But hiding in an alley wouldn't get her a shower or a place to stay tonight. Old Town's not the only place to hang out, she reminded herself. I'll find somewhere better, near Lincoln Park or in Uptown. She shoved her feet back into her ill-fitting sandals and, as a precaution, shook the remnants of charcoal from the bandanna to tie it around her head like a pirate's disguise. Leaving her sunny nook, she headed north, looking for opportunities, searching for anyone she might recognize and score a toke or a place to crash, something to eat. Maybe sell or trade jewelry. On Fullerton, she paused at a plate glass window to admire the Five-and-Dime's gleaming chrome lunch counter and its intoxicating photos with their mouth-watering descriptions. "Deluxe Grillburger with Fried Onions on a Fresh Bun." Only $1.20, but that was more than she owned. A "Refreshing Fruit Plate" meant for dieters: glistening squares of green Jello, two peach halves, and a mound of cottage cheese on lettuce. Best of all was "Delicious Ice Box Cheese Cake." For such a treat, she was willing to part with thirty-five cents.

Through the revolving doors and into air conditioning so cool that it almost tasted minty green. She swiveled in anticipation back and forth on her stool until the cheese cake arrived, presented on a little paper doily, and she ate in teeny bites to make it last as long as possible. After she'd swallowed every crumb, licked the fork clean, and drunk two glasses of ice water, there was nothing to do but leave her coins on the counter.

With her stomach momentarily content, she browsed the store aisles that brimmed with bottles of nail polish in a hundred brilliant colors, packages of stockings, emery boards, little toy trucks, pink plastic baby-dolls. Tin boxes of band-aids, delicate feather dusters, drinking straws and pipe cleaners, tubs of Lincoln Logs, cheap kaleidoscopes that rattled when she peered through the little hole at their colorful designs. A spinning rack held dozens of comic books for anyone wanting to be entertained by the adventures of Archie, Lulu, or Casper the Ghost. The rack squeaked as she sent it twirling but creaks continued from somewhere else.

Curious, she followed the sound to the dim rear of the store where white mice ran feverishly on their squealing metal wheel, around and around. In a neighboring tank, a striped snake lay motionless on its bed of sand, ignoring them. A large rectangular aquarium held dozens of turtles no bigger than silver dollars. The turtles were piled on top of each other as if to avoid the murky pool of water; their little clawed feet paddled feebly in the air. Beyond the turtles were more cages containing lavender and teal parakeets, sunny yellow canaries, and a pair of listless silver-gray doves. Every birdcage was outfitted with little round mirrors, plastic trays of seed and water, perches and swings where the birds twittered and chirped as they sparred over where to cling. Sometimes a ruckus broke out between two canaries, their clipped wings beating furiously as they pecked at one another. Curled feathers floated in the air.

In the topmost cage, a single azure blue parakeet drooped upon its perch. Katya poked her pinky finger between the slim bars; the bird did not respond. Why didn't this one have any playmates and companions like the others? She whistled and cooed but it didn't lift its head. What offense could it have made to be locked in solitary confinement? There was no one nearby to answer her indignant questions. When an announcement brayed over the PA system ("Cosmetics, line two!"), the parakeet shrank within itself as if trying to disappear.

It took no more than a moment to glance over her shoulder, another to pop open the small door. Her hand darted into the cage, her fingers wrapped around the parakeet's soft feathers, and he was liberated! He weighed nothing. As she slipped her hand into her pocket, the bird wriggled and his claws snagged against the edge of the fabric. She held her breath, afraid that she might damage his delicate feet, and sidled out of the Five and Dime while her heart pounded and the parakeet quivered in her sweaty palm.

Around the corner was a small park. Only two concrete benches and a couple of elm trees but, still, it was nature. Other birds probably lived there, maybe jays or wrens, and her parakeet could join their flock. At least he would have real branches to sit in, and sky above him. In the shade of an elm, she gently unhooked the caught claw.

"Ow!" Pain shot through her finger as his sharp beak bit her. Involuntarily, her hand jerked, flinging her attacker into the air. In a flurry of blue, the parakeet tumbled to the ground and lay still. Aghast, she crouched down to rescue the bird, careful not to stain his feathers with her blood. But her care was too late. As she nudged him, the weightless body shifted, his head flopped sideways, and his wings fell open. Clipped. Flying had never been an option for this little bird—only life in the cage. "I'm sorry," she whispered. "I was only trying to help."

She tried to dig a grave, using the handle of one of her paintbrushes but the dirt was rock hard, and when the brush snapped in half, she gave up. All at once, she was lightheaded with fury, sick to death of this ugly city and all its cages, of the alley cats who would likely find the little body and eat it. As she stomped away, her heels struck hard against the pavement, jolting her body and all the extra weight that she carried. It hurt to walk like this, but the pain somehow seemed right, justified. She deserved it.

A trash truck roared past, enveloping her in its foul stench. Katya covered her nose, brewing resentment with each step. Chicago was incapable of being quiet. Buses rumbled and screeched all night through the streets, black fumes pumping from their tailpipes. Subway trains thundered below the sidewalks, sending torrid blasts of air and noise up through the grates, and rattled precariously overhead on the elevated tracks, throwing down shards of rust from the iron girders. Soon, full summer would descend and then thousands of dead alewives would be disgorged onto Lake Michigan's beaches to stare at nothing with their lifeless eyes. Everyone agreed the die-off was awful—the stink of rotting fish, their silver bodies curling in the sun—but what could you do? Alewife Season was an annual event. Just avoid the lake for a week or two until bulldozers cleared the beaches and then forget about it until next year.

But she couldn't forget: what mysterious poison from the lake's depths could kill so many fish at once?

As the evening shadows lengthened and the streetlights buzzed on, she cupped her bloodied hand over her belly and the unseen being inside her: *I might not want you, but nobody's going to hurt you. I won't let you grow up in this hard, unforgiving place.*

Chapter Twenty-eight

If you go chasing rabbits

Robert was deep in a dream, following a woman who meandered through a green field, her long white bathrobe trailing behind her, when his telephone rang. He groped for the heavy receiver and mumbled a hello.

"I might've found our girl. How soon can you get here?" Huck's voice was urgent and hushed, as if he didn't want to be overheard.

Robert sat up. "Where are you?"

"LaSalle and Wacker Drive. Wear dark clothes and bring some cash. Hurry."

The morning was already humid and it would turn oppressively hot soon, so he dressed for comfort: rubber-soled shoes, short-sleeved shirt, soft gray cotton hat. He skipped shaving; wherever Huck planned to take him, a clean-shaven face wouldn't count for much. By the time he parked and found their rendezvous spot, the sun was well up, gleaming against the shiny towers of steel and glass that lined the Chicago River. Across the river sat the printing presses for all four daily newspapers, each with its own loading dock to receive the enormous rolls of paper that traveled through the Great Lakes. Warning bells clanged as the Michigan Avenue drawbridge ground open to let a ship ease through, its wake sloshing in crazy patterns on the river's gray-green surface. A fetid breeze lifted from the water, as if drawn up with the bridge. Green trucks slowly trolled by, tossing out bundles of Sunday papers to thud onto the pavement.

"Doc!" Huck beckoned from a shaded entranceway. Cigarette butts littered the sidewalk around his feet and he smelled as if he hadn't showered in a couple days. Robert tried to get a look at the younger man's pupils to see if they were pinpricks or had dilated into black saucers, but those unruly curls hung in the way.

"Ready?" Without waiting, Huck hefted a bulky knapsack over one shoulder and darted to a nearby railing where a stairway led into the shadows. He disappeared down the steps, leaving Robert no choice but to follow into a thick pungent darkness where he stood, blinking. This was no subway station, but an intersection of dim sidewalks leading into a labyrinth of cramped alleys that still carried the faint mark of their original paving stones.

"Hey, man! Keep up!" Huck paused ten feet ahead of him, impatient to get going.

"What is this place?" Robert's voice stalled as if the dank air were too thick to carry sound. His hand still gripped the railing, unwilling to release the cool metal that connected him to the upper sidewalk. He craned his neck to peer back up the stairs, catching a glimpse of pale shins scissoring past.

"Lower Wacker Drive. You never been down here?"

Robert had a vague idea that delivery trucks traveled streets hidden beneath the skyscrapers and avenues of downtown. But the underground was a piece of Chicago lore that was half myth, like Mrs. O'Leary's cow starting the famous fire. Or so he had thought.

Huck moved back toward him. "I heard there's a tribe crashing down here and they've got some girls

with them. They're kind of . . . freaky, so stay close."
Robert reluctantly released the railing and followed.
The soles of his shoes stuck to the sidewalk as he tried
to sidestep a puddle of vomit. Soggy brown paper bags
reeked in the gutters. Rusted signs hung from the blackened ceiling, giving clues as to what lay above: LaSalle
Street, State Street, Randolph. The throb and rumble of
a bus overhead shook the few pallid lights, setting them
atremble.

South, west, south again. Huck seemed to be navi-
gating by memory but Robert strained to hold the grid
in his mind as he journeyed through passageways lined
with battered padlocked doors that must lead into the
basements of unseen towers. The further they walked,
the thicker and more humid the air became, and the
intersections were lit too weakly to make out what the
letters spelled. His ankles ached from negotiating the
uneven cobblestones. Something about the walls troubled him, so black, so blank. And then he had it: no graf-
fiti. These abandoned streets were shunned even by the
gangs. The Blackstone Rangers and Disciples alike must
know there was no point in bringing their spray cans to
leave their lurid marks here, for who would ever see
them?

"Huck?" Robert's voice scratched his raw throat.
The young man slowed his pace and inclined his head to
show that he was listening. "Let's rest a moment." They
paused at another grimy corner. Robert wiped his face
with a handkerchief. There was no place to sit, no un-
soiled spot to lean. Huck's hair was limp with sweat. The
shadows pressed upon them; the last stairway leading
out had been many turns ago. "Who lives down here?
How could they?"

Huck shrugged as he pulled a box of Marlboros from his shirt pocket. "Some people wanna go underground." His lighter clicked and flared. "Maybe they dig the scene. Maybe they think it's safer than up above." He spoke nonchalantly but his face looked grave, his eyes dark and impenetrable.

"This isn't safe," Robert protested. "Disease, vermin, rat bites, bad air . . ." Huck smoked in silence, not disagreeing.

Let us descend into the blind world . . . Robert had read Dante's *Inferno* decades ago, when he was in the company of other boys sporting pink cheeks and small frowns as they puzzled over the text in a sunlit classroom. How could they have understood what Dante meant? Nor had he—until now.

Huck flicked his butt into the gutter and pulled against the straps of his knapsack to ease his shoulders. "We're almost there. Let's go."

Robert folded his damp handkerchief back into his trouser pocket. *"Now therefore, rise,"* he recited. *"Control your breath, and call upon the strength of soul that wins all battles . . . There is a longer ladder yet to climb: this much is not enough."* His voice gave out a little on the last word.

"Wow." Huck shook his head, grinning for the first time. "Come on then, let's go climb some ladders." They left the safety of the lone street light, plodding onward, close together in the clammy dark. After a few minutes, Huck pointed silently to the right, into a cramped corridor. They entered tentatively, trying to muffle the sound of their footsteps as they walked side by side, their elbows occasionally bumping. Robert could barely see ahead; he began to imagine an open manhole, a yawning pit of some kind that would appear beneath them without warning and his legs faltered. When Huck grabbed the back of his shirt, Robert halted instantly, teetering on some unseen brink.

"Keep quiet." Huck's breath was hot against his ear. Then his voice rang out, "Joshua!" The echo bounced back in a thinner, less confident, version. A weak light flickered ahead of them, as if someone waved a signal. "Okay, we're good to go." He kept one hand on Robert's back as they stepped forward, perhaps to keep the doctor from fleeing, perhaps to steady himself.

At the end of the passage they angled left, and emerged into a space lit by a Coleman lamp that cast long shadows up the walls. A handful of ragged people stood in its glow, upended crates in a rough circle behind them. Lit from below, like children around summer campfires holding flashlights beneath their chins, their elongated faces had turned ghoulish, their eyes haunted hollows and their mouths gashes. As Robert's vision adapted to the gloom, he made out a dozen women and girls huddled deeper in the passage near a raised platform piled with blankets. He strained to peer at them: could he spot the distended belly that Cathy surely must have by now?

"Who enters my domain?" The voice—a nasal whine —came from the only figure still seated beside the lantern. He unfolded himself to his full height, easily six and a half feet tall, looming over the others. His wild hair threatened to brush against the dingy ceiling.

"Friends, Joshua." Huck didn't bow his head, but his tone was deferential, as if asking a crocodile for permission to cross a river. "We come with offerings." He elbowed Robert, who turned to him blankly. "Give him the dough," Huck hissed.

"Oh. Right." Robert pulled a handful of small bills from his pocket and stepped forward.

"Stop!" Joshua snapped. Two of his smaller companions leapt in front of him, eyes locked on the intruders, waiting for a command. Joshua towered above them, a kind of fury twisting his face. "Do not approach Joshua. Your presence is not clean, old man."

Not clean? Bewildered, Robert gazed about the dank chamber: what could possibly be considered clean here? Huck snatched the bills from his inert fingers and gave them to the nearest person, a bedraggled woman who might have been twenty-five or fifty-five; it was impossible to tell. She peered at the pieces of paper as if she could not recognize them, turning them over before passing them, one by one, to the guards, who silently handed them to their leader. Joshua glanced at the money before secreting it within the folds of his dirty robes.

"What do you seek, old man? Joshua will grant you one wish."

If Robert had been aboveground and not lost in a dark labyrinth, he might have laughed out loud. But he answered cautiously, unsure whether he should regard this all as an elaborate theatrical production or as madness.

"I, uh, seek a girl. She—"

"Joshua's women are not for sale! Your tainted lucre cannot pluck them from the hand that holds them. They follow the true path now." Behind him, the women clustered together as if they feared being torn from their protective shadows.

Huck spoke up. "Hey man, be cool. We only want to know if this one girl is with you. No hassles."

"If she is with Joshua, she will not leave. When she is here, there is no other place to be." His voice rose higher, as if the words were squeezed through a bagpipe. "The light drains from this realm of darkness. The serpent is eating its tail. Soon the new world will be born . . ." He nodded in beat with his words and his followers, huddled around the lantern, mimicked his movements. While Joshua brayed on, Robert surveyed his colony. Did any of the girls bear that mark hidden beneath the dirt on her chin? They clung to one another, goggling at him and Huck as if they were spacemen, landed on some distant dark moon.

"The phoenix will rise from the ashes of Gomorrah! Its wings will be of silver, its tail of gold. It will bear Joshua and all who follow him to Heaven. We will walk with Buddha and Jesus and Mohammed. In Heaven will be the Lizard King . . ."

None of the girls looked familiar, no one appeared to be pregnant. "She's not here," he told Huck, although he couldn't be absolutely certain. But the idea that she might have become one of these trapped mole-people was too much to bear. It couldn't be possible. "Let's go."

Joshua shoved his guards aside and lunged toward them. "*You* cannot speak!" he yowled. Robert stumbled back, smacking against something hard and jagged. "You dare interrupt while Joshua is speaking the Word?" His clan howled in response.

"Oh shit," muttered Huck. "Move it. Go!" He pushed Robert toward the entrance. The room rang with that mad, shrill voice: "The serpent will devour you! Light will drain from the world of darkness!" They staggered through the corridor, Joshua's prophecy following them out of the lantern-lit chamber and back into the gloom. A stone struck the back of Robert's neck and two or three more cracked against the walls around them. Huck shoved something small into his hand. "Here," he urged. Robert flicked the lighter once, twice, before it caught.

Behind them, Joshua's clan crowded into the passageway, their hands heavy with bricks and rocks. Huck yanked the knapsack from his back and tore open the top. Holding onto a strap, he flung the pack into the air and dozens of bright oranges flew out. They tumbled to the ground, rolling and bumping against the filthy walls. Two girls fell to their knees and grabbed at the oranges as if they were made of gold. Then, with a savage cry, the entire mob scrambled after the fruit.

"Go, go, go!" Huck was already jogging, holding Robert's arm so that the lighter could shed some small illumination for them both. The scrabbling noises behind them faded as they broke free of the narrow passage and emerged again into the dim and nameless street. Huck released him there and began to slam his body into the walls, cursing as he careened from side to side.

"What the hell are you doing?" Robert still held the lighter high, its little flame hissing and sputtering. His leg throbbed and both arms stung from scraping against the bricks. His hat was lost somewhere in the sooty maze behind them.

"Looking—" Huck grunted as he banged his shoulder into another spot, "for a way—out! There aren't—dammit!—any stairs near here—Ha!" The wall sprang open with a metallic clang as an unmarked door yielded to his force. Robert limped through and Huck slammed the door shut behind them.

"What was all that with the oranges?" Robert panted.

"Back-up plan." Huck sounded proud of himself. "I figured fruit might distract those wackos if things got hairy."

"Good thinking. Where we are now?"

"Basement of some building." Huck took the lighter and waved it around. To Robert's relief, there was a freight elevator. They yanked open its doors and staggered inside. A minute later, they burst through a fire door and found themselves in an alley. Robert was giddy with relief, blinded by sunlight. He squinted at his watch: only quarter past eleven.

"Shit. Lost my smokes." Huck's curls were plastered to his head, his shirt and hands smeared with dirt.

"You look like hell, my friend."

"Same to you, old man."

It was true. Brown slime coated Robert's shoes. Spots of blood stained one trouser leg and his arms were streaked with dirt. He hobbled to the end of the alley and looked around. "Well, at least *I* know where we are," he said, with satisfaction. "Follow me."

Chapter Twenty-nine

Break on through to the other side

Robert withdrew a small ring of keys from his pocket, held the service door open, and ushered Huck into the safety of the Shenandoah Building. On the seventh floor, he unlocked his office, handed Huck the key to the men's room, and showed him where he could clean up. Fingering the lump on the back of his neck, he drank in the quiet atmosphere of his Women's Bureau. Mrs. Watkins' orderly desk, the worn chairs, his clean examination room, had never looked so welcoming. During the week, an empty office and a silent telephone could make him anxious; this morning, he appreciated how peaceful they were.

Huck reappeared with clean face and hands, and handed the key back to Robert for his turn. When he'd finished in the washroom, he found his friend in the exam room, idly spinning the metal stirrups attached to the table. A drawer hung open.

"Find what you're looking for?" Robert asked from the doorway. Huck wheeled around, holding a shiny duck-billed utensil.

"What's this, Doc?" He looked not the least bit guilty for having been caught snooping.

"That," Robert crossed the room to take it from him, "is a speculum. I use it for pelvic exams. Would you like to know the details?"

Huck flushed. "Uh, no, that's okay."

"And these," the doctor continued, mercilessly, "are stirrups. The patient places her feet in them for the exam." He swiveled the stirrups and raised them to their full height. Huck looked at the floor. Robert replaced the speculum and closed the drawer. "Any questions? Want me to explain the rest of the equipment?"

"Okay, Doc, I get it. No touching!" Huck held his hands up in surrender and allowed Robert to steer him back to the office, where he unlocked a desk drawer and pulled out a bottle of bourbon.

"So early?" Huck pretended to be shocked.

Robert smiled. "You have to admit, it's been a long day already." He poured them each a shot. The flimsy Dixie cup trembled slightly in his fingers as he held it in a toast. "Here's to oranges. And to being prepared." They sipped in companionable silence for a few minutes, listening to the air conditioner wheeze and the venetian blinds rattle against the window frame.

Huck propped his feet on the edge of a wastebasket and pointed at the closet door. "What's back there?"

"A small laboratory. Basic chemistry equipment, a centrifuge, test tubes, autoclave." Robert lifted his trouser leg to tend to a cut with hydrogen peroxide and gauze. "How about you, young man? Any parts that need doctoring?"

"Nah, I'm cool. Just a few scratches. No biggie. Why'd you want to be . . . this kind of doctor, just for chicks?"

"An OB-GYN? Not for the money—obviously." Robert rubbed the worn surface of his desk blotter. "Women's health is much more than delivering babies, and very rewarding in other ways. We can detect early signs of breast cancer, teach women how to use contraception, prevent infections. Believe me, young men like you benefit when your sexual partners get good care!

"What frustrates me is when patients don't want to listen. Or their church forbids them to use birth control even when it could improve their health by spacing their children more prudently. They could take better care of their existing children by raising smaller families. Even the government gets in our way. For a long time, we couldn't even discuss contraception."

"For real?" Huck shook his head. "Damn."

"In some states, we still can't provide contraceptives to unmarried women." His voice rose. "Well, it's not my place to inquire whether a patient has a marriage license or whether that ring on her finger is real or not! If she's a miss or a missus isn't my business! My job is to provide them with the best care that I can and often that means helping to ensure they don't end up with an unwanted pregnancy!" He swallowed. "Sorry for the speech-making."

Huck dropped his feet to the floor and leaned forward with a triumphant look. "Cathy's knocked up, right? So that's why you want to find our gal!" Robert turned away to watch a sparrow vainly search for crumbs on the sill. "You don't have to cop to it; I can see it in your face. Clock's ticking and we gotta find her before she pops." The older man remained silent. "Okay, Doc, I can take a hint. But I know what I know."

"Would you like another?" Robert raised the bottle in an effort to change the subject. At least he knew now that his young companion took their mission seriously. "Our" gal. This was more than just a free lunch to him.

Huck gazed at him quizzically. "Are *you* going to have another?"

Robert tilted his head as he considered. "Yes. Yes, I will." Suddenly bashful, he admitted, "It's my birthday, so we might as well celebrate."

"Happy birthday, man, and down the hatch! You always celebrate with an adventure underground?"

Robert chuckled. "Hardly. How did you think to search for her down there?"

"I got a lot of connections you know!" Huck puffed up with mock pride, but then added, more earnestly, "I tried to suss out what would be the worst place a chick might end up, and focused on that. Like you would."

Robert nodded solemnly. "Indeed." His fears had first flown to the emergency room and the morgue, ignorant of other kinds of dangers. Of men like Joshua. Or worse. He drained his paper cup.

"Well, it's a good thing she wasn't with that batshit Joshua. I don't know how we would've got her away from him. And it's sure no place for a baby." Huck sprawled in the wooden chair, legs spread wide.

"Yes, I'm relieved we didn't find her there too. I'd have had to call the police or the health department."

"I dunno, man. Cops beat the crap out of people that weird. Anyway, his tribe knows all the tunnels and passageways. They'd have scattered like rats and we would've just lost her again." Huck crumpled his paper cup and flung it in the general direction of the wastebasket, suddenly looking deflated that the morning's effort hadn't paid off. But, without Huck's forethought and street smarts, who knows what might have happened? He was out for himself, sure—opportunistic and a bit manipulative—but generous, too. Robert found himself wishing that Huck was somehow the father of Cathy's baby and together they would find her, she would be happy to be reunited and . . .

Nonsense. No more bourbon. He put the cap back on the bottle. "Tell me about your family, Huck."

"Ah-ah-ah." Huck wagged his finger at him. "Nothing doing, Doc. I'm not telling you where I'm from or what my name used to be. No point in even trying to go there."

"But you know *my* name, my telephone number. Even my birthday. And now you've visited my office. You have me, as they say, at a disadvantage." Rebuffed, Robert heard how his words became overly formal, but Huck wasn't intimidated.

"Yeah? Well, tough. You got nothing to hide."

"How do you know? I might have secrets." He thought of the letters to the draft board that he typed, coming in early before Mrs. Watkins arrived, always careful to replace her typewriter cover just as she had left it. Only the other day, she had complained that the ribbons didn't seem to last as long as they used to.

Huck snorted. "No way. You're so straight, you probably pay all your taxes and on time, too. You're a good guy, Doc, one of the white hats. That's why you want to find Cathy, right? To help her out. So, tell me about *your* family. You got a wife, grandkids?"

"I was married. My wife died; we had no children." His simple words fell into the room like the last tones of a clock striking midnight.

Huck didn't know how to acknowledge this loss. He gazed away from Robert's face, out the window, around the room, until he spotted Cathy's drawing, pinned to the wall. "Was that her?"

"Yes."

"She was a fox. You know, beautiful. A real lady, you can tell."

Robert nodded. "Yes, she was. And Cathy made that drawing."

Huck boosted himself from his seat to take a closer look. "She's pretty good. Cathy, I mean."

"Yes." Robert suddenly felt woozy. Too much alcohol on an empty stomach. "Let's go to the Artist's Snack Shop. They should be open by now."

Huck jumped up, always ready for a meal. "Sure. But you didn't tell me everything, you know. You never copped to having the hots for that waitress." Laughing, he strode to the elevator and waited for Robert to catch up.

Chapter Thirty

When the moon is in the seventh house

If you were an itinerant jewelry maker with no funds to purchase an official spot at the Lincoln Park Art Fair, you could still squat on the curb, hoping to catch some of their customers. Inside the fence, vendor booths were stuffed with wooden carvings and bright fabrics imported from West Africa or Haiti. Crafters sold tie-dyed T-shirts, macramé plant hangers, and rings formed from the handles of old silver spoons. For only a couple of bucks, caricaturists drew exaggerated versions of faces, making noses bigger and eyebrows bushier. Potters offered their hand-thrown mugs and bowls beside painters, photographers and sculptors. Katya watched for customers and for girls who seemed sympathetic and who might lend her a couch or mattress for the night. She'd given up asking guys. They thought she should give them a blow job in exchange for a bed. Didn't seem like a fair trade to her.

A shadow passed before the sun and lingered there. As the sultry air rumbled in anticipation, a dusty wind whipped through the fair booths, setting frames rattling against the wooden stands. Artists hastily tossed tarps over their paintings; easels clattered to the ground. Thunder boomed as a summer storm rolled in from the west and the crowds ran for shelter. Katya hurried to protect her delicate paper earrings from the rain. Once wet, they might leach mulberry dye everywhere, maybe disintegrate. As she tucked her wares into the satchel, wind threw soot in her eyes like an insult. Trash and litter flung itself across the asphalt towards her. A pink paper wrapped itself around her leg and even after she had escaped to the protection of a store's awning, the flier still clung to her calf. She peeled it away to read what had been delivered to her.

Need to know what the Future holds? Astrological, Tarot, and Psychic Readings. Books and Paraphernalia on all Matters Occult. Jewelry, Cards, Candles, Incense. The House of the Rising Moon. Open 7 Days a Week. A shop that sold jewelry, and promised certainty and prediction as well! And the address was only a few blocks away. It was meant for her.

After the rain, the sidewalks steamed like bread, fresh from the oven, and the air was washed clean. The shop was easy to find: its entrance was an emerald green door, down a few steps from the sidewalk. Two display windows on either side held clues as to what she might find inside. In the left frame, a crystal ball almost as large as her head rested on a bed of green velvet, while the other held a black candle in the shape of a human hand. Little flames licked the tip of each finger and the wax dribbled down the sides. Looking at it, her own hands felt sticky.

The brass door knocker was shaped like a crescent moon and rapped more loudly than she had meant, sounding rude. A muffled voice called from behind the door: had it told her to enter? As she hesitated, the door swung open.

There were two more steps to descend into the room but she lingered on the threshold, nearly choking on incense. The shop was dim and wonderfully cool, lit by an elaborate chandelier and candles in brass holders on every tabletop. Shelves lining the walls were crammed full of books and pamphlets. High-backed armchairs upholstered in velvet and brocade invited her to sit. Behind the glass counter, long strings of black beads hung, shielding an arched doorway that led to another space, too dark for her liking.

"Hello?" she called.

The beads clacked, revealing a large woman draped in a purple robe adorned with gold stars, planets, and astrological symbols. A matching turban atop her massive head looked as if it might tumble off at any moment. Her broad face was smooth and unlined as if she never exposed herself to the sun. Against the pale expanse of her skin, her eyebrows flamed over deep green penetrating eyes.

"Come forward; approach, child." Her chins wobbled as her deep warm voice rang out. Uncertainly Katya descended from the little zone of safety by the door. The woman held out pudgy hands, drawing the girl to her, and without intending to, Katya allowed her own hands to be swallowed by the warm flesh. "Let's have a look at you and we shall see what we shall see." The words rolled into her ears, seemed to echo inside her head. She held her breath, waiting to be inspected, her humiliating belly once again assessed and judged. But the shopkeeper flipped Katya's hands over so that her palms faced upwards and scrutinized them. Aromas of patchouli, sandalwood, and tobacco drifted into Katya's nostrils.

"Scorpio," the woman declared. "With moon in Gemini, no less. You are resourceful, clandestine, intense." Deep laughter shook the purple turban, and the billowing sleeves of her robe seemed to nod in agreement. "Don't be so surprised, child! I read it in your palms. It's all there for the viewing."

Katya peered at the faint lines that told her no more than a telephone wire stretched across the landscape. "What else do you see?" Immediately, she regretted asking. Harlow's palm reading had been bogus, but this woman might really see things. What future could be visible in those lines? Was her past written there as well: the lies she told, the secrets she kept?

"What would you like to know?"

So many things. Where she could stay tonight. Did her family wonder what had happened to her? Were they looking for her? Time was narrowing down to a sharp horizon when she'd have to think about what she most wanted to avoid. What would she do when the baby fought its way out? How much would it hurt? Where would she go? When Katya didn't respond, the seer added, "What do you most desire?" and the simple question filled her with loneliness. Did Harlow miss her? Had he ever loved her? No, she knew the answer to that. But would anyone love her again? She dropped her gaze to the carpet, unwilling to have her pain recognized.

"Sit, child. Rest yourself." Strong fingers guided her toward one of the royal chairs, pushed her into the velvety seat. "We should meet properly." The woman drew a leather hassock over and settled herself onto it. Once safely in place, she dabbed at her damp chins with a flowered handkerchief. "I am glorious!" She laid one hand upon her heaving chest. Her ornate gold and silver rings glinted in the candles' glow.

Glorious! That was her name, not a statement of her own wonderfulness. Although perhaps she had meant it that way as well. Was a curtsy called for? "I'm . . ." For the first time in months, Katya hesitated. Should she say "Cathy" or "Laura"? Neither choice seemed true anymore, and Glorious would surely know she was lying. But her dilemma was brief.

"No! Don't say it. Whatever name you use out there," the psychic gestured grandly toward the green door, "in the House of the Rising Moon, you will be known by your spirit name. Let us discover what it is." She placed a hot heavy hand against Katya's forehead, pushing her back in the upholstered chair. Closing her eyes, Katya felt herself pressing toward sleep, toward strange dreams. "You are creative . . . artistic . . . curious . . . open to others. But—you have been hurt! Deceived! Distressed. You are traveling far, not in miles but in worlds, always seeking. That is why you are here."

Her eyes flew open. "Yes! That's why I came . . ."

"Hush," intoned the shopkeeper and Katya obeyed. "A new life grows within you. Your hidden talents have not been appreciated but they will emerge in time." Glorious' breath whistled like a teakettle and somewhere, bells were faintly ringing. "I will now tell you your spirit name, I will present it to you, and you alone." Alone? Was anyone else in the shop? She dared not peek. "It is to be uttered aloud only in special places like this, where the vibrations are pure. Do you understand?"

"Yes," she whispered, although she did not.

As Glorious released her damp hold on Katya's skull, she opened her eyes again. The room glowed, as if the candle flames had doubled in size, and Glorious' green eyes burned in her flushed face. "Starchild." The name came forth without her lips moving. "That is how you will be known within these walls."

Disappointment flooded through Katya. She had hoped for something artistic and sophisticated. Not "child." Not a name that would remind her of her youth and her growing belly at the same time.

Glorious received Katya's frown with amusement. "But you *are* a child. Like the poem." She gestured toward a photograph on the wall, showing a little child at the ocean's edge, her back to the camera. Flowing, nearly indecipherable, white script ran along the bottom of the poster. Glorious recited the words from memory: "You are a child of the universe, no less than the trees and the stars . . ." Then she clapped her hands as if everything was settled. "Now, Starchild, show me what you have brought. Bring forth what you have carried here."

Again, Katya was astonished by what the woman seemed to know. She unwrapped the purple-black earrings and while Glorious examined the jewelry, Katya peered into the glass case. Packs of Tarot cards, gold and silver amulets, sharp-edged crystals, tiny bottles of liquid. And some oddly shaped items that looked like bracelet charms but, peering more closely, she realized were miniature erect penises. She stepped back, cheeks burning as Glorious chuckled.

Hoping there were no more embarrassing sights, she browsed the rest of the shop, admiring the velvet cushions and intricately carved furniture. One wall held a framed photograph of a bald man carrying a pentangle. His intense dark glare seemed to follow her as she moved about the room. Planets and stars had been painted on the ceiling, with lines drawn between them to indicate the constellations. Little cards labeled each bookshelf in ornate black calligraphy: *Astral Projection, Astrology, Auras, Kirlian Photography, Metaphysics* . . .

"These will do nicely, Starchild." Glorious sounded so approving that warmth blossomed in Katya's chest. "I will pay you half of each sale. Is that acceptable to you? Are we *cool*?" She uttered the word like a joke.

"Well, how much will you sell them for?" No customers had entered the shop yet. Would any of her creations sell here or would she be better off taking them back to the streets?

"Five dollars for the big earrings, four for the small. And if they sell quickly, can you make more?" Glorious' voice was suddenly efficient and clipped. Katya agreed immediately, thinking how she might come up with a new design. Mulberry season was over, but perhaps she could use wire to form stars or pentangles . . . What had Glorious just said? Something about dining? She was disappearing through the black beads. Was Katya supposed to follow? If there was something to eat, she would brave whatever might lie beyond the curtain.

To her surprise, she found a Formica-topped table and matching chairs in a small, clean kitchen. A toaster oven and hotplate sat on a rolling cart. Glorious was pulling dishes and jars out of a small refrigerator like clowns emptying out of their tiny circus car. It seemed impossible that one fridge could hold cheese, bread, jam, sardines, pickles, sliced ham, liverwurst, cherries . . . and nothing had ever looked as magical as that pecan pie. Katya wolfed down the first sandwich so quickly that it wasn't until the final bite that she could taste the ham and spicy mustard. Glorious refilled her plate with heaps of sardines, pickles, and crackers. Salty and sour flavors danced on her tongue, followed by the sweet pie and a cold glass of milk.

Glorious poured herself a glass of shimmering amber liquid from an unlabeled bottle. "One didn't need psychic powers to see your hunger. When was the last time you ate?" But Katya didn't want to make that calculation. Hunger was in the past. What mattered was right now: this kitchen, the kind woman, the empty plate, how sleepy she had become. She dozed in her chair until that damp hand was again placed upon her head.

"Time to close up, Starchild."

Katya blinked. "I'm so tired. I need a place to stay. Do you have any extra room at your place?"

Glorious shook her head. "But you may sleep here tonight. The sofa is quite comfortable."

In the shop? With its dark corners, and the human skull she had spotted peering down from a high shelf? "Thanks. That's really nice of you. But . . . how 'bout here, in the kitchen?"

Glorious chuckled. "Why not?"

They pushed aside the table and chairs to make room. While Katya arranged sofa cushions on the kitchen floor, her new friend bustled about in the front room. The cash register drawer rang open and slammed shut, fabric rustled. The beads clacked and there stood Glorious, transformed. Gone were the robe and turban, releasing brilliant orange hair, dangling in corkscrews. A black dress clung to her curves and rolls of flesh. Beneath the flaring skirt, her robust calves sloped down to trim ankles above doll-like feet, buttoned into shiny Mary Janes.

"I've extinguished all the candles. Eat anything you like, read what catches your fancy, and never mind the telephone. I'll be back in the morning at nine. Under no circumstances are you to open the doors, either in the front or this one." She meant the wooden back door, barricaded by a piece of lumber across its blank face. "Even if a visitor insists that they need help immediately, do not respond. Don't reveal that anyone is within."

The remainder of the pecan pie inside the fridge suddenly seemed an insufficient reward. "But . . . why would anybody do that? What kind of help are they looking for?" Katya croaked, her mouth dry.

"Oh, you know, psychic emergencies." Glorious waved her hand, dismissing the idea of crises like a gnat. "They'll come back when the shop is open. Now, don't forget to jiggle the handle if the toilet keeps running, and lock up behind me." And with that, she opened the back door and trundled down the alleyway, leaving Katya to wrestle the heavy board back into place.

How often did psychic emergencies happen? And how did Glorious know about them if she wasn't there to open the door? Unless, of course, she truly had powers. And if she did, was everything else known to her too: Katya's real name, all that had happened to her? All that lay ahead? The lumpy cushions slid apart every time she rolled over, bumping her hips and elbows onto the floor. Sleep was impossible. The room was too stuffy but the single, barred window was not to be opened. She would have to brave the sofa after all.

Katya tiptoed into the front of the shop where the air smelled of wax and something earthier, a funky, nearly rotten aroma. She rummaged beneath the counter in search of a flashlight. No matches, no cigarette lighter . . . How did Glorious light all those candles?

Waving both hands before her like antennae, she groped against the walls until she found an electric switch and a single lamp came to life beside the armchair. Skipping over books whose subjects sounded too weird (Kabbalah, Alchemy, Witchcraft), she chose a volume about flower remedies, another filled with color photos of crystals, and a third on exercises to improve eyesight. There was so much to learn here. Tomorrow, she would figure out a way to convince Glorious to let her stay.

Chapter Thirty-one

The time of the season

Despite Mrs. Watkins' pessimism, the shorter schedule hadn't harmed the Women's Bureau. It turned out to be more efficient to cluster appointments together and somehow, patients seemed to know to arrive before closing time, even at two in the afternoon. Robert reveled in a new freedom: hours spent visiting church basement coffeehouses, walking through parks and beaches where he studied faces, always searching for the elusive Cathy. He lost weight and his legs felt stronger than they had in years. Twice a week, he worked at the Free Clinic alongside volunteers who seemed to treasure his knowledge and experience. And he spent more time with Louise, although never on Thursdays; she held that day sacrosanct without saying why or what kept her so busy. How different she was from Phyllis, who had effortlessly changed the topic whenever the conversation drifted to anything controversial or that might cause disharmony. Louise was more straightforward, not hesitating to tackle difficult subjects: politics, the war, the latest bribery scandal—all of it interested her. True to her word, she had attended Frances Flannery's trial and was eager to tell him about it over dinner at a Chinese restaurant.

"Ever been to that new courthouse downtown, the one with the giant pillars? No, I guess in your line of work, you wouldn't have any cause to. I asked the security guard which courtroom to go to and he pointed to a bunch of photographers and cameramen, and said, 'Just follow them,' so I did. We all squeezed into the elevator together and went up to the fifth floor. They had to wait out in the corridor with their cameras, but I got to go in. It doesn't look like on Perry Mason or Twelve Angry Men. No windows, uncomfortable plastic seats, not much wood at all.

"A door off to the side opened and a matron brought Frances in. She looked terrible, Robert, her skin all splotchy and hair unwashed. Dressed in clothing like leftovers from a church rummage sale. Some of the jurors stared at her so meanly. You know, with contempt."

She paused to drink tea, her gaze distant.

"Here's what broke my heart the most. No one was there for Frances except her lawyer. Not a single friend, not one family member. I'm sure of it because I looked. There were sketch artists from the papers. Some cops. Everybody else was a reporter, scribbling away in their little notebooks. Well, the court stenographer and the bailiff and the judge, of course. But I was the only one who came even though it wasn't my job."

Robert's thoughts flew, as they often did, to Cathy. If she gave birth alone, if her baby died, and she was arrested—would her parents sit in the courtroom to support her? She'd said they made her drop out of high school. What kind of parents didn't want their child to get an education?

Louise went on, her cheeks flushed. "The prosecutor argued that the reason Frances didn't name the father was she *couldn't*—she must have slept with more than one boy and had no idea who the father was! He didn't come right out and call her promiscuous but his meaning was pretty darn clear. It was disgusting, and I hated to see the women on the jury buying it. I wanted to stand up and shout, 'Don't you see what he's doing?' but I couldn't.

"Anyway, the jury only took half an hour to decide. Guilty, of course. She'll be in jail for a long time. Guess I can't be surprised at how little sympathy they had for her situation. The baby died, after all. Still, I hope my women's group can raise funds for an appeal."

"Women's group?" Robert hadn't imagined Louise was a women's libber and the idea made him uneasy. Didn't they burn their bras? Wasn't she a bit, well, old for those kinds of stunts?

She fiddled with her chopsticks, mumbling, "Yeah, sort of like a support group."

Why would she need support and for what? He hesitated to ask. "That's good of you," he ventured. "Let me know if I can help, I'd be glad to contribute." She looked away without comment. Did she not want his money? She'd let him pay for the movie tickets and dinner; perhaps she wasn't a women's libber after all. An awkward silence followed, interrupted by the welcome arrival of fortune cookies. His slip of paper was unhelpful: *Look in the right places to find what you seek.*

Louise chuckled when she read it. "Guess you haven't looked in the right places for that girl yet. You'd have said so if you found her."

"No," he admitted. "Still searching. I'm traveling to parts of the city I haven't visited in years. Hunting for her has been an adventure. But I wish I knew what became of her. She's so young, and so talented."

Louise broke open her cookie and passed her fortune to him. *Nothing is impossible to a willing heart.* "Like her drawing of your wife?"

He nodded. "Yes, like that. I'd only just met her when she gave it to me. It's a beautiful likeness and I was quite touched by the gift."

"Maybe I'll see it for myself someday."

"Of course," he replied, trying to mask his surprise. Was she hinting to visit his office? The thought of introducing her to Mrs. Watkins made him uneasy. He couldn't imagine them in the same room . . . He pictured Louise standing in his drab waiting room and how it would look even duller by her presence. Or did she want to learn more about Phyllis?

"Am I boring you?" she teased. His eyelids flew open.

"No, no. Let's talk about you. Where'd you grow up? Tell me everything about yourself." He filled their cups with jasmine tea.

"Everything? Well, I live alone in a studio apartment, my big indulgence is season tickets to the Lyric Opera, and I enjoy being a waitress. It's like being a detective, counselor, minister, town crier, and a mother, all in one. You learn a lot about people and most of them get pretty happy when they see you bring their food! . . .Ah, I bet you're wondering if I've ever been married! Nope. Not even engaged. Right guy at the wrong time, once. Later, it seemed like the right time, but the man was all wrong. I guess I've never wanted marriage badly enough to compromise." She sipped her tea and regarded him from over the rim of the green and white cup, measuring his reaction.

"Good for you," he declared, and he meant it. "Not something to be entered into lightly."

Louise was a woman who knew what she wanted and what she wouldn't stand for. She was solo without being lonely, content with herself, unlike any other woman he'd known. Yet here they were, making plans to meet again tomorrow night. Giddiness seemed to waft in the air like the scent of jasmine from the tea. He placed his hand on the table, palm up: an invitation. And when she laid her hand in his, happiness washed over him.

At the front door of her apartment building, she faced him. Nearly his height, he needed only to angle his head forward to reach her lips with his own and linger in a shared kiss. Throughout the evening they hadn't rushed, and neither of them was in a hurry now or in the days to come. Often, after a long shift of waitressing, Louise wanted to put her feet up, so they went for drives, listening to WFMT as they rolled north to admire the gleaming white Bahai temple and south to visit the Japanese gardens in Jackson Park.

In her good-natured company, Robert saw more clearly how shriveled his life had become in the years since Phyllis's passing. Sealed in a cocoon, he had denied himself pleasure and joy—anything that could wound him. But now, he was emerging, squinting and blinking, into a new day where it wasn't enough to simply dust old habits off and put them into practice. Times had changed, women expected less adoration, more respect; they had support groups now! Still, he tried to be a gentleman at all times: he wrestled open every door, helped her with her wrap, pulled out her chair. Happily, Louise didn't seem to mind those courtesies although he suspected she could practically hear rusty springs and gears squeaking as he tried to remember how to court and flirt. Her lips always promised more, and his answered, *I will be ready.*

When that night finally arrived, uncovering their bodies was an awakening: a reminder of old urges and sensations, along with new discoveries of stubborn joints, lessons in obtuse angles, the need for cantilevers. Robert stroked Louise's buttery skin with pleasure, but each of her curves seemed to contain a concave memory, a lingering nostalgia. Phyllis hovered between them until at last he imagined turning Cathy's colorful portrait to face the wall. With those eyes no longer watching, he could focus on Louise's abundant ripe flesh; their movements brimmed with plentitude and hunger, and then with satisfaction, and finally, they fell together into a peaceful sleep.

Chapter Thirty-two

One two three, what are we fighting for?

Glorious allowed Katya to sleep on the sofa in exchange for helping in the shop. She never mentioned pregnancy or babies, and Katya gratefully gave her attention to learning which herbs smelled sweet and which like smelly socks, how to answer the phone ("You've made contact with the House of the Rising Moon!"), and not to stare at the customers, no matter how strange they looked. A midget came in regularly for astrology readings, and once, a woman who was completely bald, her scalp gleaming like the full moon. Men with elaborate tattoos snaking up their arms bought amulets for protection against mysterious fears; women who spoke with heavy accents pored over the jars of remedies. Happily, some customers also bought Starchild's earrings, and a little treasure of coins and bills nestled at the bottom of her bag. Soon, she'd get more wire and beads, and come up with new creations. If she bought clay, maybe she could make some of the little totem figures that Glorious sold from her glass case.

But today, her dreary task was to pull each book from its shelf and wipe off the dust. She sneezed dramatically, but Glorious continued to placidly spread her Tarot cards upon an octagonal table nearby. Katya had started with Alchemy this morning and it would take at least a week to reach Zoroastrian on the other side of the shop. Balancing shakily on a footstool that wobbled as she rubbed her itching nose, she wondered why everyone always wanted to make her into a drudge. If only they would just let her draw and paint . . .

"Do people really believe all this stuff?" Katya waved her feather duster petulantly, sending a shower of motes into the air.

"And why not?" Glorious didn't look up.

"I dunno. It's just that some of it seems impossible. Like UFOs. Or that guy last week who said sugar is an instrument of the CIA." It's in everything, he'd told her, glaring at the sandwich she was eating. "They've put it in your bread, in the peanut butter, the jelly. That's how they control us; if you eat sugar, you can't see the truth. They want us to be like sheep, doing their bidding, no questions asked." His theory didn't make sense to Katya, but she'd eaten her sandwich anyway, so maybe she wasn't able to see the truth.

At last, Glorious raised her head. She wore an annoying amused expression, as if she knew many things that her young helper did not. "We are concerned with the occult here, with what lies beyond ordinary knowledge or understanding."

"Well, what about astral projection?" Katya argued, gesturing at the shelf devoted to that topic. "Or telekinesis! I mean, have you seen stuff move all by itself?" Glorious leaned back in her chair and suddenly Katya felt uneasy. If people really could levitate objects with their minds, maybe Glorious was getting ready to prove her wrong. Would she need to duck if candles and books starting flying around the room? As a precaution, she stepped down from the footstool.

But all that stirred was the psychic's ample bosom, rising and falling with her breath as she said, "Starchild, have you ever eaten a piece of ripe fruit outdoors on a summer day? Perhaps a peach or strawberries. Or watermelon." She aimed a toothy smile at Katya.

"Yeah . . ."

"And did a fly or a bee, perhaps a gnat, show up, so that you had to shoo it away?"

"I guess."

"And did you not wonder how that one insect, flying through the entire vastness of nature, knew to arrive at the very moment you bit into your beautiful fruit? I'll tell you! When you broke into the peach's flesh with your teeth, perhaps you smelled how sweet it was. There are thousands more aromas than our feeble human noses can detect and those invisible scents were released into the air all around you, unseen, unnoticed. But the gnat noticed, the bee picked up the signal. That fly caught it from yards away, which is like miles to us."

Katya pictured how the scent could waft in the air, riding tiny currents. Every time she moved to take another bite or swat the imaginary insect away, she would create ripples of breeze that carried the fruit's scent further and further, reaching still more insects where they hovered.

"Why, then, would it be so difficult to believe that other hidden forces around us can move and carry signals? Even though most people are not attuned to such vibrations, that doesn't mean they don't exist. Perhaps we should work on opening your third eye, to make it easier for you to perceive the occult."

That sounded as if it might be painful. "Um, maybe later. I've got a lot of books to dust." Katya stepped back onto her stool and Glorious smiled as she resumed dealing her cards.

The door flew open, sending windchimes jangling and extinguishing several of the candles. The midget rushed in. "Gimme a reading! You've got to tell me—"

Glorious rose to her feet, raising a hand against his outburst so that he fell silent. Sweat trickled down his long, angular face. "Starchild, go to the kitchen and brew us a pot of oat straw tea. Don't come out until I summon you."

Stung by her dismissal, Katya scuttled into the kitchen. She strained her ears but no matter how quietly she ran the water and handled the teacups, all she could make out were murmurs. Oddly, sometimes it seemed as if there were more than two voices. She sat alone at the kitchen table as the tea steeped, then cooled. At last, she heard the door open and shut, and Glorious bade her return. The little man was gone. No one drank the tea.

As she lay upon the sofa in the darkened shop that night, she tried to still her mind and listen with all her senses to whatever might be vibrating in the ether. The rooms were quiet except for the refrigerator humming as its motor cycled on and off, on and off. In the alley, a dog barked wildly and then fell silent. Warm air surrounded her bare arms and legs. She could smell the ever-present incense, and musk oil where she'd dabbed a sample on the inside of her wrist. Flavors of raw onion and mustard still coated her tongue. There was a lump in the cushion beneath her hips and a faint glow of streetlight beneath the door. But if there was anything beyond these sensations, Katya couldn't perceive it. Glorious said that you needed to be open if you wished to receive. Is someone there? She repeated the words in her mind, over and over. She could imagine someone, maybe on the other side of the world, who was sitting quietly under a palm tree, legs crossed, asking the same question at this very moment. Perhaps their thoughts could meet somehow, like the fruit's scent reaching the bee's antenna. Was this only a wish or could she make contact?

Is anyone there? she asked again, holding her breath. The only answer came from the baby inside her, kicking furiously. *Don't forget,* it seemed to say. *Don't forget me.*

* * *

Robert wearily stripped the rubber gloves from his hands. It was after eight o'clock, he had finished with his last patient at the Free Clinic, and he looked forward to a meal, even if only a solo TV dinner while Louise met with her women's group. But when he walked into the waiting area, Huck sprawled on the sagging couch.

"Bout time you got done, Doc. Let's go eat. I'm taking you to dinner."

"Really? *You'll* take *me*? This is a first!"

"Why don't we go to my place?" Huck pulled a set of keys from one pocket. Jingling the key ring, he grinned like a kid who'd just hit a home run.

"Where'd you get those?" Robert had a sudden urge to pat his own pockets, as if Huck could have somehow spirited his house keys away.

"Relax, Doc. This is legit. Honest." He held up one hand in an incongruous Boy Scout's gesture. "It's not far from here. All we need is to pick up some food. And maybe a couple beers."

Robert couldn't help his own smile from breaking out. Of course, Huck would be angling for a free meal. Well, why not? Better than the frozen supper at home. "All right. Give me a few minutes."

"Cool." Huck stubbed out his cigarette. Robert packed his medical kit and helped the interns lock up for the night. The two men walked to a nearby ribs joint. "Don't sit down," Huck said. "We'll get our order to go." He left Robert to pay the bill while he ducked into the liquor store next door for bottles of Pabst. A couple of blocks away, he unlocked the front door of a modest brick apartment building and ushered his guest up to the second floor without once looking over his shoulder so, apparently, he had permission to be there.

Robert set the paper bag of ribs down on a coffee table littered with magazines. Pop stars and politicians stared at him from their covers. *Life* featured a bikini-clad girl frolicking on a California beach beside the headline: "Cambodia: the tottering wreck we leave behind." The usual juxtaposition: sex and war. Then he spotted the name on the address label.

"Ethan? This is Ethan's place?"

Huck chuckled at his unmasked secret. "Yep. He and his roommates have a spare room and they offered it to me."

"Just like that?"

"Yep." Huck began heaping stacks of barbecued ribs onto two plates.

"But . . . not to rain on your parade, but how will you pay rent? You don't have a job, as far as I know, never seem to have any money."

"That's the coolest part! They already split the rent three ways and said they don't need a fourth. You know, with med school and the clinic and working at the hospital and everything, these guys have no free time. They need somebody to get their laundry done, take in the mail, keep the plants from dying, stuff like that. So, it's like a gig in exchange for free rent. And I even get my own room."

"That's great!"

"Yeah, well, don't act like you had nothing to do with it. I know you probably told Ethan I needed a place to crash. So, thanks, man. Truly. It's been a long time since I could stop roaming around . . ."

"I'm pleased. I'll be able to call *you* on the phone, if I need to! And I won't have to worry so much about you."

Huck laughed. "You don't gotta worry about me. Save that for your patients!"

"Oh, I do, young man. I do."

They carried their supper out to the back porch and sat side by side, overlooking a small yard. The day's heat still simmered from the brick wall behind them. Damp laundry drooped in the humid air, as if exhausted, from a clothesline stretched diagonally across the neighboring porch. Robert watched Huck lick barbecue sauce from the corners of his mouth, feeling grateful that, for now, his unlikely friend had a haven.

"Man, you're freaking me out, staring at me like that." But Huck grinned to signal that he didn't mean it.

Robert took a sip of beer, mulling over what he wanted to say. When he set the bottle down, marks of his fingers remained visible in the condensation on the glass as if a ghost had been drinking. "What will you do if you get drafted, Huck?"

"They gotta catch me first," he bragged. "No way I'd go to Nam! I left home before my notice showed up in the mail. I didn't even want to read those words, 'You are hereby ordered to report . . .' My old man probably framed it and stuck it up over the fireplace in place of my picture."

"He supports the war, then?"

"He's a fucking hawk! We used to fight about it all the time." He gazed at the blank windows on the building next door.

"What about your mother?" Robert asked, gently.

"She never got much chance to say. It's not like my old man ever asked her what she thought about anything." Huck shambled into the kitchen, returning with more beers. He popped the tops and handed one to Robert. "Anyway, they better not ever catch me." Huck's voice was thick. "I'm July 9th."

Robert groaned. A few weeks earlier, the draft was changed to a lottery system. Clean-cut "youth delegates" spun plastic drums to randomly select the order in which recruits would be called up. July 9th was the first date pulled: all 19-year-olds with that birthday were now at the front of the line, first to be sent into the jungle carrying their M16s and white phosphorus grenades. "Are you only nineteen?" he asked softly.

Huck nodded, his mouth tight. Was that barbecue sauce or had he bit his lip? The dark shape of a bird cut across the dimming sky, angling down and then veering away. Below them, a door banged and a figure shuffled through the dark yard to the trash cans. She lifted the lid, dropped a bag in, set the lid down again. In silent agreement, the two men remained still, watching her. Halfway back to the building, the woman stopped and looked up, not at the porch where they sat, but at the sky, as if she were gazing at stars. Robert tilted his own head up. What did she see? The sky was a murky sodium-vapor haze which no star could penetrate. When he looked again, she was gone.

The doctor rested a hand on his friend's slim shoulder. "This war is a nasty business. I see too many young men desperate to get their 4F. They're willing to do almost anything to stay out of the army and some of them make stupid decisions. I don't want you to get hurt—or to hurt yourself. I've learned a lot about CO status, and other ways to get around the system. I could write you a letter for a medical deferment."

"Thanks, Doc." Huck swallowed hard.

"Or you could enroll in college. There are still student deferments."

"Nah. Not my thing. You gotta go full-time to stay out of the army, and I'd need a whole new identity to sign up."

"What is your 'thing', then? If there was no war, if you could do whatever you want, what would it be?"

Huck hesitated for a long time. His answer, when it came, was surprising. "You know, I really like rapping with folks at the clinic. Maybe you and Ethan and the other guys are rubbing off on me, but it feels good to help people when they're freaking out. Keep them company on their journeys. So, I dunno, maybe I could become some kind of counselor. Not a shrink exactly, but more of a personal guide who listens to their problems and then helps them figure out what to do."

"That's a great idea." Robert sat quietly for a minute before making his next offer. "Huck, if you need to go to

Canada, I'll figure out how to help you get across the border."

"Thanks, man." Huck's voice was hushed. "For now, I think I'm good. Nobody except you and Ethan knows where to find me. I never use my old name. War's gotta end sometime, right? Long as I don't get busted, I'll be okay." He hurled his empty bottle into the alley where it shattered into bits, sparkling beneath the streetlight like fallen stars.

Chapter Thirty-three

In the summer, in the city

Robert's new routine was to rise early, slip into his office and, with clumsy fingers peck out letters documenting weak knees, flat feet, allergies. He described wasted, flaccid bodies that no one—not even the Army—would want. As often as he could, he stretched the truth rather than create an outright lie: a suspicious cloud on a chest x-ray could mean exposure to TB. A pacifist's persistent cough might indicate bronchial asthma. As he typed, he pictured himself as a kind of defense lawyer, speaking up on behalf of the innocent, like Clarence Darrow, his letters a shield that would protect kids from dying in the jungles of Viet Nam. But with each report to the Selective Service System, his anxiety grew. Too many letters from a single physician might lead to an investigation. He wasn't certain what charges could be filed, but surely dire consequences awaited anyone caught lying to the federal government. He could lose his license, his reputation, maybe even his freedom.

To cushion the danger, he ordered new letterhead which listed only his name and address, omitting mention of the Women's Bureau and his specialty in gynecology. How odd the top of the page looked: as if signaling a future when the Bureau would no longer exist. Still, he typed diligently and signed with a bold hand, determined not to let a tremor reveal his worries. Before he released the envelopes down the mail chute, he made a small wish, and then watched them vanish into the dark.

Between patients, he read medical journals and textbooks, learning about the latest treatment for gonorrhea or brushing up on procedures he might need to use at the Free Clinic. At lunchtime, Louise kept the best seat open for him, marking his spot with a folded newspaper so no one else could claim it. She served him special dishes, topped with extra cheese or a toothpick bearing a tiny flag. After the Bureau closed for the afternoon, he went home for a quick nap before driving to the northside, pausing at street corners along the way to post his fliers on telephone poles. Unable to shake the memory of those lost girls who'd huddled behind mad Joshua or the sad fate of Frances Flannery and her dead baby, he prayed that somehow, against all odds, Cathy remained safe. Maybe she'd gone home, wherever that was, after all. Or she could have ended up in the care of an adoption agency. Although he harbored little hope of locating her, he still offered his unclaimed reward.

The Free Clinic was often a wild carousel of busted lips and bad trips. He peered and prodded, swabbed and sutured, forced niacin tablets down the gullets of ranting youths who'd swallowed too many psychedelic mushrooms. The blast of vitamin B^3 produced a massive rush of heat, followed by jolting restoration of a state of mind much closer to Robert's own version of reality. Once a week, the staff assembled to discuss new ploys young men were using in their efforts to win a 4-F from the draft board. Their patients were like mad scientists, performing reckless experiments on themselves, often with botched results. Those crude methods could be dangerous and carried no guarantee of success: eat peanut butter all night until your intestines become hard as a rock; tattoo "Fuck the Army" on the outer blade of your hand so whenever you saluted, they'd get the message.

"Some guy got rejected yesterday for pimples! Army doc told him that skin infections are rampant in the jungle, so now bad acne is on the exclusions list." They all cheered to learn of any new legal way to escape. But such good news was infrequent, and Robert continued to patch up the self-medicating and self-mutilating. He helped them to purge, to come down from their trips, to breathe more easily. And, to erase their despair, he composed more letters attesting to heart murmurs, vitamin deficiencies, allergies.

Huck showed up to hang out one day, and then he returned again. Soon, he had become a regular visitor. His casual presence brought a measure of calm to the waiting room and he was especially adept at handling stoned kids who saw angels (or devils!) falling from the ceiling. Robert was impressed, watching Huck reassure a fretting Appalachian mother that her wailing child with an ear infection was going to feel better "real soon."

And so the summer slipped by. In the evenings, Robert met Louise with weary pleasure, sometimes at her studio apartment, more often at his bungalow. He'd given her a key and when he opened the door, it was a joy to be greeted by her smile along with aromas of onion and rosemary, pot roast or lamb. They talked about the patients he'd seen and the patrons she'd served, shared funny stories, held hands. As their long days wound down to a willing end, they undressed in low light, still shy at being seen. Joints and bedsprings creaked as they settled between the sheets. Her cotton-soft thighs pressed against the flannel of his skin, his feathery fingers brushed her ample breasts. They traced lines and wrinkles with fingers and then with their tongues, exploring loosened and pliant flesh. Old pangs melted into a warm and urgent ache; breath became gasp, groans turned into deep moans; and, for a brief time, their heavy bodies became fire, then liquid, and then air.

* * *

"We can avoid the Labor Day weekend traffic if we leave early. Let's go on Thursday."

Robert had suggested they go away together for the weekend and to his delight, Louise said yes. He visited the AAA office to browse through their travel brochures and they'd settled on a quaint bed-and-breakfast in the river town of Galena. There, they could browse antique stores or sit in wicker chairs on a front porch and watch the Mississippi flow by. Secretly, he hoped that over a romantic dinner, he might bring up the subject of marriage, more pointedly this time.

But now her easy demeanor changed and she set her pinochle cards on the table, face down.

"You know I have my women's group on Thursdays."

"Oh surely, you can skip it this one time."

She crossed her arms and set her jaw. "Robert, I wouldn't ask you to skip out on your obligations."

"Well, they're not exactly equivalent, are they? You all talking together and me, providing care to my patients?"

Clearly, this was the wrong thing to say for Louise flushed with anger. "On top of missing out on my tips and paycheck for those days, you want me to drop my commitment, too?"

It was understood (at least, he hoped it was) that he would foot the bill for their trip, but he couldn't insult her by offering to make up the difference in her lost wages. "I apologize. I guess I've never understood how the group means this much to you. I don't know why it's so important." He must have looked crestfallen, for her stern look faded.

"Actually, I think you'd find that a lot of our talk *is* important. We discuss the same things you do with your patients: birth control, health care, sex education." She lowered her voice, although no one else occupied his living room. "Abortion."

"I don't counsel women to seek abortions. You know I can't."

"But would you, if you could?" She looked at him intently. There was something more pressing behind her question. He poured another inch of beer into their glasses while he considered his response.

"When I worked in the hospital years ago, I sometimes treated women who were giving birth to their eighth or ninth babies. Their bodies were wasted from childbearing and most of them couldn't afford that many children but they didn't have much choice. Now, with the Pill and the diaphragm, big families are more unusual. But I still see pregnancies that are unwanted—that will wreck my patient's health or reputation or career or education. And the damage from botched abortions . . ." He shook his head. "So yes," he said. "If I could help women obtain abortions without going to jail or losing my license, yes, I would do so. Otherwise, it's too risky." Then, thinking of the letters he secretly composed to the draft board, he looked away. Someday, he should tell Louise how he already rolled the dice. But not now.

"I would hate to lose your company for a few years if you were locked up!" Her half-smile set him more at ease. "But, sorry, you'll have to continue to do without mine on Thursdays. Let's just plan on making as early a start as we can on that weekend. How's that sound?"

It would have to do. Robert wondered why she'd asked that pointed question but, still a bit tender from their testy exchange, he left it alone. Even when they had snuggled together in bed, he didn't know whether he should mention marriage over Labor Day weekend. Or at all.

Chapter Thirty-four

Hope you got your things together

Katya flapped her long robe in an effort to cool herself. A couple of weeks ago, Glorious had presented her with a gift: this voluminous lavender garment, covered with silver stars. Katya admired the embroidery and hoped its ample folds would help hide her shape. But no such luck: every woman who entered the shop took one look at her and knew she was pregnant and they all had the same question: "When are you *due*?" As if she were a library book that had been checked out and needed to be returned.

The robe was too hot for August but Glorious expected her to wear it each day. The fabric scratched the back of her neck and its long sleeves often got in the way. She longed to inhabit her own body again and be finished with carrying this weight. But she dreaded the day when this intruder would emerge into the world.

"Glorious, when is my due date?" The distracted mystic didn't seem to hear as she pored over a pile of opened mail spread across the glass countertop, sighing "Bad moon, bad moon." Katya asked again and at last the medium lifted her head from her own troubles.

"Lord, child, don't you know?"

Embarrassed by her ignorance, Katya said, "I thought maybe you could foretell it for me." She picked at her robe with nervous fingers.

Glorious pushed the troubling mail aside. "Come here." They faced each other over the table set aside for Tarot readings. Glorious lightly touched Katya's green mound of belly. "Relax. Keep your mind open." The medium's emerald eyes probed her own. "I cannot tell you the precise day; not even the most trained physician knows for certain. But this child will definitely be a Libra."

Katya exhaled. Safe for now, the sun still in the sign of Leo. Plenty of time to figure out a plan, to find answers to all the questions she hadn't yet asked. But then, in a flash, time's telescope collapsed in on itself and her heart raced with anxiety: September was just around the corner, and only a few weeks remained until whatever grew inside her would force its way out. What bloody pain awaited her?

Before she could ask more questions, the telephone rang. Glorious lifted the receiver and listened without speaking. Then she said, "No," and dropped it back into the cradle as if it burned her hand, muttering again, "Bad moon.

"Who was that?"

"Nothing for you to worry about."

"But what does 'bad moon' mean?"

"Remove your robe." All warmth had vanished from Glorious' face. She moved hastily about the shop, snatching doilies from the backs of the high upholstered chairs. Obediently, Katya pulled the heavy fabric over her head and stood in her sleeveless blouse and drawstring shorts. Her bellybutton protruded like a pale thimble. "It's time we laundered some of these items. Take all your own clothes along and the kitchen towels.

You may as well make a full load or two. Here are some quarters for the machines."

"Okay." Katya gathered up her things and stuffed them into a pillowcase.

Glorious gave her a small bottle. "Peppermint soap. Use it sparingly; it's highly concentrated. The laundromat is on Belmont, about six blocks down. Bring your robe. And your satchel; you might find things to draw." She punched buttons on her old-fashioned cash register and pulled out a twenty-dollar bill. "Also, go to the bank and get a roll of quarters. I've given you all the ones I have."

Thrilled by the trust that the psychic was placing in her, Katya tucked the twenty into the innermost pocket of her satchel. She slipped her feet into a pair of flipflops and grinned at Glorious.

"Anything else?"

"Indeed." Glorious paused. "Come here." She pulled Katya to her expansive body, enveloping her in sandalwood and tobacco. "Be safe, Starchild," she murmured. "Be well, may the spirits watch over you." She pressed something flat into Katya's palm. "Put this in your satchel."

Katya wiggled free of the hot embrace. "I'm only going to the laundromat! I promise not to get sucked down the drain or anything." But she paused with one hand on the doorknob. "It'll take a little while, I guess, because of the bank and I want to get some wire and stuff to make more earrings. Okay?"

Glorious was busy resetting her turban around her hair. "I know, Starchild, I know." She pushed through the rattling bead curtain. Katya waited for her to return but even after the beads had ceased clacking, she didn't re-appear. Katya opened the door and carried her bundle into the glaring day.

The Suds-O-Mat was nearly deserted, giving her the opportunity to fill three machines in a row. While the washers agitated their loads, Katya lumbered to the bank for quarters and then to a hardware store to buy copper wire. By the time she returned to the laundromat, the machines had finished. Her cumbersome belly got in the way as she reached into the washers. Like Meadow had done, she snapped each wrinkled piece to release its creases before tossing it into the dryer. It gave her a strange sensation to mimic Meadow's gestures, as if she might turn around to find a nameless baby wailing in a wicker basket.

She fed quarters into the dryer slots and dropped heavily into a molded plastic chair near the cigarette machine where discarded newspapers littered the floor. She picked up a page of the *Sun-Times* to read Ann Landers' advice column (*Dear Ann: I think my husband of twenty-nine years is having an affair . . .*) and checked her horoscope (*Rome wasn't built in a day. Don't expect castles to last if you form them out of sand.*) before she realized that the paper was four days old. Scuffing her sandals against the papers, she idly scanned the headlines of news that had already occurred. The Senate wanted to curb the president's powers in Cambodia. Some banking deal that looked complicated and boring. And then, a headline that stopped her breath.

Union Stockyards Shuttering for Good.

For good? There was nothing good about closing the stockyards. Her pa and the father of every kid she'd grown up with worked there. With a grunt, she bent forward to snatch the paper from the floor. Her gaze raced

over the page: declining profits ... increased costs ...
Swift and Armour relocating operations to other
states ... meatpacking in a downturn ... hundreds out
of work by the end of August. Above the text, a black-
and-white photo of the Stockyard gate, its wide opening
flanked by what had always looked to her like window-
less castle towers. Gazing down from the top of the arch
was the sculpted head of Sherman, the bull who placidly
watched thousands of his brethren herded through the
gate each day to slaughter.

Her Tata. About to lose his job. She saw his big
hands spread upon the kitchen table, his swollen fingers
tarnished by tobacco, thin lines of dried blood beneath
his nails that never washed away. And his face: those
deep furrows across his broad forehead, his bushy eyebrows above tired, heavy eyes, his gray hair cut close to
the skull in what he thought was a more American look.
What would happen to her family? Her mother already
worked five nights a week. Piotr might have to leave
college and then he could be drafted.

And what about Katya? She was less than no help.
She had given her family only pain and sorrow, turned
them into disgraced subjects of neighborhood gossip.
Hunched with misery, she re-read the article, slowly
this time. The union had tried offering concessions, but
those weren't enough; Chicago was no longer "Hog
butcher to the nation." In eighth grade she'd been
assigned that poem to memorize and had recited it to
her parents. Tata disapproved of the word "half-naked"
but he was proud to learn that a poet had written about
his city, his own work. A line from the poem echoed
through her mind now: "Laughing even as an ignorant
fighter laughs who has never lost a battle." There was

nothing to laugh about. Tata, his friends, their whole Southside neighborhood had lost their battle. The fluorescent fixtures buzzed above her like flies circling a dead animal.

The dryers blared that they were done. She tore the article from the newspaper but it didn't yield easily; jagged rips severed the sentences in two. Carelessly, she crammed hot clothing into the pillowcase and slung it over her shoulder. The walk back to the shop seemed to take a long time. Sweat trickled down her back beneath the bundle of warm laundry and twice, she had to stop to rest. Should she try to call home? Was Tata already out of work?

She needed advice, and not the kind that Ann Landers wrote. Glorious could give her a full Tarot reading. Maybe cast the runes too. Toss the I Ching. Use every means of communicating with those unseen forces that might tell the future: crystal ball, Ouija board, astral chart. Glorious, peer into my palm and my irises, feel the bumps on my skull. Go ahead and open my third eye! Just tell me what to do. I'll even go to church and light a candle to Saint Jude.

She rounded the corner with hope, hastening her pace. But something was wrong. A sign had been taped upon the door and its shocking words sprang out at her: *Closed by order of the Bureau of Revenue . . . tax delinquency . . . Trespassers subject to fines and penalties . . .* The door's beautiful green paint bore gouges from a large padlock dangling from a metal hasp screwed into the frame. Through a chink in the curtains, she could see that the room was vacant and the cash register's open drawer gaped like a mechanical jaw. Katya pulled on the heavy lock; she hammered with the knocker and yelled for Glorious; she pounded her fists against the wood until her hands swelled. But all she heard was a great emptiness echoing from the shuttered House of the Rising Moon

Chapter Thirty-five

If you go, no one may follow

Katya sat outside the astrological shop, disheartened and bewildered. If she'd been inside when the authorities arrived, what would have happened? The idea drove her to her feet; it wasn't safe to stay here. She plodded down the sidewalk, dragging the heavy bundle of laundry behind her. All her earrings and bracelets were in the padlocked store and she had nothing to sell. But, knowing that something bad was coming, Glorious had tried to protect her by sending her on that needless errand. And by giving her the twenty dollars now converted into a heavy roll of quarters. Enough money for the YW. With a solution in mind, she headed for the El to catch a southbound train.

Rush hour had seized the city in its grip; crowded buses angrily roared past her and taxi drivers leaned on their horns if she didn't scuttle out of the crosswalk quickly enough. Was it her imagination or did every face bear a grimace? All of Chicago seemed irritable, turned cranky by the sultry August air that left her short of breath. Or maybe it was the intruder who pressed against her ribs so that she could scarcely inhale. Made clumsy by her bundles and bulk, she was unable to side-step sticky patches of tar and chewing gum that littered the sidewalks, and she bumped into people as they emerged from their office buildings. "Watch it!" someone snapped at her. "Get out of the way!"

It was a relief to push through the doors of the YW, into a lobby that was slightly cooler than outside. But her respite was brief. Even as she approached the window's grille, the clerk pointed to the exit.

"I'd like a room . . ." Katya began. "I have enough money." The clerk shook her head emphatically and continued to stab the air with her finger, indicating the door.

"This is the Young Women's *Christian* Association! We don't accept guests in your condition."

Katya dropped the laundry sack to wipe her perspiring face. "Out!" the clerk yelled, like rebuking a bad dog. Determined not to slink away, Katya lifted her chin and walked slowly toward the door while her mind raced: *What now?* Her back ached, her legs were sore. A few blocks away, she found a phone booth with a tattered Yellow Pages chained to the shelf. It took several calls to find an affordable motel, and she splurged on taxi fare to get there, rather than subject her swollen feet to the long trek to Roosevelt Road.

The motel bore mysterious stains on the lobby rug, a squeaky ceiling fan chopped feebly at the stale air, and she hoped there would be no bedbugs. But the desk clerk regarded her with a reassuring indifference. "Use the ashtrays, no dogs, checkout by ten a.m.," he drawled. Only when she asked to borrow a pair of scissors, did he shoot her a suspicious look and made her promise to use them in the lobby. Digging the lavender robe out of her sack, she hacked off its long sleeves. It still wouldn't completely hide her shape, but at least it would be cooler to wear. She tossed his scissors back onto the counter.

The air conditioner in Katya's rented room wheezed valiantly but managed to produce a weak stream of relief. Unfortunately, its asthmatic gasps weren't loud enough to drown out the noises that emanated through the thin walls. She chained the door and shoved a chair under the knob before she felt safe enough to strip off her clothes and stand in the shower. Blue veins threaded across her stomach like a road map of her distressed journey, while a new dark line descended from her navel and disappeared somewhere below the horizon. She stood beneath the tepid water for a long time, scrubbing her scalp with the motel's cheap bar of soap until it melted into a thin sliver. If only she hadn't overlooked Glorious' little bottle of soap back in the laundromat, she would have the scent of peppermint to waft around her.

The TV set provided little companionship; its knob was stuck on one channel where cowboys shot at Indians. Still, she sat on the edge of the bed and watched the Indians fall off their horses again and again. How long could she stay here before she ran out of money? For once, even the idea of drawing or making jewelry failed to stir her; the effort seemed too great. Perhaps she could fake her way through giving palm readings. But only someone younger and stupider than she was would pay for that. Besides, it wouldn't feel right to pretend to be Glorious. She'd never felt so inglorious, so defeated. In the next room, something slammed into the wall; as if in answer, the stowaway inside her knocked against her ribs. Little Libra, reminding her that only one of them had an escape plan. Soon this baby would insist on pushing its way out and that future was a terrifying bottomless pit.

Katya curled into a ball and wept, but the mattress springs kept poking her, prodding her to sit up, to think. Other homeless kids slept in parks or dozed in rigid plastic chairs at the Greyhound Bus station until they got rousted by security. But those kids weren't pregnant. Wherever she went, she risked someone seeing her and calling social services, and she'd end up imprisoned in that Home for Bad Girls.

There was only one solution and the longer she allowed herself to consider the possibility, the brighter it seemed. With the stockyards closing and Tata soon out of work, everything was up in the air. She wouldn't be the biggest problem any more. She could help around the house so that Ma wouldn't be so tired after cleaning offices all night. Maybe Piotr could stay in school after all. Together, they'd figure out what to do about Tata's job and about this baby. They needed her now. That's what families are for, she told herself, to help each other. It was time to go home to her old bedroom with its pink flowered wallpaper and its view of a scrawny tree that always dropped all its leaves at once, as if surrendering even before winter arrived.

After a restless night, Katya slept late, only roused by the housekeeping crew pounding on her door. She decided to abandon the sack of laundry; it was too much to carry and besides, once home, she'd have no use for those ill-fitting clothes and silly lace doilies. Maybe the cleaning ladies would want them. She donned the lavender robe, feeling Glorious' embrace wrap around her. Across her chest, she looped her worn green satchel's strap so that her battered collection of sketch-books and pencils wouldn't be left behind. At a greasy spoon, she ate a tasteless meal, thinking of her return to a kitchen filled with aromas of pork sausage, fish soup, and dumplings. As she walked to the bus stop, flipflops rhythmically slapping against her swollen feet, she assured herself Ma would be happy to see her again, enormously relieved and grateful that her daughter had come home at last.

It took a long time for the right bus to show up. There was no bench and she squatted uncomfortably in the sparse shade of a building whose bricks radiated too much heat. A one-legged pigeon gimped around her feet, hoping for crumbs. It cocked its gray and purple head at her hopefully, but she had nothing to spare, and it hopped away.

At last, the 61 arrived, blasting its black diesel exhaust into the thick air. Southside buses never had working AC; climbing aboard was like stepping into a sauna. The driver punched her wilted paper transfer without glancing away from his smudged windshield. In the rear of the bus, men drank from bottles hidden in brown bags, the paper twisted around the bottle's neck as if trying to strangle it. As the bus lurched away from the curb, she stumbled into a seat. Katya was the only white person on board and she tried not to look intimidated. It felt important to appear neither cocky nor afraid, but whenever a shadow passed over the window, her pale reflection flashed at her: haggard and worried. She tried to comb her hair with three fingers, wishing she still had a brush.

The bus lumbered down Martin Luther King Drive. A wide grassless strip in the median held rusted barrels that overflowed with trash and old men, gray trousers hitched high on their waists, turned their vacant, clouded gaze at the bus as it passed by. Two years ago, when Dr. King was killed, the ghetto had exploded into flames: liquor stores, barbershops, grocers, all torched. Harlow had told her how Mayor Daley personally ordered city workers not to clean up the riot debris. Teach them a lesson by making them live in the mess they'd made, the mayor said. And it looked like Harlow was right. Blackened, skeletal remains of storefronts gave ominous warning, like a body swinging from the scaffold in a western ghost town. Most of the windows had gaping holes or were blinded with plywood. Whenever the bus lurched to a halt and its doors screeched open, she caught the acrid scent of ruins, as if they still smoldered.

As the bus approached Pershing Road, she tried to signal a stop but the cord sagged uselessly in her hand. "Stop, please," she said as she trundled down the aisle to the rear door. One last transfer, one more bus, and she would be home. Standing on the steps, she waited for the bus to slow but it rolled through the intersection. "Out here!" she called to the driver. The bus crossed 40th Street, then 41st. Soon it would enter deeper ghetto, areas she did not know, didn't dare explore. She kicked the door. "You missed my stop!"

A slurred voice rang out from the rear seats. "White girl wants off! Stop the damn bus!" A raucous chorus of laughter cheered whoever had spoken as the vehicle slammed to a halt, throwing her off balance as her elbow banged painfully against a metal pole. The doors hissed open at last and she tumbled to the sidewalk under a sky tinged gloomy orange by the steel mills' belching smoke.

The new bus, blessedly cooler, rocketed to her old neighborhood, street signs flashing at her like a pop quiz in sixth grade: "Dearborn," "Union," and the laughably named "Normal." Katya stepped to the curb at Pulaski's Bakery, its windows dark, but the smell of sugar still hung in the air. She remembered how she had gorged on *kolatchy* and *paczek* on the day she left home, and her stomach moaned at the memory. Early evening shadows lengthened as she traveled the last few blocks, warily observing each familiar house and shop. How much smaller they looked now, how shabby and worn. She prayed that none of the neighbors would peek out their windows. Not Mrs. Novotny, not old Mr. Cervik. How disgusted they would be to see her cowcatcher of a belly. *Just let me reach the house, get safely in the door.*

The house next door looked as tidy as ever. Mr. Nowicki was always passionate about his lawn and kept it neat and trim as a green crewcut. But a strange sign stood in his yard, declaring *For Sale* in bold blue letters ringed with red and white stars. Her own yard looked odd too, as if something was out of place, the bushes too big or the fence the wrong color. Before she could reach the stoop, her front door opened and a thin black woman in a flowered housedress stood on the threshold. As Katya heavily mounted the three steps, the woman folded her arms over her chest and scowled.

Katya pushed her tangled hair away from her forehead. "Ma?" she called. There was no answer. She tried to peer around this person who was blocking her way into the cool, dimly lit house. Raising her voice, she cried again, "Ma, I'm home!"

"Stop." The woman raised both hands. Her palms glowed pink in the fading daylight. "You stop that hollering right now."

Katya gawked at her in astonishment. "But . . . I live here."

"You do not. Now, git."

"I *do* live here. My parents and my brother and me!" But even as she insisted, her voice rising like an indignant child, she realized the drapes in the window were ivory instead of white, and the umbrella stand in the front hallway was gone. From somewhere within the house, Roberta Flack's voice rose, rich and mournful. "Hey, that's no way to say goodbye . . ." Katya fell silent.

"That's right," the woman said, sounding satisfied. "*I* live here now. So, take yourself and your baby belly on outta here." Katya's mouth was too dry to swallow. She wanted to sit down, to be somewhere cool, to rearrange everything back to where it belonged. The music trailed off.

"But . . ." Katya croaked. Were her parents so ashamed when she ran away that they abandoned their own neighborhood?

"But what?"

Katya looked up and down the street, searching for what she wanted to ask. The streetlights blinked on, casting their sickly yellow glow onto For Sale signs stuck in a dozen lawns. The posts tilted as if they'd been planted in haste. "But . . . where did they all go?" Her voice was a whisper in the dusk.

"I wouldn't know. When your people run out of the neighborhood, they don't leave a forwarding address with *us*."

Katya's throat ached. She longed to run into her old bedroom, close the door, climb into bed and pull the crisp white sheets over her head. But that room had vanished. It existed nowhere—not in this house, occupied by strangers, and not wherever her family had gone. As she turned back to the sidewalk, she heard the door close behind her, giving its familiar squeak. She stared at the pavement: her chalk hopscotch squares had been erased long ago, leaving only those grooves in the cement that she'd tried to avoid as she chanted, *Step on a crack, break your mother's back.* All around her, life glowed from behind curtained windows where happy families sat, eating their dinners. Would any of them take her in? Could she go to the Slezaks? Even if they hadn't moved away, she knew they'd be horrified to find her on their doorstep like this: pregnant, dirty, sinful. *Step on a line, break your mother's spine.* She was a stain on the Warshawsky name.

It was fully dark by the time Katya found a phone booth outside the butcher shop. She rummaged in her satchel for a dime and listened to the familiar number ring and ring without answer before she dropped the receiver. It dangled at the end of its cord like a hangman's rope. She was drained of hope, emptied out, and she missed Glorious with an ache that spread through her whole body.

What was it that Glorious had given her to slip into her satchel? Frantically, Katya turned it upside down. There, on the floor of the phone booth, among her scattered pencils and notebooks, was a Tarot card. The sun beamed upon a gaily dressed lad who carried a flower while a small dog frolicked at his feet. Glorious had said it was a powerful card that represented new beginnings and courage but to Katya, the Fool, with his bundle slung over one shoulder, looked like a runaway. His face tilted up to the sky as he stepped to the edge of a precipice, never seeing the chasm about to swallow him.

Chapter Thirty-six

Take another little piece of my heart

Katya spent the night dozing behind the hedge outside St. Stanislaus Church and woke with sticks in her hair and the taste of blood in her mouth, as if overnight she had turned feral. She was tired, sore, and hungry, but soon, she would be home again. At the first glimmer of light, she sat up and began to brush the dirt from her clothes. At this hour, her father would be sitting in the kitchen, drinking his glass of strong tea while her mother still slept. Then he would leave the house to meet up with his pals, all of them workers at the packinghouse, and walk to their jobs together.

But no, that was his old routine. What kitchen was he in now? She could only picture the room she'd always known, where for her whole life she'd eaten every breakfast and supper until last October. She could picture the green linoleum, worn from four pairs of shoes scuffing against its surface. She saw the checkered curtains hanging at the window over the sink, and the painted cupboards holding dishes, plain and fancy, and a porcelain soup tureen that was only brought out on holidays. Where Ma kept her grocery money, the money Katya took when she ran away.

She'd be held accountable for that theft, she knew, and for all her other sins: the worry and pain she'd caused, and this new trouble she carried within her body. But she hoped that her father's dilemma and her own might balance each other somehow like scales at the fish market. Her family needed her now and she could be a comfort to her mother. Wherever the new kitchen was, Katya could help with the cooking and even ironing. Ma would figure out what to do about the baby. And later on, who knew? She could still make jewelry, maybe sell it in some nice shops. Or assemble a portfolio and somehow, someday, go to art school.

But first, she needed to reach the packinghouse before her father started work or she'd have to wait all day until his shift was over. Union Avenue. Almost there. Around her, men traveled in groups of four or five, dressed alike in their muted grays and blues, carrying lunch pails and thermoses. Katya knew they were headed to the stockyards and to the Swift and Armour packinghouses beyond. She knew the familiar foods in their pails: immigrants' lunches of salted cod, dark bread, pickled beets. And she knew how these weary men would plod home at the end of their workday, reeking of blood and raw meat and bone.

They gave her sidelong glances, but no one spoke to her, and she didn't recognize anyone among the grim faces. She hastened as best she could, unable to run, awkward in the long robe and belly. The knots of workers walked slowly, as if they were part of a funeral procession, somberly greeting one another in Polish and Czech, occasionally English. Her father had never learned much English. Maybe that was why he hadn't come to parent events at her school, not Back to School Night or Open House or the art show where she'd won a prize. She'd talked about the art show last October, on what was her final night at home, although none of them knew that then. How foolish she was, to think that a piece in the school show meant anything. It couldn't have saved her from the life that her parents planned for her: marry, have babies, be a housewife and clean offices at night like her mother.

She reached the gate and stood where she could watch the workers approach. And what now? There would be no husband, no church wedding. Could she really live at home again, with a baby sleeping in Piotr's old room or in a crib next to her girlhood bed? It was impossible; this whole plan was a bad idea . . .

There he was! She recognized Tata's gait: he had a certain roll to his walk as if his legs weren't quite even, or the ground gave a little beneath one foot. His hair was the same brush cut as always but he looked older, the lines in his face grooved more deeply than she remembered.

"Tata." She stepped forward and held out her hands. His disinterested glance flicked over her and away. How terrible she must look, like a beggar with her outstretched palms. No one could tell that stars had once adorned her wrinkled gown: the silver embroidery was shredded and frayed. "It's me, Katya."

Her father halted as if he'd smacked into a plateglass window. His eyes grew big. As his lips parted to say her name, disgust turned his face into a dark mask.

"I came back," she said. "I tried to go home, but—"

"*Nie!*" He commanded her to stop. Other workers stopped to stare at the disheveled pregnant girl outside their gate. "*Nie ma tu domu.*" You have no home here.

"Please, Tata! I have no place to go . . ." Her voice became shrill with panic, but he turned away from her, gripping his lunch pail so tightly that it seemed the handle would bend in his fist. She couldn't breathe; he squeezed her heart with that iron hand.

"Janusch!" a fellow in a checkered cap called. "Is that your daughter?"

Her father strode toward the gate's broad opening, his back rigid. "*Nie mam córki*," he snapped. I have no daughter.

Anger tore through her. What a fool she was to have hoped for forgiveness from this hard, proud, small man. For a moment, she felt herself become large and substantial, as if her new bulk protected her. "You tell Ma!" she shouted after him in Polish, to be sure he would understand. "You tell her you saw me! That I wanted to come home. Tell her the truth!"

But he walked on, never faltering or acknowledging her words until, from behind, her father was nearly unrecognizable. Just another worker in his drab clothes, his head bowed as if it were the end of the day and not a new morning. The last workers trickled through the sturdy limestone arch. Katya was alone and deflated. From his spot above the gate, the stone bull stared down impassively while the unseen intruder kicked her again and again, as if she hadn't been punished enough.

Chapter Thirty-seven

When you're weary, feeling small

Shall we call it a week, Mrs. Watkins?"

She looked up from her jumble puzzle, irked at being interrupted just as she'd been about to unscramble the letters PRJEINU. Doctor stood jingling his keys, ready to lock up, although the clock hadn't even struck one. Obediently, she stood. The wheels on her chair rattled as it scooted away from her. "I'll need to water the plants," she said. He glanced at his watch. Goodness, she thought, he's more impatient than some of the girls who come to see him. He wore a new tie today, green with blue and white stripes. Rather festive for no particular occasion. It had been evident to her for some time that he was courting a mystery woman and he must have a big date planned tonight.

"Why don't you go ahead? I'll finish up here."

"Are you sure?" He sounded like a schoolboy, eager to leave but trying to be polite.

"Of course." She brushed a speck of lint from her sleeve.

He placed one hand on the brass doorknob, then hesitated, his gray brows pulled down. "Perhaps I should wait for you . . ."

"Nonsense! I certainly know the routine." She folded her arms across her bosom but softened her voice to ease his concern. "You run along. I can use the spare key to lock up."

"All right, then. I'll see you Monday."

The door closed before she could correct him. Through the frosted glass, she saw his shape disappear. "No, Tuesday," she told the empty room as his footsteps echoed down the corridor. "It's Labor Day weekend." Time to put away her white shoes and purse for another season. Just as well: white wasn't practical in such a dirty city. She always had to be careful where she stepped, where she put her handbag down. She wondered whether his date would carry a white purse with her.

"Barbara Watkins," she chided herself. "It's none of your business. You straighten up and go home." But she remained where she was. Dust motes floated in the dim sunshine that had managed to penetrate the sooty window. It had been years since window washers last hung on the outside of the building. They used to dangle from their ropes like daredevils and soaped the glass with big sweeping motions as if waving hello. As their squeegees scraped the panes clean, they grinned at her and sank from view.

How foolish she was today, wishing for strange men to smile and wave at her. Better give those spider plants a good drink before leaving for the long weekend. She stood and picked up her watering can.

"Please. I need to see the doctor."

Startled, Barbara splashed water onto her shoes. A pregnant girl in a long, bedraggled dress stood in the doorway. Strands of greasy hair hung over a dirty face, and worse, her bare feet were black with filth. Barbara moved quickly, determined to keep her from stepping further into the room. "He's out. Do you have an appointment?" she asked automatically, knowing there was no one scheduled. She hadn't meant to sound so formidable, but the girl collapsed into a chair as if her legs could no longer hold her up. Sobs burst from her in hoarse staccato barks.

"Calm down. You'll go into hysterics the way you're carrying on, for goodness' sake." But her words only seemed to frighten the girl into hiccupping between her sobs. Barbara filled an empty coffee cup with the watering can and pressed tissues into the girl's hand. "Drink. Now, take a breath. Another." The cup rattled against her teeth. Barbara caught a glimpse of shiny earrings and some kind of mark beneath the dirt on her chin before the girl turned away to blow her nose. Hadn't lost all her manners even if she did look like a hobo.

"He wanted me to come back. I need . . ." But the weight of all that she might need seemed to strike her mute. Hadn't there been another barefoot patient, some months ago, back in the spring? An odd girl, very quiet, thin. Yes, she remembered her now—and the fact that she never returned to pay her bill. The girl's voice was faint; Barbara was met by an unpleasant odor when she leaned closer to hear. "Somebody stole my flip-flops while I was sleeping. I've been riding back and forth on the El for a couple of days and then, I looked out the window and saw this building, and I remembered how nice he was."

Barbara checked her watch. Doctor couldn't have reached home yet and she had helped discontinue that expensive answering service years ago. She should insist that the office was closed and send this vagabond on her way. But she pulled open a drawer where she kept soda crackers for women suffering from morning sickness and handed the packet over, saying, "What's your name?"

There was no answer for some minutes while the girl wolfed down crackers. But finally, after a big gulp of water, she spoke. "Katya." No last name was offered. "Thanks. I haven't eaten today. Or yesterday."

"I'm Mrs. Watkins, Katya. Do you need bus fare to go home?"

"They don't want me. Not anymore." The girl looked so mournful that Barbara knew it would be fruitless to press further.

"Well. I suppose I must ask: Are you in labor?"

Katya shook her head. "I don't think so. I don't have pains. The baby's been quiet lately."

"Not eating or drinking can have that effect. You're probably dehydrated. Have another cup of water." Barbara's thoughts raced as she finished tending to her plants and pulled the blinds against the afternoon sun. Should she give the girl enough money for a meal? But no restaurant would let her in, looking like that. Stay here until they could reach Doctor on the phone? With his dinner date or whatever he had planned, they might be waiting a long time. What does one do with a homeless pregnant waif, who even had the shoes stolen off her feet? She stuffed the jumble puzzle into her handbag.

"Come along. My bus is due in five minutes." Then, looking again at the girl's haggard face and filthy feet, she changed her mind. "On second thought, we'll take a taxi."

* * *

Barbara draped a clean sheet over the girl's sleeping form. It had taken three tubs of hot water to wash off all the dirt, and then another to shampoo and rinse that tangled mass of hair. (Discreet checking for lice had, thankfully, yielded none.) In the lamp light, Katya looked younger than before, her cheeks softened in sleep, the crooked scar gleaming white against her tanned skin. She'd said her family had moved away and left her behind. She had nowhere to go, no one to take her in, refused to give her last name. Perhaps it had been an error in judgment to have brought her here but Doctor still wasn't answering his phone, and Barbara couldn't just send the poor thing out into the night.

She left a lamp on so that Katya wouldn't be disoriented if she woke, and turned to searching through the closet for a garment the poor girl could wear in the morning. Most of Barbara's outfits were fitted styles, neat shirtwaist dresses fastened with snaps and buttons or snug little belts. She prided herself on having gained only one size over the past fifteen years. (It was a vanity, she knew, but she had so few, she allowed herself this one.) At the back of the closet, she found an option. Three years ago, she'd planned a winter vacation to visit her sister Marjorie in Florida. In anticipation, she purchased a muumuu: a loose tent of a dress covered in large tropical flowers. It had been ill-advised, even at Wieboldt's prices, and she'd had to cancel the trip after Marjorie's husband fell ill. Crimson orchids were a bit much for a young girl, but nothing else would fit. And, if she were to iron it, using lots of spray-starch, the fact that Katya wore no brassiere might be less evident.

It was almost midnight, but Barbara dialed Doctor again. The round white circles beneath the black dial glared at her like ten accusing eyes as his line rang. Where could he be? But she knew the answer. She climbed into bed and switched off the lamp. When

Doctor began closing the office early, it was clear he had somewhere else to go. She prodded the pillows, trying to find a comfortable spot. She'd seen how grief-stricken he was when his wife died, and it wasn't her place to judge if he was seeing another woman now, but one might think that, after working together for seventeen years, he would confide in her. Instead, he'd turned out to be little different than those window washers—giving a wave and a grin before disappearing.

In the living room, the girl moaned. Katya was very young to be on her own. Barbara directed a stab of anger at the unknown boy who had done this. And where was he tonight? She imagined he sat in a bar, telling stories to his drinking buddies, laughing and pushing his hair away from his forehead with the same careless manner that Eddie had. She sighed and rolled over. She didn't want to think about Eddie. He hadn't been in her life for two decades now and should have been long forgotten. Except that she saw his name again each time she wrote her own. Perhaps she should have returned to using her maiden name, but then it would have been obvious to anyone who knew her as Barbara Watkins that she'd been divorced. It was easier to allow them to believe she was a widow; after the war, there'd been plenty of them. And even Doctor didn't know the truth.

Katya mumbled in her sleep. *We're all restless tonight: me, the girl, her unborn baby.* Of all the thoughts pressing in on her in the dark, Barbara was not going to allow any memories of how she had once wished for a baby, very early in her marriage before it turned sour, and then brutal. *Enough,* she chided herself. *You're being melodramatic. Get up and drink some warm milk.* But she stayed where she was, listening to the soft sounds coming from the next room. It was pleasant to have another person in the apartment, to hear someone other than the lead-footed neighbor upstairs. Tomorrow, they would go shopping for proper clothes. No need to splurge at Marshall Fields—Sears would do for a few nice maternity outfits and some decent undergarments. And a pair of shoes; Katya must have shoes.

Chapter Thirty-eight

Distant as the Milky Way

For the past hour, Katya had copied images from Barbara's display of Christmas plates. Barbara had bought one for herself many years ago and the purchase had become her annual tradition. Every year, a new plate was issued bearing a scene of old-fashioned holidays with the date inscribed beneath it in gilt: a horse-drawn sleigh dashing over the snow, stockings hung before a blazing fire, furry animals gazing at a Christmas tree in the woods. 1943-1969: her collection nearly filled the living room wall.

Already, the girl appeared healthier and happier. She gulped down glasses of milk, ate anything that Barbara offered, and occasionally remembered to say "please" and "thank you." All she had asked for was paper to scribble on with her dirty bits of charcoal, and she seemed thrilled when Barbara gave her a blank note-book to use.

"What will you do when you run out of room?" Katya bent over the drawing, adding tiny details to an image of merry children sledding down a hill.

Barbara stared at the wall. It was as if she'd been asked what would happen when she ran out of time. "I don't know." What could she do? Quit buying them? Remove the first few years of plates to make room for new ones? How maudlin her collection looked now, these sentimental depictions of a life she'd never lived, one that had never really existed except in Currier and Ives prints. Twenty-six expensive fictions: what did that say about her?

She picked up the phone and dialed the doctor's home again and, for the twentieth time, listened to it ring and ring before she replaced the handset with increasing irritation. Doctor had someone else in his life now; she should, too. He wasn't the only one who deserved to be happy. After Katya was asleep, she pulled the telephone into her bedroom and called her sister in Florida. "You won't believe it!" She told Marjorie all about her young houseguest. Barbara didn't admit that she fantasized about keeping Katya and her daughter (surely, the baby would be a girl) but Marjorie seemed to know just the same.

"Oh, Barbara," she chided. "What's got into you? You know you're not the mothering kind. You're just not cut out for that kind of thing."

Barbara hung up and stared at the ceiling, deflated. Marjorie was right, of course. In her years at the Bureau, Barbara had seen a hundred other girls who'd got themselves in trouble and had never tried to help any of them, never fed them or gave them a place to sleep. It really wasn't her job; there were programs and places to help those girls. After all, what did she know about Katya, or her background? Or about babies, for that matter?

On Monday Doctor still did not pick up his phone and with every unanswered call, her resentment grew. Now that she had come to her senses, it would be best to get the girl out of here as soon as possible. It was Labor Day and everything was closed, there was no place to go, and nothing to do. To keep busy, she scrubbed the kitchen floor and had Katya iron a stack of pillowcases.

"Tomorrow, we'll go see Doctor," she said, as she passed the salad bowl to Katya over dinner.

"What do you think he's going to do?"

"I presume he'll examine you, make sure the baby's all right. And then make arrangements for you to give birth in a hospital. Probably at Cook County, given your situation."

"But then what?"

The girl was nervously chewing her lower lip. It would be best to present her with a plan, let her know that she wouldn't have to go back to the streets. "Oh, Social Services will take care of everything—finding your parents, getting the baby adopted if that's what your parents want. If they can't locate your family, they'll take you to a foster home. I'm sure there are excellent ones."

Katya picked olives out of her spaghetti sauce and lined them up on the edge of her plate. For the first time all weekend, she didn't finish her meal but "I'm tired," was all she said. After Barbara washed the dishes, she joined her guest in the living room so that they could watch "The Doris Day Show" together. Only a re-run, but Connie Francis was on. Katya fell asleep before it ended.

It was nearly ten o'clock when at last Dr. Lewis answered his phone. "I've been calling you," Barbara said, sounding more peevish than she had intended. "Many times." She held onto the reason why, keeping it out of reach for a few more moments.

"We—that is, I—was away. In Galena," he added, unnecessarily. "Is there a problem?"

"Yes. I have one of your patients here."

"Oh?" He sounded perplexed. "Where are you?"

"At home, where else? But if I'd known how difficult it would be to reach you, I never would have brought her home with me." (Although, in truth, she had no idea what else she might have done.) "I've had her all weekend. She's a runaway!" She heard the disapproval in her voice, how her anger with Doctor was unfairly heaped upon the girl, but she couldn't stop herself. "Dirty, underfed, and very pregnant."

"One of my patients?"

"Yes." Was that so difficult to understand? "She came in last spring sometime."

He inhaled sharply. "By any chance, does she have a scar on her chin?"

"Yes she—"

But Dr. Lewis interrupted her, to exclaim to a companion, "She's been found!" Then he spoke into the phone again. "Mrs. Watkins, this is remarkable! What's your address? Let me get a pen."

"Doctor, it's very late . . ."

"Yes, but you see . . ." And Barbara stood stunned, clutching the receiver in a tight hand, while her employer excitedly told her how he'd searched for the girl sleeping on her couch. All summer long, when he left the office, he'd gone hunting in coffeehouses and cafés. He'd hung out (he said that: "hung out"!) at Grant Park. "After all this time, she has returned! And you have her in your care. You don't know what this means to me!"

She dropped into a chair. The impact of her tailbone against the wooden seat sent a sharp jolt up her spine as his words jarred her, the realization hitting her like a headache. *All this time.* The entire summer he'd been engaged in his quest and never said one word. He'd shortened their clinic hours without telling her why. He'd raided her file box looking for clues, had roamed around the city, talked to strangers. But he hadn't confided in her. No, she didn't know what this meant to him; she wasn't sure she knew him at all. He was still speaking but she couldn't focus on his words.

"No," she managed to croak. She cleared her throat and repeated more firmly, "No. She's sleeping and needs her rest. You may fetch her in the morning. At eight-thirty."

"Thank you," he said, "for taking care of her." He sounded more emotional than she remembered him being since his wife passed away.

But, unmoved, Barbara replied, "I didn't do it for you, Doctor."

Chapter Thirty-nine

She's a rainbow

Tempted as he was to glide through a four-way stop or race down a deserted side street, the risk of being delayed by a traffic ticket kept Robert's foot light on the gas pedal. So many ways he had hoped to find Cathy—in response to Huck's ad or encountering her outside a coffeehouse or even the unlikely serendipity of her showing up at the Free Clinic—but never had he imagined that Mrs. Watkins would be the one to secure her safe arrival. He'd phoned Huck last night with the good news, then stayed up far too late drinking celebratory tea with Louise.

"I wonder if she's had any medical care at all," he said. "Anyway, now's my chance to make sure she's all right, and that she'll deliver a healthy baby. And I want to thank her—to acknowledge that my search for her has widened my life."

"And then what?" Louise asked.

"And then we'll see," was all he could answer.

But Louise's sensible question echoed in his mind as he parked in front of Mrs. Watkins' tidy apartment building. Other concerns weighed on him as well. What if it was a different girl instead—the wrong girl? She'd said "Katya," not "Cathy." No, the scar was too much of a coincidence; it had to be her. His voice shook as he identified himself through the intercom to be buzzed in.

The door to 3A stood ajar and he rapped once before pushing it open.

Just as she had done last May, a girl sat hunched over a drawing pad, long loose hair shielding her face from view. She wore a brightly colored dress and her bare arms were tanned. For a moment, there was no sound other than the rasp of charcoal against paper.

Mrs. Watkins appeared in the doorway to the kitchen. "Coffee, Doctor?" The chilliness in her voice puzzled him; something to figure out later. For now, he needed no extra stimulant; his heart pumped vigorously enough. When he declined, Mrs. Watkins retreated to a corner of the room where she was taking decorative plates down from the wall and noisily wrapping them in paper.

Robert hesitated to sit beside the girl, afraid that, like a skittish animal, she might spook easily. If he knelt on the floor, his knees would complain and the struggle to stand again could be difficult. It was so important for him not to blunder now. He pushed a hassock closer to the couch, sat, and cleared his throat.

"Hello, Katya." He reminded himself to use the unfamiliar name after months spent thinking of her as Cathy. She looked up and he recognized her immediately, as if the image had never faded from his memory: her hazel eyes, green flecks among the brown; that crooked white scar; her serious expression. And a wariness that hadn't been there last spring, her elfin look vanished. Dark circles lingered beneath her eyes, like the smudges of charcoal on her fingers. Better check her iron levels, she might be anemic. "You never came back for your test results."

Katya let out a harsh bark of laughter. "Guess I know what it said." There was no need to gesture to her prominent abdomen. Clearly, third trimester.

"Indeed," he responded. "Have you had any prenatal care?" She looked at him guardedly. "Seen any doctors in the last few months? You and your baby could suffer without adequate nutrition, the right vitamins."

"I did suffer," she said with bitterness, and looked away.

Robert let a minute of silence go by and watched her slash marks across the page. "Remember, you gave me one of your drawings?" She nodded. "I had it framed, and it hangs on my wall in the spot we chose together."

"Yeah?" Her cheeks turned pink. "Cool. Nobody ever framed one of them before."

"Well, no one ever gave me a signed piece of art before." She smiled shyly at his praise, then winced and grimaced.

"Baby kicking you?"

"I guess."

He chose safer ground. "What are you drawing today? May I see?" She thrust the paper at him as if she didn't care. In thick black lines, a forbidding building towered above a steep flight of steps. Tapered window panes bore prison bars and the large door was stippled with black dots like a hobnailed boot. "What is this place?"

"Where you're gonna take me, I guess," she mumbled.

Startled, he moved to sit beside her. "But why would you say such a thing? How on earth did you get this idea? I don't know what that building is."

A shadow of confusion passed over her face. She glanced across the room at Mrs. Watkins and whispered, "She said you'd take me to Cook County Hospital and then to social services. I'm going to a foster home, or someplace worse . . ."

"Well, that's not true." He raised his voice so Mrs. Watkins would hear him above the racket she was making with her china plates and wrapping paper. "No one will take you anywhere you don't want to go." The girl's tight frown eased a little. He opened his black bag. "Right now, I'd like to give you a brief check-up. Just listen to the baby's heartbeat and measure your blood pressure." He should get a blood sample, find out if she was anemic, but better not to rush. He knew his hands trembled with emotion and he doubted whether he could find a vein without needing to jab her repeatedly.

Mrs. Watkins withdrew into her bedroom while he gave Katya a cursory exam. Apart from some scabs and old bruises, she was in reasonably good shape. Gestation would be tricky to calculate: she didn't know when her last menstrual period had been but the infant was still high in her abdomen, not yet engaged. Oddly, she insisted that the baby wouldn't be born until late in September for reasons that had something to do with the zodiac. Robert couldn't make sense of it, but he was relieved to confirm that her pressure was normal and the fetal heartbeat was strong.

"Would you like to listen?" He inserted the ends of his stethoscope into her ears and carefully placed its resonator against the rise of her abdomen. For a minute, she listened to the rapid thud of her baby's heartbeat. Abruptly, she pulled the instrument from her ears and handed it back to him.

"Here." Her jaw was rigid. "I don't want it."

"Don't want what? To listen more?"

"This baby." Her voice cracked with the admission and she stared out the window as she continued, growing louder and more agitated. "I don't like having it inside me, and I'm afraid of it getting born. I can't go home or back to ... the guy who used to be my boyfriend. I can't keep it, I'm not a mother! I don't want *any* of this."

Robert thought for a few minutes before he answered, waiting until her breathing subsided. "This must be overwhelming for you. We'll figure something out. Right now, I'd like to bring you back to my office so that I can take samples of your blood and urine, make sure that everything is as it should be. After that, if you like, you can stay at my home. Louise—my lady friend—and I would be glad to host you. There's an extra bedroom and you're welcome to it."

She regarded him warily. "Do I have to clean your house?"

"Of course not! Why?"

"Cause seems like that's all most people think I'm good for," she muttered.

He held up one hand as if swearing an oath. "You will not be my housemaid. Truly."

And then, for the first time that morning, Katya smiled. "Okay." With effort, she stood, looped the strap of a dilapidated green satchel over her shoulder and vanished into the bedroom to say goodbye. When she emerged, she carried a baby blue round suitcase, like stewardesses toted in the airline commercials. He took the incongruous luggage from her and waited but Mrs. Watkins did not come out to witness their departure.

* * *

Mrs. Watkins had fed her well, given her a garish dress to wear and, best of all, bought her a blank sketchbook. It had been wonderful to finally have plenty of shampoo and conditioner too, to use cotton swabs for her ears, and nail clippers. But Katya hadn't felt welcome with Mrs. Watkins. How tightly the old lady pressed her lips together and how she watched from beneath those penciled eyebrows, too high upon her forehead. Maybe Katya had bothered her too, for being knocked up or something. After she drew a picture of those decorated plates, Mrs. Watkins had taken them all down from the wall, as if somehow they were tainted.

The doctor helped her into the passenger seat of his car, put the keys in the ignition but didn't start the engine. Katya waited uncertainly, watching him grasp the steering wheel and release it, grasp and release. Finally, he turned to her.

"I've been looking for you, Katya. For a long time. Ever since we first met."

She stared at him, speechless, while he told her how he had put up fliers, and notices in *The Seed*, had hunted at parks and coffeehouses. He'd offered a cash reward! The idea that he'd been willing to pay someone to tell him where he might find her, money that could have fed her on so many occasions, she couldn't make sense of it. So many times when she'd felt alone and abandoned, when she wondered if anyone could be trying to reach her telepathically, when she'd wandered and worried, all that time he had been searching. For her.

"Why?" Her voice was thick with emotions she couldn't express. "Why did you do all that?"

Robert's answer was the simplest one that he could give, short and true. His voice was husky, almost shy. "Because I care about you."

Katya dropped her head into her hands and wept.

They sat in the car together for a long while. He gave her his handkerchief and patted her shoulder from time to time, letting her sob as much as she needed to. Harlow had been cruel, Tata had spurned her, and her mother was who knows where. But this kind old man, who barely knew her, had made it his mission to find her. She cried for the sharp irony of it, for the cosmic joke of it all. That's what Glorious would have said and she cried again at the knowledge that she couldn't share this moment with Glorious. When she had no more tears left, she took a deep, shuddering breath. Her cheeks were damp, but even the air seemed fresher, cleaner somehow.

"Ready to go?" he asked. Katya nodded. She did feel ready. Whatever was coming next was bound to be better than what was behind her.

* * *

His car sailed down blocks that had once taken her hours to travel. How odd, to swiftly roll along the same streets she had wandered so many times. She remembered stumbling over an uncleared bank of snow and ice on that corner, and straggling slowly through the heat of a July afternoon past this one. She had the strange notion that if she turned her head at the right moment, she would spot another version of herself, alone and on foot, still hunting for a safe place to spend the night.

Now, she sat safely on a cushioned seat, shielded from sun or rain, with the dashboard radio playing soft music.

"Here we are," he said, cheerily, as he ushered her through the front door. She moved slowly into a small living room furnished with brown leather chairs and sofa pulled up before a brick fireplace. Above the mantel hung an oil painting of a meadow erupting in red and gold blossoms. She caught glimpses of oak furniture and glass-fronted cabinets, gingham curtains, white stove. Everything cozy and old-timey, like in picture books she'd loved as a child, where furry bears lived in cottages with thatched roofs.

"This is Louise. And here, at last, is Katya!" He emphasized her name as if so much was contained in those two syllables. A middle-aged woman moved toward her, smiling as she wiped her hands on her apron. Chunkier than Mrs. Watkins and much friendlier looking.

"I'm so glad to meet you," she beamed. "Are you hungry?"

"Always."

"Good! I've been cooking and it's almost ready . . ."

Doctor R. and Louise showed her to a room on the first floor ("So you won't need to climb the stairs," he explained). Most of the space was taken up by a bed covered with a white quilt and a bureau holding twice as many drawers as she would need. She pulled aside the lace curtain to peek out the small window at a grassy backyard. Her hosts filled the doorway as they lingered together, awaiting her judgment.

"It's nice. Really nice." It was almost embarrassing, how relieved they looked at her words, exchanging satisfied smiles with each other. The doctor set the baby blue luggage next to her new bed.

"I suppose you'll want to unpack."

"It won't take long. Most of my stuff got lost or stolen but . . ." Ashamed and uncertain, could she really ask for more? He nodded at her as if to say: go on. "I only have two things to wear now. This—" she opened the little suitcase and pulled out the bedraggled lavender gown whose sleeves she had amputated weeks ago. No amount of washing would remove its stains. "And this one." She gestured at the bright muumuu covering her body. "And it's so loud, you can probably hear it coming."

Doctor R. burst into laughter. "That's loud, all right!"

"I don't really want to wear either one," she admitted. "They're not me. I feel sad . . ."

"No need to explain."

"So, after we eat, maybe you could give me a lift to the Free Store? That's where I usually find stuff. And everything is free there, you just leave a donation if you want to."

Louise put a hand on the doctor's shoulder and he took her silent hint. "I'll be glad to take you anywhere you'd like to shop. To *real* stores, I mean. Don't worry about the money, it's fine."

In Louise's company, and with money to spend, no one would mistake Katya for a shoplifter. They could go to an import store; she could choose her own wardrobe, maybe a loose Mexican shift or a wrap-around skirt. Katya wanted colorful outfits that matched her mood at this moment: hopeful and at ease.

"I'll start a list," Louise said. "You're going to need maternity bras, diapers, baby clothes, blankets, bottles . . ."

As if it knew it was being talked about, the baby butted against her ribs, reminding her in painful Morse code: *You can't leave me behind.* And, in an instant, Katya's happiness drained away.

Chapter Forty

Going where the water tastes like wine

After months of searching, Robert was reluctant to let Katya out of his sight. He closed the Bureau for the rest of the week, leaving it to Mrs. Watkins to reschedule his appointments, and made sure that every time she woke from a nap, someone was there to keep her company. Louise came after work and helped wash her hair. Huck treated Katya as if she were a little sister, teasing her, even offering to rub her swollen feet. He brought copies of *The Seed* and comic books, and the two of them read them together while Robert and Louise eavesdropped with pleasure on the laughter spilling from the front room.

But serious conversation was required too, and Robert invited her into the backyard on a sunny afternoon, bringing cookies and lemonade to sweeten the task. Her belly hung low these days, forcing her to waddle as she made her way to the lawn chair.

"I've let you settle in for a few days, but time is working against you. We need to make arrangements," Robert began. Katya seemed more interested in a small brown sparrow hopping about on the flagstones in search of stray crumbs than in having this discussion, but he persisted. "There are several hospitals you may choose for the delivery. I can recommend a doctor to attend you as well."

"*You're* my doctor! I don't want anybody else."

"You need a qualified obstetrician, dear. I don't have hospital privileges and I haven't delivered a baby in years."

She stayed silent, so he tried a new tack. "Have you decided whether you're going to keep the baby? Or give it up for adoption? We need to prepare either way . . ."

Katya frowned. "When I was on the street, I was so busy figuring out where to sleep and trying not to get busted, I couldn't think about it. And now . . . It's like this bumper sticker I saw once. It said: 'The past is just a memory, the future's but a dream.' Something like that. It's too hard to plan for tomorrow."

Her attitude troubled him. Didn't she realize that the future was already upon her, impossible to escape, like the shadow that spread beneath her folding chair? He tossed a crumb toward the sparrow. It fluttered off, but quickly hopped back to pounce upon the morsel. Perhaps Katya was not so different from this little bird: easily deterred but willing to come back. He waited, forcing himself to be patient.

"I know I'm supposed to feel something towards the baby . . . something *more* than I do. I wish Glorious was here."

"Who is that?"

"A friend of mine but she's gone now." She heaved a sigh. "What I *don't* want is so much clearer than what I *do* want!"

"All right, let's talk about what you *don't* want." Another bird fluttered to the ground, searching hopefully a safe distance from his outstretched feet.

"Okay. I don't want to go to any hospital. I don't want to be knocked out or cut into."

"You mean anesthesia and episiotomy?"

She nodded. "You're the only doctor I've ever been to. And I don't like the idea of a bunch of strangers doing things to me."

Perhaps he could introduce her to another obstetrician before she went into labor and that would ease her anxiety. But it would be tough going to persuade her that the hospital would not be as dreadful as she feared, to explain the procedures and reassure her that anesthesia was effective.

"And . . . I know I don't want to keep the baby." Her eyes welled with tears. "Is that terrible of me?"

He patted her shoulder, relieved that at last she was voicing a decision. "Not terrible at all. I'm sure an agency can find a wonderful family who will be grateful to adopt this baby."

"But that's the thing!" She pulled away, gesturing with her glass and sending lemonade sloshing over the rim. "I hate the idea of handing it over to some social worker to give it away to strangers. That seems so wrong." Robert wanted to assure her that the adopting parents would be carefully screened, but she wasn't done venting. "It's so . . . secondhand! And what if that family doesn't treat it right? What if they won't let the kid do things, things that matter . . ." He had the sense that she might be thinking of her own family, her own past. "Stop asking me questions. I'm going to take a walk now." With difficulty, Katya pushed herself out of her chair. "By *myself*."

Robert watched her waddle out of the yard and slowly move down the sidewalk. He willed himself not to follow. He had to trust that, this time, she would return.

And when she did, several worrying hours later, she glowed with excitement. "I know where I'm going to give birth, and who can have the baby!" she declared as she came in the door. Robert insisted she sit down and elevate her feet before she launched into her story: she had read something in the *Seed* about a roving band of hippies traveling east in a kind of gypsy.caravan "They're looking for land and they're going to start a commune," she told him, admiration in her voice. They were camping out in a nearby vacant lot so she had plodded over there to see what they were all about. Turns out, the "tribe" included pregnant ladies and midwives, she'd met them all, they were very cool, and—the midwives would be happy to deliver the baby right there in one of their own buses!

A hundred objections flew through Robert's mind. Hadn't we done away with birthing at the hands of amateurs in unsterile environments for good reason? Who were these so-called midwives and where did they get their training, if they had any at all? How on earth could Katya trust these people with her health and well-being, simply because they were hippies?

"This is a *good* idea, Doctor R.," she insisted. "You'll see."

Katya watched him, waiting for his response. Somehow her time on the streets hadn't completely robbed her of idealistic visions: she looked more hopeful and eager than he'd ever seen. Wasn't he the one who had failed by not living up to his own ideals? Didn't he believe in trust, in being honest and open to new ideas, and in giving people second chances?

He tried to think of a question that wouldn't sound too skeptical. "If they're hunting for land, what are they doing in the middle of Chicago?"

"Some of their buses broke down so they have to make repairs and try to raise some dough. Anyway, the caravan's closer than a hospital and it's a lot more comfortable. This'll be *so* much better."

"I doubt that," he said, drily.

She stubbornly locked her jaw. "It's my decision, isn't it? You said so. You can't force me to go to a hospital."

I probably could, he thought, but I won't. Despite her stubbornness, he was pleased to see her show some spunk. She would need that kind of fortitude in labor. Especially if she gave birth in a bus with hippies! He rubbed his forehead. "I'm worried, that's all. How qualified are they?"

"Just talk to them. You'll see how mellow they all are."

"All right, in the morning."

"No, now. What if I go into labor tonight and you've never even met them?"

"Well, what if they leave town before you start labor?"

She smiled. "That's not going to happen. Just trust the universe."

He sighed. "All right, you win. Let's go."

"I'm too tired. Go without me." She rolled over, and in a few minutes was asleep. Robert placed his hat on his head and picked up his black medical bag. Who knew? He might need it.

The caravan was impossible to miss: two dozen old school buses and delivery vans crowded into a vacant lot, with a few more parked nearby. Every vehicle was painted in bold vibrant colors; images of suns, stars, flowers, and vines wrapped around the sides. Headlights had been transformed into exotic eyes. Warm light shone through curtained windows, while a bonfire crackled in the center of the lot. An earthy, spicy aroma that reminded him of Louise's goulash rose from a large pot hanging over the flames. Lanky figures danced to the rhythm of drums. The night was warm, many of the men were shirtless, and the firelight glowed on their rippling muscles and torsos. It was impossible to ignore the allure of such young, healthy physiques. Perhaps this, too, was part of the tribe's appeal to Katya.

A knot of young women watched over half-naked toddlers romping a safe distance from the smoky fire. Robert was struck by how modest the young women appeared in their long skirts, and all of them wore their hair in Katya's style: parted in the middle and flowing loose. When they caught sight of him, their quiet conversation ceased. The children stopped frolicking and pressed shyly against their mothers' legs. He was accustomed to such a response; although he had given up his shiny shoes several months ago, there was no hiding his age or that he was a foreigner to their chosen life. But he had confidence now in his ability to talk with younger people. He would never be one of them, but he knew how to help and how to offer friendship, if they were open to it.

"Good evening, ladies." He removed his hat as he spoke, deliberately adopting old-fashioned courtesies. "I'm Doctor Lewis and I'm looking to speak with your midwives." At those words, a woman with long brown braids appeared in the doorway of a bus and beckoned him inside. He blinked at the onslaught of paisley, radiating suns, repeating prints. The entire interior was covered in gaily patterned fabric—not only the walls and the curtained windows, but the ceiling too, and a large bed where rows of seats had once stood. A heavily pregnant woman reclined on the bed, while three others rubbed her arms and legs with oil. She murmured with pleasure at their ministrations. Sticks of incense sent fragrant smoke into the air. At the rear of the bus, he spotted a crude kitchen, little more than a large water jug and hotplate. So at least there was the possibility of sanitation.

The braided woman tapped his arm. "I'm Lucy, the senior midwife here." With her high, untroubled forehead and smooth cheeks, she looked scarcely older than Katya. But streaks of gray in her braids betrayed her age, and her voice carried a mature steadiness. "Katya told us you'd show up. This is our midwifery bus. Please, rest yourself." She offered him a wooden chair and seated herself sideways in the driver's seat to face him. The symbolism did not escape him: she wanted to demonstrate that she was in charge, but he spoke first.

"I'd like to understand how you manage labor and delivery."

Lucy gave an easy laugh. "We don't like to use those words, they create their own energies, you know." At his puzzled look, she went on. "You call them 'labor pains'; we call them 'rushes.' Women have a spiritual, holy experience giving birth when they're not anesthetized, not separated from their babies or from their men."

She nodded at the woman on the bed. "When her time comes, her old man will be beside her, smooching and giving her good energy. Right now, we're trying out different kinds of oil—coconut, almond, olive oil. We encourage ladies to massage oil on their bellies as they grow, and onto the perineum." She watched to see how he took this information. "With a stretchy perineum, there's no need for cutting."

"So, you never perform episiotomies."

"No need to. And we birth the babies slowly, so the mother doesn't tear."

"Where did you train? And how many babies have you delivered, may I ask?" He hoped his rudeness wouldn't end the interview too soon.

She sat up straighter, but the calm smile never left her lips. "We have three midwives. Two of us have nursing backgrounds. All of us are mothers and we gave birth naturally ourselves. We learn through experience, reading, and from the wisdom of others. I was blessed to study with midwives in Mexico, where they still birth at home, and with an older midwife back in California who delivered hundreds of babies before the medical establishment shut her down. We're not opposed to doctors even when you're opposed to us."

Lucy held up her fingers. "So far, we've welcomed six new souls, four born right here on the bus, and they all had excellent Apgar scores."

The hippies were familiar with that scoring method to gauge a newborn's health: a pleasant surprise. Perhaps they weren't as primitive as he had feared.

"Birth isn't a medical problem, Dr. Lewis; it's a natural event, not an illness." She gestured to his gray hair, his wrinkled face. "I'll bet you're the right age to have been delivered by a midwife yourself."

She was right; Robert remembered how his mother told him that the midwife had arrived in a horse-drawn wagon. As a child, he'd mixed that story up with an old nursery rhyme: "Ride a cock horse to Banbury Cross, to see a fine lady upon a white horse. Rings on her fingers and bells on her toes, she shall have music wherever she goes." He'd pictured the midwife decked out in colorful jewelry and silver bells; gazing at these hippie women, with their hair ribbons and dangling earrings, his childhood image hadn't been wrong after all.

Yes, birth could be miraculous. But it could be risky, too: prolapsed umbilical cords, hemorrhage, retained placenta. It wasn't always possible to avoid a C-section. He worried the soft brim of his hat with his thumbs as new objections came to mind. He tried to express them lightly so she wouldn't decide he was bringing negative energy into the bus. What if the caravan went on its way before Katya gave birth? (He tried to avoid saying "labor.") What then? Lucy was unconcerned. "It's the full moon in a few days. I'm sure that will kick her rushes into gear."

"But, what medications do you have? What if you need forceps? Katya's very special to me. What will you do if there are complications?"

Lucy's smile became beatific, almost as if she'd been waiting for him to ask this question. "Ah. You can be with us, helping and teaching. We know we have much to learn. Your experience will help us prepare for any problems, and we can show you our ways."

"You mean, I'll be with her during labor and delivery here?" The midwife nodded, her brown braids gently bobbing in agreement.

How rusty were his skills, how much had he forgotten? It had been more than seven years . . . But what was that delightfully naive statement Katya had told him? How, after seven years, he had been completely renewed. Well, maybe so . . . He had revived plenty of techniques at the Free Clinic this summer; Katya was young and healthy; and if problems developed, the nearest hospital was only ten minutes away. "And she agreed to this plan?"

"It was her idea. She wants you here. She trusts you."

Those words lifted his heart. From the afternoon he'd first met her, sitting cross-legged on the floor of his office as she drew the portrait of Phyllis, he had wanted to protect this vulnerable, talented, mystery girl. And now she trusted him to do so. He bent his head in agreement, feeling no need to say anything more.

Lucy showed him how they layered the birthing bed with clean linens and sheets of plastic. Robert showed her the contents of his medical bag. All three midwives sidled to the rear of the bus with him to inspect their supply cupboard. Rudimentary items mostly: rubber syringes, eye drops, gloves, clamps, but also several fetoscopes. And herbal remedies of goldenseal ("to dry the umbilical stump") and black cohosh (they said it helped to expel the placenta).

"What's in these capsules?"

Maria answered. "Cayenne pepper. It does wonders if her blood pressure drops after giving birth."

"I'll bet it does!"

Attitude seemed paramount in their view; as long as they balanced "good vibes" with emergency care, they seemed confident they could handle almost anything. It was reassuring when Lucy finally acknowledged that the midwives wouldn't adamantly oppose hospitalization if it were necessary. But only in an extreme case. Did they know the signs of fetal distress? He described how to spot green or brown meconium stains in the amniotic fluid or a prolonged change in heart rate. He showed them which part of the thigh to inject with Pitocin if the mother hemorrhaged and the midwives took careful notes on everything he said. Teaching might have been like this, if he had chosen that path. But perhaps he wouldn't have been fortunate enough to find such eager students.

There was just one more problem to discuss. Had Katya talked with the midwives about her intentions for the baby? Did they know that she didn't want to keep it?

For the first time, the radiance in Lucy's face dimmed as she nodded at the women giving massages. "See Jenny there? The lady in green?" She whispered that Jenny had had a stillbirth last week, a little boy.

"Wait a minute. You said you've delivered six babies, no complications!"

"I did say that. Jenny and Marcus gave birth in a hospital in Iowa City on the way here. I don't know if the outcome would've been different if they stayed with us. But it's been a heavy time for them ever since."

"I imagine so." Great circles beneath Jenny's eyes spoke of her grief as she slowly ran her oiled fingers along the other woman's calf.

"Katya is a compassionate soul," Lucy said. "She's giving her baby to Jenny and Marcus."

Katya had created a solution for her dilemma. A wave of emotions surged through Robert: surprise, relief, confusion, worry, and—although he had had nothing to do with it—pride. He released a long exhale, as if he had been holding his breath for days, and Lucy laughed.

"Now you know what a rush feels like, Doctor!"

Chapter Forty-one

Outlaws in the eyes of America

I've got the munchies." Katya moaned softly as she peeked through her lashes at Huck, trying to look pitiful. They had waited until the doctor went to bed before creeping into the backyard to giggle over a shared joint. Now the two of them lounged on the sofa, with only the flickering TV images lighting the room.

"Yeah? Maybe Doc's got some chips in his pantry."

"I need a milkshake. Or wait—apple pie," she sighed. "This thing keeps kicking me, saying it wants pie! Want to feel?"

Not really. But before he could refuse, she lifted her blouse, grabbed his hand, and placed it on her bare belly. The taut surface quivered beneath his fingers splayed against her pearly skin. Then an angular shape glided across her abdomen like a fish floating past the glass in an aquarium, pressing against his palm. He snatched his hand back.

"Damn! That's weird."

"I know. I keep picturing odd stuff in there like a submarine or maybe a rocket ship with fins 'cause of the poky parts. But I guess those are really knees or elbows."

Huck rubbed his palm against his jeans to erase the sensation, then lit a cigarette and exhaled a long stream of smoke toward the ceiling. "Hey—I got something for you."

"Yeah? Hope it's pie!"

He reached into his grubby knapsack and pulled out a small metal box. Katya opened it to reveal a dozen chalks in rainbow hues. Her delighted face made it worth the risk he had taken, boosting from the art supply shop, palming the box in defiance of the sign that warned shoplifters would be prosecuted to the fullest extent of the law. He did like a challenge.

"Ooo, thanks. Hand me that."

Huck leaned over and snagged the drawing pad with one hand. She flipped it open to a blank page and propped the pad against her belly. "Turn on the lamp. I'm going to draw your portrait. Hold your head that way. Not so much. There. Keep still, like that."

"Oh, man," he mock complained, but held the pose, listening to the faint scratch of chalk on paper, his own breath, a clock ticking in the hallway. From time to time, he glanced sideways. Katya frowned in concentration as she worked. As she brushed a loose strand of hair away from her forehead, she smeared green chalk across her temple. "Don't move!" she commanded. At last, she put the chalk down and examined her work.

"Lemme see," he said, stretching his neck to work out the kinks.

"Okay, but don't touch or it'll smudge."

He held the page as if it were a treasured LP. Katya had turned him into a proud pirate. Brown curls tumbled from beneath a tri-cornered hat topped by a feathery plume. An emerald green parrot clung to his gloved hand and both of their noble profiles stared into the distance as if trying to determine where the bird might fly.

"Far out!" he exclaimed. "I love it." Wanting to do more for her, he asked, "Still hungry?" She nodded, stifling a yawn. "I could hoof it to the 7-11 and get a treat to keep that little submarine quiet. Maybe not pie, but ice cream or something. You going to keep awake until I get back?"

"I dunno. You could take his car."

Doc's Fairlane was parked at the curb. Huck had ridden in it plenty of times but had never been invited to drive.

"It'd be a lot faster. He'll never know. I'm really hungry . . ."

Huck knew he shouldn't. But the keys dangled temptingly from a hook near the front door and so he said, "Chocolate or vanilla?"

"Both!"

Huck flashed her a peace sign, lifted the keys from their hook, and slipped out the door.

* * *

"Wake up. Please, wake up!"

Robert sat up, throwing off the blankets. "You all right? Labor pains?"

"No, not that. But something's wrong."

He flipped the light on, squinting in the glare. Katya looked scared, her face tight with anxiety.

"Huck went out. For ice cream. 'Cause I asked him to. But it's been a long time. He took your car. I made him do it." She hung her head. "I fell asleep and he's still not back. I'm so sorry! I never thought . . ."

His mind leapt through possibilities—flat tire, ran out of gas, a crash . . . Huck heading for California or fleeing to Canada with no intention of returning. Or perhaps just joyriding and planning to sneak the car back before dawn.

The telephone on his bedside table rang. They both stared at the black instrument. Would lifting the receiver bring bad news? Still, it had to be done. "Doctor Lewis speaking," he announced formally, as if he were sitting in his office.

"Captain Connolly, Fourteenth Precinct. We got your grandson here. You wanna come ID him?"

Grandson? For a moment Robert thought he might still be asleep, caught in an odd dream. Then it dawned on him in a flood of new dread. Huck had been arrested. "Yes! My grandson, of course. Is he all right?"

"Yeah, but you got to come down to the station."

"Give me the address and I'll come right now." When he hung up, he patted Katya's cheek. What a child she still was. "It's all right, don't worry. Go to bed and I'll tell you everything in the morning."

But it wasn't all right; he hadn't even thought to ask what the charge was. What if they fingerprinted Huck? How quickly could they find out he hadn't registered for the draft? He telephoned Checker Cab and dressed hurriedly.

The cab driver grunted without surprise when told the destination. Where else did you go at this hour except to the hospital or jail? Round blue lights identified a boxy building as the precinct station. The entry reeked of bleach and booze, and when he pushed through the door, he saw why. The floor was freshly cleaned, the mop still leaning against a bench where a wino in grimy clothes snored and muttered in his sleep. Robert hesitated to walk across the wet linoleum, but there was no sense in waiting for it to dry. A bored-looking desk sergeant called to him.

"Help ya?"

Robert was acutely aware that he was unshaven, his face as rumpled as his shirt. At least he had put on a tie while waiting for the cab to show up. He crossed the room and offered his card to the sergeant in hopes of impressing him. "I'm Dr. Robert Lewis. I understand my, uh, grandson is here." He carefully avoiding saying "in custody," praying that Huck hadn't been arrested, but only detained.

The officer stood and slowly approached the counter. "What's his name?"

Oh Lord. If only Huck had confided in him . . . But of course, the lad would be too cautious, too smart to use his real identity. And the answer came to him. "Robert," he answered with false assurance. "Bobby. Named after me." He held his breath, crossed his fingers in his pocket. This had to be right. The sergeant pawed through some papers, seeming in no hurry to find the right document. From somewhere down the hall, metal clanged against metal in a reminder that Huck was locked behind bars. Robert gritted his teeth as he waited.

"Looks like little Bobby left his wallet at home. No license, no ID . . . What was he doing, out so late, driving after curfew?"

Robert cleared his throat and lied. He was surprised how easy it was. "I was attending a patient and needed some items from my office. Not wanting to leave her alone, I sent him to fetch them. It's been damned inconvenient having to wait all this time!"

The officer scratched his head. "Hmm. Well, who's with your patient now?"

"I had her transported to the hospital," he replied, easily. "May I have Bobby now? Or, are you charging him with something?"

"Naw, we'll let him off with a warning. This time. Sign here to show that you're taking responsibility for this juvenile. Your car's at the impound lot. You can pick it up after nine."

Juvenile? Huck had succeeded in convincing them he was underage? Clever of him. Better to face any charges as a juvie than an adult. Plus, avoided the question of the draft.

A few minutes later, Huck stumbled through the doorway as if someone shoved him from behind. His hands were cuffed in front of him, his jacket torn at the collar. His weak grin was at odds with a large red welt next to one eye and a gash on his cheek. Robert spoke to the desk officer in barely suppressed fury. "What happened to him?"

The officer gave him a hooded look. "Must have tripped in his cell. Isn't that right, kid?" Huck locked eyes with Robert. "Yep," he said, flatly. "That's exactly what happened."

The wino snorted in his sleep and rolled over. Robert wanted to wrap an arm around Huck's shoulder and hustle him out of this stink-hole. With agonizing slowness, the desk sergeant rooted around to locate the envelope of Huck's belongings: lighter, Robert's car keys, a few coins. A second cop, burlier than the first, unlocked the handcuffs and made "Bobby" verify that none of his things had gone missing. Huck's hand shook as he signed the inventory release.

At last they could leave. When they were one step away from the door, the burly cop warned, "We pick you up again, we won't be so easy on you!" The sergeant added, "And Gramps, don't let Bobby drive your car until he gets a haircut." Their laughter followed Robert and Huck down the steps.

Outside, Huck took long gulps of air. Silently, the two men walked east toward the sky's pearly glimmer and found a bench at the lakefront. They watched the water brighten from sable to amethyst to blue as the sun rose and greeted the day, glinting upon every wave.

"I only got a couple blocks from the house when they pulled me over and busted me. Claimed a tail light was out. Hope Katya's not too bummed 'cause I never got her that ice cream."

"I think she'll get over it," Robert said. "Let me see your wrists." Huck obediently pulled back his sleeves to allow the doctor to examine the scrapes. "Not too bad. But you'll have a black eye. Again! Your ribs okay? Anything else hurt?"

"Nah. They mostly wanted to hassle me, see if I would piss myself. But I stuck to my story: I'm seventeen years old, driving my granddad's car. And—sorry about that." His voice quavered. "Really, truly. I never should of . . ."

"No, you shouldn't have," Robert growled. But he was too relieved to be angry. "Let's go get the car. Katya will be fretting." They began to walk north along the shore's riprap. "How on earth did they believe that you're only seventeen?"

Huck gave a lopsided smile. "They couldn't prove otherwise, could they? And then my 'Gramps' showed up to spring me. Thanks for being so sharp, Doc. I was counting on you to figure out the name I gave them."

"Luck was on your side today, my friend. How much longer can you keep being lucky?"

Huck had no answer.

Chapter Forty-two

I saw myself as you knew me

Robert was glad to send his last patients out the door. He found it difficult to focus on his appointments, his mind often straying to thoughts of home where Huck was keeping Katya company. They had both promised to call right away if she showed any signs of going into labor.

"May I come in?" Mrs. Watkins rapped on the doorframe. Rather than wait for his invitation, she dropped a white envelope on the ink blotter before him.

"What's this?" His name was typed across the front.

"My two week notice. I believe that is the standard practice." She crossed her arms and stared him down.

"But why?"

She made an unnecessary adjustment to the narrow belt on her plaid dress. "I've been aware for some time that your needs and mine are not entirely compatible."

Something didn't add up. She'd been unusually aloof all week, ever since he'd arrived at her apartment to reunite with Katya. Speaking little, banging her typewriter keys. Her attitude toward the patients hadn't altered; what had changed was how she regarded him.

"Do you mind that Katya is staying with me?"

"Of course not," she snapped. "I'm not her mother."

He hesitated. "I know I've been distracted . . ."

"Indeed. Running all over town, hunting for her."

Should he confess that searching for Katya had been why he'd shortened their work day? Or that he spent his afternoons at the Free Clinic, his evenings with Louise? All the changes he hadn't confided in her. "It never occurred to me to inform you."

Her thin lips pressed firmly together. "I matter so little to you."

"That's not it," he protested. "I didn't think you'd be interested." But a hot reproach shot through him: the lack of interest had been his own. He'd wanted to dodge that steely glare, her evident disapproval.

She stood ramrod straight, framed against the open doorway behind her. "My sister has long urged me to retire and join her in Florida. It's past time for me to do so. I trust you'll be able to find an adequate replacement." But despite her polite words, she sounded skeptical. Who else would put up with him?

"I'll be sorry to see you go, Mrs. Watkins." It was a half-truth. But she was right—as she often had been; it was past time for a change. She gave a curt nod and withdrew. A moment later, he heard the thud of the door closing, the clop of her heels tapping down the corridor. Robert continued to sit, his hands resting uselessly on the unopened envelope. He'd been thoughtless and inconsiderate, flaws high on his list of personal failings to avoid whenever possible.

When he was a lad, Robert's friends had teased and called him: "Straight-arrow Bobby." He never crept out of a window at night or cheated on tests, had never needed to lie to his parents about where he'd been or what he'd done. But now—at his age!—he'd spent the summer chasing adventures as if he were some careless teenager, sidestepping confrontations, avoiding hard truths. His discreet use of Mrs. Watkins' machine to type the deferment letters seemed furtive and sneaky, a shameful act rather than a heroic rescue. He'd surrounded himself with people who hid their identities— the patients who gave false names, Huck's close-mouthed history, Katya's true past—and, as if contagious, he'd become evasive and shifty himself, lying to the draft board, to his secretary. He even kept the woman he loved in the dark. It was too late to make amends with Mrs. Watkins, that was clear. But perhaps he could still remedy his other shortcomings.

* * *

He picked Louise up at the end of her shift, saying only, "Let's go for a drive," and they sat in uncharacteristic silence as long shadows crossed the Outer Drive. The trees in Lincoln Park had turned dull green, the first sign that autumn was taking hold, readying the leaves to wither and drop. Further north they drove, until he turned down a short street and parked at the lakefront. Together, they watched light drain from the sky and the waves turn blue, then indigo, then purple-black.

Robert spoke first. "I've got a stone in my shoe. Not a real one. I mean, something's troubling me and I've got to get it out."

Louise angled to face him. "Go on."

"I want you to know that I think the world of you. I'm grateful every day that I came into the Artist's Snack Shop and that you spoke so kindly to me. You're a wonderful, generous, lovely person. I enjoy our time together. All of it." He stopped, uncertain how to proceed. A pair of white gulls sailed above the blue-black waves.

"But?" Her face grew somber. He clasped her hand; her palm was clammy against his own.

"But I'm not sure I want to go on like this."

Louise pulled away. "I thought we were happy . . ."

"Oh, I am! My dear," he brushed her cheek with trembling fingers. "I mean, I don't know whether I can continue without knowing that we are moving toward something more permanent and stable." He paused. "I'm older than you, and you may not want the burden of caring for an old coot . . . but . . . but I'm not the kind of man who dates a woman—is intimate with her—without offering to marry her."

In the rearview mirror, a last sliver of sun glowed a brilliant orange as it sank behind the El tracks. His heart hammered painfully in his chest while he waited for her to respond.

Louise cleared her throat and spoke quietly. "I'm not bothered by your age, Robert. I'm fifty-six, by the way, so there's not that much difference between us. To tell the truth, I'm not too keen on marriage. I don't especially want to change my name—"

He interrupted. "Do you love me, Louise? Because I love you." What a relief to say it and to hear her reply: "Yes, I do." Her words sounded enough like a wedding vow that he took her hand again and this time she squeezed his affectionately. "I'm happy with the way things are, spending a lot of time together, but we each have our own place, too. Why change now?"

Robert had thought about this all afternoon, rolling the answer around and around in his mind, like a stone being polished by the waves. "Because I know how quickly life can change, how abruptly and completely we can become diverted from the path we're on. I didn't expect to outlive Phyllis, and certainly not by so many years. I never thought I would love again." She gave him a warm smile. "I certainly didn't anticipate that I'd chase all over the city in search of a pregnant girl—or spend hours at a free clinic or let the police think that Huck is my grandson! The point is, although I'd like to believe that you and I have plenty of time to be together, many happy years ahead of us, I can't trust that we will."

"But marriage won't give us more years. It guarantees nothing."

"That's true, there are no guarantees. Maybe I've been spending too much time with Huck and Katya and all those young people who never plan ahead. I can't see what's coming next. Life is so unpredictable; the only certain future is, well, its end. I know that sounds morose and I don't mean to be a pessimist. But that's why it's important to embrace the happiness we have right now—and not risk waiting for a day that might never come!"

She shook her head. "I don't know. We've only known each other for a few months . . ."

Did she sense that he had kept secrets from her? He wiped his forehead with a handkerchief. "You're right. And you should know more. Something I've done, or rather, that I'm still doing, I haven't told you about it, but now I'd like to." The interior of the car had grown too dim for him to read her expression. A mosquito whined around his ear. He should start the car, raise the windows, and turn on the AC but it was more important to reveal everything while he still had the courage. And could still hold onto the hope that Louise wouldn't spurn him as Mrs. Watkins had done or be terribly disappointed in him for having hidden the truth. He took a deep breath.

"I write letters to the draft board to help inductees get disqualified from service. I've been doing it for a couple of months now."

"And?"

"And it's dishonest. I'm vouching for ailments and limitations, illnesses, that these young men, um, may not actually have."

To his surprise, Louise laughed.

"It's a serious matter!" he protested. "I'm falsifying records! Placing my medical license in jeopardy if I'm caught . . ." But she continued to laugh. Another mosquito. He turned the key, pressed the button to raise the windows. Moths swirled drunkenly in the headlight beams. "I don't understand why you find this so amusing."

She wiped her eyes. "First, I think it's wonderful that you care so much. I'm sure those draftees are grateful to be spared. What's funny to me is something else: how all these hippies and Yippies and young people talk about changing the world. You know, how they grow their hair long, drop out, protest all the time. But you and I: turns out, *we're* the revolutionaries."

"I still don't understand." The AC fan whined its complaint along with him.

"I've kept a secret from you too. Not because I wanted to, but out of loyalty . . ." she trailed off.

"Go on," he said, hoping that he sounded more encouraging than nervous.

"It's how I spend my Thursdays. Involved with other people."

Was there another man, someone she saw once a week? He swallowed hard. "Better tell me everything."

She said simply, "I'm part of Jane."

"What?"

"Jane. You know, like Katya mentioned when she first came to see you."

"Katya was looking for you?" It made no sense. Robert twisted in his seat, knocking an elbow against the horn which blared like a warning, startling them both.

"Not me, the group of women I meet with. We're all Jane. It's a code. When Katya used it, she meant she was looking for an abortion."

"You mean?" He was having trouble figuring out what to say first. "You said it was a support group."

"It is. We help women terminate unwanted pregnancies. That's the support we give."

"So, you refer them to a physician who—"

"No. We did use a doctor before, but now—some of us—we do it ourselves."

Robert broke into a fresh sweat as anger flooded through him. "How? With what training? What skills? Don't you know what kind of risks you run? Prison for yourselves, but far worse for those women . . ."

Louise snapped on the overhead light and he squinted at her in its yellow glare. She looked as cross and flushed as he felt.

"Robert! Listen to yourself! We were trained by the doctor we worked with, and our outcomes are good. It's not that complicated to do a D-and-C. We're cleaner than back-alley abortionists and we're not drunks like some of them are!" For a long minute, they eyed each other, until he dropped his gaze in surrender. She was right. He'd known for a while that someone was providing clean, safe procedures and he'd secretly approved of them, whoever it was. Why should he object now that one of the outlaws sat beside him? An outlaw who he loved dearly.

"I apologize for lecturing. I certainly never thought that you or your friends would be cavalier . . . But why do you take such risks, Louise?"

"I could ask you the same thing, couldn't I? Both of us, we're doing what we think is right to save lives." She paused to gather her thoughts. "I've known too many people whose lives were upended, hurt. Maybe they needed an abortion and couldn't get it; maybe they were hurt by an unclean procedure. It's the secret history of shame and relief that nobody talks about. But the Janes brought it out of the dark. We kept talking about it until we decided we had to actually do something, not just talk, not wait for the laws to change."

Meekly, he asked, "May I ask what exactly you do— not all the Janes, just this one?" He patted her knee.

"I can tell you that I'm pretty much the old lady of the group. Most of the Janes are younger than me, grad students, young mothers. We're very careful: only a few people perform the service. Most don't even know where it takes place, and the location changes often. I return messages, screening out callers who might be trying to set us up or women who're too far along to be helped. I might meet a woman on a street corner and hand her off to somebody else. I might sit with her afterwards to make sure she's all right. I don't think I should say more than that. The more people who know, the greater the danger. To all of us."

"Are you afraid I'll betray you? Even accidentally? Is that why you kept this from me?"

"No, it wasn't that. After twenty years of waitress-ing you learn who's going to skip out on their tab or be a lousy tipper. I knew right away you were a good guy." At her words, the tightness in his jaw eased. "But when you left your card and I saw you're a gynecologist, I didn't want you to think I was only interested in your connections. You know, like recruiting you to help us get supplies. And I didn't know if you would disapprove; lots of people do. But if they saw how hopeless these girls are . . ."

"I know. I've seen it myself too many times."

She fiddled with the air conditioning vent, directing more cool air onto her face. "And I worried you might want me to quit and then I'd have an awful choice to make . . ."

He shook his head firmly. "I won't ask you to do that. You make your own decisions. I respect that."

"Good. I wanted to protect you, too. You could be in big trouble if you're involved, even in the smallest way."

"But I am involved, aren't I? Because we're . . ." He searched for the right words. "A couple. In each other's life!"

"Yes, we are. Anyway, that's the long story of why I laughed. 'Cause you and me, we're more radical than most of the kids."

He chuckled. "I see what you mean. And maybe you're right about marriage too. Perhaps it isn't the next step. We can keep on as we have been—even better, now that our secrets are out. Or, we could move in to-gether like the youngsters do. After all, we are revolu-tionaries!"

Chapter Forty-three

Tears and fears and feeling proud

Katya sat on a kitchen folding stool with her feet planted on the lower step to ease the pain in her lower back while Louise bustled about, occasionally placing a bowl beside her for her to help stir or mix. It was clear that her assistance wasn't necessary but when Louise said, "It's always nice to have another woman in the kitchen," Katya felt a stir of pride. For once, she was being treated like a grown-up. She wielded the potato masher with extra vigor, only pausing at another sharp tug low on her abdomen.

Louise paused chopping carrots. "Everything okay?"

"Yeah, I guess. Doc Robert says these aren't real contractions, they're more like practice for later."

"Looks like you're done practicing on those potatoes," Louise said, removing the bowl and handing Katya a dish towel to wipe up the potato mash she had splattered onto the table and her forearms.

"Hey, gals! What's happening?" Huck loped into the room, a bounce in his step, as if he had springs hidden in his boots. His mouth fell open in mock surprise as he stared at Katya. "Omigod, you're pregnant!"

"Ha-ha, very funny."

Huck made a silly face as he reached over Louise's shoulder for a taste. When she deftly swatted his hand away, he winked at Katya. She was glad to see that his black eye, which made him look more like a pirate than ever but gave her pangs of guilt, was fading.

Robert arrived in time to set the table with his best china and cloth napkins. Katya draped her napkin across the top of her belly, like Tweedledum from *Through the Looking-Glass*. Candles illuminated their four faces in a warm glow. As she idly listened to them talk, the candle flames seemed to burn more brightly. The back of her head felt weightless, dissolving. Huck's voice filled her ears but she couldn't make out what he was saying. The room held a radiance that was more than light: it had a texture like velvet, and a color both red and gold. Another contraction pulled deep within her, leaving her dazed and disoriented.

One candle burned its last remnant of wax and extinguished itself with a small hiss. In the faint glow, Doc Robert, Huck, and Louise looked unbearably tender as they regarded her with shimmering expressions of affection and concern. How she cherished them! She had found a trio, after all—not the young singers she chased after, but these three friends. Love swelled in her, like a balloon lifting her heart. And, in response, something stirred within her, a hidden rupture.

"Feeling all right, Katya? You look strange."

"I'm fine," she managed to say, ducking her head to wipe her mouth with the napkin. When she looked up again, she inhaled sharply. Her mother sat in Louise's chair, wearing a flowered housecoat and kerchief as if ready to go out on her night cleaning shift. And there was Tata, at the head of the table, smiling at her. Huck had turned into Piotr: as always, shoveling dinner down his throat. For a moment, it seemed like the most natural thing in the world to be at the square kitchen table again, surrounded by these beloved faces she hadn't seen in nearly a year. Her father no longer scowled; everyone ate and drank calmly as if she'd never left. Why had she missed them so fiercely when they were right here, in front of her?

But as the candle flames flickered, the Warshawskys vanished and the doctor, Huck, and Louise resumed their places. The realization struck her like a blow: I've replaced one family with another. Once again, she was the little sister, the obedient daughter, that meek girl who never climbed on a bicycle after scarring her chin, who obeyed the rules—until the day she left home.

Was this where all her travels had brought her? Around in a circle and back home again? A wave of anguish washed over her. It hadn't taken seven years to change into a different person: she'd done it in one. After being known as Cathy and Laura and Starchild, she had returned to being Katya, and yet, she wasn't the same girl who had run away from home. She knew she'd never go back to high school. She couldn't pretend that she hadn't been pregnant, hadn't slept in People's Park. Would never forget that she'd made love with Harlow, and had her heart broken. All that suffering couldn't have been just to settle back into another comfortable bungalow, even if it was nicer than the one before. Louise rose to clear the table, nudging Huck to help. Katya watched them ferry the dishes to the kitchen, still caught in what she had seen. This new loving family is an illusion, just like the images of my old one. Huck is not my cooler, older brother; these are not my parents or grandparents. They're offering me an easier, comfortable life. But it's not mine.

She would need to leave once again. And over and over, if necessary, until she found what she sought. So much lay ahead of her even though she could not name it, couldn't quite picture her new life, and didn't know where to go. But not right now. Katya took a deep breath and, with difficulty, rose to her feet.

"I think the baby's coming."

* * *

Louise helped Katya change her clothes and pack the silly round suitcase. Robert snapped on an overhead light and opened his bag to re-check his supplies. With such a slow trickle of amniotic fluid, there was no urgency but it would be best to make the short trip to the caravan now, before labor commenced in earnest. Syringes, stethoscope, hemostat, Pitocin. He liked to have his own instruments, to know exactly where they were when he needed to lay his hands on them.

"What about me? What do I do?" Huck's voice was high, strained by anxiety. He lit a Marlboro although one already burned in the ashtray before him. Clearly, he needed a task.

"Why don't you check the car? Make sure there's plenty of gas and the tires are inflated." If a trip to the hospital was needed later, it would be prudent to be prepared. Robert tossed him the keys and Huck rushed out. From the next room, Louise asked, "How are you feeling?"

"Good," Katya replied, panting audibly. "I mean, it's exciting and a little scary, but it doesn't hurt any worse than those Braxton-Hicks. Guess it's going to be easier than I thought!" Oh dear. Well, she would be experiencing the real thing soon enough.

Huck dashed in to announce that the chariot was ready. He'd tell the Free Clinic that Robert would be out for a day or two, and Louise offered to call Mrs. Watkins with the same message in the morning. At the front door, Katya halted, one hand pressed against her belly, the other clutching the doorframe, reluctant to let go. "Time to say goodbye," Robert urged. The girl moved slowly, as if she mistrusted whether the ground would support her weight. He recognized her unsteady gait and knew that she was already withdrawing into that altered state, pulling deep within herself to concentrate her energies on the journey ahead.

Despite the late hour, a light burned in the window of the midwifery bus: an old-fashioned oil lamp like the ones from his childhood. The three midwives welcomed them without a trace of surprise as if they had expected Katya's arrival.

"Let's get you settled," Maria said, placing an arm around the younger woman's shoulders. She seemed unflappable, a good trait for midwives. "Want to change into a nightgown? Or, you can go without. Lots of ladies do. Up to you."

While Katya changed her clothes behind a curtain, Lucy spoke quietly to Robert. "Babies come out in much the same way they started. If they're conceived in light and love and togetherness, they'll arrive with the same vibes. But if there was some hassle or hang-up, the relationship was in a bad space, then it's likely the birth will get hung up too."

Did Lucy think Katya would bring bad vibes to her birth? How little Robert knew about the missing boyfriend or whether he'd ever loved this vulnerable girl who was about to suffer. Even the most peaceful labor was still a travail. He offered a more relevant piece of information, something he had observed firsthand: "She ate dinner about thirty minutes ago."

"That won't last long. Most ladies clean out their systems in the early stages. It helps speed up the rushes."

Sure enough, fifteen minutes later, Katya vomited into a bucket. Pale and clammy, she begged to lie down on the waiting bed. Robert reached for her wrist and checked her pulse.

Crystal said, "You can, but I think staying upright is a better idea. Let's walk around a bit, you'll have plenty of time for lying down later. Or you can stand, squat, whatever makes you comfortable." She ushered Katya out of the bus while telling how she'd given birth kneeling on all fours. Maria handed Robert a cup of tea and he sipped its odd, earthy flavor as he watched the pair make a halting circuit within the ring of dark vehicles. Katya paused often, one hand pressed against the small of her back, or leaned upon the taller woman for support. Her white nightgown glowed in the dim, eerie light. Nothing else moved, no one awake at this late hour; the buses and vans sat quietly like sleeping animals while the two women slowly shuffled by. From time to time, Robert heard a faint moan but whether it came from Katya or elsewhere, he couldn't tell.

"Full moon," Maria observed. "The time when most babies are born." Robert remembered nurses at the hospital saying the same thing. Perhaps it was true after all. How long had it been since he had looked outside when the moon was at its fullest? Even with the streetlights' orange glow down the block, the moon gave a shimmering aura to the trodden grass and to some folding chairs left beside the doused campfire and to Katya's hair as she bent over to rest.

At last Crystal helped Katya back up the steps and onto the mattress.

"May I?" Robert lifted the white nightgown to expose her taut flesh. Already, she seemed to have lost any bashfulness. Expertly, he palpated her belly for the baby's position. "Just what we like to see," he assured her. "Head down and engaged, and the baby is facing your back." He had each midwife take turns placing their fingers against the subtle bumps of the infant's spine and the two points of its bottom, high above Katya's navel. She groaned as another contraction passed through her body.

"Relax your face," soothed Maria. "Blow air through your lips, but keep them soft. Don't hold your breath. Let the rushes arrive and pass, like waves breaking on the shore. That's it." Katya puffed and moaned, but then retreated into herself between bouts of contractions, as they grew stronger. The midwives practiced listening to the baby's heartbeat with fetoscopes between contractions while Robert watched.

Mindful of his promise to help teach, he began to explain, "In some maternity wards, physicians become concerned when the rate drops below one hundred beats per minute and they'll start prepping for a C-section."

"Shush!" Lucy's command was murmured but firm. "No need to speak of such things now."

Rebuffed, Robert crouched on a small seat near the bed. Years ago, he had spent long nights leaning against the wall outside a labor room, waiting until the mother progressed into the second stage and it would be time for him to assist. Patience is part of the practice, he'd told himself then. And he was out of practice now. So he waited. Time became its own presence in the room, slow and thick. Katya struggled out of her nightgown, too sweaty to care about modesty any longer. Crystal wiped her brow and neck with a damp cloth while Lucy checked on the cervix's dilation.

The crowded room grew dimmer; the moon must be sinking beyond the city skyline. Maria whispered, "The veil between the worlds is thin . . ." Somewhere far off, a train whistle hooted. Soon, dawn would peek over the distant lake. He listened to Katya's breath as she puffed through another rush, and to the quiet rustles as the women moved about to check her vitals and massage her back. In the warm glow of the oil lamp, their faces were golden and smooth, their movements gentle and unhurried. Katya sprawled against a pile of pillows, her round body flushed and abundant and working hard, as beautiful as any Renaissance painting he had seen.

"Oh god, here comes another one," she cried. The midwives surrounded her, like worker bees attending their queen. They urged her to breathe. "I can't do it!"

Lucy took charge. "Oh, but you can. Squeeze my hand, but keep your mouth relaxed. That will help. You're almost through transition. Day will break soon, and you're going to push this baby out, and everything will be beautiful. Right now, women all over the world are doing the same as you: using their strength to birth their babies. You're not alone. We're all here with you."

"I need to push!"

"Not yet, not yet. Short breaths, like a puppy dog." Katya panted, her eyes wild. "Let's take a look at you."

Lucy aimed a flashlight at the dark crown of the baby's head pressing against her distended pink flesh, stretching it impossibly. Robert saw how tightly her perineum strained and reached for his scissors. Just a small snip to prevent her from tearing. Lucy placed a hand on his arm. "Wait. We'll ease the head out." He met her gaze; she was calm and determined. All right. For now, he would continue to trust them but he pulled on a pair of rubber gloves, just in case.

The women tucked themselves into place, Crystal and Maria on either side to hold Katya's hands, wipe her face, or help her into position while she held her knees. Lucy squatted on the floor at the end of the bed. Robert held the flashlight steady as she dribbled olive oil over Katya's bulging vulva and the baby's crowning head, massaging lubricant into the perineum. At every push, the head emerged a bit further, but the midwives continued to encourage Katya to resist giving in to the urge to force the baby out. As the contraction subsided, so did the pressure, and the cup of the infant's head would regress again.

Push and subside, push and subside, like the ebb and flow of the tide. Robert no longer paid heed to how he sat or when he leaned forward to observe or whether he panted along with her. Lucy spread her hands against Katya's bottom, wide so that the skin between finger and thumb resembled another straining perineum, taking the pressure into her own flesh. Bulge forward, ease back, forward, back. After each panting bout, Katya laid back with her eyes closed, drawing into some dark and private space before her body forced her the return to the rigors of the present. Never had he witnessed a birth transpire so patiently, with such an incremental and rhythmic pace. At last, the head emerged halfway, revealing a preternaturally long forehead and the tops of delicate ears, flattened against the blue-tinged skull.

Lucy reached for a clean towel. "Push all you like."

Katya looked at Robert and extended her hand. Too weary to speak, she opened and closed her fingers against her palm like a toddler's gesture that says, "Come here. I want you." The room grew brighter as he stood, stripped off his gloves, and awkwardly traded places with Crystal in the cramped space.

Months ago, those delicate fingers had glided into his palm, cool against his warm hand. Now, Katya gripped him with hot ferocity, no longer the tentative girl. He stoically willed himself not to wince, knowing that she would draw strength from him. She could not spare one ounce of attention from the great bearing down she needed to do.

"The head's out," Crystal declared. Katya attempted to see, but the bulwark of her belly was in the way. Maria took her hand and guided it. "Feel that?"

"Ohhh," Katya inhaled in awe.

"Open your mouth wide and pant while we ease the shoulders out." Robert wondered for a moment whether the midwives would know what to do if the umbilical cord happened to be around the neck. But they were practical; they would ask him for help if they needed it. Right now, he was Katya's friend and protector; no need to be Doctor.

"One more push. Push now!"

Katya seized his hand again as a deep lion's roar issued from her, a bellow—not of pain, but of triumphant release. The room rang with the sound, while somewhere, distant bells chimed. Far away, in his peripheral vision, the midwives bustled about, wrapping and wiping and suctioning, but he had no need to watch, for Katya still clung to his hand. Her face glowed with a radiance that seemed to surround her and her eyes shone, more green than brown now. His heart was too large for his chest and a lump in his throat threatened to choke him.

The infant cried, a high wail. "I did it," she whispered. Tears streamed down her cheeks and soaked into the pillow.

"Yes! Yes, you did," he stammered. "I knew you could. So proud of you." He wiped her cheeks with his free hand, letting her tears run into the hollow of his palm. "Everything is wonderful. Just perfect."

Maria edged to the other side of the bed. "Would you like to hold him?" So, a boy. Robert caught his breath as Katya released his hand to reach for her baby with both arms. Maria placed him on Katya's chest, skin to skin, his rosy flesh against her own, still flushed with effort.

"He looks like an alien," she murmured, happily.

Robert chuckled. "Yes, his head is long. Babies' skulls are soft and the bones move easily. He'll round out in a day or two."

She cupped his tiny bottom in her palm. "But I won't have him in a day or two." She traced the shape of his delicate ear with the tip of one finger. "Look at him. I didn't know I could make something so beautiful . . ."

Robert moved closer to her, their heads together as if posing for a portrait. He smelled her shampoo and the pungent aromas of iron and vernix, heard his own breath and the whoosh of blood in his ears. The baby's rosy lips were parted as if already wanting to nurse. Its long forehead was clear and untroubled, untouched by the pain and endeavor it had brought on its journey to life.

"He's looking at us," Katya marveled. It was true. The child's eyes were a pure newborn blue and it watched them with a deep timeless gaze, its azure irises like stars. As a medical student, Robert had been taught that newborn eyes could not focus and were capable of discerning only light and motion, perhaps vague shapes. But looking into this baby's wise stare, he couldn't believe there were any limits on its vision. For the rest of his life, whenever Robert looked at photos of tropical waters or those profound images of Earth from space, or watched fireworks dazzling the night sky, he remembered this candescent, fulfilling moment and the miraculous sense of being recognized: *I see you. I know you.* This tiny being seemed to perceive beyond their smiles and tears; it dove into Robert's essence, and what it found there was met, not with joy or judgment, but with a solemn dignity, taking his measure.

A tug on his sleeve. Lucy beckoned for him to join the midwives hunched at the foot of the bed. Reluctantly, but ever the doctor, he complied. They conferred in a whisper. "She hasn't passed the placenta yet."

"How long has it been?" He had no idea how much time had passed, had forgotten to look at his watch, and the sun was fully up, flooding through the bus windows and the open door.

"Six minutes. Maybe seven."

He checked for bleeding and noted with admiration that Lucy had been correct: no tearing. "Well done," he congratulated the trio. "Katya," he raised his voice to her. "We're going to palpate your abdomen now." She scarcely glanced in their direction, absorbed in her newborn. With practiced motions, he showed the midwives how to assess the firmness of her uterus and how to gently encourage it to contract until, a few minutes later, the placenta emerged. He and Lucy examined it together, confirming the red and purple mass was intact.

"Do you have a garden?" Crystal asked. "Placentas are great for growing rose bushes."

Robert shook his head, unable to consider the idea of digging in the garden. He stretched his back, trying to ease muscles which suddenly were chiding him, commenting on his age and the long night he'd spent. All the wonder and amazement ebbed from his weary limbs. He would leave Katya to rest, knowing she would be well looked after, and return in a few hours, after a nap.

As he stepped down from the bus into the cool morning, he spotted Jenny and Marcus in the shadows, waiting to meet their child. He wanted to tell them to go away, leave Katya in peace. Give her more time, let her change her mind. But, too tired to speak, he merely nodded at them and turned away.

Chapter Forty-four

You, who are on the road

R obert's car seemed to float slowly through the city
as he drove. Small details caught his eye: the ruddy,
rough bricks of a six-flat; spiky green leaves on a plant
in a window box; a street sign hanging drunkenly from
its pole. He clicked the radio on and hummed along to a
Mozart piano concerto for a few minutes before the
effort felt too great.

The house was still: Louise had left for work, Huck
snored on the couch, deep in sleep, one arm across his
face. Robert scrawled a message for him. *All is well—a
little boy. I'll go back after a nap.* He removed his shoes at
the bottom of the stairs to creep up and set his alarm
before he fell into bed.

Up again at two, he showered and shaved, and felt
almost refreshed by the time he came downstairs to find
Huck pouring coffee in the kitchen. Huck handed him a
cup, saying, "Drink up. I'm coming with."

"The bus doesn't have much room."

"You're not leaving me behind, Doc!"

"Fine. But we may have to take turns visiting her."
They grabbed pieces of toast and climbed into the car.

A few blocks later, Huck yelled, "Wait! Stop!" Robert pulled to the curb, braking hard.

"What's wrong?"

Huck sprang out and vaulted over the low fence sur-
rounding a front yard. He plucked a handful of yellow

chrysanthemums, bolted back to his seat, and slammed the door. "It's traditional to bring flowers, isn't it?" He grinned.

"Yes," Robert answered, drily. "But, traditionally, one visits a florist shop."

"We ain't got time for that. Her kid's gonna be out of diapers by the time we get there. You drive awful slow."

Robert rotated his steering wheel to the left with one hand, preparing to point to the midwifery bus. Trampled weeds and tracks crisscrossing the dirt offered ghostly reminders of the departed caravan. Only one vehicle sat at the curb, a lanky fellow tinkering under the hood. A spray of orange bittersweet lay crushed beneath its tires.

Robert ran to the van. "Where is everyone?" He wanted to believe that they'd gone to gas up the vehicles or get supplies of some kind, but he knew those answers didn't make sense. The mechanic slowly wheeled around, keeping a firm grip on his wrench. A lock of his hair was tangled in the hoop he wore in his left ear.

"Who the hell're you?"

Robert drew a sharp breath. No point in alienating him. "I'm a doctor. I was here last night attending a birth in the midwives' bus. I need to know where they are."

The mechanic nodded. "Yeah, I heard about that" He looked at Huck and the yellow mums he was clutching. "You the daddy?"

"No, man, we're her friends. More like her family."

Robert jumped in. "You all swore you'd be here for another week! She's just delivered a baby and I need to make sure she's all right." His jaw clenched in anger and frustration.

The mechanic set his wrench on the fender and took a step away from the van to light a cigarette. "Yeah, well, your Chicago PO-lice had different ideas. Unmarked cars showed up around noon, claimed we were trespassing. Gave us ten minutes to clear out or they'd start busting us."

"Fuckin' pigs!" Huck spat on the ground.

"Why are you still here, then?"

"Guess they didn't want to bother for just one collar. Anyway, soon as I get the engine fixed, I'm outta here, man."

Robert scanned the vacant lot as if it held some answers. Nothing but a few scraps of paper, blown by the wind. It was as if he had dreamed the whole event... "But how will you find them?"

Mechanic laughed. "Hey, man. Just 'cause we haven't reached the end yet doesn't mean we don't know where we're going! We always map out the next stop, in case we get separated."

Robert grabbed his sleeve. "Where's the next stop?"

"Don't touch me, man!" The mechanic pulled his arm away. "Ann Arbor. We won't get hassled there."

"I didn't mean to hassle you," Robert began to apologize, but Huck interrupted him.

"C'mon, Doc, let's go get our gal." He handed a flower to the mechanic who tucked it into his shirt pocket. "Take it easy."

* * *

They moved quickly, eager to get on the road before rush hour seized the highways in its frenzied grip. But first, a stop at home for maps and a supply of cash from

Robert's locked desk drawer. He telephoned Louise at the Snack Shop but her manager said it was too busy for her to take the call.

"All right. Please tell her that Robert and Huck are going to Ann Arbor to get Katya."

The manager replied slowly, as if trying to write it down, "Rob and Huck and Ann are going . . ."

"Never mind. Just say that Robert will call her at home later this evening. No emergency, just a change in plans."

"Will do."

While Huck scrounged in the pantry and fridge, Robert walked into Katya's room. Dresser drawers stood open and the rumpled bed looked as if she had just flung off the covers. Hanging on the doorknob he found the bulging green satchel that she always kept with her. Her artist's bag, left behind in the rush. He placed it carefully on the front seat and climbed behind the wheel. Huck heaved a cooler into the back seat. "So we won't have to stop too soon."

"I hope we won't stop at all. I don't know how fast those old buses can travel, but I'm guessing they don't have too much speed. We might catch up to them on the way. Two hundred and fifty miles to Ann Arbor . . . What do you think? Five hours to get there?"

"Hell, no. We can make it in four. Maybe less."

"I'm not going to get stopped for speeding."

Huck grinned. "I don't want another run-in with the fuzz any more than you do, Gramps." He tuned the radio to WXRT, blasting rock-and-roll into the car until they were too far out of town for the signal to reach them.

After exiting the toll road in Indiana, Robert pulled over to let Huck drive. To his surprise, Huck first checked and re-set the mirrors. He placed his hands at ten and two before putting the gearshift into drive. Beneath that disheveled exterior was a careful driver. Once on the road, he swiftly moved the Ford into the fast lane and pushed the cigarette lighter in, saying, "Relax. Take a nap."

But Robert knew he wouldn't sleep. Instead, he undid the fasteners on Katya's satchel and pulled out her notebooks and papers: here was the story of her journeys, rendered in pencil, crayon, charcoal. The most dog-eared sketchpad must hold her oldest artwork. The first few images were childish horses and trees; they showed some promise but were commonplace, derivative. More talent was in portraits of an older couple, perhaps her parents, and a young man who resembled Katya around the eyes and in the shape of his unmarked chin. The older folks wore dour expressions, as if they disapproved of whatever they saw before them. In the last few pages, their faces had changed, looking softer and more sentimental, perhaps drawn from memory.

She had filled every inch of the remaining pads, rendering certain people over and over: a handsome fellow with long, fair hair; a large woman wearing a turban. Clearly, Katya had worked on faces, and her improvement was evident as she became more adept at capturing expressions with only a few strokes of her pen. In each notebook, her work became more passionate and mature.

"Look, here's Louise and me."

Huck glanced at the page. Katya had drawn them from behind as they stood together at the kitchen sink, their shoulders and hips touching to form a two-headed being. "No wonder she wanted to go to art school. She's good."

Robert recognized the drawbridges over the Chicago River, Adler Planetarium's dome, and the graceful dolphins that adorned Buckingham Fountain. He might have found her sketching in Lincoln Park beside the zoo's entrance or outside the Aragon Ballroom. So many times, she had been nearby, just around the corner while, all summer long, he had chased behind. Just like he was doing now.

A troubling thought pulled at him. Portraits, landscapes, experiments in texture and shadow, birds, buildings . . . He leafed through the papers again. Of all the models available to an artist, her own is the most reliable, the easiest to find. But there were no images of her body as it progressed through the changes of pregnancy, and none of her own face in a mirror. Katya had chosen to ignore her self. She was as absent from her work as she had been during the months he had searched for her.

He gathered her sketchbooks together, careful to repack them in their original order. "How much further, you think?"

"Maybe fifty miles."

"If we don't spot them before reaching Ann Arbor . . ." Robert trailed off, unsure of what came next but Huck had a quick answer.

"We'll go to the campus and find the nearest head shop. Start asking around. We'll find them."

"You know, you're a lot more organized than you look, young man."

Huck chuckled. "You know what they say: you can't read a book by its cover."

Robert was going to point out that the adage was about judging, not reading, but the words caught in his throat. Coughing, he gesticulated at the vehicles in the slow lane ahead: radiantly painted buses lumbering in a long line like elephants bearing their ornamented howdahs.

"Is that them?" Without waiting for an answer, Huck shot across two lanes of the interstate and pulled up beside the last bus, honking. Robert rolled down his window to flag down the caravan. Hands popped out of the windows, flashing peace signs. He shouted at them but it was impossible to be heard in the rushing wind. Huck accelerated past the buses to catch up with the lead vehicle, a shiny red delivery van adorned with mandalas and a green dragon. The driver cupped his hand around his left ear.

"Pull over!" Robert yelled. The driver nodded and pointed to a highway sign: rest area, one mile. Robert gave a thumbs-up and Huck tooted the horn once more before racing ahead to the exit ramp.

The rest stop parking lot was deserted. Padlocks hung on the scarred restroom doors. A field of ripe weeds, grown tall behind the small buildings, rippled in the wind. Robert watched a breeze silently ruffle over the field like an invisible hand, running its fingers through golden hair. The whine of passing traffic and a red-winged blackbird trilling in the distance were the only sounds.

"Doc?" Huck touched his shoulder; the caravan was rumbling in. With a last look at the wind caressing the field, Robert turned back to the world. He made a beeline for the bus where he'd spent last night.

Lucy greeted him at the doorway. "It's so cosmic that you're here!"

"I need to see her." The midwife stepped aside and he climbed into the bus. Katya sat up in bed, alone. Her hair was neatly braided and she showed good color in her cheeks.

"Huck and I came to take you home."

"Oh, thank god!" She held out her arms. Robert's knees gave way as he sat on the edge of the bed, but Katya was reaching for her satchel. "Thank you. I thought I'd lost my art forever." She patted the bag as if to assure herself it was real.

The mattress sagged beneath him. "How are you?" Too simple a question.

"Everything hurts. I've got cramps. My belly's sore, and my back, and . . . between my legs."

"It's normal to have a few days of discomfort. Cramps too. Are the midwives helping you with the pain?" He should check her blood pressure. But where was his medical bag? At home, back in Chicago, left behind. What had happened to his mind?

"Yeah." She gestured at a teapot on the windowsill. "Tastes nasty but I drink it anyway."

"And the baby?" he asked, gently. There was a long silence during which he felt a sharp pang for the absent infant. Was that her longing or his own?

"I named him Jesse." Her voice was soft, her face twisted in grief. "It means 'gift.'"

"A good name."

"'Cause I gave him away. I know it's right but . . . it hurts." She stared at the teapot as if its contents could ease this pain.

"You can still change your mind. He is your baby."

"No, he's not." She turned to face him, wincing. "I mean, I was in the middle of all those rushes and cramps and everything, I saw . . . something. Like I was a passageway between this world and another place. Like the baby didn't really come from me at all. Jesse was already in the universe." She wiped her eyes with the edge of the sheet. "I saw forwards and backwards at the same time. I know what he's going to look like when he grows up, and I saw my parents and how happy they were when I was born. He came through me, and now he's here, and he's so pure . . . Maybe we never get to be that pure again. We're all so flawed, you know?"

"Some flaws don't mean anything, Katya. They're only on the surface." Robert gently traced the mark on her chin.

She gave a wan, grateful smile. "For so long, I resented Jesse. I didn't want to be pregnant, I didn't want to think about it, I didn't even like feeling him move inside me. But now, he's here and I have to protect him because the world is such a terrible place."

"Oh, no, Katya. No." He wanted to assure her that her breaking heart would heal someday but she shook her head, refusing to let him convince her.

"There's the war, and violence, and bad scenes. Oh, I know there are good people, too—I've met plenty of them." She took his hand. "The best way I know to keep Jesse safe is to give him to Jenny and Marcus, to the whole tribe, really. Once they have their land, he'll grow up in the country, with plants and animals all around, and people who care about him. The government will never find him, he can't be drafted, won't ever be sent to war."

All along, he had wanted Katya to have more choices, and she had made one. How could he question her decision now? He and Louise couldn't raise a child, and he had no better solution. He would have to trust that her faith in these ragtag vagabonds would be earned, that they could create a new, loving kind of family.

"And what about you? Ready to come back with Huck and me now?" She paused for a few breaths, an eternity. But he already knew what her answer would be, had seen it as he watched the silent ripples across the golden field of weeds.

"I'm going to travel with these folks. Not to keep Jesse, and I don't think I'll be a farm girl on their commune for long. But I can't go backwards, not any more than the baby could. If you want to be born," she smiled sadly, "you got to move ahead, right?"

Someone rapped on the window beside her head. "We need to get going," a voice called, as if affirming Katya's conclusion.

"Two more minutes," he answered. "I should send Huck in. He wants to see you too."

"Wait!" She threw both arms around his neck and Robert held onto this beloved girl who had given him so much. For a long speechless moment, they said everything that needed to be said except for the word "good-bye." And then he released her and left the bus for the last time, holding the door open for Huck to bound aboard. He sat behind the wheel of his car as the caravan buses started their engines. They flicked on their headlights against the gathering dark and began to slowly creep down the entrance ramp to the highway. Without intending to, he counted the vehicles, the moments, the sad beats of his heart. He told himself he would linger until the last bus had departed before turning the ignition key and finding his way home. He would wait as long as he could. The caravan was still rumbling past him when Huck leaned through the open window.

"Not going to leave without me, were you, Doc?

Robert swallowed. "I wasn't sure you were coming. Thought maybe you were tempted to . . ."

"Nah, this ain't my scene. I'm a city boy." Huck gave a crooked smile. "But our gal looked good, didn't she?"

"Yes, she sure did." He could barely get the words past the lump in his throat.

"You look whipped, man. I better drive." Robert slid over and closed his eyes, glad to yield the steering wheel to his friend's steady hands. Too exhausted to feel his body against the seat or the bumps in the road, he seemed to be suspended outside of himself. In the space behind his eyelids, a rapid slideshow of images flickered by: there was Huck, sprawled in a restaurant booth in his carefree posture, and here was the cramped waiting room of the Free Clinic, crowded with anxious young men. Now, the grassy vistas of Grant Park where he'd spent so many hours watching passersby, and now, his lab where his test tubes gleamed their telltale, chartreuse omens. A slender girl frolicked down the corridor in bare feet, and now, her heavy body moved through the grand halls of the art museum. Mrs. Watkins' disapproving frown appeared, then faded away. And he saw Louise turn to welcome him as he entered the café.

All his experiences had brought him to this instant that immediately became another moment, and then another. As he watched the swift picture show, he felt a rush of certainty, a joyful surge of confidence, that as surely as he knew the past, he saw what was to come. He would hire a new assistant, someone younger and friendlier than Mrs. Watkins, a woman who might call the patients *Ms.* The kind of woman who Louise would choose for a friend. Together, they would paint the Women's Bureau in shades of sky-blue and lavender. Colors that Katya would have liked. And he would find a partner to run the practice with him so that the Bureau could benefit from his wisdom and experience, and from a younger doctor's energy and spirit, melding past and future into a vibrant present. They wouldn't hesitate to talk about abortion when it was needed, to give women as many choices as they could, asking the right questions and offering to unlock the secret chain of referrals to the Jane network. Katya had once told him that neither past nor future exist. How wrong she was! Robert carried all of yesterday's memories with him into this instant. *Before* and *after* were what gave *now* its symmetry. The tires struck a rhythm of "Now, now, now," but the melody he heard was created by what came before and what lay ahead.

As the car raced along the dark highway, speeding toward Louise waiting for him, Robert wished a final farewell to Katya. His fears for her had kept him awake at night; searching for her had brought him adventure and love. Now it was time for him to leave this girl who had eluded him, inspired him, brought him so much life. *Goodbye*, he thought and then heard, as if in echo, *hello*, as he saw again Jesse's wise eyes—that sapphire gaze that had greeted him and found him good and held him all the way home.

July 1999

A fly landed on Hannah's bare leg and tiptoed across her pale hairs until she brushed it away. From her hammock, she watched her mother behind the window overlooking the back yard. Emotions flickered over Katya's face like clouds passing before the sun, creating shadow and light, shadow and light. She wiped her cheeks with the back of her hand as she read the letter that had arrived in the morning's mail.

For her whole life, Hannah had secretly watched her mother, observing how she swept her hair away from her forehead when she was hot or exasperated, and how she held her fork upside down to spear bits of potato from the plate. She knew which colors were her mother's favorites (forest green and russet; autumnal shades, like a fox in the woods), which textures she liked best against her skin, and the names of the musicians whose records she played most often. She studied Mom's habits so that, when she was old enough, she could dress like her and move with her unconscious grace. Even now, when she could be so embarrassing (did she have to wear those paint-spattered shoes when she dropped Hannah off at school?), Hannah watched her from under half-closed lids, observing through her lashes.

Whatever was contained in that letter was making her mother happy and sad and happy again. There, the sign that she was nervous or troubled: she rubbed the scar on her chin, that mark from when she tried to ride her brother's bicycle. Hannah had been told the story a dozen times, had asked to hear it again and again. How unbelievable that people once had said girls shouldn't be allowed to ride bikes! No wonder her mother let her have a skateboard when she turned ten. "If you fall, you fall," Mom said. "Then you'll get back up."

Her voice was unconcerned but Hannah knew that if she were ever hurt, her mother would be at her side before she had recovered a breath. Once, when she stepped on a yellowjacket near the peony bush, she had just had time to cry out before Mom flew out of the house and scooped her into her strong arms, still smelling of paint and turpentine. With the flat side of a silver knife, her mother had scraped the stinger away, and made a poultice of baking soda to soothe the welt ("So that the scent will disappear and the rest of the wasps won't find you"), and she laid Hannah on the bed the wrong way, so that her foot could rest on a pillow. Then she snuggled in beside her with warm arms and cinnamon breath, and told stories for an hour, both of them facing the headboard decorated with images of badgers and rabbits. Mom had painted that, and the frieze around her bedroom wall, and the seascape over the fireplace, and all the stacks of canvases that filled the studio and hung on every wall.

Many of the paintings were of Hannah. She didn't mind posing: sitting still was one way she could watch her mother without being noticed. While Mom concentrated on her brush strokes and frowned at her charcoal lines, Hannah studied how she held the brush between her fingers, as light as a feather, but decisively. Momentary hesitation followed by a choice, a direction.

Now, Mom stared through the window, but not at the hammock or the trees or the vegetable garden where the tomatoes waited to be picked. Her hands lay still on top of the pages and she seemed to see nothing that existed here, where Hannah lived. It gave Hannah an odd sensation, as if without her mother's gaze she became invisible. If she waved, would her mother blink and recognize her again? Bring her back to life?

Her mother's blank face seemed to recede; she was on a ship departing from the dock. Hannah was pricked by fear but just as she opened her mouth to call out, Katya blinked. She looked at her daughter, smiled, and beckoned: come inside. She had returned from the unknown and Hannah tumbled out of the hammock, eager to run into her mother's welcoming arms and listen to the tale she would tell.

ACKNOWLEDGMENTS

Writing is a solitary act, but one that occurs within a larger community of readers and friends. I benefitted enormously from the participation and support of many, some who read certain chapters, others who stuck with me through countless drafts. Erika Mailman and the members of her Mailstrom writing group, Karien van Ditzhuijzen, Kat Ferreira, Kathryn Pritchett, Kristy Lin Billuni, and Lisa Beazley were all thoughtful and encouraging. Kate Crofton and Patrick Sutton provided valuable medical advice as well as good cheer. Karen Bender, Erica Eisdorfer, Nina Grimaldi, and Gini Grossenbacher gave constructive critique and spurred me onwards. Gay Guard-Chamberlin taught me how to read and gave this manuscript loving scrutiny. Dylan Kome reminded me of days gone by, as did the collective memories of Hyde Park Classics: a diverse, unruly and opinionated group from my home turf. I want to particularly thank David Hutchinson, Ian Wilson, Lois Ann Abraham, and Marilyn Reynolds. Without their unflagging love and friendship, I might have allowed Katya and Robert to remain unknown.

I'm also grateful to Richard Ljoenes for his beautiful cover design, bringing the story to life in ways I could not imagine.

Readers who are curious to learn more about Katya and Robert's world may want to explore other works including these that aided and inspired me:

- "Free health centers: A new concept?" by Irene Turner, *American Journal of Public Health*, 1972
- *Spiritual Midwifery* by Ina May Gaskin, revised edition, 1978
- *The Birth of the Pill* by Jonathan Eig, 2014
- *The Caravan* by Stephen [Gaskin], 1972
- *The Healer's Tale: Transforming medicine and culture* by Sharon R. Kaufman, 1993
- *The Story of Jane: The legendary underground feminist abortion service* by Laura Kaplan, 1995
- Personal stories shared at the Vietnam War Draft Lottery site www.vietnamwardraftlottery.com

ABOUT THE AUTHOR

Anara Guard grew up in Chicago. Her lifelong love of reading has led her to jobs as diverse as minding a Chicago news stand at the age of nine, working as a librarian in a small New England town, fact-checking manuscripts for Houghton Mifflin, and writing book reviews. An award-winning poet, she has had short stories published in the anthology *Twenty Twenty: 43 Stories from a Year Like No Other*; in her collection, *Remedies for Hunger*; and in various literary magazines. She attended Bread Loaf Writers Workshop and the Community of Writers. She is currently working on her second novel.

www.anaraguard.com

A reading guide for *Like a Complete Unknown* is available at

www.newwindpublishing.com